A STOLEN HEART

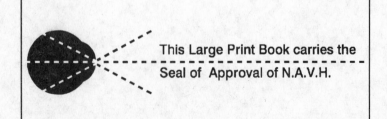

This Large Print Book carries the
Seal of Approval of N.A.V.H.

A STOLEN HEART

AMANDA CABOT

THORNDIKE PRESS
A part of Gale, Cengage Learning

GALE
CENGAGE Learning·

Farmington Hills, Mich • San Francisco • New York • Waterville, Maine
Meriden, Conn • Mason, Ohio • Chicago

GALE
CENGAGE Learning

LIBRARY OF CONGRESS CATALOGING-IN-PUBLICATION DATA

Names: Cabot, Amanda, 1948– author.
Title: A stolen heart / by Amanda Cabot.
Description: Large print edition. | Waterville, Maine : Thorndike Press, a part of Gale, Cengage Learning, 2017. | Series: Cimarron Creek trilogy ; 1 | Series: Thorndike Press large print Christian romance
Identifiers: LCCN 2017003274| ISBN 9781410499776 (hardcover) | ISBN 1410499774 (hardcover)
Subjects: LCSH: Large type books. | GSAFD: Christian fiction. | Love stories.
Classification: LCC PS3603.A35 S76 2017b | DDC 813/.6—dc23 LC record available at https://lccn.loc.gov/2017003274

Published in 2017 by arrangement with Revell Books, a division of Baker Publishing Group

Printed in the United States of America
1 2 3 4 5 6 7 21 20 19 18 17

For Virginia Chapman, former classmate, friend, and prayer warrior *extraordinaire*. Ginny, I'm so glad you took the time to reconnect with me. It's wonderful having you back in my life.

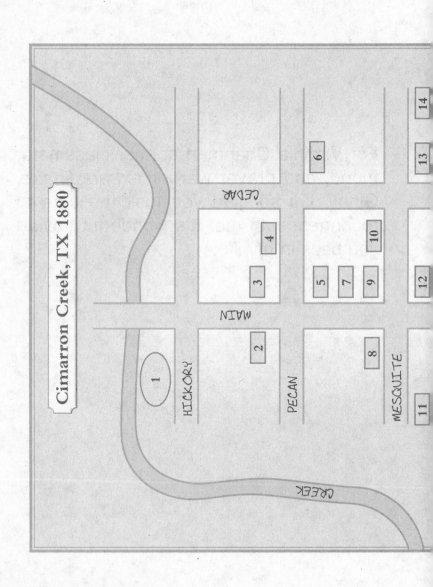

Cimarron Creek, TX 1880

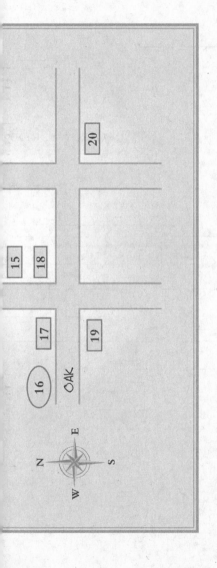

1 – Town park
2 – Silver Spur saloon
3 – Livery stable
4 – Porter and Hilda's home
5 – Mercantile
6 – Aunt Bertha's home
 (a Founder's house)
7 – Apothecary
8 – Doc Harrington's home and office
9 – Dressmaker's shop
10 – Travis's home
11 – Catherine's home

12 – Sheriff's office and jail
13 – Jacob Whitfield's home
 (a Founder's house)
14 – Charles, Mary, and Warner Gray's
 home
15 – Mayor's office/ post office
16 – Cemetery
17 – Church
18 – Cimarron Sweets
19 – School
20 – Matthew Henderson's home
 (a Founder's house)

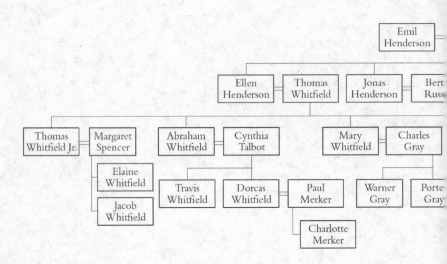

FOUNDING FAMILIES

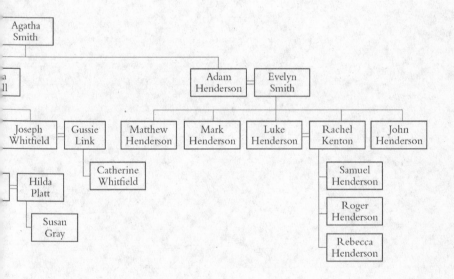

1

No matter what anyone said, she wouldn't believe this was a mistake. Lydia Crawford glanced at the other passengers, wondering whether her hours of sitting here, remaining silent but keeping a smile firmly fixed on her face, had done anything to lessen their hostility. She had considered pulling a book from her bag and spending the day lost in one of Jane Austen's tales but had feared that would only rile her companions more.

Though Lydia wanted nothing beyond a peaceful journey and some pleasant conversation, she suspected that was impossible. The two sisters who were traveling together and the mother and son had given her friendly smiles when they'd boarded the stagecoach in Dallas, but the moment she'd opened her mouth, those smiles had turned to frowns, the friendliness to hostility.

"She's a Yankee," one of the sisters had

announced. "Mebbe a sister to one of them carpetbaggers. She's sure makin' a mistake coming to Texas." They both glared at Lydia for a moment, then turned away, refusing to even look in her direction.

The mother had taken more drastic action. Though she and her son had chosen seats next to Lydia when they boarded the stagecoach, once Lydia had spoken and they'd realized she was a Northerner, they'd moved to the less comfortable backless bench in the center of the coach rather than risk being tainted by her presence.

Lydia had endured snubs before, but none of this magnitude. Though she'd tried to slough it off, she'd been unable. Not only had the woman's shunning hurt but it made Lydia wonder if she would face similar rejection in Cimarron Creek. *Nonsense,* she told herself. *Edgar would have warned me if that were the case.* But of course there had been no word from Edgar. The night he left, they had both agreed it would be far too risky for him to send a letter or telegram. He would go to Texas and make a home for them, leaving Lydia to join him as soon as the school could find a replacement for her. Though it wasn't their original plan, it was the only one that made sense after what had happened outside the tavern. Surely it

12

wasn't a mistake.

Lydia's gaze moved past the disapproving sisters to the dark-haired boy in the center of the coach. With little else to occupy him, he'd been staring at her. Now he leaned forward, his hand extended as if he wanted to touch her. Lydia shook her head slightly, knowing nothing good would come from encouraging the child. A second later, though his mother had been gazing out the window, seemingly oblivious to the curious looks her son had been giving Lydia, she turned abruptly and yanked him back onto the bench.

"Silas, you stay right here. I don't want you talkin' to that person." She spat the final word as if it were an epithet. Lydia refused to cringe. She'd been called worse, especially once she'd crossed the Mason-Dixon line. Though the war had been over for more than fifteen years, the enmity caused by four years of bloodshed and the disastrous era known as Reconstruction remained, at least in some hearts.

"But, Ma," the boy protested, "she's real purty. I nebber seen hair like that."

This time Lydia did cringe, wishing she'd been Silas's teacher. The boy was clearly old enough to attend school, but his poor grammar told her that if he was being taught, it wasn't well.

Silas's mother continued to frown. "You do as I say, young man, or I'll tan your hide."

"Yes, Ma." But, despite his mother's admonitions, Silas smiled at Lydia.

"Silas!"

He looked up at his mother, his expression one of feigned innocence. "I ain't talkin'."

Though Lydia was tempted to grin at the boy's cheeky response, she didn't want to get him in any more trouble, and so she turned to look out the window. At least the scenery would not protest a Northerner's gaze.

Texas bore little resemblance to central New York. It wasn't simply the heat, although that was far more intense than she had expected, especially since summer hadn't officially begun. The towns she'd passed through were smaller than the ones near Syracuse, with few of the two-story houses so common at home.

Lydia hadn't been able to identify many of the crops, and the trees — she'd heard someone call them pecans and live oaks — were unlike the elms, maples, and sycamores that lined the streets in Syracuse. The grass was different too, and though she hadn't

14

thought it possible, the Texas sky seemed even deeper blue than a summer sky at home.

Lydia shook herself mentally. Syracuse wasn't home any longer. Her family was gone, and she'd resigned her position at the academy where she'd spent most of her life, first as a student, then as a teacher. With her ties to central New York severed, there was nothing to return to. Her future home was with Edgar in Cimarron Creek, Texas. Thank goodness that was only a few hours away. She was equally thankful that none of the other passengers would be disembarking there. Surely the residents of Cimarron Creek would be more welcoming.

She leaned against the seat back and closed her eyes, not wanting to see the unfriendly faces opposite her. The journey that had been long and at times grueling was almost over. Before the sun set, Lydia would be with Edgar. By the end of the week, she would be Mrs. Edgar Ellis. It might be four months later than they'd planned, but soon — very soon — she would be wearing the beautiful ring he'd shown her their last evening together. Lydia bit the inside of her cheek, remembering how the ring had gleamed in the moonlight when he'd held it in his bloodstained hands.

Stop it! she admonished herself. She had resolved not to think about that night and the reason Edgar had fled. When the police had questioned her, she had been able to answer honestly that he hadn't told her where he was headed. But even though no names had been mentioned that night, she'd known his destination. Months earlier, Edgar had shown her a map of Texas and had pointed toward the town where he wanted them to raise a family.

"It's right in the heart of what they call the Hill Country," he said. "Germans settled a lot of towns, but this one was founded by three men from the North."

Edgar's enthusiasm had been contagious, and Lydia soon found herself imagining their life in a new state.

"It'll be warm and beautiful," he told her. "Best of all, we'll be able to open our own business. No more working for others."

Independence had always been Edgar's dream, though the details seemed to change with the phases of the moon. One day he wanted to run a mercantile. A week later he would talk about buying a hotel and restaurant. The one thing they'd both agreed on was that a saloon had no place in their future.

Lydia had soon realized that all that truly

mattered to Edgar was being his own boss, and she'd accepted the vague explanations. It didn't matter to her whether they ran a mercantile, a hotel, or something else. What mattered was being with Edgar.

Soon. She opened her eyes again and gazed at the landscape. The bluebonnets she'd heard so much about were no longer blooming, but other wildflowers dotted the grass, and the flat terrain had turned to gently rolling hills. Lydia sighed with pleasure. Texas was beautiful, a place where dreams could come true, where promises would be fulfilled. She'd been right to ignore the advice one well-meaning woman had given her. There was no reason to turn back. In a few hours she would be with Edgar and all her questions would be answered.

It was not a mistake.

Trouble was coming. Travis Whitfield could feel it in the air as he strode toward the mercantile. The stagecoach was due in ten minutes. As it did each weekday, it would bring mail. Today it would also bring Travis's father, the source of the impending trouble.

Travis tried not to frown, but the fact was, with Pa in Austin, this last month had been more peaceful than any he could recall since the town had asked him to wear the sheriff's badge. Wasn't that a sad commentary? Though he wasn't satisfied with Doc's verdict that Sheriff Allen's death had been an accident and though a man had gone missing, Travis was calling it a peaceful month.

The peace was about to end. Dorcas's latest letter had warned him that not even the sight of his first grandchild had mellowed Pa's temper. He was still telling anyone who'd listen — and even those who wouldn't — that his son had no business accepting the appointment as Cimarron Creek's sheriff when he was already serving the town as a lawyer. Never mind that Travis was doing both. Once Pa stepped off the stagecoach, he'd start haranguing him again.

Tipping his hat to a woman whose overflowing bag indicated she'd found several garments to her liking at the dressmaker's shop, Travis had to admit there were days when he agreed with Pa. He'd known being sheriff wouldn't be easy, but it had proven to be more difficult than he'd expected. For a town of barely a hundred and sixty, Cimarron Creek seemed to have more than its share of problems.

Travis looked down the street. Perhaps he

was prejudiced, but he believed his grandfather and great-uncles had chosen wisely when they'd laid out the town. They'd insisted that trees be cut only if absolutely necessary, with the result that the stores on Main Street were shaded by live oaks. He'd seen other towns where residents had to contend with the blazing sun, and the sheriffs of those towns had admitted that tempers frequently flared when the mercury rose.

Travis couldn't blame heat for the latest problem. It hadn't been hot the night the town's newest resident had disappeared. There hadn't even been a full moon. Some folks — his own father among them — claimed mischief was more likely when the moon was full. That hadn't been the case last week. No heat, no moon, just one missing man.

Opal Ellis wasn't going to be happy that Travis had nothing new to report, but it wasn't for lack of trying. When his own search had turned up no clues to the whereabouts of Opal's missing husband, Travis had sent telegrams to the sheriffs of all the surrounding towns. They'd had no more success than he had.

"Howdy, Sheriff."

Travis nodded at the trio of schoolboys

lounging against the one empty store on Main Street. With school over for the summer and crops not ready for harvest, they had little to occupy their time. Fortunately, they hadn't gotten into trouble. Not yet. But they would. Remembering his own boyhood shenanigans, Travis knew that was inevitable. He only hoped the antics wouldn't be too serious and that no one would ask him to intervene. He had enough work already, with the missing Edgar Ellis on top of his list.

Travis didn't like unsolved mysteries. That was the reason he'd asked for his cousins' opinions. The three of them had been playing horseshoes in Porter's yard when he'd brought up the subject. As he'd expected, neither man was reticent about expressing his beliefs. What he hadn't expected was that the men who were as close to him as brothers had disagreed.

Porter claimed Edgar had left town of his own volition once he'd learned he was going to be a father.

"Babies are a lot of work," he declared. "I ought to know." As the youngest of what some townspeople called the Three Musketeers but the only one who was married and had a child, Porter liked to boast about his status.

20

Wrinkling his nose as if he were tired of listening to his brother's tales of fatherhood, Warner disagreed with Porter's assessment. Instead, he speculated Edgar had been run out of town — or worse — by someone still fighting the war. If Pa had been in Cimarron Creek at the time, he might have been Warner's primary suspect, but Pa was in Austin, making Dorcas's life miserable.

Though he'd done everything he could, Travis had no idea where Opal's husband had gone. As much as he wished it were otherwise, that was one mystery he was unlikely to solve today or anytime soon.

As he approached the drugstore, Travis pulled his watch from his pocket and nodded. He'd left too early. Since there was no point in standing in front of the mercantile simply waiting for the coach to arrive, he might as well see what Warner was doing this afternoon. Travis pushed open the door and inhaled the pungent smells of the county's only pharmacy.

On the opposite side of the store, his cousin glanced up from whatever he was grinding with his mortar and pestle. As tall as Travis but with hair a lighter shade of brown and eyes that were blue rather than gray, Warner had the firm jaw they'd both inherited from their great-grandfather.

"You don't look too happy," he said.

"Pa's due in with today's mail. Would you be happy if you were in my boots?"

Warner shook his head. "I can't say that I would, but my own boots are feeling mighty uncomfortable today."

Though Travis had hoped for a bit of sympathy, it appeared he'd be the one dispensing it. "Someone didn't like the potion you made for them?"

As Travis had intended, Warner rose to the bait. The town's first pharmacist was proud of his training and insistent that he be treated with the proper degree of respect. He was not, he had informed both his brother and Travis, a pill peddler.

"How many times do I have to tell you they're not called potions? That sounds like something a witch brews. I concoct medicines."

Travis looked around his cousin's obviously prosperous business. Tall glass-fronted cabinets filled with bottles in every size, shape, and color lined the back wall. Many of the bottles were patent medicines Warner purchased ready-made, but others were created right here using formulas Warner had learned during his years of training in Philadelphia.

Raising his hands in mock surrender,

Travis conceded his cousin's point. "All right. Let me rephrase my question. Did someone not like the medicine you concocted for them?"

"I wish that was the problem. I could deal with that." Warner continued grinding whatever it was into a floury powder. "You're not the only one with parent problems. My father stopped by to remind me it's time for me to do my duty. I'm expected to marry and produce grandchildren, preferably boys since Porter has already presented Ma and Pa with a granddaughter."

Though his own father had similar sentiments and wasn't shy about voicing them, this was the first time Travis had heard that his uncle was pressuring Warner. "What does he expect you to do — send for a mail-order bride?"

Warner shrugged. "That idea was mentioned. I don't think he cares how I find a bride so long as I do. The gist of the speech he gave me was that as the firstborn it's my responsibility to ensure that the Gray name is carried on." Warner poured the finely ground substance into a small glass bottle and capped it. "You know as well as I do how unpleasant Pa can be when he's riled, so if you happen to see a beautiful single woman walking the streets of Cimarron

Creek, send her my way. I'll make her an offer she won't refuse."

Though Warner sounded serious, he waggled his eyebrows and pretended to twirl the ends of a nonexistent moustache. Travis began to laugh. "Thanks, cousin. I needed a good laugh."

Travis was still chuckling at Warner's parody of a melodrama villain while he waited for the stagecoach. The arrival of a single woman, much less a beautiful one, was as unlikely as Pa suddenly regrowing the leg he had lost at Gettysburg, and Warner knew it. Still, his cousin had joked instead of ranting about his father's demands.

Perhaps that was something Travis ought to do. The problem was, joking didn't come easily to him. Even before he'd assumed the sheriff's badge, Aunt Bertha had told him he took life too seriously. He couldn't argue with that. Life was serious, and it had become more so after his mother's death five years earlier. Since then, Aunt Bertha had done her best to cheer him. Lately, though, she'd been so caught up in whatever was troubling her that she hadn't chided Travis, and he found he missed the gentle yet firm advice she used to dole out.

Travis's smile faded. His aunt had supported him when he'd needed her, and how had he repaid her? He'd left her alone, even though he'd known she must be lonely after Uncle Jonas's death. That would end. While being Cimarron Creek's sheriff was important, Travis was also Bertha Henderson's great-nephew. That was important too. It might only be for a few minutes, but he resolved to visit her every day. Tonight he would . . .

Before Travis could finish his thought, he heard the distinctive rumbling of the coach and saw the cloud of dust that accompanied it during most of the summer. Girding himself for the coming encounter with his father, he waited until the coach stopped, then fixed a smile on his face as the driver climbed down from his perch and opened the door.

Travis had expected a one-legged man with a scowl on his face. He did not expect the first passenger to disembark to be a beautiful young woman. Golden-haired and dressed in a more formal style than any of Cimarron Creek's ladies, she was a vision of loveliness. Travis stared, trying not to let his jaw drop open in shock. Had God answered Warner's prayer? It hadn't been an official prayer, but his cousin had definitely expressed a need for a beautiful young woman, and here she was. Travis hadn't seen a woman this beautiful in . . . The simple truth was, he couldn't recall the last time he'd seen anyone who came close to her. Catherine was easy on the eyes, but she was his cousin. This woman was not.

The woman looked around, clearly assessing the town while the driver unloaded her baggage. Did she find Main Street as pleasing as Travis did with its well-kept stores and the tree-branch canopy, or was she expecting something grander? Though she'd said not a word, her clothing and hairstyle made Travis believe she'd come from a large city, probably one in the East. Which raised the question of why was she here. It didn't appear that she was expecting to be met, which made the woman's arrival distinctly odd. Unaccompanied, unexpected women simply did not come to Cimarron Creek.

Who was this woman? Just as importantly, where was Pa? Pa moved slowly, and of course he would have let the lady leave the coach first, but he should have disembarked by now.

Travis took another step toward the stage-coach, only to see the driver close the door, then drag the two trunks onto the board-walk.

"No more passengers for Cimarron

Creek?" Travis asked. Though he recognized most of the drivers on the line, he'd never seen this man before.

The driver shook his head. "No, sir. That's all." He tipped his head toward the beautiful woman standing in front of the mercantile. "I reckon the other passengers will be glad to see the last of her. Purty near every time we stopped, I got an earful about her."

Unwilling to engage in gossip, Travis refused to ask the driver why the others had objected to the lovely lady, but the driver took his silence as license to continue. "She's a Yankee, you know," the man said as he climbed onto his perch. "Like those confounded carpetbaggers."

Just what Cimarron Creek didn't need. Edgar Ellis's arrival had caused enough of a stir, and though he'd gradually gained acceptance, Travis suspected the only person who truly regretted his disappearance was his wife.

When the stagecoach pulled away, leaving a cloud of dust in its wake, Travis saw that the woman hadn't moved. Perhaps she was waiting for someone after all. He wouldn't count on that.

"How can I help you, ma'am?"

The stranger turned, apparently startled by the friendliness of his tone. If the driver's comments were accurate, she hadn't been welcomed inside the coach. Travis's official duties didn't include welcoming strangers to town, but he was a Whitfield, and Whitfields were expected to maintain Cimarron Creek's reputation as a friendly place.

The woman dipped her head slightly and managed a small smile. Travis took a deep breath. Close up, she was even more beautiful than she'd been at a distance. Her features were as perfect as the ones he'd seen in those ladies' magazines Aunt Bertha favored, her eyes as blue as the summer sky. And when she smiled, well, a man would have to be blind in both eyes not to be dazzled.

"I'm looking for someone," she said slowly. "My . . ." Breaking off whatever it was she had planned to say, she shook her head. "I'm looking for Mr. Ellis, Edgar Ellis. Can you tell me where I might find him?"

Travis felt as if he'd taken a mule kick to the stomach. "I wish I could." He saw the woman's confusion. Truth was, he was confused too. When Edgar had arrived in Cimarron Creek, Travis's impression had been that the man was a loner. He'd never spoken of family or friends, and like many men who'd headed West, he'd chosen not to speak of his past.

Travis narrowed his eyes, considering the woman who wanted to find Edgar. Though he saw no other resemblance, the stranger had the same coloring as the missing man. Perhaps she was his sister. Travis wouldn't blurt out his question. That would be rude, and if there was one thing his mother had taught him, it was to be polite to ladies. Even though his position as sheriff occasionally required a firm interrogation, there were other ways to get the information he needed from this woman.

"I'm sorry, ma'am. I seem to have forgotten my manners. I'm Travis Whitfield, and I'm the sheriff here. I'll do whatever I can to help you, Mrs. . . ." He let his voice trail off, encouraging her to volunteer her name.

"It's Miss. Miss Lydia Crawford."

Not Ellis. That meant, unless they had different fathers, Miss Crawford wasn't Edgar's sister. Perhaps she was a cousin. Or perhaps she was no relation at all, but in that case, Travis wondered why she'd come.

"I would appreciate it if you could direct me to Edgar." Her voice was clear, each word carefully enunciated. It was a pleasant voice, but it was also a Northern voice that would garner her few friends in Cimarron Creek. The townspeople might not be as outspoken as the other passengers on the stagecoach had been, but they did not welcome Yankees.

Travis wished it were otherwise. He also wished he did not have to disappoint this woman who looked like she needed a friend, but there was no way around it. He was going to disappoint her. "That's the problem, Miss Crawford. I can't direct you to him. Edgar disappeared last week. No one knows where he's gone."

Miss Crawford recoiled as if he'd hit her, and for a moment Travis thought she might crumple onto the boardwalk. "Edgar's gone?" Her voice was filled with disbelief.

"That's right, ma'am. I wish I could help you, but I've been unable to find him." There had to be something he could do for her. Travis thought quickly. "Would you like to talk to his wife?"

This time there was no doubt about it. Miss Crawford was going to faint. As blood drained from her face, Travis stepped forward and put an arm around her. She looked up, those beautiful blue eyes filled with pain, and the words came out as little more than a croak.

"His wife?"

2

Lydia took a deep breath, then exhaled slowly, all in a desperate attempt not to faint. She had never fainted, not even when Hortense, her closest friend at the academy, had laced her corset too tightly. Unfortunately, tight corsets were nothing compared to this.

Edgar was married!

She'd survived the long journey; she'd endured the many snubs; she'd even managed to keep her composure when she learned Edgar was gone; but she'd come unraveled when the sheriff had mentioned Edgar's wife.

Lydia felt the blood drain from her face, and black spots danced in front of her eyes. It couldn't be true. The sheriff must be mistaken. But if he wasn't . . . Lydia's legs grew weak and her spine threatened to crumble. *Stop it!* she told herself. *You're not going to faint.* But her body refused to obey,

31

and before she knew what was happening, the sheriff had put his arm around her.

She should object. After all, it wasn't proper for a strange man to be touching her. Even though she and Edgar had been betrothed, he had never been so bold in public. Lydia opened her mouth to protest, then closed it again. She couldn't object when the sheer strength of the sheriff's arm was doing more to calm her nerves than her careful breathing.

Edgar was married!

She took another breath, exhaling slowly as she tried to make sense of a world that had suddenly gone topsy-turvy. Though the sheriff's words had lodged inside her, Lydia refused to believe them. Edgar couldn't be married. He simply could not. She hadn't given up her comfortable life and traveled all this way to meet a man who'd found himself another wife.

"Do you want to talk to Mrs. Ellis?" The sheriff's voice was low and somehow reassuring, as if he were trying to keep a frightened animal from bolting. Lydia wouldn't bolt — there was no place to go — but she needed to regain her composure before she met Edgar's bride.

Grateful for the comfort the sheriff was providing, she restrained herself from shrieking that she was the one who was supposed to be Mrs. Ellis. That was why she'd come here, to marry the man she loved, the man who'd claimed to love her. But he hadn't. That much was clear. If the marriage was real — and Lydia had no reason to believe it was not — there was nothing she could do to change it. What she could do, what she had to do, was learn why Edgar had broken his promises.

"Yes, I would like to speak with her," Lydia said as firmly as she could when her limbs were trembling, "but I think I'd better sit down for a moment." Despite the sheriff's firm grip, her legs still felt on the verge of collapse.

"Of course. I should have thought of that." Keeping his arm around her waist, he led her to a bench in front of the mercantile. Though she'd thought he would step away once she was seated, the sheriff remained close enough to catch her if she fainted and tumbled forward.

"Would you like a glass of water, maybe a cup of tea?"

Lydia looked up at the man who was trying to comfort her. If she'd been asked to picture a man as different from Edgar as possible, it would be Cimarron Creek's sheriff. Travis Whitfield was several inches taller than Edgar and more powerfully built. Though his clothing was ordinary, he wore it with more self-confidence than any man she'd met. His features were more sharply defined than Edgar's, his chin square, his nose finely chiseled. But the biggest difference was in the two men's coloring. Unlike Edgar with his blue-eyed blond good looks, Travis Whitfield sported hair so dark it was almost black and gray eyes that shone with intelligence and, at this particular moment, concern.

"My aunt claims a cup of tea makes everything better."

"I have a friend who said the same thing." Lydia nodded slowly. Hortense believed tea to be a panacea, but all the tea in China wouldn't change the fact that Edgar had married someone else. Lydia's heart recoiled at the thought that he might have given his wife the filigreed gold band he'd bought for her. Had he also told his new wife she was the only woman in the world for him?

"Cream and sugar?"

Lydia blinked as she looked up at the man who'd rescued her. What was he talking about?

"In your tea," he said, his voice once again low and somehow intimate, as soothing as the breeze that was a welcome relief after the stifling heat of the stagecoach.

"Oh." She'd let thoughts of Edgar distract her. When she'd nodded, Sheriff Whitfield must have thought she was asking for a cup of tea. "Thank you, but I don't need tea. I feel better now." Rising from the bench on legs that were once again steady, she fixed her gaze on the sheriff. "Where might I find Mrs. Ellis?" Though it hurt to pronounce that name and know it belonged to another woman, Lydia forced the words out.

The sheriff gestured to the north, his eyes darkening from silver to the shade of a thunderstorm. "I hope you don't mind my saying it, Miss Crawford, but right now you look like a good wind could blow you over."

He bent his arm and waited for Lydia to put her hand on it. "I'll take you to the saloon. It's only a block away."

"The saloon?" Lydia hadn't thought he could shock her again, but he had.

The sheriff nodded. "That's where they've both been working. Faith hired Edgar the day he arrived. Said she's never seen a man so good at keeping the peace." For the first time since she'd met him, the sheriff's lips curved into a smile. "Maybe Edgar should have been sheriff."

Lydia wasn't smiling. Today, the day she'd

thought her dreams would come true, had turned into a day of shocks. Not only was Edgar gone but he seemed to have changed. Nothing Lydia had heard sounded like the Edgar she'd known. That Edgar had sworn he would never set foot inside a tavern, but now he was working in one. That Edgar had claimed he loved Lydia and that she was the wife he wanted, but he'd married someone else. Promises, promises. He'd broken them all, just the way Papa had.

"Shame should not be shared," Mama had always insisted, and so Lydia wouldn't tell the sheriff about Edgar's false promises, but the way he was looking at her made it clear she had to say something.

"I can't picture Edgar with a star on his chest." Fear of men in uniform had driven him from New York.

Sheriff Whitfield shrugged. "Some folks couldn't picture me with one, either, but here I am — the one and only lawman in town. When I pinned on the star, I made a promise to keep everyone in town safe. I'm doing my best, even though I don't always succeed."

Lydia wondered whether he was referring to the mystery of Edgar's disappearance but wouldn't ask. After he'd assured her that her trunks would be safe in front of the mercantile, they'd been walking as they talked, going diagonally across what the sheriff had identified as Main and Pecan Streets. While Main was, as its name implied, the primary avenue in town, Pecan separated the mercantile and other high-class shops from the livery and saloon. Though both of those establishments were well maintained, Lydia knew enough about small towns to realize that neither was considered as respectable as the dress shop and drugstore she'd spotted in the same block as the mercantile.

As the stagecoach had lumbered into town, Lydia had stared out the window, eager to see her new home. Edgar had chosen well. The various houses and businesses on Main Street were attractive, and the presence of mature trees made Cimarron Creek an appealing town. Even the Silver Spur, as she learned the saloon was named, appeared to be a cut above the saloons Edgar had described.

Constructed of what Lydia assumed was native stone, it boasted an attractive sign over the traditional swinging half doors. Were it not for the door and the windows, it could have been almost any business, but the windows were darker than normal. Perhaps they were designed to keep the sun from baking the interior, but she thought it more likely they were meant to protect the identity of the saloon's patrons.

"Ready?"

Though Lydia doubted she would ever be ready to enter a saloon, when she nodded, the sheriff pushed the door open to allow her to precede him. It took a few seconds for her eyes to grow accustomed to the dark interior, but she soon discovered there were only three men seated at the polished wood bar and two others at one of the small tables. As she had expected from the well-tended exterior, the inside of the saloon held well-made furniture and was surprisingly clean. Lydia had envisioned sawdust on the floor along with scarred tables and broken chairs.

Though she said nothing, a woman stood behind the bar, her light blue eyes regarding Lydia with open curiosity. Dressed in what Mama would have called flamboyant clothing, the woman had auburn hair that could only have come from a bottle, but the silver wings at her temples were probably natural.

"Afternoon, Faith," the sheriff said as he and Lydia approached the bar. "I'd like you to meet Miss Lydia Crawford. She came all the way from . . ." He let his words trail off,

38

obviously expecting Lydia to complete the sentence. It appeared that open-ended phrases were Sheriff Whitfield's preferred method of interrogation. She almost smiled, remembering how she'd tried that technique with her pupils. It hadn't been particularly successful.

Seeing no reason not to answer, Lydia looked at the sheriff as she said, "Syracuse."

His reaction was unexpected. While he made no comment, Lydia knew she wasn't mistaken in the confusion that had momentarily clouded his eyes. "Syracuse," Travis Whitfield said firmly. "She's come from Syracuse, New York, to see Edgar." There was a second's pause, as if he were waiting for the woman behind the bar to respond. When she said nothing, he continued. "I explained what happened, but I was hoping Opal might be able to tell her something more."

The sheriff turned slightly so that he was once again facing Lydia. As if suddenly recalling his manners, he began the introductions. "Miss Crawford, this is Faith Kohler, the owner of the friendliest saloon this side of the Rio Grande."

When the woman's face flushed at the compliment, Lydia tried to smile. "It's a pleasure to meet you, Mrs. Kohler." That was an exaggeration. Nothing that had happened since Lydia had stepped into the stagecoach had been a pleasure.

"Just Faith," the saloon's owner said, "and the pleasure is all mine. Any friend of Edgar's is welcome here." Her eyes narrowed as she studied Lydia for a second or two before saying, "I'd like to help you, but like the sheriff said, I'm not the one you want to see." She turned toward the door that led to the back of the saloon. "Opal! Come up front."

Though Lydia tried to brace herself, she was not prepared for her first sight of Mrs. Edgar Ellis. The woman who emerged from the back bore little resemblance to what Lydia had been expecting. She'd expected a woman at least as old as herself, maybe even closer to Edgar's nine and twenty years. Instead, his wife was very young, probably only eighteen or nineteen. She was also very tall, only an inch or so less than Edgar's height. Though no one would call her beautiful with her carroty red hair and a face covered with freckles, her light green dress highlighted eyes of the same shade.

Lydia tried to keep her eyes from drifting lower, registering what she'd seen the second Opal Ellis had entered the room, but she failed. The pretty green dress highlighted more than Opal's eyes. It also accentuated her swollen abdomen. Opal wasn't simply Edgar's wife; she was also the mother of his child.

This had to be a nightmare. Any moment now Lydia would waken and find herself back in Syracuse. But as desperately as she wished it were otherwise, she knew this was no dream.

You're the only woman I'll ever love. Edgar's promises echoed through her mind, and for a second Lydia thought she might be ill. The man she'd believed loved her had been as false as her father, promising everlasting love, then marrying another when his fancy strayed.

"You okay, miss?" Edgar's wife asked, her eyebrows knitting with concern. "You look like you seen a ghost."

The ghost of her dreams. They'd been killed as surely as if someone had thrust a sword through them.

"I had hoped to see Edgar, but the sheriff told me he's gone." Though Lydia could see the questions in Opal's eyes, telling her she had expected to marry Edgar would only cause pain. It was best to say as little as possible.

"I don't know what happened. Some folks say he run away, but he din't. He was happy

41

about the baby." Opal laid her hands on her stomach, as if to protect the life within, and as she did, Lydia saw she was wearing the ring Edgar had bought for her.

"Edgar would never abandon us," the young woman declared.

But he'd done exactly that to Lydia.

3

The woman had secrets. Travis's instincts told him there was more to Lydia Crawford's relationship with Edgar Ellis than she was admitting. If they were cousins, she would have mentioned that to Opal, but instead she'd just stood there, as stiff as a fence post, while Opal told her what little she knew about her husband's disappearance.

Travis had the impression Miss Crawford was afraid to move lest she shatter like one of Aunt Bertha's china figurines. It was only when it was obvious that Opal had nothing more to say that he'd taken Miss Crawford's arm to lead her outside and across the street.

Though she had been visibly shaken by the sight of Opal, Miss Crawford's distress had begun before that. She'd said nothing, but Travis knew he hadn't been mistaken in thinking she'd been uncomfortable entering the saloon. The truth was, he shouldn't have taken her there, at least not to the front door. Even Aunt Bertha, who felt free to go anywhere within the borders of Cimarron Creek, avoided Faith's establishment. Travis should have used the rear entrance, where their arrival would not have been so public. It was too late to change that. Now he'd have to try to undo the problems he'd unwittingly caused.

When they reached the other side of the street, Miss Crawford took a deep breath, then let it out in ragged little pants that told him as surely as a blue norther chilled his skin that she was still upset. More than upset. She looked physically ill. This was worse than when he'd told her Edgar had disappeared. He wasn't sure what to do other than keep an arm around her while he figured out what to do next.

Doc Harrington might be able to help her, but Travis had heard enough from Cousin Catherine to fear that the doctor could just as easily harm Miss Crawford. Like it or not, she was Travis's problem. He may have only been the messenger, but he was the reason the smile had left her face. Now it was up to him to make her time in Cimarron Creek as pleasant as possible and to unravel her secrets. The first was his duty as a gentleman, the second his responsibility as sheriff.

Travis glanced down the street as he tried to form a plan. There was no sign of the schoolboys, nothing that needed his attention other than Miss Crawford. He didn't want to let her go anywhere until he discovered the reason for the inconsistencies in her story. She claimed to be from Syracuse, but Travis was certain Edgar had said he was from Dayton. One of them was lying.

And then there was the timing. It could have been coincidence that Miss Crawford arrived here so soon after Edgar's disappearance, but Travis wasn't one to believe in coincidences. No, sirree. If he were a betting man, he would have bet there was a connection between her arrival and Edgar's sudden departure. The way he figured it, Edgar hightailed it out of Cimarron Creek at about the same time Miss Crawford left Syracuse. Assuming, of course, that Edgar had left voluntarily. That had yet to be determined. In the meantime, Travis had a decidedly uneasy woman on his hands.

"We need to find you a place to stay tonight," he said as kindly as he could. "It's my responsibility to keep everyone in Cimarron Creek safe, and that includes visitors." The way she nodded told Travis his words

45

were barely registering. The visit to the Silver Spur had shaken her more than he'd realized.

"The northbound stagecoach is due in at noon tomorrow." By then he should have some answers. He'd telegraph the authorities in Syracuse to see how much of her story was true. And while he was doing that, he'd check on Edgar too. There'd been no reason for Sheriff Allen to contact anyone in Dayton when Edgar arrived, but matters had changed. Sheriff Allen was gone and Edgar was gone, leaving Travis determined to learn what he could about the young woman who'd come in search of a missing man.

She looked up at him, her beautiful blue eyes filled with determination. "I'm not leaving tomorrow." A light breeze teased the curl that had come loose from her chignon, bouncing it against her cheek. Seemingly oblivious to the way it softened her face, she flattened her lips as she said, "I won't leave until I know what happened to Edgar."

Travis was surprised, and yet at the same time, he wasn't. For as much as Miss Crawford seemed fragile, he sensed a strong will underneath that apparently soft exterior.

"It could be weeks, even months, before we find Edgar." When she didn't so much as flinch at the thought of spending that amount of time in Cimarron Creek, Travis continued. "I don't mean to pry, but do you have the funds to stay that long?" The town had no hotel, and though he might be able to find someone who'd allow her to board with them, it was unlikely anyone in town would take a stranger — especially a Northerner — without expecting to be paid.

Miss Crawford inclined her head slightly. "That shouldn't be a problem. I'm not destitute, if that's what you were thinking."

It wasn't what Travis had been thinking. Her clothing was well made and, though slightly dusty from travel, appeared to be new. Still, if she'd expected Edgar to provide a home, and Travis suspected that was the case, she might have brought little more than her personal belongings. Those trunks were probably filled with nothing more than clothes and the frippery women seemed to prize.

"I can work," she continued. "I used to teach school."

Travis bit back a smile at both her slightly imperious attitude and what it revealed. He now recognized the starch he'd seen in her. Every teacher he'd known had been determined. Unfortunately, although he'd begun to like Miss Crawford, he was going to have to disappoint her again.

"We already have a teacher."

Another woman might have wept or at least clenched her fists in frustration. Miss Crawford was not one of those women. "I'll find something else to do."

She was determined; she was probably a hard worker, but that didn't mean she would succeed. Though Travis hated to dash her expectations, he wouldn't hold out false hopes. As far as he knew, none of the storekeepers needed an assistant, and if they did, they would be reluctant to hire a beautiful single woman who was likely to get married the next month. It would be difficult for Travis to convince anyone to hire her, even if she were a native-born Texan. As for a Yankee . . .

"There's not a lot of opportunity," he told Miss Crawford. "Most of our girls marry as soon as they're out of school."

The blood drained from her face, then rushed back, and he saw unmistakable pain in her eyes. "Marriage is the last thing I want," she declared.

It was odd that she protested so vehemently. Most women wanted to marry. In fact, Travis couldn't think of a single one who didn't. He'd bet anything that Miss Crawford was lying.

As the wheels began to spin, Travis realized there was a perfectly logical reason for her arrival in Cimarron Creek: she had come to marry Edgar. If she was one of those mail-order brides he and Warner had discussed, the fact that she was from Syracuse and Edgar from Dayton made sense. What didn't make sense was that Edgar would marry Opal if he had a lady like Miss Lydia Crawford coming to be his bride. Opal was a nice enough girl, but she couldn't hold a candle to Miss Crawford. Even if they hadn't exchanged likenesses, Miss Crawford's letters would have shown Edgar that she was educated and genteel.

Travis wouldn't think about marriage and how the woman standing so close to him was exactly the kind of bride Warner claimed he wanted. Warner might be as close as a brother, but somehow the thought of him marrying Miss Crawford seemed wrong. Besides, she said she wasn't looking for marriage.

"Be that as it may, we need to find you a place. I doubt you'd want to stay at the saloon, even if Faith had room for you." Miss Crawford was obviously uncomfortable around Opal.

"No, I wouldn't. What about a boarding-house?"

"We don't have one." There'd never been a need, because unlike some towns, Cimarron Creek had few temporary residents.

"Who needs a boardinghouse when we've got those three big houses?" Pa had demanded one night. Though Pa had always been disdainful of the houses the first generation had built, claiming they were pretentious, Travis suspected it was a case of sour grapes, that Pa wished he'd been the son to inherit his parents' mansion instead of it being passed to his older brother, while he'd been left living outside the town limits on the family's ranch.

"Look at Bertha rattling around all by herself. It's a sin, I tell you," Pa had said that same night.

Travis didn't believe it was a sin any more than he believed it was coincidence that particular memory had resurfaced at the precise moment he was trying to find lodging for Miss Crawford. Pastor Dunn had preached a whole sermon about how what many believed to be coincidence was actually God's hand at work. This was the perfect example of that.

"I have an idea," Travis said slowly as he tried to consider the thought from every angle. This might be just what both Miss Crawford and Aunt Bertha needed. His aunt didn't need money, so that wouldn't be an issue, but she did need something to occupy her time. And if Miss Crawford lived with her, Travis wouldn't worry about his aunt so much. He could stop by every day and check on both of them. He almost grinned at the prospect of seeing Miss Crawford every day. No doubt about it, having her live with Aunt Bertha was a good idea, maybe even a great one.

"My aunt — great-aunt, actually — has a large house," he explained. "I think she might agree to let you stay with her. She's been living alone since my uncle died last year, and though she won't admit it, she's lonely."

Miss Crawford's shoulders sank in relief, but she said, "I don't want to impose on anyone."

"You won't." Travis could promise that. "If Aunt Bertha doesn't want you to stay, she'll tell you."

"Of course you can stay." Mrs. Henderson, the woman Travis had claimed treasured her role as the matriarch of Cimarron Creek, nodded vigorously. With her silver hair and green eyes, her patrician nose and a jaw line that was still firm, she was clearly a force with which to be reckoned.

As for the house, Travis had not exaggerated when he'd described it as large. It wasn't simply large; it was magnificent. Lydia's breath had caught at the sight of what could only be described as a mansion. Two stories high with six columns on the front and four more on each of the sides, it dominated the corner of Cedar and Pecan.

When Lydia had gasped, unable to hide her surprise, Travis had laughed. "If you look down Cedar, there are two more equally big houses. When the two Henderson brothers and their brother-in-law founded Cimarron Creek, they each built a house large enough for a dozen children. As it turned out, there were only nine children among the three of them, but the houses remain as monuments to their dreams of a dynasty."

Lydia's awe increased when Mrs. Henderson opened the front door, revealing an expansive foyer and a curving staircase.

"I'm glad Travis brought you here," Mrs. Henderson said when he'd explained Lydia's situation. The three of them were seated in the parlor. In keeping with the size of the house itself, this room was larger than the main gathering room at Lydia's former academy, and that had been designed for two dozen pupils, three teachers, and the headmistress.

"Everyone in this town has told me on at least one occasion that this house is too big for one person," Mrs. Henderson continued. Somehow she managed to speak without pausing to breathe. "Why, Xavier Cready even went so far as to say I ought to marry him just so I didn't have to live alone. Imagine that. Me married to Xavier Cready."

Though Lydia had no idea who Xavier Cready was or why anyone would consider the thought of his marrying the sheriff's great-aunt to be ludicrous, one thing she did know was that she had never met a woman like Bertha Henderson. Lydia might not have seen a tornado, but she'd read about them and how they flattened everything in their path. This woman was like a whirlwind. Woe to anyone who stood in her way.

"You'll be part of the family," Mrs. Henderson had announced a minute earlier. "That means there's no need for formality. You may address me as Aunt Bertha, and my nephew is Travis. I trust you won't object if we call you Lydia."

Though Lydia had been raised in an

establishment that valued etiquette and would never have dreamt of addressing a woman of Mrs. Henderson's stature as "aunt," she merely nodded her agreement. She liked being called Lydia, and it was certainly easier to think of the tall dark-haired man who'd been so kind to her as Travis rather than the sheriff.

"I don't know Xavier Cready, but I believe a woman should not marry unless she's in love and is sure the man loves her," Lydia said as calmly as she could with Travis Whitfield standing only a few feet away, his gray eyes seeming to catalog each move she made. Though he'd said nothing after performing the introductions and explaining Lydia's dilemma to his aunt, he showed no signs of leaving. Lydia should have had no reason to feel uncomfortable, and yet she couldn't dismiss the feeling that Travis had looked inside her head and knew she'd come to Cimarron Creek expecting to marry Edgar.

"Exactly." Aunt Bertha inclined her head in a gesture that would have made Queen Victoria proud. "I knew the minute I set eyes on you that we'd get along. You've got a good head on your shoulders."

"Are you certain you want me to stay?" Though Lydia had felt an instinctive liking for Travis's aunt, she did not want to take advantage of the woman's loneliness. "I'm sure you can tell that I'm from the North."

"What of it?" the older woman demanded. "So am I."

"Most of the people on the stagecoach weren't exactly welcoming. They seemed to think I was a carpetbagger."

Aunt Bertha lifted one elegantly clad shoulder. "The carpetbaggers left an unpleasant legacy. No doubt about that, but don't you worry. The Henderson name wields a lot of power here. It was my husband, his brother, and their sister's husband who founded this town more than forty years ago. We're all from Illinois." But that had been before the war. Much had changed since then.

Aunt Bertha changed the subject without taking a breath. "You can blame the men for the name. I tried to tell them that the Cimarron River didn't flow through Texas, but they wouldn't listen. The minute they set eyes on the creek, they decided to rename it Cimarron and call the town after it. The only thing I can say about that is that Cimarron Creek sounds a whole lot better than Muddy Creek."

She smiled at Lydia. "But you're not worried about names, are you? You needn't worry about the townsfolk. Once you're living with me, no one will dare say a word against you." For the first time, Aunt Bertha paused for half a second before she amended her statement. "Except for Abe."

"And who might he be?" Having been forewarned, Lydia would do her best to steer clear of him just as she'd steer clear of the saloon. Not only were saloons places no decent woman frequented, but Lydia had no wish to see Opal Ellis again. That would only remind her of what should have been hers.

"Abe is Travis's father. He's a stubborn coot who's as ornery as the hills are old." Aunt Bertha gave her nephew a look that challenged him to disagree. "Don't bother trying to deny it. You know there's no excuse for his rudeness."

Lydia wasn't certain which surprised her more: Aunt Bertha's outspokenness or the fact that Travis merely nodded. Apparently Lydia wasn't the only one who bent to Bertha Henderson's will.

The older woman narrowed her eyes as she fixed her gaze on Travis. "I imagine you've got some sheriff's work to do. You don't need to worry about Lydia anymore. Just make sure someone brings her trunks over here."

As Travis headed for the front door, Aunt Bertha rose from her chair and gestured toward Lydia. "Come along, my dear. Let's find you a room. You've got ten to choose from. Once you're settled, we'll have a cup of tea and get to know each other."

Lydia couldn't help smiling. The woman really was a whirlwind, but that might be just what she needed: a good strong wind to blow away the cobwebs of the past.

4

Lydia had never slept in a room so beautiful or so large, but after seeing the rest of the house, she shouldn't have been surprised. It was evident that Mrs. Henderson — Aunt Bertha, Lydia corrected herself — was a wealthy woman and, as Travis had said, a lonely one. Though she smiled and chattered, Aunt Bertha's eyes held an expression Lydia had no trouble recognizing. She'd seen it in her mother's eyes from the day Papa left them until the day Mama had closed her eyes for the last time. Loneliness, sorrow, and, unless Lydia was mistaken, regret haunted her benefactress.

Though the same emotions roiled through Lydia as she unpacked her smaller trunk, placing garments in the beautifully carved bureau and matching armoire, they were overshadowed by anger. How could Edgar have wed someone else when he'd promised to marry her? The laughter that burst from her lips was harsh and brittle, devoid of mirth. The answer to her question was found in Opal's swollen belly. That explained the marriage, but it did not explain why Edgar had forgotten the words he'd spoken to Lydia, the promise to love and honor her for the rest of his life.

She sank onto the edge of the bed and buried her head in her hands as she tried to make sense of everything that had happened. There was no undoing Edgar's marriage, and she wouldn't want to even if it were possible, not now when she realized just how shallow his love had been. It was almost as if he'd forgotten Lydia the minute he left Syracuse.

One thing was certain: he hadn't told Opal she was the second woman he'd asked to marry him, because when Lydia had introduced herself, there had been no flicker of recognition in Opal's expression. Opal had no idea she was wearing a ring her husband had bought for someone else.

Lydia couldn't blame Opal. There were only two people to blame: Edgar and herself. She must have done something wrong, something that made it easy for Edgar to walk away from their betrothal as easily as Papa had walked away from his family. Perhaps when Edgar returned — if he returned — she'd discover what it was. In the meantime, she needed to put her anger aside and learn what God had in store for her.

Lydia pulled the Bible from her valise and began to read.

"Something smells good, Aunt Bertha."

Lydia looked up from the egg she was cracking and saw a slender, dark-haired woman about her height enter the kitchen. The visitor was unexpected, but then again, everything about Lydia's time in Cimarron Creek had been unexpected. In less than twenty-four hours, her hopes and dreams had been shattered, and yet at the same time, though she wouldn't have believed it possible, she had found sanctuary and something more: a sense of peace.

The sanctuary had come quickly, the result of Aunt Bertha's unconditional acceptance of her and the offer of a room for however long Lydia wanted to remain in Cimarron Creek. The peace had been hard won, coming only after Lydia had relinquished her anger and begged for understanding. Though there'd been no words carved on stone tablets, no donkeys providing guidance, the peace that settled over her as she thought of the town she'd seen so briefly told Lydia she was meant to stay here.

But she wouldn't stay unless she could do something to repay Aunt Bertha's kindness. When she'd come downstairs for the evening meal, Lydia had told the older woman that she needed to feel useful.

"I've been working since I was eight," she explained. "First helping my mother with her housekeeping duties at the academy, then teaching. I don't know how to be idle."

Aunt Bertha laughed, but though Lydia had suggested a variety of tasks she could perform, cooking breakfast was the only thing she had agreed Lydia might do. It might be only one meal a day, but Lydia was determined to make it a memorable one. That was why she'd been in the kitchen for almost two hours before the visitor arrived.

"Who are you?" the young woman demanded as she took another step into the kitchen. Her posture and clothing told Lydia she was not a servant, yet she'd chosen to enter the house through the tradesmen's door. Dressed in a freshly laundered white shirtwaist and a stylishly bustled navy skirt, the woman could have graced the pages of *Godey's Lady's Book* if it weren't for her raised eyebrows and decidedly suspicious expression.

"I might ask the same question," Lydia said as she reached for another egg. Aunt Bertha had requested breakfast at eight o'clock, and Lydia didn't plan to be late. "Mrs. Henderson didn't tell me she was expecting a visitor."

The woman's frown deepened, reminding Lydia of the other stagecoach passengers' reaction when they heard her accent. It appeared the pretty brunette shared their disdain for Yankees. "I'm Catherine Whitfield, her great-niece."

If Lydia was supposed to be impressed, she was not. "And I'm Lydia Crawford, her new boarder," she replied, matching the visitor's tart tone.

Unbidden, Catherine walked around the kitchen, her eyes cataloging both Lydia's appearance and the meal preparations. "I don't suppose you mean her any harm," she said, her wariness diminishing. "You'd hardly be cooking breakfast if you meant to rob her."

Though the thought was ludicrous, Lydia tried to put herself in Catherine's shoes. Many Texans believed they'd been robbed by the carpetbaggers and were understandably suspicious of Northerners. Catherine had no way of knowing how firmly Lydia tried to adhere to the Commandments. She would not steal any more than she would kill.

"I assure you I did not travel all the way from Syracuse to take advantage of your great-aunt or anyone in Cimarron Creek. Cooking breakfast is the only thing she'll let me do to help her." When Lydia had suggested preparing all the meals, Aunt Bertha had refused but admitted that it was becoming more difficult for her to move in the morning and that she would appreciate being pampered then.

"Jonas always wanted me to hire a cook," she'd explained, "but I told him that would be pretentious. What else was I going to do with my days?" And so they'd settled on breakfast at eight.

Aunt Bertha might claim that she was being pampered, but it was no hardship for Lydia to prepare meals here. Like the rest of the house, the kitchen was generously proportioned. Cupboards lined one wall; a huge range dominated another, but the room's most notable feature was the marble-topped table. Large enough to seat six, it could also be used as a work space.

Catherine laid her hand on the table, perhaps enjoying the coolness, and stared at Lydia. Lydia had no idea what changed

Catherine's mind, but as quickly as suspicion had blossomed, it seemed to fade, and Lydia found herself being favored with a tentative smile. It appeared Catherine had decided to trust her.

A rush of pleasure swept through Lydia at this latest evidence that coming to Cimarron Creek had not been a mistake. Travis had helped her, Aunt Bertha had welcomed her, and Catherine had accepted her. After the shunning she'd experienced on the stagecoach, Catherine's smile felt like balm on an open sore, and Lydia resolved to do whatever she could to foster it.

"Would you like to join us for breakfast?" She'd made more than enough rolls and bacon for three, and it would be a simple matter to scramble a few more eggs.

"I already ate," Catherine admitted, "but whatever you have in the oven smells absolutely delicious."

"Then stay for them. They're cinnamon rolls."

The last hint of suspicion vanished. Catherine perched on the edge of one of the chairs, her ankles crossed the way Lydia taught her pupils was proper for a well-bred lady. "If they taste as good as they smell, I'm going to come here every morning. I may even try to convince you to bake some for my pupils."

Lydia gave Catherine another appraising glance. Though she appeared to be a year or two younger than Lydia, she suspected they could become friends, especially since it seemed they had something in common. "That sounds like you're the schoolteacher."

"The one and only." Catherine echoed Travis's phrase, making Lydia wonder whether it was a characteristic of the town or only the Whitfield family.

Lydia cracked the last egg, then began to beat them. She would wait until Aunt Bertha arrived before she cooked the eggs, but she wanted everything to be ready.

"I taught in Syracuse," she told Catherine. "A small, private boarding school for girls."

"That must have been nice. No boys to get into mischief." A smile crossed Catherine's face, as if she were remembering a particularly amusing incident, and in that moment, Lydia realized Catherine wasn't simply pretty; she was beautiful.

"My girls managed to find their share of trouble," Lydia assured her visitor. "I wouldn't have minded having some boys, though. The variety might have been fun."

"Fun?" Catherine raised one perfectly shaped eyebrow. "That's a word I've never associated with teaching."

"Then why are you doing it?" Though Aunt Bertha hadn't shared any details, she had made it clear last evening that the Whitfield and Henderson families had had more than their share of financial successes. Surely Catherine wasn't teaching only for the salary she received.

"I'm a Whitfield," she said, as if that explained everything. "In this town, Whitfields and Hendersons are taught to do everything they can for the other residents."

"Noblesse oblige."

Catherine nodded. "That's it. We're the closest thing to nobility this town has, and we have obligations. I'm luckier than most of my cousins, though. Girls are only expected to have jobs until they marry. For the boys, it's a lifetime sentence."

Lydia wondered if that was how Travis viewed being sheriff, if he'd taken the position only out of a sense of obligation. That might explain his comment about Edgar being a better sheriff.

A week ago, Lydia would have scoffed at the idea of Edgar as a lawman, but today she wasn't scoffing. When she'd wakened this morning, it was to the realization that the Edgar she thought she knew was gone — not simply from Cimarron Creek but from her life. He was a married man now, soon to be a father. The only thing he owed her was a few answers, and those would come only if he returned. For Opal's sake, Lydia hoped he would. Until he did, she would do her best to put him out of her mind. It was less distressing to talk about the handsome sheriff. As far as she knew, he hadn't lied to her.

"I've only met one of your cousins so far. Travis."

Catherine's smile broadened. "He's a good one. If I had a brother, I'd want him to be like Travis. Of course, Warner and Porter are pretty good too. Folks used to call them the Three Musketeers because they were always together. Mama claims Warner and Porter are the brothers Travis should have had."

As she heard footsteps on the stairway and realized Aunt Bertha was approaching, Lydia tested the frying pan. The drop of water danced across the surface, telling her the skillet was ready. "I haven't heard about Warner and Porter," she told Catherine as she poured the beaten eggs into the pan. "Are they Whitfields too?"

Catherine shook her head. "They're Grays, but their mother was a Whitfield until she married Charles Gray. Just so you know, Uncle Charles owns the livery and stable. He's training Porter to take over when he dies. Warner — he's the older son — runs the drugstore." Catherine's smile turned mischievous. "We're not supposed to brag, but Aunt Mary and Uncle Charles were proud as could be when Warner graduated from the Philadelphia College of Pharmacy. I don't think they'll let anyone in town forget their son's accomplishments."

Though Lydia wanted to ask about Travis's family and how long he'd been sheriff, Aunt Bertha entered the room. Unlike yesterday, when she'd worn an elaborately bustled gown, she was dressed in a simple morning frock today.

"Good morning, Catherine," she said when she spotted the visitor. "I didn't expect you, but it looks like you and Lydia are getting acquainted. I overheard you telling her about Warner and Porter. Did you tell her about the Gospels?"

When Catherine shook her head, Aunt Bertha explained. "My brother-in-law Adam and his wife had four sons they named Matthew, Mark, Luke, and John. You can see why everyone calls them the Gospels. Matthew is our mayor and postmaster, while Mark . . ." Uncharacteristically, she paused. "That can wait for later. I should probably draw a family tree so you can keep all the aunts, uncles, and cousins straight, but right now something smells wonderful."

"Just breakfast. I invited Catherine to share it with us," Lydia said as she stirred the eggs. They looked good, and so did Aunt Bertha. She'd seemed tired after supper and, though she'd claimed nothing was wrong, had been out of breath when she'd climbed the stairs last night. Now she appeared healthy and happy.

"That's an excellent idea." Aunt Bertha sniffed, then smiled. "Are those cinnamon rolls I smell?"

"Yes, ma'am."

Aunt Bertha's smile turned into a full-fledged grin. "You, my dear, can stay here forever. The only thing I like better than cinnamon rolls is fudge."

Catherine rose to give her aunt a quick hug. "If I didn't know better, I'd say Porter inherited his sweet tooth from you." She turned to Lydia and added, "If you're ever invited to Porter's house for a meal, you can expect a very sweet dessert."

The conversation continued as the three women filled their plates and took them to the dining room. When she'd swallowed the last bite of cinnamon roll and washed it down with a cup of coffee, Catherine looked from Lydia to her aunt. "Thank you both. There was a reason why I came over today, and it wasn't simply to eat two of those delicious cinnamon rolls. Mama asked me to invite you for supper." Turning to her aunt, Catherine said, "I hope you'll come. It'll do Mama a world of good to have company. And, Lydia, of course we'd love to have you come too."

Aunt Bertha nodded. "How is Gussie?"

Lydia filed the name away for future reference at the same time that she noticed Catherine had made no reference to her father. She wouldn't ask. Not only would that be rude, but in all likelihood there would be no need to ask. Aunt Bertha seemed determined to provide Lydia with the entire history of Cimarron Creek and its founding families.

"You'll have to see for yourself. She's following the doctor's advice, and she still claims we'll go to Europe this summer, but as far as I can tell, she's not getting any better." Catherine frowned and took another sip of coffee. Judging from the way her hands trembled, Lydia guessed the coffee was meant to hide her distress. When she'd laid the cup back on its saucer, Catherine looked at her aunt. "Maybe you can convince her all those bleedings aren't good for her. She won't listen to me."

Aunt Bertha nodded as she said, "Gussie always had a mind of her own, but I'll see what I can do." She rose and gestured toward the back of the house. "You two go outside and enjoy my garden. I'll wash the dishes."

Though Lydia tried to protest, it was like trying to stop a waterfall, and so she followed Catherine to the gardens she'd admired from her bedroom window.

"I'm sorry your mother is unwell," Lydia said as she and Catherine strolled between the rosebushes, enjoying their sweet perfume. "What does the doctor say is wrong?" It might be prying, but Lydia couldn't help being concerned by the seemingly frequent bleedings. The doctor who'd treated pupils at the academy claimed bleeding was dangerous and should be used only in extreme cases.

Catherine's brown eyes reflected anger. "Doc Harrington is an old fool. He says Mama suffers from bad humors and that the only way to cure her is to drain them out. I'm afraid he'll kill her, and if he does, I don't know what I'll do. Mama's more than my mother. She's my best friend and my whole family."

"What about your father?" The question

slipped out before Lydia could censor it. She'd said she wouldn't pry, but here she was doing exactly that.

Catherine didn't seem offended. "My father was killed in the war. I don't remember him at all."

As far as she knew, Lydia's father was still alive. Unlike Catherine's father, he had spent eight years with his daughter, leaving her with many memories. They'd been a family. If anyone had asked her, Lydia would have said they were a happy family, but she would have been wrong. Her father had left the home they'd made together when he found a woman he loved more than her mother.

Lydia looked at Catherine, seeing the sorrow in those chocolate brown eyes. Her own story was no happier than Catherine's, but there was no need to share it, especially when Catherine was so worried about her mother.

"I wish there were something I could say other than 'I'm sorry.' "

Catherine fingered a yellow rose whose petals were tipped with blush pink. Idly, Lydia wondered whether that had been a deliberate attempt at cross-pollination or a fortunate accident.

Turning her attention back to Lydia,

Catherine shrugged. "Sometimes there's nothing else to say." As she took a deep breath and straightened her shoulders, Lydia could picture her in front of a schoolroom, controlling unruly pupils with her no-nonsense posture. "Let's talk about happier things. You didn't tell me what brought you to Cimarron Creek."

That wasn't necessarily a happier subject. Lydia sniffed a red rose as she chose her words. "I came to visit a friend." She had no reason to admit that Edgar had been more than that. Nothing would be gained, and Opal would be hurt if the full story were known.

Catherine smiled. "It must have been Edgar Ellis."

"How'd you guess?"

Catherine's shrug said the answer should have been obvious. "He's the only other Northerner in town. Or I should say, he *was.* The grapevine's been buzzing with speculation ever since he disappeared."

It was the opening Lydia needed. Neither Faith nor Opal had known anything more than that Edgar had left the saloon one night, saying he needed some fresh air, and had never returned.

"You can imagine how surprised I was after traveling all this way and then discovering he's not here. That doesn't sound like the Edgar I knew." While she might not want to share her and Edgar's relationship — former relationship, Lydia corrected herself — with anyone, she was curious about Catherine's view of the man who had been Lydia's fiancé. Perhaps Catherine had seen something that would explain why he'd changed so much and why he'd left town so suddenly.

"I can't say I knew him well, but Mama and I used to talk to him and Opal after church," Catherine said slowly. "He seemed like a nice enough man. I know Opal's been happier since Edgar arrived, and I've heard Faith is pleased with his work." Catherine shrugged. "I wish I could tell you more, but I have no idea why he left."

There was one scenario Lydia had no trouble imagining. As a light breeze stirred the air, she asked, "Did he get into a lot of arguments?" An argument that had escalated out of control and left a man seriously injured was the reason Edgar had fled Syracuse.

Catherine shook her head. "Not that I heard, and I would have heard if there were any. Cimarron Creek is small enough that there are very few secrets here."

That was a daunting thought. Secrets were

meant to be kept secret.

Catherine fingered a petal on one of the pink roses, her lips moving as if she were practicing a speech, though no words were audible. A moment later she looked up. "I'll tell you one of my secrets if you promise not to tell anyone, not even Aunt Bertha."

"Of course." Lydia was surprised by how flattered she was that Catherine wanted to confide in her. Once Catherine's initial distrust had disappeared, Lydia had found herself as drawn to the woman as a hummingbird to nectar. It wasn't simply that they were both teachers or that they shared a connection through Aunt Bertha. Lydia felt as if they were kindred spirits. If she stayed in Cimarron Creek — and it seemed as if she would — it would be wonderful to have a friend like Catherine.

"I promise not to tell anyone."

"The nice part about this secret is that it could help you. If you really like teaching and decide to stay here, there's a good chance the town will be looking for a new teacher next year."

Given what Catherine had told her about the Whitfields' sense of responsibility, Lydia knew there was only one reason for a possible vacancy. "You're getting married?" A pang of regret speared her. If everything had gone the way she'd expected, today might have been Lydia's wedding day.

Catherine's smile broadened. "I hope so. No one knows — not even my mother — but he told me he wants to keep company with me." She pulled a petal from the rose and crushed it between her fingers. "Oh, Lydia, he's the handsomest man I've ever met. Most people think I'm level-headed, but everything changes when I'm with him. My heart beats so fast that I can hardly breathe, and all I can think about is how much I want to be his wife."

Lydia tried not to stare. How was it possible that, although she had planned to marry him, she'd never felt that way about Edgar? It was true she'd enjoyed being with him and had felt safe confiding her dreams to him, but Edgar had never left her breathless, and her heart had never raced, not even the two times he'd kissed her. If that was the way love was supposed to feel, perhaps it was just as well she wasn't marrying Edgar. But she wouldn't say that. Instead, Lydia smiled and said, "I hope he loves you as much as you do him."

A radiant smile was Catherine's response. "He does. I know he does."

"So, who is this lucky man?" It was difficult to imagine a man more handsome than Travis Whitfield, but Lydia was certain Catherine wasn't in love with her cousin. Though there'd been no sparkle in her eyes when she'd spoken of him, her eyes were as bright as the North Star now.

This time Catherine shook her head. "I'm not superstitious, but I don't want to say his name until we're officially courting. All I'll say is that he's wonderful." She tossed the crushed petal to the ground. "The other thing that's wonderful is that you came to town. I needed a friend like you."

5

"Why ain't anything cooking?"

Travis clenched his fists, then slowly straightened his fingers as he reminded himself of the futility of being annoyed. It wasn't as if he hadn't heard criticism before; it wasn't as if getting angry would solve anything. Pa was Pa, and though Travis wished it were otherwise, he was certain the man would not change.

Travis had gone to meet the stagecoach again today, and this time his father had been on it. They'd walked home together, a journey of less than two blocks, but by the time they arrived at the house they shared, Travis's tongue had hurt from the number of times he'd bitten it rather than vent his annoyance. He'd remained silent while his father had voiced a litany of complaints. He didn't like Dorcas's husband. All the baby did was cry. The stagecoach ride had been too rough. Now he was complaining about the lack of a pot of stew simmering on the stove.

"Porter invited us to have supper at his place," Travis said, hoping to end the tirade. "Warner and their parents are going to be there too."

Pa nodded grudgingly as he ran his hand through hair the same shade of brown as Travis's. Though he'd inherited his gray eyes from his mother, Travis had his father's color and build. He hoped the similarities ended there, because Cimarron Creek did not need two cranky Whitfields.

"All right," Pa said. "That wife of Porter's may be scrawny, but she sets a good table."

Though Hilda would not be happy to be described as scrawny — she was slender, not skinny — Porter would appreciate the compliment to his wife's cooking. It was well known that his mother was at best a mediocre cook who managed to put lumps in everything. Aunt Mary's gravy was particularly bad.

"You want to wash up before we leave?" Travis asked when he'd carried his father's bags to his room. There'd been no word of thanks, but Travis had learned not to expect any. Ever since Pa had sold the ranch and moved in with Travis, their relationship had been best described as strained. Travis told himself that it was understandable that his father hated being dependent on someone, particularly his son, but there were many days when he wondered if he'd done the right thing by offering to share his home with Pa.

"I suppose I better."

Half an hour later, they set off again, this time headed toward Porter and Hilda's home. Catty-cornered from Aunt Bertha's, the youngest Gray couple's house was only half the size of the Henderson mansion but had similar classical lines.

When the building had been under construction, Warner had teased his brother about creating a poor imitation of their parents' home, claiming he preferred the simpler lines of Travis's house. That was the one time Travis could recall Porter's anger being directed at his older brother. Though they'd tussled as children, once they'd become adults, the fights had stopped . . . until that day.

The truth was, Porter cared about appearances. That was why he wanted columns marching around his house. Travis didn't care about columns and friezes. The home he'd built had no furbelows, but it did have enough room for a family. What mattered to him was whether the roof and windows were tight enough to keep the elements outside. After listening to Aunt Bertha complain about rain making its way into her attic, Travis had gained a new appreciation for roofers.

But today, as he and Pa walked by his aunt's house, Travis had little thought for roofs. Instead, his mind wandered toward the people living beneath that roof. Correction: toward the beautiful young lady living beneath that roof. Lydia Crawford.

As he'd expected, Travis had received responses to his telegrams this morning. Lydia Crawford was what she claimed, a well-respected schoolteacher from Syracuse, New York. Edgar Ellis, on the other hand, had never set foot in Dayton, Ohio. Interesting. Travis wondered if Opal knew that at least part of her husband's story was false.

But it wasn't Opal who'd haunted Travis's thoughts all day. It was a lovely blue-eyed blonde. Though he'd thought she might venture out, he hadn't seen Lydia in town. That was probably just as well. Until Aunt Bertha paved her way, Lydia's introduction to Cimarron Creek's residents might be difficult.

"About time you got here," Porter muttered when they arrived. "My ma's been singing to Susan, and you know what that's like." Though Aunt Mary was an excellent pianist and served as the church's organist, her singing voice was as notorious as her cooking.

Within minutes they were all seated, with Porter and Hilda at the head and foot, Travis and Pa on one side facing Warner and his parents on the other.

"I hear you've been holding out on me, cousin," Warner said as soon as his father had blessed the food.

Charles Gray had an impressive voice, one the townspeople claimed should belong to a preacher. Others claimed that his voice, combined with his rugged good looks, was what had convinced Mary Whitfield to marry below her station. Though Uncle Charles had turned the livery into a profitable enterprise, Pa claimed that when he'd first come to town, Charles had been as poor as a church mouse.

Right now, Uncle Charles appeared as puzzled as Travis by his son's words.

"What do you mean?" Travis asked. The expression in Warner's eyes belied his slightly amused tone. Whatever was bothering him, he was serious about it.

"You didn't tell me about the young lady who came to town yesterday. What kind of Musketeer are you? You should have introduced her to me as soon as you learned she wasn't married."

"Maybe Travis is keeping her for himself," Porter suggested.

Pa looked up from the slice of bread he was buttering and frowned. "What's going on? We got someone new here? When did this happen? Seems a man can't leave town without the place changing."

Travis suspected that no matter what he said, his father would be unhappy, especially when he learned Lydia was a Northerner. Though Pa's parents had been born in the North, the war had changed his view of everything and everyone north of the Mason-Dixon line.

"A young lady arrived yesterday," Travis said calmly. If Pa exploded when he heard the story, there was nothing he could do. "I met her, because I was waiting for the stagecoach that I thought was bringing you. Your telegram said you were arriving yesterday."

Pa had made no explanation for the delay when he disembarked, and he said nothing now. Though Hilda and Aunt Mary appeared to have little interest in the newcomer's arrival, Uncle Charles's expression radiated curiosity.

"It turns out the lady had nowhere to

stay," Travis continued, "so I took her to Aunt Bertha's. As far as I know, she's still there."

Pa seemed to accept the explanation, but Porter frowned. "You forgot the most important part. The way I heard it, she came looking for Edgar Ellis."

Travis could only speculate who'd spread the story. It wasn't Opal or Faith. Both of them valued privacy and extended it to others. It had to have been one of the men who'd been in the Silver Spur yesterday afternoon.

"That's right." He confirmed the rumor, knowing he was setting fire to tinder.

There was a second of silence before Pa reacted. "She's a Yankee?"

Travis nodded.

"You escorted one of the Cursed Enemy around town? You took her to my aunt's house?" His voice escalated with each question. "You shoulda run her out of town."

Though his father was practically shouting, Travis kept his voice at a conversational level. "There was no reason to run her out of town or even to ask her to leave."

The meal forgotten, Pa turned and glared at Travis. "Mark my words. That was a mistake. A big one."

■ ■ ■ ■

"I'm sorry, Travis," Warner said an hour later when the meal had ended and he, Travis, and Porter had taken refuge on the front porch while the older men smoked cigars in the parlor. "I didn't realize Uncle Abe would get so riled or I wouldn't have said anything at supper."

Travis shrugged. "He's more ornery than usual today. I think the stagecoach ride must have hurt his leg. He'll settle down."

"I hope so." Warner leaned against the railing, crossing his legs in front of him as if he were relaxed. Only the glint in his eye told Travis he was intent on learning something. "Now that he can't hear anything you say, tell me about the new lady. Is she beautiful?"

The question shouldn't have bothered Travis, and yet it did. "She is," he said. *More beautiful than anyone I've met.* But that wasn't something he planned to tell Warner. Let him make his own observations.

"And she's single?"

"Yep."

Warner's eyes narrowed with interest. "What else do you know about her?"

"She used to teach school."

"Beautiful and smart. Perfect." Warner turned toward his brother, who had appropriated the larger of the rocking chairs and appeared to be ignoring the discussion of Miss Lydia Crawford's attributes. "Doesn't she sound perfect to you, Porter?"

"If you call a Northerner perfect." Porter's tone left no doubt that he did not.

Warner shrugged. "You know Pa doesn't hate Yankees the way Uncle Abe does."

Travis suspected that was because Uncle Charles had been one of the few men to remain in Cimarron Creek during the war. Though he groused about the carpetbaggers along with everyone else, his life hadn't been changed the way Pa's had.

Warner continued speaking. "All he cares about are looks. He's already informed me there are no women in town pretty enough to be the mother of his grandsons. I tell you, Travis, Miss Crawford is perfect." He uncrossed his legs and straightened his back. "When do I meet her?"

"Are you sure you don't mind doing this?" Catherine pointed toward the bowl of dough she'd just punched down.

It was still early morning, but the two women had been working in Aunt Bertha's kitchen for over an hour, with Catherine trying to make her first batch of cinnamon rolls. Though Lydia could have done it faster herself, she didn't regret inviting the young schoolteacher to join her. It was surprisingly enjoyable to have company as she prepared breakfast.

"Of course not. We're both teachers, Catherine. This is what we do. Teaching you to make cinnamon rolls is no different from teaching someone to write." Lydia reconsidered her assertion and said, "Actually, it's easier, because you're motivated. Now, sprinkle flour on the table, and then you're going to roll out the dough."

As she complied, Catherine nodded. "I certainly am motivated. I kept thinking about those rolls all day yesterday, and you should've seen the way Mama's eyes lit when I mentioned them. I'd love to be able to make them for her and one day for my husband." A blush stained her cheeks as she pronounced the final word.

Lydia did not want to think about husbands. "Once you've mastered these, I'll show you how to make stollen. That's one of my favorites." She watched as Catherine carefully rolled the sweet dough into a half-inch-thick rectangle, then spread the cinnamon and brown sugar mixture over it. "Now comes the hardest part," she told the pretty brunette. "You need to roll this carefully so the filling doesn't escape while you're forming the log. Once that's done, you'll cut it into slices and put them in the pan for the second rising."

As Lydia had expected, Catherine's attempts were far from perfect, and yet she knew the result would be as delicious as if Catherine had managed to cut each of the pieces the same size.

"Your mother must have been a wonderful cook," Catherine said when she'd covered the rolls with a towel and poured herself a cup of coffee.

Lydia shook her head. "Mama considered cooking a chore, not a pleasure, but luckily for her, she didn't have to cook."

"Because she hired a cook." Catherine's smile turned into a grin. "Everyone who eats one of Aunt Mary's meals wishes she'd do that."

"That's not quite the way it happened." Lydia chose her words carefully. Though she'd told Catherine that her mother had died two years ago, she had not explained what had happened to her father. "Once Papa was gone, she needed a way to support us. We were both fortunate that she found a position as a housekeeper at a girls' boarding school. They let me live there and allowed me to attend classes."

Laying her cup on the table, Catherine leaned forward slightly. "Is that where you taught?"

Lydia nodded. "It seemed like the right thing to do. I enjoyed tutoring the younger girls, so when the headmistress suggested I attend Normal School, I agreed. After that, teaching at the academy gave me a way to repay the headmistress for her kindness to both Mama and me."

Catherine took another sip of coffee, the furrows between her eyes leaving no doubt of her confusion. "But if your mother didn't cook, how did you learn to make such delicious baked goods?"

"I helped the cook. She taught me how to make simple foods special with a few herbs and spices." Lydia smiled, remembering the hours she had spent with Mrs. Fitzgerald. "I enjoyed that, but what I really loved was making candy."

"And she taught you that."

"No. I worked at a confectionary during school holidays. It was a way to earn a little extra money, but mostly I gained an appreciation for a piece of good candy."

"You're making me hungry for some." Catherine glanced at the wall clock and wrinkled her nose. "Whoever heard of eating candy before breakfast?"

Lydia raised an eyebrow. "I did, but only to ensure that it was ready for customers." Though she'd tried to keep her voice solemn, she couldn't control her smile. "That was the excuse I used for the first piece. The second, however . . ."

As she'd expected, Catherine laughed. "Your life sounds so exciting compared to mine."

Exciting was not a word Lydia would have used to describe anything about herself. "If you call shoveling knee-deep snow for months on end exciting, then I guess it was. Teachers weren't supposed to have to do that, but we all pitched in to help our handyman when his back began to bother him."

Nodding when Lydia offered to refill her coffee cup, Catherine asked, "Is that why you left Syracuse?"

"Not really. The snow was beautiful, and summers are glorious, but after my mother died, there was nothing holding me there. When Edgar said we would be able to build new lives here, it sounded like a good idea." It still did, although Edgar wouldn't be a part of whatever life she built.

"So you and Edgar were friends." Catherine looked as if something about that bothered her.

Though Lydia wouldn't admit that they'd been more than friends, she wasn't lying when she said, "He was my best friend." And that was why it hurt so much to discover that he'd broken his promises. Friends didn't do that.

She must have frowned, because Catherine reached across the table and patted her hand. "Don't worry. Travis will figure out where he's gone. He's a good sheriff, and," she added with a conspiratorial smile, "in case you're interested, he's one of the most eligible bachelors in Cimarron Creek."

But Lydia wasn't interested. It didn't matter how handsome Travis was, even though he was more handsome than any man she'd met. Marriage wasn't for her. That was one lesson she'd learned the hard way.

Marriage. Travis took another swallow of coffee in the hope that it would clear his head. Normally he enjoyed the somewhat bitter brew, but not this morning. Even an extra spoonful of sugar hadn't made it palatable.

He frowned and looked around the kitchen as he sliced bread and prepared to toast it. If he wasn't careful, he'd become as ornery as his father. He couldn't let that happen, but he also couldn't dismiss the thoughts that had been storming through his mind all night, keeping sleep at bay better than a quart of coffee.

Marriage. He should have left the game when it had been apparent that that was going to be the primary topic of conversation. Instead of concentrating while they'd been playing dominoes last night, it seemed all Warner could do was talk about Miss Crawford and how she might be the perfect wife for him.

And then there was Nate, the goat farmer who formed part of their quartet. He didn't say much, but he'd hinted that he had his eyes on someone and that they might tie the knot next year. Only Porter had remained silent, perhaps because he was already married.

Travis took another swig of coffee, frowning when he noticed how ragged the bread was. Pa would be sure to complain. The man seemed to spend his time looking for reasons to complain. But Pa wasn't what was bothering him this morning. Warner and Nate were. His good friends were on the verge of making a huge mistake.

Hadn't any of them looked around and seen what marriage meant? Once the thrill of those first few months faded, the promises of happiness disappeared, replaced by the reality of life with a virtual stranger, a life of endless misery. Travis had seen it enough times to know that was the rule, not the exception.

His mother had tried to hide it, and when he'd caught her crying, she'd claimed she had sensitive eyes, nothing more, but Travis knew better. Ma was unhappy, and Pa was too. Though neither would admit it, at least not to Travis, their marriage had been a mistake.

Aunt Bertha and Uncle Jonas's life wasn't much better. When he had been a small child, Travis had loved to play in their yard, but then everything had changed. By the time he began to study law with Uncle Jonas, he could see the strain between them. And then there were Porter and Hilda. Travis couldn't tell anything about Hilda — she kept a smile on her face whenever Travis was around — but Porter didn't act like a man who was boots over Stetson in love with his wife.

There had to be some exceptions. The logical part of Travis's brain told him that, but the other part, the part that could not forget his mother's tears, knew that marriage was a risk. A risk he wasn't willing to take.

6

"I'm sorry, my dear, but the answer is the same." Aunt Bertha held out three more slips of paper as she entered the parlor where Lydia was tatting an edging for a handkerchief. For the past day and a half, the notes had been arriving regularly, the result of the inquiries Aunt Bertha had sent on Lydia's behalf when she'd insisted she wanted to find a way to earn some money.

"No one admits to needing an assistant." Aunt Bertha frowned and crumpled one of the sheets. "No one said it, but I suspect word of your beauty has spread through town faster than dust in a summer windstorm. The men are afraid their wives would be jealous if you were in their stores all day, and the single women shopkeepers don't want competition for the bachelors' hearts."

Though she was disappointed, Lydia wasn't surprised. Travis had warned her this was likely. Instead of dwelling on her seeming inability to acquire employment in Cimarron Creek, she focused on Aunt Bertha's explanation. Lydia didn't believe the older woman's rationale. Aunt Bertha was being kind, not wanting to admit that no one in town wanted to hire a Yankee. The thought that Lydia's appearance had anything to do with the rejections was ludicrous.

"I'm not beautiful," she said firmly.

Aunt Bertha shook her head. "You're as beautiful as my hair is gray." She gave her silver locks a pat. "If you don't believe me, you need only look in the mirror." Without a pause, she continued, "Pride may be a sin, but not acknowledging God's gifts is equally sinful. He gave you that beautiful face just like he gave you the ability to teach. They're both valuable. And before you try to contradict me, let me remind you that not everyone can instill the love of learning in young minds. Catherine struggles." Aunt Bertha's eyes narrowed, and she nodded. "That might be the answer. When school resumes, you could help her."

Though Lydia knew she would enjoy that, she also knew it wasn't the solution to her dilemma. "Travis told me the town has no money for a second teacher." And Catherine wouldn't be ready to resign for another year.

Aunt Bertha shrugged. "That may be true, but I've told you money doesn't matter. I have more than I'll ever need, so why would I expect you to pay me for the little food you eat?"

It was not the first time they'd had this discussion. Lydia smiled at the woman who'd offered her a home. "You know I want to earn my keep."

"And you do. Not having to cook breakfast has made my mornings easier, but that's not all you do. Just having you here to talk to has helped me more than you'll ever know. I wouldn't admit it to Travis, but I was lonely. You've filled a place that's been empty ever since . . ." For the first time, she paused, swallowing deeply and staring into the distance.

When Aunt Bertha spoke again, it was obvious she hadn't wanted to continue that train of thought. "If you want to help, you can go to the drugstore this afternoon. My nephew has some digestive tablets for me. I usually go myself, but I'm feeling a mite tired today." She turned her gaze back to Lydia. "Do you know where the drugstore is?"

Lydia nodded. "Next to the mercantile. I saw it when I arrived. Catherine told me how proud Warner's parents are of his profession."

Aunt Bertha gave Lydia a warm smile. "You remembered his name. Good work, Lydia. Maybe I won't have to give you a list of all the relatives after all."

Once the lunch dishes were washed and put away, Lydia donned her hat and gloves and headed for the drugstore. It felt good to be out and about. Though it had been three days since she'd arrived, Aunt Bertha had insisted she stay at home, claiming she would introduce Lydia to the townspeople at church on Sunday.

"Some of them need a while to get used to the idea of another Yankee in Cimarron Creek," she explained. "By Sunday, speculation will have died down, and with you by my side, no one will dare to be rude."

Aunt Bertha had made an exception the night they'd had supper with Catherine and her mother but had not stopped to converse with the few people who'd been outdoors while she and Lydia walked to Catherine and Gussie's home. Though Lydia had been happy for the opportunity to meet Catherine's mother, after seeing how frail Gussie Whitfield was, she shared Catherine's belief that they would be unable to travel to Europe this summer. It appeared that merely walking the block from their home to the doctor's office would sap Gussie's stamina.

Today it was Aunt Bertha's stamina that was failing, and that worried Lydia. Though the older woman continued to insist that nothing was wrong, she could not disguise her breathlessness when she climbed the stairs. But Lydia was strong, healthy, and glad to have the opportunity to stretch her legs. More than that, she was happy to be able to do something for her benefactress, even something as trivial as running an errand.

She walked briskly toward Main Street, enjoying the warmth of the sun on her shoulders, and her lips curved into a smile as she pushed open the door to the drugstore. It would be interesting to see if it resembled the ones she'd visited in Syracuse.

As her eyes adjusted to the relative darkness, Lydia saw the same glass-fronted cabinets with the same array of multicolored bottles, the same long counters she'd encountered when she'd bought patent medicines for the headmistress. Though it was more than a thousand miles away, this apothecary had much in common with the ones in Syracuse. There was, however, one difference.

"Good afternoon, Miss Crawford." The look the man behind the counter gave her made Lydia's smile falter. She had expected Warner Gray to be close to Sheriff Whitfield's age, and he was. She had thought he might bear some resemblance to Travis, and he did. But she had not expected him to subject her to what could only be called close scrutiny. No one, not even the single men who'd ridden the stagecoach, had looked at her like that. Some of those men had displayed interest, but it had been a warm interest, not this cold cataloging of her features.

Lydia nodded briefly, acknowledging the pharmacist's greeting. Though he was the same height as the sheriff, his hair was lighter than Travis's, his eyes blue rather than gray. Right now, those eyes were assessing her, moving slowly from the crown of her hat to the toes of her high-buttoned shoes, looking at her as if she were a specimen under a microscope. Was this what men were taught at the Philadelphia College of Pharmacy? Lydia doubted it.

"I must say that I'm flattered you came in person rather than having Aunt Bertha send a note," Warner Gray said with a smile that did nothing to warm Lydia's heart. "Unfortunately, my answer is the same as my fellow shopkeepers'. I hate to disappoint a pretty lady like you, but I have no need of a clerk or an assistant. On the other hand, perhaps . . ."

She didn't want to hear what alternative he might propose. It might be wrong to form a snap judgment, but Lydia knew she did not want to work for this man.

"You're not disappointing me, Mr. Gray." She used the stern voice that never failed to keep mischievous pupils in line. "Possible employment was not the reason I came." Her firm tone appeared to have no effect on him, for Warner Gray continued to regard her as if she were a piece of merchandise he was considering purchasing. If this was how the other storeowners would have reacted if she'd visited their shops, Lydia was grateful Aunt Bertha had not let her approach them. It was far better to have received their responses in writing than be subjected to such scrutiny.

Since Texans were noted for their friendliness, she could only surmise that Warner Gray's rudeness was caused by her being a Yankee. Fortunately, the sheriff had never stared at her. He'd been as polite and as helpful as any man could be.

"I'm here as a customer. Aunt Bertha," Lydia said, using the familiar name deliberately, "asked me to pick up a package you have for her."

Apparently surprised by the request, Warner nodded quickly. "Yes, of course." He reached beneath the counter and withdrew a small rectangular tin with familiar lettering. Lydia had purchased the same brand of digestive tablets for one of her fellow teachers. "You can tell her I added it to her account."

"Certainly. Thank you, Mr. Gray."

"The pleasure was mine." He gave Lydia another of those long looks that made her wish she were somewhere — anywhere — else. "Welcome to Cimarron Creek, Miss Crawford. I hope to have the opportunity to get to know you better."

Lydia had no such hopes, but rather than be rude, she simply slid the package into her reticule and nodded. As she turned to leave, the door swung open, and a man strode in, knocking Lydia aside in his impatience to reach the counter.

"Do you have the rat poison I ordered?" he demanded.

Lydia took a shallow breath as she regained her balance. Though the man was the same height as Warner, the similarities ended there. Less formally dressed than the pharmacist, he appeared to be a farmer or working man with broad shoulders, clearly defined muscles, and a hat that had obviously seen better years. His hair was almost as pale blond as Lydia's, and she suspected his eyes were a lighter blue than Warner's. But what made him distinctive was not his appearance. It was the scent of mint that clung to him.

The man took another step, then stopped, as if he'd suddenly registered Lydia's presence. He turned, his cheeks flushed red with embarrassment. "I'm sorry, ma'am," he said, doffing his hat. "I hope I didn't hurt you. I didn't see you, what with the darkness and all. I assure you I'm not always so rude, especially around pretty girls. My mama taught me better."

"I'm fine, sir. No harm done," Lydia told him. This man hadn't intentionally shoved her out of his way, but Warner Gray had most assuredly intended to stare at her. Even if it hadn't been his intent to embarrass her, he should have recognized her discomfort and stopped.

The blond-haired man turned toward Warner. "Go ahead, man. Aren't you going to introduce us?"

Though the pharmacist appeared unhappy with the request, he complied. "Miss Crawford, this is Nate Kenton. Despite his ap-

102

parent lack of manners, I feel duty bound to tell you he grows the best peaches in the area, and his goats are without rival. Nate, this lovely lady is Miss Crawford. She's staying with Aunt Bertha while she's in Cimarron Creek."

Nate Kenton nodded gravely, and as he did, Lydia saw that his eyes were indeed the blue she'd expected. "It's my pleasure to meet you, Miss Crawford."

"And mine to make your acquaintance." It was the polite rejoinder, the standard reply. And, though she wouldn't describe it as a pleasure, Lydia had appreciated the fact that while Nate Kenton had inspected her, he hadn't been as blatant as Warner Gray. His had been the appraisal a single man often gave a woman.

Lydia dipped her head in farewell. "If you'll excuse me, gentlemen, I need to leave." As she turned, she saw Warner sling a bright yellow sack onto the counter. "Here you are, Nate. Guaranteed to kill rats."

Though the fastest way to Aunt Bertha's would be to retrace her steps and walk north on Main, then east on Pecan, a distance of less than two blocks, Lydia was in no hurry, and so she headed south.

"Lydia!"

She turned, startled by Travis's shout but

103

pleased by the prospect of a conversation with a man whose courtesy was never in doubt. He appeared to have been walking down the boardwalk on the opposite side of the street, but now he was striding across the street toward her.

"Good afternoon, Sheriff," she said as he approached.

Those eyes that could change from silver to thundercloud gray shone with amusement. "I thought we'd agreed on first names."

"We did, but I wasn't certain of the etiquette when you're working."

Amusement turned to a chuckle. "I'm always working. That's one of the disadvantages of the job, but let's not talk about that. I'm glad to see Aunt Bertha let you out of the house. She can be a tad protective."

Though Lydia doubted Travis meant to be critical, she was quick to say, "Your aunt has been nothing but kind to me. She's planning to introduce me to everyone on Sunday, and in the meantime she's asked all the shopkeepers if they need help."

Travis tipped his hat to the trio of women emerging from the dressmaker's store before he said, "No luck." It was a statement, not a question.

"No."

"I was afraid of that. There's not much for single women to do here except —"

Before he could complete the sentence, the sound of boot heels pounding on the boardwalk made both Travis and Lydia turn. Nate Kenton was approaching at the same pace that he'd barreled into the drugstore. It appeared this man did nothing in slow motion.

"No fair, Sheriff," he said when he reached them. "You can't monopolize the prettiest girl in town just because you've got a star on your chest." Nate pulled a small bottle from his pocket and handed it to Lydia. "This is for you, Miss Crawford. I never had call to buy it before, but Jacob Whitfield at the mercantile told me the ladies like this scent the best."

Lydia stared at the perfume, not sure what to do. The etiquette lessons she'd taught in Syracuse had stressed that flowers, books, and candy were the only gifts a lady could accept from a gentleman other than her husband. Items as personal as clothing or toilet water were strictly forbidden. But this was Texas, not Syracuse. Perhaps customs were different here.

"I'm sorry that I can't accept this," she said, her regret at rejecting a friendly overture sincere. Though she had no interest in Nate Kenton as a suitor, Lydia did not want anyone in Cimarron Creek believing her to be standoffish. "We've only just met."

Nate nodded, as if he'd expected her response. "This isn't an ordinary gift, Miss Crawford. It's an apology for the way we met. I don't want you thinkin' I'm some kind of lout who doesn't respect a lady." He looked down at the glass bottle. "Take it . . . please."

His plea was so heartfelt that Lydia could not refuse him. "Thank you, Mr. Kenton." Not only did she accept the perfume, but she opened the top and sniffed the contents. "It's very pretty. I'll enjoy wearing it." And she would. It had been years since she'd had toilet water. Though many scents were not costly, she and Edgar had agreed to save every penny they could for their move to Texas. He had given up tobacco, and she'd forgone luxuries like perfume and fancy handkerchiefs.

The smile that lit Nate's face turned him from good-looking to downright handsome, almost as handsome as the sheriff. He ducked his head in apparent shyness but managed to say, "I'd be mighty pleased to escort you to Mrs. Henderson's."

Though he'd remained silent until now,

Travis shook his head. "There's no need, Nate. I was heading that way myself."

His smile turning into a scowl, Nate stared at the other man for a long moment before he said, "You surprise me, Sheriff. I heard you say you weren't lookin' to get hitched."

"You heard right, but that doesn't stop me from escorting Miss Crawford home." He bent his arm, not moving until Lydia placed her hand on the crook of his elbow. "Aunt Bertha's waiting."

But she wasn't.

When Lydia entered the house, she found a note saying Aunt Bertha was napping. Not wanting to possibly disturb her by going upstairs, Lydia carried the package from the drugstore into the kitchen and laid it on the table. There had to be something she could do. While the room that Aunt Bertha and her husband had turned into a library had a large collection of books, today reading held no appeal for Lydia. She needed something more active, something that would keep her from thinking about the three very different men who'd spoken to her this afternoon.

Supper, in the form of a stew, was already simmering on the stove, and it was too soon to make biscuits. Perhaps she should see if the garden needed weeding. But the kitchen drew her. As she looked around the room, Lydia remembered Aunt Bertha saying the only thing she liked better than cinnamon rolls was fudge. That was it. She'd make a batch of fudge. Unlike some confections, it required only simple ingredients. Surely the kitchen had them.

Within minutes, Lydia was stirring the chocolate concoction, watching for the telltale change in the size of the bubbles that indicated it was approaching soft-ball stage. The stirring and watching ought to have kept her mind occupied, but Lydia still found herself thinking about the men who'd made such an impression on her.

Though their approaches were different, it was clear that both Warner and Nate were looking for wives. Warner appeared to believe finding a wife was like choosing a saucepan at the mercantile, while Nate had a gentler, more traditional strategy. And then there was Travis, who claimed he had no interest in marrying. Why not? He was the most attractive of the three, and not simply because of his appearance. Unlike the others, he had the knack of making a woman feel comfortable around him. It was no wonder Catherine claimed he was such an eligible bachelor.

Lydia dipped a teaspoon into the saucepan, dropping a small quantity of the chocolate into the glass of water she'd placed next to the stove. Perfect. She lifted the pan from the stove and placed it in the large bowl of cool water, then continued beating. Though others might disagree, she'd always believed that the cool-down beating was the critical step in preparing fudge.

Within minutes, the fudge was ready to be spread in a dish, but the question of the sheriff's disinterest in matrimony continued to whirl through her brain. He was a handsome, eligible bachelor with a respectable job. The only negative thing she'd heard about him was that he had a cranky father, but surely that was no reason not to marry. The only explanation that made sense was that, like her, he'd been disappointed in love. If that was the case, Lydia understood completely. It would be a long time, if ever, before she risked her heart again.

"Something smells delicious."

Lydia turned, her heart pounding at the unexpected sound of Aunt Bertha's voice. She'd been so lost in her thoughts that she hadn't heard the older woman's approach.

"I hope I didn't disturb you with my cooking."

Aunt Bertha shook her head. "I didn't

hear a thing, but when I woke, a heavenly smell was coming up the stairs. I thought I was dreaming, because it reminded me of a wonderful candy store back in Illinois. My mother used to take me there for a treat or when we had something to celebrate. They made the best fudge in the world, and this smells just like that." It appeared that Aunt Bertha's nap had accomplished its goal of restoring her, because she was back to normal, speaking for what seemed like minutes without taking a breath.

Lydia smiled at the combination of energy and enthusiasm. "I won't claim mine is that good, but I thought you might like a piece. It'll be ready in a few minutes — just enough time for me to make a pot of tea to go with it."

"Oh yes." Aunt Bertha settled into one of the chairs next to the table and nodded as Lydia prepared the tea. Ten minutes later, she bit into a piece of fudge, closed her eyes, and sighed. "Where did you learn to make that? It's even better than at the shop back home."

Shaking her head, Lydia said, "After what you said, I can't believe that, but I'm glad you like the fudge."

Aunt Bertha took another bite, washing it down with a sip of tea. "Did your mother teach you to make fudge?"

"No. When the school where I taught was closed during the summer and for holidays, I worked in a confectionary. That's where I learned to make everything from ribbon candy to fudge." Lydia smiled, remembering the small shop with the delicious confections. "My favorites are chocolate-covered creams."

"You're making me hungry," Aunt Bertha said as she bit into a second piece of candy. "That shouldn't be possible, not after all I've eaten. I love Cimarron Creek — it's my home now — but I do wish we had a confectionary." Without a pause, she fixed her eyes on Lydia. "Are you really going to stay here?"

"I'd like to." She couldn't leave without learning what had happened to Edgar, but even more than that, Lydia felt as if God had brought her here for a reason. The reason wasn't clear, but she felt his hand leading her to this particular town at this particular time.

"Do you like making candy?"

Lydia nodded. "Even more than I do teaching."

"And you can make chocolate creams and ribbon candy in addition to fudge?"

"Peanut brittle, penuche, and peppermint

sticks too." Lydia smiled, remembering the hours she had spent learning to make virtually every kind of candy.

"Then I have a proposition for you."

7

Another dead end. Travis looked around his office and at the empty jail cell. He hated dead ends. The citizens of Cimarron Creek had elected him sheriff because they believed he could keep them safe, but so far he'd failed to do that for at least one person. Edgar Ellis was still missing, and Travis was no closer to finding out why.

The widow Brown had insisted Travis visit her this morning, claiming she had important information. When he'd arrived at her house, she'd given him some fruitcake so steeped in brandy that it turned his stomach, although for the sake of peace within the town, he'd eaten half a piece, then agreed to take the rest back with him. It was only after he'd suffered through the fruitcake and a cup of tepid weak tea that she'd informed him she'd seen Edgar riding out of town on his horse. There were only two problems with her story: no horses were missing, and though the widow claimed she'd seen Edgar's face by the light of the full moon, there had been no moon the night Edgar had vanished.

As if that weren't enough to sour the day, there'd been Nate's obvious infatuation with Lydia. Travis couldn't blame the man — she was the most attractive woman to come to Cimarron Creek in a long, long time — but the idea of Nate making moon eyes at her didn't sit well with him, nor did Warner's declaration that he planned to court her.

Though he couldn't put his finger on the reason, Travis couldn't picture Lydia with either of them. Even if she overcame her reluctance to marry, and Travis suspected she would once she had a chance to realize that Edgar hadn't been the right man for her, she shouldn't marry either Nate or Warner. He knew it wasn't his call, but somehow the prospect of his friends courting Lydia rankled.

And now this. Travis fingered the note with Aunt Bertha's distinctive script that Curtis Wilkins had delivered. It wasn't the first time Aunt Bertha had used Curtis as a messenger. Ever since he'd discovered he could earn a penny running errands, the boy's favorite place to play had become the street in front of Travis's aunt's house. When Curtis handed him the envelope, Travis had thought Aunt Bertha might be inviting him to dinner, but instead she said she needed legal advice. Surely she hadn't picked today to decide to revise her will.

Travis rose and reached for his Stetson. He might as well go right away, because if he didn't, he'd spend the rest of the afternoon wondering what was wrong.

"Thank you for coming so promptly," Aunt Bertha said as she ushered him into the parlor where Lydia was seated next to a small table that held a pot of tea, three cups, and what appeared to be a plate of fudge. "We need to talk, but first have a piece of fudge."

Travis tried not to let his annoyance show. Though he knew his aunt was lonely, surely this was going too far. He had a job to do. "Thank you, but I'd rather get down to business. Tonight is Pa's night to host his poker buddies. I've got a lot to do to get ready." If he needed another reason to feel grumpy, poker night filled the bill. The quartet of men who met for the weekly event might be relatives, but somehow they fueled Pa's cantankerous side, with the result that Travis's father was even more caustic than normal after they left.

Aunt Bertha shook her head, apparently dismissing Travis's objections, as she poured a cup of tea and handed it to him along with a piece of fudge. "The fudge is business. Taste it."

Fearful of a repetition of the fruitcake disaster, Travis took only a small bite. To his surprise, the flavor burst that hit his taste buds was so good that he quickly took another bite. He had never tasted fudge quite like this. "Whatever you put in this, it's delicious. I could eat a whole plate."

Aunt Bertha gave Lydia a look that seemed to say "I told you so." Nodding, she extended the plate to Travis, offering him a second piece. Though he probably should have refused, he did not.

"I told Lydia the fudge would be a success," his aunt said smugly. "It's sure to be a bestseller."

"Bestseller?" Travis tried to imagine what Aunt Bertha meant. "Are you planning to sell fudge at the Fourth of July celebration?" While some of the town's women earned a little extra money by providing special foods during the parade and the afternoon festivities, he knew his aunt had no need of additional income.

"No," she said, her expression telling Travis he was mistaken and should have had the sense to realize it. "We're going to open a store — a confectionary — and sell fudge and other candies all year long. That's why we need you: to make it legal." She gave Lydia a fond glance as she said, "Lydia and I are going to be partners. She does all the work, and I invest a little money."

"I see." The truth was, Travis didn't. He'd heard that people sometimes did strange, almost irrational things the first year after a spouse's death and wondered if that was Aunt Bertha's case. "Do you mind if I talk to Lydia alone?"

Though his aunt shook her head, her green eyes twinkled with what appeared to be suppressed mirth, almost as if she had read his mind and found his thoughts amusing. Her next words confirmed Travis's supposition.

"If you're worried that I'm off my rocker, I can assure you that's not true. But go ahead." She made a shooing gesture with her hands. "Have your talk in the garden."

Though her reluctance was apparent, Lydia rose and led the way outside. When they reached the rose garden, although a stone bench beckoned visitors to tarry, she remained standing. "You're obviously concerned by the whole idea," she said, her face as serious as her voice. "Are you afraid no one will want to buy candy from a Yankee?"

"No." That thought had never crossed Travis's mind. "One taste of your fudge, and they'll buy it all. My concern is for my aunt. What will she do when you leave? She can't run the store alone, but she's not a person who admits defeat easily. She's also reluctant to ask for help. It's a difficult combination."

Lydia nodded, as if she'd experienced that trait, and perhaps she had. She certainly hadn't been defeated when she'd arrived in Cimarron Creek only to discover that Edgar was missing, and she was adamant about not being dependent on Aunt Bertha. The difference was, Lydia was younger and more resilient than his aunt.

Travis tried not to frown as he said, "I'm afraid Aunt Bertha will insist on keeping the store, and it'll be too much for her. She's not exactly a youngster anymore."

To his surprise, Lydia nodded again. "I agree with you completely. It would be a mistake for her to try to open or operate the store alone. There is, however, one fallacy in your thinking. The problems you've outlined are based on my leaving Cimarron Creek, and I'm not planning to do that."

Travis blinked. "I don't understand. Even though you hadn't said it, you obviously came to Texas to be with Edgar." Travis wouldn't go so far as to say "to marry Edgar," since that might embarrass Lydia. "The problem is, Edgar's not here and if what I fear is true, he'll never return."

As her face blanched, Lydia took a step backward as if trying to distance herself from the possibility Travis had raised. "You think he's dead."

"Yes." There was no point in pretending otherwise. Travis had searched, the neighboring counties' sheriffs had searched, but no one had found a trace of him. "It's the only logical explanation for his absence. I don't believe Edgar simply vanished. It's true that a determined man can disappear, but I don't think he left Cimarron Creek voluntarily. Either Edgar had an accident or he was the victim of foul play."

As Lydia closed her eyes for a second, Travis saw the anguish on her face. No matter what had happened between them, she had deep feelings for Edgar. The sheen of tears deepened the blue of her eyes as she opened them and looked directly at Travis.

"And you believe it was the latter."

He wouldn't lie. "I do. The question is, are you sure you want to live in a town where accidents that might not have been accidents keep happening?"

Travis hadn't thought Lydia's face could lose any more color, but it did. "Accidents. Plural." She clenched her fists, then released them slowly as she sank onto the bench. "What else happened?"

Travis admired the steadiness in her voice. Though she could not hide the trembling of her limbs, somehow Lydia's voice did not reflect her distress.

"Our last sheriff fell off his horse and broke his neck." Travis frowned, remembering the day he'd seen Lionel's body being carried back into town. "Everyone wants to believe it was an accident, but the fact is, he was the best horseman in the county."

"Even good horsemen fall."

Travis's lips tightened. "They're much more likely to do that if their horses are spooked. I haven't told anyone else this." He paused, uncertain why he was confiding in Lydia, a woman who was almost a stranger. "I found a bruise on his horse's flank. It looked like someone was playing David and Goliath and hit him with a rock."

"Oh." Her eyes registered her understanding.

"So I repeat my question: do you want to live here?"

Lydia was silent for a moment, as if collecting her thoughts. "No place is totally

120

safe. I learned that in Syracuse. You can try to run away like . . ." She paused, obviously uncomfortable with the direction she'd led the conversation, then said, "Running away doesn't solve anything. There comes a time when you have to take a stand." She straightened her shoulders as she took a deep breath. "It may sound silly, but opening a confectionary here is my form of taking a stand. Yes, Travis, I plan to stay."

The knock on the door startled Lydia. She and Aunt Bertha had been sitting in the parlor, and for once the older woman had been silent, leaving Lydia lost in her thoughts.

"Would you mind seeing who's there? I'm a mite tired." Aunt Bertha straightened her spine, but there was no ignoring the lines of weariness that marred her face.

Lydia wasn't surprised by Aunt Bertha's fatigue. Though she'd taken a nap, it had been a busy afternoon spent formulating plans for the confectionary, and the discussion had continued through supper. At first Lydia had been surprised when Aunt Bertha had summoned Travis, wondering why the sheriff needed to be involved in establishing a candy store.

"He's not just the sheriff," Aunt Bertha

explained. "He's also Cimarron Creek's only attorney. Practically from the day Travis was born, my husband was determined that he would follow in his shoes. It didn't take much to convince Abe that his son should study with Jonas — he always did want him to have an easier life than he did as a rancher. Fortunately, Travis has a mind that's well suited for the law. Jonas wasn't a man given to praise, but he claimed Travis had the makings of a first-rate attorney. That's why he made him a full partner so quickly."

Lydia had smiled, both at the enthusiasm in Aunt Bertha's voice when she spoke of her great-nephew and at the realization that Travis was an even more intriguing man than she'd first thought. The fact that he'd agreed to become sheriff when he already had an important role within the community spoke to his concern for his hometown. It would have undoubtedly been easier to say no and remain Cimarron Creek's attorney, but Travis had not taken the easy road.

It had been almost amusing to watch his initial impatience with what he obviously thought was nothing more than a social call turn to pure professionalism when he learned what Lydia and Aunt Bertha were planning. When he'd finished his second piece of fudge and had begun discussing the business itself, Travis had been helpful, explaining what legalities were involved. Fortunately, they were not too onerous, perhaps because almost everyone involved was part of the Whitfield-Henderson clan.

The only point of disagreement had been the store's name. Aunt Bertha had wanted to call it Lydia's Sweet Shop, but neither Travis nor Lydia had been comfortable with that. Though he hadn't voiced his reasons, Lydia suspected he still doubted she would remain in Cimarron Creek. Her discomfort with the proposed name was simpler: she didn't want to take credit for something that was only partly hers. Eventually they'd all agreed that the store would be called Cimarron Sweets.

Tomorrow she and Aunt Bertha would visit the building Travis had suggested. In the meantime, they'd hoped to relax, but that wouldn't happen until Lydia answered the door. She rose and walked through the wide hallway to the front door, trying not to frown when she opened it and saw the visitor. If there was one man in Cimarron Creek that she did not want to see again, it was this one.

"Good evening, Miss Crawford." Warner

Gray held out a light gray box tied with a piece of fancy ribbon. "I'm sorry our conversation was cut short this afternoon, but I wanted to welcome you to Cimarron Creek and hope you'll accept this small token of my esteem."

Lydia shook her head slightly, refusing to take the proffered gift. She had no regrets over the brevity of their previous conversation and hoped this one would be even shorter. "Thank you, Mr. Gray, but there's no need. You've already welcomed me."

Lydia remembered those uncomfortable seconds in the drugstore when she'd felt as if she were being inspected. Though his expression was warmer now, she had the same feeling of being evaluated, and so she returned the favor, her eyes moving slowly from the crown of Warner Gray's hat to the tips of his boots. The man was undeniably handsome, and some women would undoubtedly consider him charming. She was not one of them.

"Warner, is that you?" Aunt Bertha's voice carried through the hallway. "Bring him in, Lydia."

If it had been up to her, Lydia would have left the man on the doorstep, but she would do nothing to upset Aunt Bertha, and so she led the way to the parlor.

"I won't stay long," the town's pharmacist said when he'd greeted his aunt. "I simply want to welcome Miss Crawford to town."

"I see." Though her words were commonplace, the way her lips twitched told Lydia something about the situation amused Aunt Bertha. "It appears you've come bearing gifts."

"Just a token." Warner offered the box to Lydia for the second time, and this time she had no choice but to accept it.

"Go ahead, girl," Aunt Bertha encouraged her. "Open it."

Lydia untied the ribbon and lifted the lid, revealing a box of nougats. Flowers, books, and candy. She tried not to frown at the realization that she'd just received one of the gifts a suitor was allowed to bring to the woman he wished to court.

"That's perfect, Warner." Once again it was Aunt Bertha who spoke. "That's exactly what Lydia needs."

Aunt Bertha was wrong. Lydia did not need a box of candy, and she most definitely did not need a suitor. Still, common courtesy required that she acknowledge the gift. She managed a smile as she said, "Thank you, Mr. Gray. May I offer you a piece?"

The man shook his head. "I wish I could stay, but my family is expecting me for a late supper." He smiled, and for the first time Lydia saw genuine warmth in his eyes. "I hope I'll be welcome to return another time. I'd like to get to know you better."

Before Lydia could respond, Aunt Bertha nodded. "Any time, Warner. Any time. And please tell your parents I sent my regards."

Though the comment was benign, a flicker of discomfort made its way across Warner's face. "Certainly, Aunt Bertha." His voice betrayed no distress, making Lydia wonder if she'd imagined his uneasiness.

When Lydia returned to the parlor after escorting Warner to the door, she found the older woman smiling. "Next to Travis, he's my favorite nephew. You could do worse."

"What do you mean?" Although she feared she recognized the gleam in Aunt Bertha's eyes, Lydia didn't want to make any assumptions. Not every woman over a certain age was a matchmaker.

Aunt Bertha's smile widened. "Warner's obviously hoping to court you, just like Nate Kenton." As Lydia started to protest, Aunt Bertha shook her head. "That toilet water was more than an apology, my dear. But back to Warner. I've heard his father is pressuring him to marry. He must consider you an answer to prayer."

Was that the reason he'd inspected her so

carefully? Lydia had felt as if she were being evaluated, and perhaps she was — as a prospective bride. If Warner's father was indeed urging him to marry, that would explain why he'd reacted to Aunt Bertha's reference to his family.

"I'm no one's answer to prayer," Lydia said as calmly as she could, "especially not where matrimony is concerned. I have no intention of marrying."

"Nonsense!" Aunt Bertha appeared genuinely shocked. "You may believe that now, but you'll change your mind when the right man comes along. He'll sweep you off your feet, and before you know it, you'll be standing in front of the parson and repeating your vows. In the meantime, it was nice of Warner to bring you some candy. You can see what your competition is." Aunt Bertha gestured toward the open box. "Try a piece."

8

"So, what do you think?"

Lydia looked at the empty building that had once been a millinery. With its large front room and the plate-glass window, not to mention its location on Main Street, it would be ideal for almost any business that catered to customers. Any business other than hers.

She tried to tamp down her disappointment. After a mostly sleepless night during which her mind had whirled with ideas for Cimarron Sweets, she had made a simpler than normal breakfast for herself and Aunt Bertha. Though she missed her friend's companionship, Lydia knew it was good that Catherine hadn't come to hone her dough-making skills this morning, because Aunt Bertha had agreed that they would meet Travis at the store at 8:30.

"I don't want to interfere with your routine," she had told him.

Though Travis had claimed he could delay his routine, Aunt Bertha had been adamant, and so here they were, inspecting the empty shop.

"I'm not sure," Lydia told Travis. Though the location was ideal, there were other considerations. "Even if we tear down the wall between them," she said, pointing to the two small rooms at the back of the building, "the space would be barely large enough for a kitchen. And if I use that for a kitchen, I don't know where I'd store the stock."

Aunt Bertha, who'd sat perched on the wide front windowsill while Lydia and Travis explored every inch of space, tapping walls to ensure they were solid, measuring each of the rooms, rose. "Why do you need a kitchen? There's a perfectly good one at my house. Oh, it'll be a bit more work, because you'll have to carry the candy over here each day, but you're young. You can do that. And if you do, there's no need for renovations. You'll have plenty of room."

Aunt Bertha took a step toward Lydia. "Think about my kitchen and that marble-topped table you used for cooling the fudge. I never did see much use for it, but Jonas insisted. He said he'd heard it was good for fancy pastries and candies, and it seems he

129

was right."

In typical Aunt Bertha fashion, she continued without a pause. "The house has been here for forty years, and no one made candy until you arrived. The way I see it, it's time someone put that expensive marble to good use on a regular basis." She shook her finger at Lydia. "Don't even try to say you don't want to impose. You're not imposing. You're giving this old lady a new interest. Isn't that right, Travis?"

He shrugged. "I can agree with most of that, but I take exception to the 'old lady' part. You'll never seem old to me."

"Oh, pshaw, boy. Save your pretty words for someone who deserves them, like Lydia here. If you're interested — and you ought to be — you'd better move quickly. She's already caught Warner's eye, and if that toilet water he gave her is any indication, Nate Kenton will be knocking on my door tonight to pay his respects."

As embarrassment sent blood rushing to her cheeks, Lydia tried to change the subject. The last thing she needed was Aunt Bertha trying her hand at matchmaking. Lydia had told her she wasn't interested in marriage yesterday, and nothing had changed since then.

"The marble-topped table is perfect," she

admitted. "In fact, your whole kitchen is. I couldn't have designed one any better suited for candy making. So, if you're certain I can use it, then this building will be fine."

Lydia gestured toward the west-facing front of the building. "I won't be able to put candy in the window because of the afternoon sun, but I might turn the sill into a window seat. If I put a small table and two chairs in front of it, customers could sit with a cup of tea or coffee and sample a couple different kinds of candy before they make their decision."

Aunt Bertha narrowed her eyes, obviously considering the plan. "Would you charge them for that?"

"No. The samples will be tiny, just a taste to convince them they want a whole box."

"Is that what the store in Syracuse did?" Though Aunt Bertha appeared intrigued, she wasn't offering an opinion yet, and Travis said nothing. To Lydia's relief, he had not reacted to Aunt Bertha's clumsy attempt at matchmaking, but neither had he said anything about Lydia's plans for the store. Perhaps he thought it was not his place to advise, but the truth was, Lydia wanted his opinion.

"No," she said, answering Aunt Bertha's question. "It's my idea. When I saw the big window, I knew it could be something special."

"I agree." Travis nodded vigorously, his apparent reluctance to join the conversation gone. "It's a good idea. You're not just a great candy maker, Lydia. It seems you also have a real head for business."

This time the color that flooded her face was due to pleasure, not embarrassment.

He shouldn't care that Warner and Nate wanted to court Lydia, Travis told himself as he strode toward his office after escorting the women back home. That was hardly a surprise. Any red-blooded male would be attracted to her pretty face. But Lydia Crawford was more than a pretty face. Today she'd proven there was a keen mind beneath that golden hair, and that only added to the mystery. Try though he might, Travis could not understand why a woman like Lydia would have been involved with a man like Edgar. Oh, Edgar seemed like a hard worker, and both Faith and Opal had nothing but praise for him, but he wasn't in the same class as Lydia. If you asked Travis — and no one had — she was better off not marrying Edgar.

"There you are, Sheriff." A boy sprinted across the street, his face red with exertion.

"Ma said to tell you another window was busted. Same as last week."

"Another rock?" This was the third time Curtis Wilkins had come with the same report.

"Yes, sir. She's mighty upset."

Travis nodded, imagining the scene at the boy's house. "Tell your ma I'll be over to investigate in a few minutes." As Curtis raced back to his home, Travis entered his office and gathered the few investigative tools he'd inherited from Lionel. Though he doubted the magnifying glass would reveal anything, he might as well take it. If nothing else, it would reassure Mrs. Wilkins to know the town's lawman was doing his best.

Half an hour later, Travis left the Wilkins home, displeased but not surprised that Curtis had been right. This crime was the same as the others, and that meant no clues. There were no footprints, no pieces of thread or other leads to the perpetrator. The only scrap of evidence was the stone that had shattered the window, and that could have come from anywhere.

As had happened the previous times the Wilkinses' window had been broken, the neighbor across the street had lost another chicken, leaving Mrs. Higgins as unhappy as Mrs. Wilkins. The chicken thief could have been a fox, but there were usually stray feathers when foxes were responsible. This time, while there were no feathers, an overturned water bucket had provided one clue: human footprints.

A man, a full-grown man by the size of the boot print, had stolen the chicken. And, since it seemed unlikely two different people were involved in crimes so close together on the same night, that man had also thrown a rock through Mrs. Wilkins's window.

Who and, more importantly, why? The questions reverberated through Travis's brain as he continued his morning rounds. The first time a window had been broken, Mrs. Wilkins had been convinced it was the work of one of the schoolboys she claimed were always bullying Curtis, but when Travis had visited the boy's home, he'd discovered he slept in the loft and that his parents were light sleepers who would have heard him if he'd tried to go outside. As if that weren't enough to exonerate him, the boy wore a far smaller boot than the print Travis had found today.

The crimes weren't serious. They didn't threaten the residents of Cimarron Creek. They didn't even cause financial hardship, because Travis had paid for the window repairs and bought new chickens for Mrs.

Higgins. But the crimes still disturbed him. He was the sheriff. It was one thing to make restitution for the crimes. That eased their effect, but that wasn't why the townspeople had elected him. They wanted him to find the culprit and ensure that the broken windows and chicken thefts stopped. Unfortunately, no matter how hard he tried, he'd been unable to do that.

Had the citizens of Cimarron Creek made a mistake in choosing him? That question kept Travis awake at night.

"Face it, Travis; you're not cut out to be a sheriff." Though he frequently bellowed, tonight Pa spoke in an almost conversational tone that made his words all the more powerful. This was the Pa Travis remembered from his childhood, whose quiet recriminations stung as much as a switch. "You're meant to be a lawyer."

Travis helped himself to another serving of beef and potatoes. "I'm still a lawyer," he pointed out, "but I'm also a lawman." While it hadn't been his choice, now was not the time to mention that, especially since he was already questioning his wisdom in pinning on the star. "The town needed a sheriff, and they chose me."

"You didn't have to agree. You were already serving the town by handling all the legal affairs."

It wasn't the first time Pa had made this argument. Travis gave him the same reply he had before. "Yes, I did have to agree." In the past, those words had been enough to send Pa into a tirade. When he remained silent tonight, Travis continued his explanation. "I wasn't about to let the town become victim to something like the State Police." Though the excesses of the carpetbagger regime were notorious, there were few that could compare with the State Police. With their extraordinary and unconstitutional powers, they had made a travesty of justice in many towns. Travis wouldn't let that happen here.

"And you think that might have happened if you weren't wearing that star?" For once, there was no belligerence in Pa's tone, only simple incredulity.

"It could have." One of the subjects discussed at last year's meeting of attorneys had been the problems two towns had experienced when the wrong men became sheriff. In one case, they'd hired an outsider who'd turned out to be both corrupt and vicious. In another, a local man's true colors had been revealed when he'd been given the star.

If Travis hadn't accepted the appointment, Cimarron Creek would have had to hire an outsider, an unknown, for there'd been no other candidates. Oh, Porter had mentioned running for sheriff, but Uncle Charles had put a quick end to that, saying Porter was needed at the livery. And the truth was, Travis could not picture his cousin as a lawman. He was a good man, a good friend, but he was also a man with an unpredictable temper. That was a quality no town could afford in its sheriff.

"You're worrying about the wrong thing." Pa shook his head as he used a piece of bread to sop up the last drops of gravy. "There's only one thing wrong with this town, and that's that we've got too many of the Cursed Enemy here." Glaring at Travis, as if he expected a challenge, he said, "Mark my words. They're behind everything."

"That's absurd, and you know it." Until Lydia had arrived, Cimarron Creek had been home to only one Northerner. "Edgar's not even here. How could he have stolen the Higginses' chickens or broken Mrs. Wilkins's window?"

"Mark my words," Pa repeated. "He's been hanging around, just looking for the chance to do some mischief, and now he's got a helper. Another one of the Enemy."

"Lydia?" If Pa had met her, he'd know how ridiculous that idea was. Lydia was kind and caring. Even if she didn't make the best fudge Travis had ever eaten, she would have been an asset to the town.

Pa nodded. "If that's her name, then she's the one."

Though he was tempted to laugh, Travis restrained himself. Nothing would be gained by raising Pa's ire. "Lydia would no more steal chickens than you would sing 'The Battle Hymn of the Republic.'"

But Pa's anger was already simmering. "You're a fool, Travis. You're letting a pretty face blind you to the truth. She's a Northerner, and that says it all. Every last one of them is a scalawag. Why, if she sets foot in church, the roof will fall down."

This time Travis did laugh.

9

She could not ignore the stares as she and Aunt Bertha walked down the aisle and took their seats in the first pew on the right, the one Aunt Bertha had informed her was reserved for the oldest generation of Hendersons, just as the one on the left belonged to the senior Whitfields. Though it was empty now, Aunt Bertha had told her that was where Travis and his father and Catherine and her mother sat with Charles and Mary Gray. Warner, along with his brother Porter and his family, occupied the pew behind them, while the Gospels and their families filed into the two rows behind Lydia and Aunt Bertha.

Though not unexpected, the open stares and a few hostile glares from the congregation left Lydia feeling uncomfortable, but once the service began, she forgot everything in the joy of worship. An hour later, her spirit restored by the familiar hymns and the minister's brief but powerful sermon about loving thy neighbor, Lydia was ready to face the congregation. They were her neighbors, and no matter what they said, she would love them. She would also do everything she could to be the kind of person they could love.

"I'd like you to meet Lydia Crawford. She's staying with me." Lydia lost count of the number of times Aunt Bertha said that, performing introductions as she and Lydia made their way down the center aisle after the service. Though Lydia tried to associate names with faces, she knew she would not succeed. Instead, she focused on smiling sweetly and doing her best to ignore the whispered comments that trailed behind them like a ship's wake. But she could not ignore the man who scowled at her. Though it was possible that the scowl was due to the leg that ended at the knee and his dependence on a cane, Lydia suspected that was not the cause. This long after the war, even phantom limb pain should have disappeared.

"Abe, I'd like to introduce you to Lydia Crawford. She . . ."

The man whose resemblance to Travis left no doubt of his identity did not let Aunt Bertha continue. "I know who she is, but if you expect me to welcome her to Cimarron Creek, you're sorely mistaken. Yankees have no place in my town."

"Now, see here, Abe." As Aunt Bertha began to sputter, Lydia placed her hand on the older woman's arm.

"It's all right, Aunt Bertha." She forced herself to keep smiling as she looked at Travis's father. "Mr. Whitfield is entitled to his opinion."

A flicker of something that Lydia hoped was grudging respect crossed the older man's face, quickly replaced by a frown. "Don't waste your time trying to change it. You'll never do that."

Travis gave Lydia a look that communicated his regret over his father's words, but he said nothing. It was Aunt Bertha who whispered, "Don't let him bother you. He's always like that."

Though Lydia tried to dismiss the man's rudeness as part of his habitual crankiness, the memory of his disapproving frown lingered. Had Travis been subjected to similar anger growing up? She hoped not.

The progress down the aisle was slow, as Aunt Bertha stopped to introduce Lydia to the other parishioners, but eventually they reached the narthex and, after praising Reverend Dunn for his sermon, emerged from the church.

To Lydia's surprise, Nate Kenton moved toward them. After glancing at Aunt Bertha, he fixed his gaze on Lydia.

"May I have the privilege of walking you two ladies home?"

Lydia's cheeks hurt from smiling, and her head ached from the strain of trying to remember names and faces. All she wanted now was to spend half an hour in total silence, but before she could formulate a polite refusal, Aunt Bertha nodded vigorously, setting her hat ribbons to bouncing.

"Certainly, Nate. Would you like to join us for dinner? I'm sure Lydia would like to get to know you better."

Lydia tried not to cringe at Aunt Bertha's less than subtle effort at matchmaking. To her surprise, Nate appeared equally uncomfortable. Perhaps Aunt Bertha had been wrong and he had no romantic interest in Lydia. Perhaps he was merely acting on Reverend Dunn's admonition to be neighborly. "Thank you, but my sister is expecting me."

From the corner of her eye, Lydia saw Catherine emerge from the church and stare at them, a frown marring her normally sweet expression. Lydia turned slightly, hoping to catch her friend's eye, but when she did, Catherine's frown deepened and she turned away.

Seemingly oblivious to her niece's displeasure, Aunt Bertha smiled at Nate. "Did you tell Lydia you're practically family?" Without waiting for a response, she turned to Lydia and explained. "Nate's older sister married one of my nephews. Rachel's a Henderson now. A lovely woman, inside and out. And she has three children that would make any woman proud. I was surprised they weren't in church today."

As Nate bent both arms so that Lydia and Aunt Bertha could place their hands on the crook of his elbows, he said, "The boys caught the measles, and Rachel's afraid Rebecca may be contagious, so they all stayed home. That's why she needs me. I promised her I'd help entertain the boys."

Aunt Bertha nodded but for once seemed content to remain silent, leaving the burden of conversation with Lydia.

Love thy neighbor, Lydia reminded herself as the trio headed north on Main. She could — and would — be polite to Nate. The man was simply taking the minister's sermon to heart and being neighborly in escorting them home. The least she could do was keep the discussion from dying.

"How old are the boys?" Lydia wondered

whether they were among the boys whose antics troubled Catherine. Though Catherine hadn't mentioned any names, she had said that the worst offenders were two brothers.

"Twelve and thirteen."

Lydia nodded. They probably were the mischievous ones. "A tough age to be sick." And to spend days inside a schoolhouse when you'd rather be outdoors doing almost anything else. It wasn't hard to understand why they'd gotten into trouble.

"They're not used to being sick," Nate confirmed. "Especially with spots all over. They won't let their friends see them, even the ones who've had measles."

"I can't blame them. Teasing can hurt." Lydia had seen the effects on her schoolgirls and knew that it could be even worse for boys, simply because they often tried to pretend the taunts didn't hurt.

"I'm not sure what I can do to help them."

Though she said nothing, Aunt Bertha's face was flushed. Deliberately, Lydia slowed her pace as she sought a way to help Nate. He was a pleasant enough man, and even though his constant chewing was a bit annoying, at least it was a wad of mint leaves rather than tobacco.

"What would you do otherwise?"

"If they weren't sick, I'd saddle some horses and go for a ride." Nate frowned. "I already asked, but Rachel said no. She thinks it would be too much for them."

"What about a wagon ride?"

For the first time since he'd joined them, Nate appeared to relax. "I hadn't thought of that. I'll bet Rachel would agree to that. Thank you, Miss Crawford."

"He seems like a nice man," Lydia said ten minutes later when Nate had escorted them to their front door, then taken his leave.

Aunt Bertha nodded as she sank onto the settee. Though they'd walked slowly, she was breathing heavily and appeared fatigued. "Nate is a good man," she agreed, "even if he does have a weak stomach. That's why he smells like a walking mint plant. I told him he ought to try some of my digestive tablets, but he claims natural remedies are better." Aunt Bertha shrugged. "He could be right. The man's got a good head on his shoulders. He's a hard worker too. Nate may not be as handsome as Travis or Warner, but he's still a good catch. That's why I'm surprised he hasn't married yet. He's close to thirty, you know. A man ought to be settled down by that age."

Edgar had said the same thing the day

he'd asked Lydia to marry him. He'd announced that he was ready to settle down. And he had. Unfortunately, it had been with another woman. But there was nothing to be gained by thinking of Edgar and his wife, the wife who was going to bear his child, the wife whose husband had disappeared.

"I thought for a while that Nate and Catherine might be courting," Aunt Bertha continued, "but that doesn't seem to be the case. Most courting couples meet up after church. The way Nate latched on to us tells me he's not interested in anyone else."

But Catherine had been visibly upset. Lydia bit her lip as she considered the possibility that Nate was the man Catherine loved. Surely that couldn't be the case, because as Aunt Bertha said, Nate did not appear to be a man who was smitten with another woman. And yet he was as handsome as Catherine had claimed. There was only one way to know if she was right.

"I thought I'd visit Catherine this afternoon," she said. "Would you like to come with me?"

Aunt Bertha shook her head. "I'm going to take a nap once we finish eating. Church wore me out more than I expected."

Lydia's concerns grew. She hadn't expected Aunt Bertha to admit that anything was wrong, and the fact that she was so open about her fatigue worried Lydia. "Is there anything I can do for you?" Though she knew the older woman would protest, Lydia would insist on washing dishes and putting the food away.

Once again Aunt Bertha shook her head. "It's nothing a nap won't cure."

And so when the meal was over, Aunt Bertha headed upstairs while Lydia made short work of the dishes. If Nate was the reason for Catherine's coolness, Lydia wanted to set things straight between them. As she filled a small bowl with several pieces of fudge and some of the chocolate creams she'd made last night, Lydia smiled. Once Catherine knew she had no interest in Nate, their friendship would no longer be in jeopardy.

"Hello, Lydia." The words were polite, but the tone was distinctly cool when Catherine opened the door and saw who was standing there. Lydia hadn't imagined her displeasure.

"I'm sorry I didn't have a chance to talk to you after church."

"It's all right." It was a perfunctory reply with no warmth behind it. This was not the Catherine who'd joked as they'd rolled out sweet dough or the one who'd shared her concerns about her mother.

"It doesn't seem all right to me. I'm not sure what I did to hurt you" — although she had a good idea — "but I want to do what I can to fix it. I don't want to lose your friendship, Catherine. That's why I brought this." Lydia held out the bowl of candy.

"A bribe?" For the first time, a smile teased the corner of Catherine's lips.

"You can call it that. I prefer to think of it as a peace offering."

Catherine nodded. "Come in." She led the way to the parlor and offered Lydia a seat. "You're right that I was upset, but I shouldn't have been. It's not your fault that Nate can't keep his eyes off you. You're a beautiful woman, Lydia."

It was what Lydia had feared. Nate was indeed the man Catherine hoped to marry. If she'd known, she would have overruled Aunt Bertha and refused to let him escort them home. "Nate is the one." Lydia made it a statement.

As tears filled her eyes, Catherine nodded. "I thought he was until I heard how he ran down Main Street to give you some perfume. He's never given me any."

Lydia wondered if that was the reason Catherine had sent the note, saying she couldn't come for her pastry-making lesson on Friday. Some friend Lydia had been! She tried not to frown as she realized that she'd been so caught up in the excitement of planning the candy shop that she'd neglected her new friend.

"The toilet water was meant as an apology, nothing more. Nate practically knocked me over when he came into the drugstore, so he was trying to make amends."

"That may have been the case then, but I saw the way he looked at you this morning." Catherine brushed an errant tear from her cheek. "He's infatuated."

Though she and Edgar had never had one, Lydia had heard of lovers' spats. She hoped with all her heart that this would prove to be nothing more than a misunderstanding and that Catherine's dreams of marriage to Nate were not permanently shattered.

"I wouldn't say he's infatuated, but even if he were, I'm not interested in him — or any man, for that matter. I'm not going to marry. I'm going to open a candy store."

Catherine nodded. "I heard that — the part about the candy store." When Lydia raised an eyebrow, Catherine managed a weak smile. "Don't look so surprised. I told you there are no secrets in this town."

She dashed the tears from her cheeks, straightened her shoulders, and reached for the candy dish, clearly signaling that the discussion of Nate was over. Catherine chose a piece of fudge and nibbled the corner. "Delicious," she said when she'd swallowed the candy. "If everything you make is this good, your shop will be a success." She took another bite and nodded again. "I think the store is a good idea for Cimarron Creek and for you. I've had a lot of time to think over the last couple days, and I'm beginning to believe women need to rely only on themselves."

Though that might be right for Lydia, she did not believe it was the answer for Catherine. "But you love Nate."

"That's true." Catherine's smile faded. "The problem is, he obviously doesn't love me. If he can be distracted so easily, he's not the man for me." Though her words were firm, the instant she'd pronounced them, Catherine burst into tears. "Oh, Lydia, it hurts."

Drawing her friend into her arms, Lydia nodded. "I know."

An hour later, Lydia left Catherine. She'd dried her friend's tears and tried to comfort her, but Lydia knew the hurt would remain. She had wanted to tell Catherine that she understood, that the man she'd expected to marry had married another woman, but she hadn't. Lydia would tell no one about Edgar, just as she wouldn't tell anyone that Nate had broken Catherine's heart.

"You look serious. Is something wrong?"

Lydia turned, startled by Travis's question. She hadn't seen him, but here he was, only a foot away from her. "No. You just surprised me."

His eyes narrowed, and he shook his head. "I went to law school, Lydia. That means I learned how to cross-examine witnesses. The first thing I was taught was to watch their expressions. Those tell more than words. You can claim you're not worried about anything, but your face says otherwise. I hope it's not my father's rudeness at church." Travis's eyes darkened. "I want to apologize for that. There's no excuse for his behavior, but even though I've tried, I can't get him to see how wrong he is to blame Yankees for everything he doesn't like in his life."

"It wasn't your father. Aunt Bertha warned me about him, and while I won't say it was pleasant, what he said was no worse than what I heard on the stagecoach."

Travis appeared relieved. "If it wasn't Pa, it must be something else that's bothering you."

Lydia nodded. There was no point in denying what Travis had seen, but that didn't mean she would talk about Catherine or Edgar. "You're right," she said as she took his arm and resumed the walk home. "I am concerned about something, and you might be able to help me. It's your aunt."

"Aunt Bertha? What's wrong?"

"She seems to tire very easily. Just climbing the stairs leaves her out of breath, and she takes long naps each day. Do you know if she's ill?"

"I don't think so." Travis was silent for a moment. "It could be her age. She's over sixty, and her husband's death hit her hard."

The explanation was logical. Lydia had seen how depressed the school matron had been when her sister had died, and losing a spouse was even more difficult.

"That's probably all it is," she agreed.

To her surprise, Travis shook his head. "Maybe not." He looked around, as if assuring himself he would not be overheard. "No one talks about it much anymore, but I've heard Aunt Bertha hasn't been the same since she lost her daughter twenty years ago."

Lydia had thought she was done with surprises for the day, but apparently she wasn't. "I hadn't realized she had a daughter. She's never mentioned her."

"That might be part of the problem. The parson always says it's important to grieve. I'm not sure Aunt Bertha did. Or if she did, she never finished."

"What happened? Was it smallpox?"

"I don't think so, but no one really knows. Joan was here one day, gone the next. Bertha and Jonas wouldn't talk about it other than to say she was gone."

"That's strange."

"It is," Travis agreed. "I probably shouldn't have told you, but since you're living with her, I thought you should know. All I ask is that you don't tell Aunt Bertha I said anything."

"I won't." But that wouldn't stop Lydia from wondering what had happened to Joan Henderson.

10

"This is even prettier than I expected." Catherine smiled as she looked around the front room of Cimarron Sweets. To Lydia's delight, her friend was the first customer to enter the store, and her genuine appreciation made Lydia return the smile.

The past three weeks had been busy, but everything had gone more smoothly than she'd dared hope, including her relationship with Catherine. Though Catherine was obviously still bothered by Nate's fickleness, she did not appear to blame Lydia. Instead, she'd offered to help Lydia prepare for the store's opening. Though Lydia would have appreciated her friend's advice on the store's décor, when Catherine had mentioned that her mother had taken a turn for the worse, Lydia had claimed that the greatest favor Catherine could offer was her opinion of the various candies. Lydia had practiced making everything from peanut brittle to penuche, from caramels to chocolate creams, and had taken samples of each to Catherine. It was little enough to offer a friend who was suffering from both the loss of a potential suitor and her mother's continued decline.

"Mark my words," Aunt Bertha had said when she returned from visiting her niece by marriage, "Gussie won't last the summer."

Lydia didn't want to think about that this morning, and judging from Catherine's overly bright eyes and slightly red nose, which were undoubtedly the result of tears, neither did her friend.

"I'm pleased with the way the store turned out," Lydia admitted, gesturing toward the glass-fronted cabinet that displayed her confections. With its polished wood top, it was an eye-catching piece of furniture. She had Warner Gray to thank for that. Though she had covered the front window with an old sheet so that passersby would not see the changes she was making to the store, Warner had stopped by Aunt Bertha's house one evening, saying he remembered the layout of the store and wondered if she needed a display case. When Lydia had admitted that she planned to ask Luke Henderson, the Gospel who was also the town's carpenter, to make one, Warner had volunteered to give her one that he insisted was gathering dust in his back room.

The window seat's velvet covering had come from Nate Kenton. Apparently Carpenter Luke, who was also his brother-in-law, had told him of Lydia's plan to have a window seat, and he'd insisted on giving her two yards of velvet he claimed to have found in a trunk when he'd moved into his house.

Though Lydia had tried to refuse, not wanting to cause Catherine any more pain, Nate would not be dissuaded. "Do I look like a man who'd wear velvet?" he'd asked when she had protested the generosity. In both cases, Lydia had insisted on paying the men, though she knew the prices they'd agreed on were far below the items' actual value.

"Everyone's been so helpful," she told Catherine. Though Warner and Nate had led the list of helpful residents, others had volunteered their services at what Lydia suspected were reduced rates. That had surprised Lydia. Even with Aunt Bertha's patronage, she was still a Yankee, and the wary looks she received from some parishioners each Sunday told her Travis's father was not the only person in Cimarron Creek who disliked Northerners.

But sooner than she'd thought possible, she had freshly painted walls and the shelves she needed in the back rooms. The only challenge had been finding a table and two chairs to go with the newly created window seat. Aunt Bertha had resolved that problem by taking Lydia to the attic and telling her she could use anything she found there. Though the nicks and gouges spoke to its age, the oval table had needed nothing more than a good cleaning and polishing to make it perfect for the spot, and once Lydia had created calico cushions for the chairs, they complemented both the table and the window seat.

"I'm not surprised that you've had help. Most of the people in Cimarron Creek are friendly. And there's the curiosity factor." Catherine wrinkled her nose, her amusement evident. "Everyone wanted to be the first to have a story about the Yankee shopkeeper. It didn't hurt that you have Aunt Bertha's support. I doubt many would want to cross her." Catherine looked around. "Where is she? I thought for sure she'd be here to greet customers."

Lydia shook her head. "I expected her too, but she told me the store was mine. She's the silent partner."

"Aunt Bertha silent?" Catherine raised an eyebrow and chuckled. "That'll be the day." She pointed toward the glass-fronted cabinet. "I came here to do more than talk. I promised Mama a pound of fudge."

While Lydia weighed the candy and slid the pieces into one of the white boxes she'd decided would be her signature wrapping, the doorbell tinkled. Looking up, she saw the young woman she recognized as Porter Gray's wife enter, a toddler clinging to her hand.

"I didn't expect to see you here, Catherine," Hilda Gray said as she took another step into the store. "I thought you'd be with your mother." Of medium height, Hilda might never be called beautiful, but her perfectly tailored gown highlighted her brown hair and helped disguise the fact that she was far thinner than was fashionable. Though Lydia had been introduced to both Hilda and Porter at church the first Sunday, she had not spoken to either of them since.

Catherine ignored Hilda's slightly waspish tone and favored her with a smile. "Mama's one of the reasons I'm here. She wanted a pound of Lydia's fudge." Catherine gestured toward the cabinet. "It's the best either of us has ever tasted."

Lydia turned to her new customer.

"Would you like a sample? I have tea and coffee to go with it."

The woman's eyes widened slightly before she nodded. "Certainly, if you don't mind my daughter." Though the child had remained silent, she had begun to fidget. "She's not the neatest of eaters yet."

Lydia gave Hilda her brightest smile. "You're both welcome to taste anything Cimarron Sweets offers. Today I have fudge, penuche, and chocolate-covered vanilla creams."

"I'll try one of the creams." Lydia's second customer shepherded her daughter to the table and helped her climb into one of the chairs. Taking the one next to her, the woman gave Lydia a small smile. "I'm not sure you remember me, but I'm Hilda Gray, and this is Susan."

"I certainly do remember you. It's a pleasure to see you again," Lydia said. "And your daughter is more than welcome. I have milk for the younger customers."

While Susan managed to spread more fudge outside her mouth than in it, Hilda Gray bit into the quarter of a cream that Lydia had placed in front of her, chewing thoughtfully, then taking a sip of coffee. "This is delicious. Porter will love it. I'll take a pound of these." She glanced at the box in front of Catherine. "Make that two, plus one of the fudge. My quilting bee is tomorrow. I always serve some kind of sweet, but it's become difficult to find something different each month. If the other ladies like these candies as much as I think they will, I'll make them a new tradition."

Lydia nodded and pointed to the small decorations she'd piped on top of each candy. "Would you prefer roses or stars? I'll normally stock two kinds of flowers, but I decided to use stars for the next few weeks in honor of Independence Day."

Pursing her lips, Hilda studied the two candies as if choosing the correct one was a matter of life and death. "That's a good idea. I'll take stars today. Next time can be flowers."

Lydia thought about the woman's desire to serve something different each month. "If you order in advance," she said as she began to weigh out the creams, "I can make a special decoration for your quilters." Her mind began to whirl with the possibilities. Perhaps Hilda would like a spool of thread or a quilter's hoop instead of flowers, or perhaps she would choose a flower that had specific significance for her group.

As she wiped the chocolate from her daughter's face, Hilda smiled. "What a wonderful idea! Would you consider doing something exclusively for us?"

"Of course."

The woman was beaming as she left the store, holding three boxes of chocolates in one hand, her daughter's hand in the other.

"How did you know exactly what to say to guarantee Hilda's patronage?" Catherine asked as the door closed.

"What do you mean?" Lydia placed the dirty dishes on a tray and turned toward the back of the store. Since neither room had water piped into it, she had had Luke Henderson construct one counter with a lower section where she could place two pans, one with soapy water, the other designed for rinsing.

Catherine stepped out of the way. "Hilda's trying to become a leader in the community. I think she has illusions of becoming another Aunt Bertha. Telling her she can have exclusive candies will help that."

Catherine was acting as if Lydia had accomplished some great feat, when all she'd done was try to satisfy a customer's needs. "I'd do it for anyone. It's easy enough to make new designs, so each one can be a little different." That was one of the reasons chocolate creams were her favorite confection. Not only did Lydia like the flavor

161

combination of the chocolate coating with the creamy interior, but she enjoyed piping a design on top.

"You may do it for others, but Hilda will be able to say she was the first. She'll feel as if everyone else is following her lead. Good work, Lydia."

Catherine picked up the box of fudge she'd left on the counter while Hilda and Susan were in the store. "I need to go home now, but I hope you and Aunt Bertha will come for supper again this week. Mama always perks up when she knows you're coming." Unspoken was the fact that Gussie Whitfield's bad days outnumbered the good ones. "Will you pray for her?"

Lydia nodded. "For you too." She hugged her friend, then watched as Catherine walked down the street, her head held high, her step jaunty, as if she had not a care in the world when inside her heart was breaking.

Only minutes later, two women entered the store.

"Hilda Gray told us you have chocolate creams," the first announced.

"I have to admit they're one of my favorites," Lydia told her, "but the penuche is also delicious."

The second woman's eyes brightened. "I

haven't had penuche in years. I'll take some. Maybe half a pound."

Gesturing toward the table and chairs, Lydia said, "Would you like a sample of both the penuche and the creams and some tea or coffee?"

The two women exchanged glances, then nodded. A quarter of an hour later, they left having each purchased two pounds of candy. Word appeared to spread quickly, because by the end of the day, Lydia had sold everything she'd made. Tonight would be a busy night replenishing her stock.

She gathered the now empty pans and locked the front door behind her. Wouldn't Aunt Bertha be pleased when she heard how well the first day had gone? She'd probably say "I told you so," and she would be right. She had been the first to predict that the townspeople would embrace the idea of a candy store, even one run by a Yankee.

Lydia's smile widened as she saw Travis approaching her. Perhaps it was silly, but the sight of the sheriff never failed to boost her spirits. Unlike Warner and Nate, both of whom gave her smiles that made Lydia fear they had listened to Aunt Bertha's matchmaking, Travis treated her as if she were a friend — nothing more, nothing less.

"You look like you had a good day," he said.

"Even better than I had hoped. I sold every last piece of candy and poured at least a dozen cups of tea and coffee."

The cups and saucers were now washed, dried, and back on the shelves ready for tomorrow's customers, assuming there was anyone else in town who wanted to buy candy. As successful as today had been, Lydia had no guarantee that it would be repeated. The curiosity factor, as Catherine had called it, would last only so long.

Oblivious to the doubts that had seized Lydia, Travis nodded. "I thought that might happen. Cimarron Creek has never had a candy store, so you're filling a need."

Though Lydia was tempted to say that no one needed candy, that it was a guilty indulgence for many, she did not. "I was afraid that once I opened my mouth, they'd leave, but no one did." There had been a few raised eyebrows, suggesting that not everyone in town had heard that the new shopkeeper was a Yankee, but no one had shunned her.

"It's time they learned that not all Northerners wear horns. I'm afraid my father will never accept that, but the rest of the town is kinder."

Travis looked up and down the street, his gaze deceptively casual. Lydia had seen him do it before and knew he was looking for anything out of place, any sign that something was wrong. As he'd once told her, a sheriff's job never ended.

"Is there a specific reason your father hates Yankees?" To Lydia's surprise, though Aunt Bertha provided a running commentary on almost everyone in the Whitfield-Henderson clan, she had said little about Travis's father other than that he had always been disagreeable.

Travis nodded again. "In one word: Gettysburg. He lost his leg and too many comrades there."

Gettysburg. The name conjured images of almost unthinkable suffering as tens of thousands of men on both sides of the conflict fought under the hot July sun. Though President Lincoln had later called it hallowed ground, his words brought little comfort to those who'd lost so much there.

"I can only imagine how difficult that must have been. The whole war is one of the saddest parts of our history."

"Yes, it is, but so is Pa's attitude. I've tried. Aunt Bertha has tried, and while he was alive, Uncle Jonas tried, but nothing we said changed the way he feels." Travis's eyes were as dark as rain clouds. "I suspect Pa would enjoy your fudge as much as I do, but I also suspect he's the only person in Cimarron Creek who'd refuse to eat it simply because of what he considers his principles."

Lydia had seen those principles at work each Sunday after services ended. Though he would nod to Aunt Bertha, Travis's father carefully avoided meeting Lydia's gaze and pretended not to hear her greetings.

"You have to respect his opinions."

To Lydia's surprise, Travis chuckled. "That would be easier if he were a little less loud when he expressed them. But let's not talk about my father. If you hand me that bag, I'll be glad to carry it home for you."

"Thanks." Lydia handed him the bag. While not heavy, it was bulky because of the number of tins she'd stuffed inside, and though she was exhilarated by the success of her first day in business, she was also tired. "Are you sure I'm not taking you away from business?"

"Even the sheriff is entitled to a few minutes off duty. Besides, I need a fresh perspective."

As he glanced toward the saloon, Lydia surmised that he was thinking of Edgar. "Is there still no sign of Edgar?" she asked.

"No, and by now even if there had been a trail, it would be cold." Travis's lips tightened into a frown. "I don't understand it. It's been over a month, and I've found nothing but dead ends. People don't simply vanish." He frowned again. "I hate unresolved mysteries, but it's beginning to look as if this will be one."

"Like Aunt Bertha's daughter." Lydia was still haunted by the realization that her benefactress had an unvoiced tragedy in her past. Not once in the four weeks that Lydia had lived with her had Aunt Bertha given even the slightest hint that she'd had a daughter. It was as if Joan Henderson had never existed.

"Yes." Travis greeted two men whose uneven gait bore witness to the time they'd spent inside the Silver Spur. When they were out of earshot, he continued. "Obviously there's no connection between the two cases other than that both of the missing people lived here, but that doesn't mean I'm happy about either one. The only logical explanation is that they both met with foul play."

Lydia thought back to what Travis had told her about Aunt Bertha's daughter. "In that case, wouldn't there have been a search for Joan? It didn't sound as if that happened."

Travis turned to look at Lydia, his expression thoughtful. "You're right. I was only a kid, but the way I remember it, Joan simply disappeared. Aunt Bertha claimed she was visiting some cousins. Then when she didn't come back, everyone knew that wasn't the case. Eventually speculation died down."

Though they'd been heading north on Main Street, when they reached Mesquite, Travis turned on it. "The story I heard was that Aunt Bertha and Uncle Jonas insisted no one in the family talk about Joan. There's always been the belief that the Whitfields and Hendersons need to set an example for the rest of the town."

Lydia smiled. "Noblesse oblige."

"Exactly."

Though he probably hadn't intended it, Travis had given her the opening to ask one of the questions that had puzzled her. "Is that the reason you became sheriff?"

"Partly."

"And the other part?" Unlike Aunt Bertha, he didn't feel the need to fill every silence with talk.

"I wanted to be sure we had an honest man in the job. I'd heard stories of sheriffs who looked the other way when their friends were involved. I didn't want that to happen here. Besides, no one else seemed particularly interested in the job other than Porter, and his father squashed that idea the instant Porter mentioned it." Travis shrugged. "Someone brought up my name, and the next thing I knew, I had a star on my chest."

"Are you happy about that?" Lydia couldn't tell from either his words or his expression.

"I'd be happier if I could find Edgar and stop the vandalism."

Lydia heard the frustration in his voice and wanted to do something — anything — to help him. She couldn't find Edgar, and she couldn't stop the vandalism, but perhaps she could boost Travis's spirits. Everything he had said confirmed her initial impression that Travis Whitfield was a man of honor, a man who knew the difference between right and wrong, a man who would keep his promises. "You're a good man, Travis. The town is lucky to have you."

Her words of praise were still ringing in his ears as Travis let himself into his house. He could rationalize the sudden warmth that had lodged in his heart, saying it was the result of a compliment, but the truth was, he'd received compliments before, and none had affected him this way. He could try to convince himself otherwise, but the fact that the compliment had come from Lydia was what had touched him. Travis knew she wasn't trying to flatter him; that simply wasn't something she would do. No, when Lydia Crawford said something, she meant it. And that made her words as sweet as the candy she sold. Sweet and unforgettable, just like the woman herself.

His thoughts still centered on Lydia, Travis stopped short when he saw his cousin in the parlor with Pa.

"I didn't expect you, Warner. Have you come for supper?"

Warner nodded. "That and some advice." He glanced at Pa but directed his words to Travis. "I asked Porter, but he was no use. All he did was laugh."

Pa looked up from the piece of wood he'd been whittling. "You could have asked me. I courted a woman once, you know."

Warner's sudden blink told Travis Pa had hit a sensitive nerve. "I didn't hear any mention of women," Travis said, trying to spare his cousin the tirade he knew would follow.

"Just look at your cousin's face and you'll know I was right. He looks like a lovesick pup."

Before Travis could respond, Warner let out a harsh laugh. "I can always depend on you to speak your mind, Uncle Abe."

"That's one of the prerogatives of age: you get to say what you think. What I think is that you could do better than to hanker after the Cursed Enemy."

Lydia? Of course. Warner hadn't been joking when he'd talked about courting her. He needed a wife, and Lydia was available.

"Now that Warner knows exactly how you feel, he and I are going outside for a few minutes." Travis jerked his head toward the door. When he and his cousin reached the backyard, he continued. "Is Pa right? Are you interested in courting Miss Crawford?" He wouldn't call her Lydia, not now.

Warner nodded. "I am. The problem is, I don't seem to be getting anywhere with her. I've gone to her store every day, volunteering to help her with whatever I could."

"And she doesn't appreciate it? That doesn't sound like Lydia." Travis frowned at the realization that he'd used her Christian name.

"Oh, she appreciates it," Warner countered. "She's always polite. She thanks me and smiles, but she doesn't treat me any differently than she does Xavier Cready."

Travis was tempted to smile at the thought of the curmudgeonly widower who'd tried to court Aunt Bertha setting his sights on Lydia.

"I see." It might be unkind to feel so relieved that Lydia wasn't showing Warner any favoritism, but Travis couldn't stop himself.

"I don't think you do see. When I asked her if I could court her, she said she was too busy getting the store ready to think about anything else."

"The store's open now," Travis pointed out. "Maybe she'll change her mind." But he hoped she wouldn't.

"I'm not sure she will. There's another problem too. Nate is determined to woo her. He's there almost as often as I am."

Remembering the farmer's expression the day Lydia had come to town, Travis wasn't surprised. "Have you considered that she might fancy Nate?"

Warner snorted. "I'm not stupid, Travis. Of course the thought crossed my mind. But every time I've seen Nate leaving her store, he looks as discouraged as I feel."

"Then it seems she was telling the truth. She's not ready for marriage. The time isn't right."

"When will it be?"

Travis shrugged. "Only Lydia knows."

11

"This house has never smelled so good." Aunt Bertha took a deep sniff as she settled into a chair in the kitchen. She'd rested for an hour after supper, but as she did so many evenings, had returned to watch Lydia make candy. Though Lydia had teased her about having a sweet tooth like Porter, she suspected the reason Aunt Bertha spent so much time here was that she was lonely.

"You're the best thing that's happened to me in many years," Aunt Bertha said without taking a breath. "I memorized Romans 8:28 when I was a little girl, but it's only recently that I've learned how true those words are. Losing Jonas was harder than I could have imagined, and there were times when I despaired of ever finding happiness again, but then you arrived." Aunt Bertha nodded. "I thank the Lord every single day for bringing you into my life. You're a true blessing, Lydia."

Lydia felt heat color her cheeks. She wasn't accustomed to praise. "I'm the one who's been blessed." She looked up from the dishes she was washing and gestured toward the pan of cooling fudge. "I enjoyed teaching, but running Cimarron Sweets is more rewarding than I thought possible. Everything seems better here. I knew I enjoyed making and selling candy, but I didn't feel this excited and energized when I worked at the shop in Syracuse."

The days were long. Even though the store was open only during the afternoon, Lydia's days began early and ended late. She caught herself yawning too often, and yet she wouldn't have changed a thing about the business. The store had been open for more than three weeks now, and while some days were slower than others, she had enough customers that she would turn a profit. If it weren't for her continuing worry about Edgar, Lydia would have said that her life was close to perfect.

"I'm not surprised you feel different." Aunt Bertha raised an eyebrow as if the reason should be obvious. "That's because the store in Syracuse wasn't yours."

"This one isn't, either."

"Nonsense! You're the one who's done all the work. All I did was offer a little money.

Now, are those peppermint sticks ready to sample?"

As she placed the last pan in the draining rack, Lydia nodded. "They are." Today was the first time Lydia had made them. She'd always considered peppermint a winter treat, but when Nate's sister had asked if she would make some, Lydia had agreed.

"I also made mint fudge. I'm not sure how popular it will be in the summer, but I thought I'd experiment. I want to offer new flavors every couple weeks to keep people coming back to the store."

Aunt Bertha took a sip of her coffee, then pointed at the fudge. "I need a taste of that before I try the peppermint stick."

When Lydia placed a small piece on a plate, Aunt Bertha bit into it. For once, she was silent for more than a couple seconds, as if trying to decide whether she liked the flavor, and Lydia felt herself tense. She'd never before mixed mint with chocolate, but when she'd licked the spoon, she had thought the combination a good one.

"It's excellent," Aunt Bertha said at last, "but I don't think this is the right time to offer it."

"I should wait for Christmas?" Peppermint was always a big seller during December.

"No, no." Aunt Bertha shook her head so vigorously Lydia thought her hair might come undone. "Not that long. Just until Founders' Day. You could make it your Founders' Day special and only sell it that week." She slid the remaining bit of fudge into her mouth and made a show of tasting it. "Everyone in town will want some, so be sure you make enough."

"I like that idea." Though she'd thought of offering seasonal specialties, Lydia hadn't considered such a limited availability. It made sense, especially given how enthusiastic the townspeople were about celebrating Cimarron Creek's founding.

"Good. Now, what are you planning to wear on my day?"

In one of her lighter moments, Aunt Bertha had pointed out that she was the sole surviving founder. "I told Matthew and the others that I'd sit on the platform with them, but I won't give a speech. That was Jonas's responsibility, and I refuse to take over. No one wants to listen to an old lady talk about the first days of Cimarron Creek anyway."

Though Lydia suspected many of the townspeople would indeed be interested in Aunt Bertha's tales, she had been unable to persuade her, and the subject had been dropped. Now it appeared Aunt Bertha was more concerned about sartorial elegance than speeches.

"Everyone comes in their best clothes," she told Lydia.

"I know. That's why I decided to wear something different to the store that day." Lydia described the purple striped shirtwaist and the delicate lace collar that she planned to pair with a rich blue skirt. "In the evening I'll wear my Sunday dress."

Aunt Bertha shook her head. "Oh, my dear, you need something more elegant for the evening. Even if you aren't a founder, everyone knows you're my protégé. They'll expect you to dress like a Whitfield or a Henderson."

Lydia wondered if that was the reason Aunt Bertha had given her six different but equally elegant pinafores to wear at Cimarron Sweets. "Those gray dresses you used for teaching will be perfect underneath the pinafores," she had said. "You'll look neat and prosperous. Perfect."

But it appeared that Lydia's wardrobe plans for Founders' Day were not perfect.

"Your skirt and shirtwaist will be fine during the day," Aunt Bertha conceded, "but there's dancing in the evening. You wouldn't want to disappoint your beaux, would you?"

It was a familiar subject. Each time either Warner or Nate visited, Aunt Bertha talked about their good qualities, and each time Lydia reminded the older woman that she was not looking for a husband or even a beau.

"You know I'm not interested in marriage."

"But Warner and Nate are definitely interested in you. They're both fine men, you know."

"I'm not disputing that." Warner no longer seemed to regard her as an item he was considering buying, and Nate had overcome what Lydia suspected was innate shyness around women and had begun to regale her with stories of his Angora goats. "It's simply that I'm not planning to marry," she told Aunt Bertha. Lydia knew she should have learned her lesson after what had happened to her mother, but it had taken Edgar's broken promises to make her realize she was not meant to be a wife.

Aunt Bertha did not appear convinced. "Be that as it may, you still need a new gown. Think of it as advertising for the store."

"That might be a good idea, but it'll have to wait for next year." Lydia's heart warmed at the thought of being here that long.

"When Camilla Dunn stopped in yesterday, she said she had more orders than she could fill. It seems every woman in Cimarron Creek wants a new gown." And though most of the women sewed their everyday dresses, they relied on Camilla for special-occasion clothes.

"I'm a fair seamstress," Lydia told Aunt Bertha, "but I don't have time to sew something new, especially if I'm going to make extra fudge. I'm afraid the town will just have to see me in my church dress all day long."

Pursing her lips, Aunt Bertha said, "We'll see about that."

Two days later when Lydia returned from the shop, she found a royal blue gown lying on her bed.

"Try it on." Aunt Bertha entered the room and pointed to the dress. "I used your Sunday dress as a pattern, but it may still need some alterations."

"You made this?" Lydia stared at the gown, amazed by both its beauty and the fact that Aunt Bertha had sewn it. The older woman had told Lydia that her fingers hurt so much from arthritis that she rarely did any handwork.

"I remade it," Aunt Bertha corrected her. "It wasn't doing any good stuffed in a trunk, and you needed something new." She picked up the dress and held it in front of Lydia. "Try it on. I hope I haven't lost my touch with a needle and scissors."

She hadn't. The gown was a perfect fit, and with its heart-shaped neckline, cap sleeves, and the apron-style draping that flowed into a bustle, it looked like something from a women's fashion magazine. The style was perfect, but what made the garment extra special was the fabric. The rich silk had subtle slubbing that shimmered when Lydia moved.

"Oh, Aunt Bertha!" Lydia twirled in front of the cheval mirror the older woman had insisted she place in her room. "It's the finest dress I've ever owned."

The clothing Lydia had worn in Syracuse had been of good quality but had been designed with serviceability in mind. Poplin and gabardine had been the fabrics of choice, not silk.

Aunt Bertha smiled her approval. "I'm happy to see it worn again."

Lydia fingered the sumptuous fabric as she admired her reflection. Though it was possible that the gown had once belonged to Aunt Bertha, she doubted it. The color was one that only a younger woman would have worn, and the fabric was too new for it to have been part of Aunt Bertha's youth. Unless Lydia was gravely mistaken, the dress had once belonged to Aunt Bertha's daughter Joan. Tears welled in her eyes at the thought that she'd been given something so precious.

"Thank you. I don't know what to say other than thank you."

Aunt Bertha's eyes shone with unshed tears. "Just enjoy it," she said. "That's all I ask. The dress was made for dancing, and so are you."

There were days when Travis was inclined to agree with Pa that he should never have agreed to become a sheriff, and today was one of them. Founders' Day was Cimarron Creek's biggest celebration of the year, bigger even than the Fourth of July. The shops all closed at noon, leaving the afternoon free for a parade, speeches, and games for the children, all followed by a barbecue. And then when the sun set, the adults would return to the park wearing their finest clothes as they prepared to dance the night away.

Travis had expected a few problems to crop up after the barbecue. Some residents could be depended on to imbibe a little too heavily from the jugs that — despite the town's edicts — contained a beverage stronger than lemonade or sarsaparilla. Tempers would rise, and at least one fight seemed inevitable. Travis was prepared for that, but he hadn't been prepared for this.

At this time of the day, Main Street was normally almost empty, but as he looked out his window a few minutes after nine, he discovered a line of women stretching in front of his office and down the street. While it wasn't unusual to see one or two women out shopping this early, this was unprecedented. It appeared that every woman in Cimarron Creek had made her way to this particular block.

"What's going on, ladies?" As he stepped outside, Travis saw that the line stopped in front of Lydia's candy store. Though normally closed until after noon, today Lydia had opened it this morning to conform to the Founders' Day tradition of closing all stores at midday. That made sense. What didn't make sense was that the entire female population felt the need to visit Cimarron Sweets this particular morning.

Travis had been pleased by the apparent ease with which the townspeople accepted Lydia. Though he'd heard a few disparaging remarks about Yankees, Lydia's unfailing courtesy and the quality of her confections seemed to have won over the majority of the naysayers. Still, the crowd that lined the street was unexpected.

"Miss Crawford made a new flavor of fudge," Mrs. Wilkins said in answer to Travis's question. "She calls it Founders' Day Fudge, and today's the first day it's on sale."

"No one knows what the flavor is, but we don't want to miss it." Mrs. Higgins continued the explanation. "She's only going to have it for a week."

And no one wanted to be left out. It was a brilliant strategy, one that ensured Lydia would sell every pound she'd made. But that strategy, Travis discovered half an hour later, could also cause problems.

He'd remained outside, talking to the women, listening to their stories of their children and grandchildren as they waited patiently for their chance to buy some of the mysterious Founders' Day Fudge. And it was still a mystery, for, no matter how many women left the store, their little boxes held as carefully as if they contained something more precious than fudge, no one would tell the others what the special flavor was. Perhaps they didn't know. Perhaps Lydia had prepackaged the candy and had sold it without her trademark samples. If that was the case, it was another example of Lydia's expertise, because the anticipation continued to increase.

The line had grown shorter, but there were still half a dozen women on the street when one woman emerged, a box in her hand.

"She only has five pounds left," the woman announced.

Travis tried not to frown, but he'd seen another three women inside the store. That meant Lydia's supply would run out before her customers did.

"I'm sure Miss Crawford will have more tomorrow," he said. He could only hope that was true, but he wasn't at all certain it was. He knew Lydia usually began candy preparations as soon as the supper dishes were done and that she continued making candy each morning, getting everything ready to take to the shop immediately after the noon meal. Since she would be at the celebration tonight, her candy-making time would be limited, meaning there was no guarantee she'd have fudge ready tomorrow.

"But I need some today," one woman said, her voice verging on hysteria. "I promised my daughter she could have some. The poor dear has measles. I thought this might make up for missing all the festivities today."

A second woman propped her hands on her hips and glared. "My son needs it just as much as your daughter. He done broke his leg and cain't get around good on his crutches."

As if on cue, all six women outside the store began to push and shove, trying to reach the door. The formerly orderly queue had become a melee.

"Ladies, please. Let me in." Travis entered the store and found Lydia looking as calm as ever. Only the tick at the side of her mouth betrayed her dismay. He made his way to the counter, taking her arm and leading her into the back room. "We'll be a moment, ladies," he said. "Please wait." As if any of them would leave without her prize.

"I heard you're about to run out of Founders' Day Fudge," he said. Though he was addressing Lydia, he'd positioned himself so he could watch the store. The last thing Lydia needed was for a fight to break out here.

"It's true. I thought I had enough, but the demand exceeded my expectations."

"I want my fudge," one woman shouted. "I waited as long as everyone."

"And you'll have it, Mrs. Schilling." Lydia raised her voice to be heard over the murmurs that were increasing in volume. She lowered it again as she spoke to Travis. "I wish I had enough to make everyone happy. I'm not Jesus with the fishes and the loaves. I can't turn these five boxes into enough for everyone."

"Maybe you need Solomon's wisdom. Remember how his threat to cut the baby in half revealed the child's true mother."

Lydia was silent for a moment before a smile crossed her face. "That's the answer." She marched across the front room and opened the door. "Ladies, may I have your attention? Please, everyone, come inside. There'll be room for you all."

When the eight women were gathered inside the shop, Lydia continued. "You've all been so patient. I appreciate that and your support more than I can say, but now I have a problem. I don't have enough Founders' Day Fudge to sell each of you a pound." She gestured toward the remaining five boxes. "I hate to disappoint anyone, and I'm sure you don't want any of your neighbors to feel left out. This is Founders' Day, after all. I've been told it's the day everyone comes together as a community."

Though Travis wasn't certain where she was heading, he was pleased by the murmurs of assent that met her statement.

"I wondered if you'd consider this," she

continued. "I'll open the boxes and sell each of you a half pound of fudge. That way everyone will have some."

Although several women nodded, one frowned. "I need more sweets. I didn't make a pie, because I was counting on a whole pound."

"I understand." Lydia's sober expression said she did. "That's why I propose to give each of you a half pound of any other candy in the store at no charge."

She gestured toward the glass-fronted cabinet with its display of assorted sweets. "The fudge is special, but there are some people in town who prefer peanut brittle. I'll admit I'm partial to the chocolate creams." Lydia pointed to a silver platter. "You'll notice that I put double Cs on them. That stands for both chocolate cream and Cimarron Creek."

To Travis's relief, a couple women chuckled, and the angry murmurs subsided.

Lydia continued her sales pitch. "I'm planning to introduce lemon drops next week. As a small thank-you for your patience and your generosity in sharing Founders' Day Fudge with your neighbors, I'll put aside a supply for you so you won't have to worry about missing out on them if they prove to be as popular as the fudge."

The women nodded, and within ten minutes, the store was empty of customers. The first crisis of the day was over.

12

Five hours later, Travis walked slowly around the crowd that had gathered in the park. This was the quietest time of the celebration. The parade was over, the games had yet to begin. For the next half hour, the townspeople would endure the annual speeches, beginning with his uncle's. It was time for Uncle Matthew to perform his mayoral duty of officially welcoming everyone to the day that honored his own parents' contribution to the town. His speech would be followed by longer ones delivered by the members of the town council. It was all part of the tradition, albeit the most boring part.

There had been a time when Travis had hated being bored, but that was before he became sheriff. Now he cherished days with no reports of broken windows, stolen chickens, or fights in the Silver Spur. The past few weeks had been unusually quiet, so quiet that Warner had even commented on the lack of petty crimes during one of their weekly dominoes games. Both Porter and Nate had chuckled when Travis told them he was happy to be bored.

But today boredom was chased away by the shout everyone in Cimarron Creek dreaded. "Fire!" A man's hoarse cry pierced the crowd, and within seconds, half a dozen men were following him toward the livery, where ominous billows of smoke poured from the door and the neighs of frightened horses competed with the townspeople's shouts. Like most of the buildings in town, the livery's exterior was constructed of stone, but the interior had more than its share of flammable materials.

Travis reached the building at the same time as Porter and joined the hastily formed bucket brigade. Other fires had taught business owners the value of keeping a supply of water close at hand, and Porter, knowing how fire frightened horses, kept more water than most inside the stable.

To Travis's relief, though the smoke was dense, the flames appeared to be confined to one part of the building, threatening Porter's supply of feed but far enough from the horses and carriages that neither was in danger. The combination of the men's help and Porter's generous supply of water soon subdued the flames, leaving the blackened back wall the only sign that a fire had taken place.

Porter had been lucky, but when he turned to Travis, his face registered a fury that matched the flames. "A fine sheriff you are." He spat the words at Travis, seeming not to care that the men who'd helped fight the fire were listening and would undoubtedly repeat everything he said. "You can't even keep your family safe."

Though stung by the unfairness of the attack, Travis said nothing but instead urged the men to return to the park. It was time for the celebration to continue.

Uncle Matthew was in the middle of his speech when Porter approached Travis half an hour later. "I'm sorry. I didn't mean what I said." But the damage was done.

As he walked through the crowd, Travis heard the rumors begin, people speculating about a rift within the Whitfield family. Travis knew there was no truth to it, but he also knew truth wasn't a necessary ingredient for gossip. Porter's angry accusation would take on a life of its own, growing in importance with each retelling. There was no knowing what embellishments the story would have by the time Pa heard it.

Travis tried not to frown at the thought of

the tongue-lashing his father would deliver tonight. He had work to do before then. It was up to him to keep the citizens of Cimarron Creek safe.

Fortunately, the rest of the afternoon passed without incident, unless you counted the minor scrapes acquired during the children's games and the bowl of mashed potatoes that two of the younger boys decided would make a good shampoo. There was nothing serious, nothing unexpected. Now all that remained was the dancing. If Travis could intercept the jugs of whiskey and keep those who imbibed away from the rest of the revelers, the day would have a successful ending.

He looked around, admiring the work the committee had done to prepare the park for the evening's festivities. After the barbecue supper had ended, the benches had been moved to the perimeter, leaving the center of the park open for dancing. Lanterns had been strung from the trees on the perimeter, and others had been placed on poles near the improvised dance floor. The fiddlers were tuning their instruments as couples returned to the park, many dressed in clothing that would not be out of place in a formal ballroom. Combined with the glow of the lanterns and the sparkle of the stars overhead, it was a scene some might call romantic.

But Travis was not looking for romance. He wasn't looking for anything other than an end to this day. Or so he thought until he saw her. She was walking slowly, her arm around Aunt Bertha's waist as if she were supporting the older woman. Her smile was more relaxed than it had been this morning, and her hair was caught up in some fancy style, but what made his gaze pause was her gown. Dark blue and shimmery, it left no doubt that she had curves in all the right places. Lydia Crawford wasn't simply beautiful; she was stunning.

"Good evening, ladies." Travis approached the two women. "I'm glad to see you here." He wasn't going to say what was in his heart, that the sight of Lydia took his breath away. That would be wrong for many reasons, not the least of which was that he was the sheriff, and he was on duty.

Aunt Bertha gave him one of those "I know what you're thinking" looks that had intimidated him when he'd been a boy. "Is that all you have to say, nephew? I thought your mother taught you better. When you see a lady as beautiful as Lydia, you're supposed to compliment her."

"That's hardly necessary," Lydia said

before he could reply. "Sheriff Whitfield has much more important things to do than hand out idle flattery."

Though he was surprised by her formality in referring to him by his title rather than his Christian name, Travis couldn't object. Hadn't he just reminded himself that he was here in an official capacity?

"I don't flatter," he told her. "Both of my parents instilled a respect for truth in me. The truth is, you're looking very beautiful tonight, Lydia, and so are you, Aunt Bertha."

His aunt grinned. "Nicely done, my boy. There's hope for you yet." She turned to Lydia. "Let's find me a seat so you can start dancing."

While Lydia looked as if she wanted to protest, she simply glanced around the park, her eyes lighting on a row of benches. Pointing to them, she asked, "Would you like to sit there?"

When Aunt Bertha nodded, the two women began to walk in that direction, with Travis trailing behind them. He wasn't sure what he hoped to accomplish. Neither woman needed his assistance, and yet he wasn't ready to leave. But then he heard the shouts.

"I saw her first!" There was no mistaking

either Warner's voice or the anger in it.

"Maybe so, but I gave her the first gift." Nate made no attempt to hide his own ire. Though the man was normally slow to anger, it was clear that Warner's words had provoked him.

Travis lengthened his stride, determined to reach the men before their argument could escalate. He had no doubt that Lydia was the subject of the confrontation and even less doubt that she would be embarrassed by it. As Cimarron Creek's sheriff, he needed to prevent a brawl. As Lydia's friend, he needed to keep her from becoming the subject of ugly gossip.

"That's all the more reason I should have the first dance," Warner declared.

"You think you can stop me?" Nate turned as if to head toward Lydia.

"I do."

Travis was three yards away when Warner grabbed Nate by the arm, spinning him around, only to find Nate's fist landing on his cheek. The fight had begun. Warner managed to get in a good punch, knocking his opponent to the ground, but the farmer was ready. Hooking his leg around Warner's, he dropped him into the dirt. If he hadn't been so disgusted with both of them, Travis might have laughed at the sight of two grown men acting like schoolboys, fighting over a girl and tussling in the dirt.

"Stop it!" He reached down and pulled the men apart. When the men were once again on their feet, he stood between them. "It's time for you both to leave."

"Not before I dance with Lydia." Warner brushed the dust from his pants, then ran an exploratory hand over his face. Though he appeared relieved to find no blood, he grimaced at the bruise.

Nate shook his head. "I'm not leaving without a dance, either."

"Sorry, gentlemen." And Travis was. This was the worst part of being sheriff, having to administer justice to people he knew. It was one of the reasons some towns preferred to hire outsiders. But Travis had taken an oath, and nothing would stop him from keeping it, regardless of the fact that the perpetrators were his closest friends.

He looked from Warner to Nate, his expression as steely as if they'd been total strangers. His cousin and his friend should never have come to blows, but they had, and now they had to accept the consequences. "You know the rules. Anyone who disturbs the peace — and you were definitely disturbing the peace — has to leave. Go home."

"But, Travis . . ."

Travis shook his head at Warner. "Go." He turned to the crowd that had gathered to watch the men's argument. "The excitement's over, folks." He tipped his head to one side, listening to the fiddlers warming up. "It sounds to me like the first dance is about to begin. You don't want to miss that."

The next hour passed quickly with no problem other than having to confiscate a jug of whiskey and send its owner home. Travis walked the perimeter, keeping watch. And if his eyes happened to stray to a certain golden-haired lady in a fetching blue gown, well . . . The point of his job was to keep everyone safe.

"I told you she was trouble."

Travis swiveled, startled by his father's voice. He'd thought Pa was on the other side of the park, spending the evening with his poker buddies.

"Look what she's done," Pa continued. "She caused a fight between two men who used to be friends. I told you, Travis, you need to run the Cursed Enemy out of town before she causes any more trouble." Pa took a shallow breath. "I wouldn't be surprised if she was behind the fire too."

The accusation was so absurd that Travis did not honor it with a reply. If he stayed here, he would only say something he might regret. *Honor thy father and thy mother.* The commandment echoed through Travis's brain. Sometimes the best way to honor was to walk away. He spun on his heel and headed toward Lydia. That might annoy Pa, but it was better than the alternative. Besides, Travis wanted to see the woman whose beauty made his heart sing. And, for once, she wasn't dancing. Though she'd had partners for every set before this, now she was seated by Aunt Bertha.

"I'm not much of a dancer," Travis said when he reached her, "but I wondered if you'd care to take a walk with me."

Lydia looked up, surprised to see Travis. Oh, she'd seen him from a distance all day, but other than the time in her shop this morning and the brief words they'd spoken before the unfortunate incident had begun, they'd not spoken. This was the opportunity she'd sought.

"Yes, thank you. There's something I'd like to discuss with you."

Ever since she'd heard what had happened between Nate and Warner, though she'd tried to keep a smile pasted on her face, Lydia's stomach had been tied in knots. The only good thing she could say was that

Catherine had not been here to witness the man she loved's foolishness. Though Lydia wished Gussie had felt well enough for her and Catherine to attend tonight's festivities, it was good they'd missed the altercation.

Aunt Bertha had told Lydia it was nothing to worry about. "Boys will be boys," she'd announced, but Lydia wasn't convinced. While Aunt Bertha tried to find the best in every situation, Travis was a realist. He'd tell her the truth.

They walked in silence until they were outside the park. It was quieter here, with less chance of being overheard, yet they were still close enough to the crowd that no one would look askance at the sheriff and the town's candy maker walking arm in arm.

Lydia opened her mouth to speak, but before she could get out the first word, Travis turned toward her.

"Are you enjoying being the belle of the ball? Not every woman has two men fighting over the honor of asking her to dance." There was a hint of humor in his voice. Ridiculous. There was nothing amusing about what had happened.

Lydia shook her head, as much in response to Travis's apparent amusement as to his question. "That's what I wanted to discuss. I'm embarrassed by what happened. I knew

I was making a mistake by coming here tonight, but Aunt Bertha insisted. She claimed I was part of the town now and needed to be a part of Founders' Day." Lydia had been a part, all right. The scandalous part.

"Aunt Bertha was wrong. I'm not a part of the town, not yet. I know that even though they buy my candy, there are plenty of people who consider me an interloper, maybe even an enemy, because I'm a Yankee. Any progress I may have made in gaining their trust was destroyed tonight."

Travis was silent for a moment, all traces of humor gone from his expression. "For what it's worth, I think you're wrong. No one could blame you for what Warner and Nate did. That's as silly as Porter blaming me for not being able to stop the fire. He apologized later, and Nate and Warner will too. Once they've calmed down, they'll realize what happened was the result of their own idiocy."

"Not everyone will think that way." She had overheard several of the women speculating that Lydia had led the men on. One had even referred to her as a hussy.

Travis must not have heard those comments, because he continued. "Look at all the men who asked you to dance. They weren't shunning you."

"That's true, but they don't buy much candy, either. I can't let the store fail." What bothered her most was the thought that Aunt Bertha's faith in her might be misplaced.

"It won't fail. The scene this morning should have proven that. Almost every woman in Cimarron Creek was standing in line to buy your fudge."

"They could change their minds just as quickly." The women on the train and the stagecoaches had been friendly until Lydia had spoken, but in an instant their welcome had vanished, replaced by disdain and in some cases outright enmity.

"I can't imagine that happening because two men got into a fight over dancing with you."

"They should have known better. I tried to tell them."

"Tell them what?" Travis tipped his head to the side, reminding Lydia of a bird listening for a worm. Only there were no worms, just the reality of her situation.

"That I have no intention of marrying them or anyone."

He nodded slowly, but Lydia sensed that Travis was acknowledging her statement rather than agreeing with it. "You've said that before, but you've never explained why. Most women look forward to marriage."

"I'm not most women."

Travis nodded. "I know that. You're stronger and braver than most women."

His words sent warmth spiraling through her, chasing away the cold dread that had settled deep inside her when she'd heard about Warner and Nate's fight.

"I still don't understand why you're opposed to marriage," he said.

Because I saw what it did to my mother. Because I almost made the same mistake. Those were the reasons, but Lydia didn't want to admit them. Though the best thing was to say nothing, unbidden the words slipped out. "Men can't be trusted."

Travis flinched and started to speak, but Lydia stopped him. "I'm sure there are exceptions. You're probably one of them, but I've seen enough to know it's true. Men can't be trusted where love is concerned."

13

She was wrong. Travis strode around the perimeter of the park, frustration making his footsteps heavier than normal. Lydia was wrong. Men could be trusted. Even his mother agreed with that. "He's an honorable man, he kept his wedding vows, and even though he's become harsher since the war, he's been a good father to you and Dorcas," she declared the day Travis had asked if Pa was the reason she was crying.

His eyes scanned the crowd, looking not only for signs of trouble but for an answer to his question. Lydia had refused to say anything more, and though Aunt Bertha would undoubtedly give him an earful of explanations, he didn't want to talk to his highly opinionated aunt tonight. He just wanted to understand why Lydia claimed men couldn't be trusted and his mother had seemed so sad.

If everything Ma had said was true, why

had she cried so often? Though she'd claimed she had sensitive eyes and that dust motes sometimes made her weep, Travis didn't believe that. He'd recognized the despair in her sobs when he'd wakened in the middle of the night and heard her crying in the kitchen. Dust motes weren't to blame. He knew that. What he didn't know was who or what was responsible for his mother's unhappiness. He'd probably never know, because Pa refused to talk about her, and Dorcas knew as little as Travis did.

Whatever the problem was, Ma had taken it to the grave with her. But Lydia was still alive. That gave him time to change her mind once he understood why she felt the way she did.

Abandoning the perimeter, Travis made his way to the center of the park, where couples were dancing to a lively tune. Though some of his aunts and uncles sat on the sidelines, his cousins were out in full force with the notable exception of Warner, who'd been banished, and Catherine.

As a lemon-yellow dress caught his eye, Travis revised his observation. Catherine was here, and since she was closer to Lydia than anyone other than Aunt Bertha, she might be able to help him.

"Evening, Catherine," he said when he

reached her side. "How's your mother?" He'd heard that Aunt Gussie was having a bad spell today and that was the reason neither she nor Catherine had attended the earlier events.

"She's sleeping now." Catherine's voice held a note of sadness. "I wanted to stay with her, but she insisted I come. I'm not really in the mood for dancing, though."

"Neither am I."

"The women of Cimarron Creek will be eternally grateful for that." The soft chuckle that accompanied her words told Travis that Catherine was remembering the times he'd attempted to dance but had accomplished little other than mashing his partners' feet.

"Since neither of us is interested in dancing, may I escort you to the refreshment table? The punch is better than normal."

Catherine nodded as she placed her hand on the crook of his elbow. "What is it you want to ask me?"

"What do you mean?" Had Catherine somehow read his thoughts?

"I'm a teacher, Travis. I've learned to read little boys' expressions. You look exactly like one of my pupils did the day he asked me where babies came from."

Travis couldn't help laughing as he wondered how Catherine had gotten through that potentially embarrassing moment and whether there had been others that were just as bad. Maybe being sheriff wasn't the worst job Cimarron Creek had to offer.

"I assure you I wasn't going to ask you that."

"Good, because I had no intention of answering. What do you want to know?"

He had planned to ease into the subject, but now there was no need. "Do you believe men can be trusted?"

Catherine's grip on his arm tightened, telling Travis he'd hit a sensitive nerve.

"In general or about something specific?" she asked.

"Something specific. Do you believe men can be trusted where love is concerned?"

"Absolutely not."

"I heard I missed the excitement yesterday," Catherine said as she took a seat at the marble-topped table.

"The fire was out almost before it started." Lydia poured a second cup of coffee and handed it to her friend. "I heard that Porter was angry and even went so far as to blame Travis, but by the time I danced with him, he was as calm as could be."

Catherine nodded. "That's Porter for you. He has a quick temper, but it subsides as fast as it flares. I wasn't referring to the fire, though. Half a dozen people told me about the fight."

The fight. If there was one part of Founders' Day that Lydia didn't want to recall, it was that. And the worst part was that Catherine had had to hear about it from someone else. Lydia had planned to tell her what had happened when she saw her this morning.

"I'm sorry, Catherine. I hope you know I didn't do anything to start it. If I'd known you were coming to the dance, I would have stayed and told you about it myself." As it was, when Aunt Bertha had admitted to being tired, Lydia had used that as an excuse to leave the festivities. She had been gone before her friend arrived.

"I know that. Nate and Warner were being like schoolboys. To tell you the truth, Lydia, seeing how Nate's been acting has opened my eyes." Catherine stared into the distance for a moment. "Mama told me there are two kinds of love. One is when a woman gives her heart to a man. That's good, but she said it's even better when he steals her heart. That's the kind of love that lasts a lifetime."

Love was something Lydia and her mother had rarely discussed, and not once had

Mama spoken of stolen hearts. That was understandable, for Mama's experience with love had been far different from Gussie's.

"Did Nate steal your heart?"

Catherine shook her head. "I thought so at first, but now I know it wasn't so. I can see that the Nate I thought I knew was a figment of my imagination and that what I believed was love was nothing more than my longing to be married. The real Nate is not the man I want to marry. That would have been a mistake."

Lydia looked up from the fudge she was stirring. "I know what you mean. I almost made the same mistake."

"With Edgar."

Lydia couldn't hide her surprise. "How did you know? I haven't told anyone."

"As I told Travis last night, I've learned to read people's expressions. Yours told me there was more than friendship between you and Edgar."

There was no point in denying what Catherine had seen. "Was. Past tense. When I learned that he'd married Opal, I realized I didn't really know him. If he could fall in love with someone else so quickly, he wasn't the right man for me."

"But the right man will come. God will

send him."

"Maybe."

Travis reached to the ceiling in a vain attempt to overcome fatigue with a stretch. What he needed was a solid ten hours of sleep, but that wasn't going to happen any more than Lydia was going to admit that she might be mistaken. He stretched again, then poured himself a cup of the now-cold coffee he'd made when he'd returned from the night's patrol.

Grimacing as he took a big swig of the beverage that would probably do little to keep him awake, Travis shook his head. He might not know why his mother had been so sad, but he did know one thing, and that was that he didn't want Lydia to become like Ma. She deserved to be happy. Right now the store made her happy, and though it might not be part of his official responsibilities to the town, Travis had every intention of doing what he could to ensure that happiness continued.

He swallowed the last of the coffee and rose. It was time to see what was happening on Main Street. Placing the empty cup next to the pot, he tried to convince himself that the only reason he spent time with Lydia was his concern for her success. It had nothing to do with the way her smile made him feel as if he were ten feet tall or that even an innocent brush of her fingers against his sent waves of pleasure through his veins. That was foolishness, and Travis Whitfield was not a foolish man.

"I'm sorry to bother you, Sheriff."

Travis spun around at the sound of Opal Ellis's voice. He'd been so lost in his thoughts that he hadn't heard the door open. That was not good. Not good at all. He needed to be alert every minute of the day.

"Morning, Opal. What can I do for you?" Though he believed he knew the answer, Travis felt compelled to ask the question. There was always the possibility that she was here on Faith's behalf.

"I wondered whether you'd learned anything about Edgar."

Opal's slender fingers pleated her skirt in an uncharacteristically nervous gesture, drawing Travis's attention to her abdomen. In the more than two months since her husband had disappeared, Opal's unborn child had grown to the point where even an unobservant man could not ignore it.

"I'm sorry, Opal, but every lead has turned out to be false. No one has seen Edgar since the night he disappeared. The only encouragement I can give you is that no one has found his body. That means he could still be alive somewhere." It was a faint hope, and Travis knew it. So did Opal, for though she nodded, she looked as if she were about to burst into tears.

"I don't know what I'm going to do." Opal's hands cupped her abdomen in a protective gesture. "Faith won't let me work at the Silver Spur any longer. She says it's bad for business. She says I can stay there until the baby's born, but I need to pay for my room and board. How can I do that when I'm not working?" Opal shook her head, her face contorted with distress. "Edgar was going to find us a house, but now . . . I don't know what to do."

The words came out in a torrent, and then she did it. She burst into tears. Travis tried not to frown as the thought came to him unbidden that Lydia might have been right. Perhaps men — or at least Edgar — weren't to be trusted. Opal had put her trust in Edgar, and now she was alone with a baby on the way.

"I'm sorry, Sheriff," she said between sobs. "I know it's not your problem."

But it was. Travis couldn't help believing that if he'd been on patrol that night, he might have been able to prevent Edgar from leaving. "I wish I had better news for you," he told the young woman as she tried to staunch her tears.

Opal looked at him through red-rimmed eyes. "You'll find him. I know you will."

If only Travis shared her optimism. When Opal left, he resumed his afternoon routine, stopping in the town's business establishments, ensuring that the proprietors and their customers knew he was looking out for Cimarron Creek's residents.

Knowing how important it was to not be predictable, lest thieves or vandals use that information to their benefit, he varied the order that he visited the shops, and while he didn't enter every home, he took the time to stroll down each of the streets whether or not it housed a business. The townspeople had a right to protection, and he was dedicated to providing it.

Today he listened to two women complaining that their chickens weren't laying as many eggs as normal and another declaring that her cow's milk production was only half what it had been last month. Though he had no idea what the women expected him to do about their problems, he nodded sympathetically. At least they weren't weeping.

By the end of the afternoon, every bone

in his body ached from fatigue, but his step was lighter as he approached the candy store. The time he spent with Lydia had quickly become the highlight of his days. Despite her protests that he had other, more important responsibilities, Travis had started stopping at Aunt Bertha's house every day at noon to help Lydia carry the newly made candy to Cimarron Sweets. He returned each afternoon at six after she'd closed the store and completed her cleanup so that he could escort her home. While the empty pans weren't too heavy for her, they were bulky.

"You look tired," he said as he entered the store through the rear door. The sweet smells of chocolate and peppermint made his mouth water. If he was fortunate, she would offer him a piece of both.

Lydia raised an eyebrow. "What kind of greeting is that?"

"An honest one." And one from a man who was too tired to remember his manners. "I told you I don't indulge in flattery. Are you getting any sleep?"

She shrugged as she handed him a plate with four pieces of candy on it. "Probably more than you are. You can't patrol all night and then expect to stay awake all day."

"And you can't cook all night and every

morning, then expect to be ready to serve people all afternoon."

While Travis devoured the fudge as if he hadn't eaten for days, Lydia said, "I'm not cooking all night. It's only a few hours after supper — never more than four or five." Lydia tipped her head to one side, smiling as she said, "I don't want to disappoint my customers. They've bought more candy than either Aunt Bertha or I thought possible. It's worth losing a little sleep."

He understood the feeling. "My night patrols have stopped the vandalism." No matter what the women said, Travis was not taking any responsibility for too few eggs or too little milk.

"But you can't continue this way." Lydia slid the now empty plate into a bucket of soapy water, then rinsed and dried it. Though she said nothing more, Travis saw the way her hands trembled slightly as she placed the plate on the shelf. Three weeks ago, that would not have happened, but three weeks ago, she had gotten more than four hours of sleep a night.

"Neither can you. Have you considered hiring an assistant?" As the idea popped into his brain, Travis knew it was no coincidence that Opal had visited him today.

"To make candy?" Lydia looked as if he'd

suggested she rob a bank.

That had been exactly what he'd thought, but it was obvious she wouldn't agree. "How about someone to cut the fudge, do all the weighing, and box the candies?" He knew that was how she spent her mornings. "If you didn't have to do that, you could sleep another hour or two." And if she agreed, he would have found a solution to another problem.

Though he'd expected an immediate refusal, Lydia looked as if she were pondering the suggestion. "That might work, but who would I hire? Several of the girls might be interested, but they'll be going back to school soon."

Travis spoke slowly, remembering her reaction the day she'd arrived in Cimarron Creek and had first met Faith and Opal. "Opal Ellis isn't going to school, and she could use a new job."

Blood drained from Lydia's face so quickly that Travis feared she might faint. "Opal? You want me to hire her?" Horror tinged every word.

Travis nodded. "If you're worried about what your customers would say, everyone knows all she did at the saloon was sing and dance. Faith didn't even let her serve drinks." When Lydia seemed to be relaxing,

Travis continued. "The problem is, she can no longer dance, and she needs a way to pay Faith for her room and board."

Though color was making its way back to her cheeks, Lydia did not appear convinced. "I don't know."

"I won't pressure you, but I think this would be a good solution for both of you."

Obviously fighting a yawn, Lydia reached for one of the bags of empty pans and headed for the door. "All right. I'll think about it." She turned, her eyes serious as they studied his face. "You need to find a way to get more sleep too." Lydia gave him a small smile. "You might take your own advice and hire a deputy."

"Maybe I should."

It wasn't a bad idea. In fact, it was a good one. The problem was, hiring help felt like admitting failure. The previous sheriffs had never needed a deputy. They'd single-handedly kept the peace in Cimarron Creek. Was Pa right in saying Travis wasn't meant to be sheriff?

"He's asking too much." Lydia hated the way her voice had turned shrill, but she couldn't seem to stop it. Though she ought to be making a fresh batch of peanut brittle and one of taffy, she'd been so distressed by

Travis's suggestion that she'd abandoned the kitchen and headed for Catherine's house, hoping her friend could help her.

"Is the problem hiring an assistant or hiring Opal?" Catherine asked. She'd led Lydia into the parlor and pointed toward the settee. Once Lydia was seated, she'd settled in next to her and put her arm around Lydia's shoulders.

"It's Opal. I don't know how I can spend every day with her. Whenever I think about her, I remember that she's Edgar's wife and will soon be the mother of his child."

Catherine was silent for a moment, leading Lydia to suspect that she was choosing her words carefully. "When I look at you, I see my friend, not the woman who caught Nate's eye."

A wave of shame washed over Lydia. She'd been thinking of no one other than herself when she should have remembered that she was not the only one who'd been disappointed in love. And even though she and Catherine had suffered disappointments, their pain was far less than Opal's. She'd lost more than the promise of love; she'd lost her husband, and her unborn child had lost its father.

"Some Christian I am," Lydia said. "I certainly failed at the 'love thy neighbor as thyself' commandment."

Catherine's reply was instantaneous. "Don't be so hard on yourself. You're only human."

"But so is Opal, and she needs help."

Once again Lydia found herself ashamed. When she'd arrived in Cimarron Creek, though she was a total stranger, Aunt Bertha had offered her a home. More than that, she had given Lydia the protection of the Henderson name and then — without Lydia having to ask — had helped her establish the confectionary. How could Lydia refuse to offer a helping hand to a woman whose need was even greater than her own?

She nodded, knowing Travis had been right. "I'll give her a chance."

14

"Oh, Miss Crawford, I don't know how to thank you. I never dreamt I could work in a place like this." Opal's eyes shone with pleasure as she looked around Aunt Bertha's kitchen. She had responded to the message Lydia had sent and had come to the house early this morning, eager to try out for the position as Lydia's assistant.

"This is so beautiful," Opal said, stroking the marble-topped table, "and the candy is as good as everyone claims."

Lydia was tempted to smile. Opal's youthful enthusiasm was appealing, and there was no doubt that she was a quick learner. Not only had she demonstrated an aptitude for cutting fudge into precise squares, but she'd proven adept at folding boxes. As long as Lydia avoided looking at the ring adorning Opal's left hand and the obvious thickening of her middle, she could admit how much help the young woman would be.

Lydia took a deep breath as she reminded herself that it wasn't Opal's fault that Edgar had married her rather than Lydia. As far as she could tell, the girl had done nothing to snare him other than being her sweet self. And she was sweet. Lydia could tell that from the hour they'd spent together. It was no wonder Faith had hired her to sing and dance at the saloon. Opal must have been a refreshing change from the jaded women who sought to attract customers with their painted faces and low-cut gowns.

"I hope you're still excited after you've been here for a week or so," Lydia said. "There's nothing glamorous about the work."

Opal looked up from the box of fudge she'd placed on the scale. "There's nothing glamorous about the Silver Spur, either, Miss Crawford. At least men won't be staring at me here."

"That's true." Even if Opal worked at the store itself, she would encounter few men. With the notable exception of Travis, Warner, and Nate, few men ventured inside. "I thought you might be able to help in the back room," Lydia said, voicing a thought that had popped into her mind when she'd seen Opal's efficiency. "You'd be in charge of washing dishes, making tea, and boxing special orders. That would mean an additional five hours of work each day. Do you think you could do that?"

The smile that crossed Opal's face turned her from pretty to almost beautiful. "Oh yes, Miss Crawford. I'm not afraid of hard work."

Lydia nodded. "Good. We'll start tomorrow. And, Opal, please call me Lydia. Miss Crawford is too formal for people who are going to be working together." Just as importantly, the use of her Christian name would mean that Lydia wasn't constantly reminded that she was still a miss, while Opal was Mrs. Edgar Ellis.

"Of course, Miss . . ." Opal shook her head at the realization that she'd already forgotten the admonition. "Lydia," she said with a shy smile. "I'm glad you came to Cimarron Creek."

And so was Lydia.

Travis was right, Lydia realized a week later. Hiring Opal had been just what she needed. The girl — Lydia still thought of her that way, even though she was married and expecting a child — had proven competent at every task she had assigned to her. Having her cut and box candy in the morning had indeed allowed Lydia to sleep an additional two hours, and Opal's work in the back room meant Lydia could leave as soon as she closed the store rather than having to remain to wash dishes. The extra time made a big difference, and so did Opal's company.

Though at first they'd talked about nothing more than which flavor fudge Lydia should make next and what designs seemed to sell the most chocolate creams, as the days had passed, their conversation had widened, touching on everything from Opal's desire to learn to play the pianoforte to Lydia's experiences as a teacher. And now, only seven days since she'd hired her, though Lydia would never have expected it, she admitted that Edgar's wife had become her friend.

"Is there anything else I can do?" Opal asked.

Lydia nodded. They were in the middle of the afternoon lull. "You can watch the store for me. If someone comes in, you know what to do."

Opal's eyes widened. Though she'd refilled tea cups and brought out the plates of tasting samples, she had never sold candy. "Where will you be?"

"I want a cloth for the table." Now that the words were spoken, Lydia realized how silly they sounded. There was no reason the addition of the tablecloth couldn't wait until tomorrow. It wasn't as if anyone had complained about the plain table. All Lydia knew was that the idea had popped into her head half an hour ago and wouldn't leave. While she'd been helping Mrs. Wilkins select an assortment of creams for her bridge party, she kept picturing the trunk in Aunt Bertha's attic and the beautiful crocheted tablecloth that lay within it. Never before had she felt such urgency, and she couldn't dismiss it.

"I should only be gone half an hour," she told Opal as she put on her hat and gloves.

Her eyes still wide with surprise and apprehension, Opal nodded. "I'll do my best."

"You'll do fine. I know you will."

Lydia walked so quickly it was almost a run, compelled by a force she could not explain. When she entered the house, she climbed the stairs, taking care to move as quietly as she could. At this time of day, Aunt Bertha was often napping, and Lydia did not want to disturb her. But as she reached the second floor, Lydia realized that Aunt Bertha was not asleep. The unmistakable sound of sobbing carried through the heavy oak door.

Lydia's heart wrenched at the despair she heard in those sobs, and she knew it was no coincidence she'd felt driven to come home. The tablecloth was simply the catalyst to get Lydia out of the store and where she needed to be, here with the woman who'd been so kind to her.

As she opened the door to Aunt Bertha's bedroom, she saw the older woman sitting on the side of her bed, a framed picture in her hand, tears streaming down her face.

"What's wrong?" Lydia asked as she sank onto the bed beside the weeping woman and wrapped her arms around her. "How can I help you?"

For a second she thought Aunt Bertha would say nothing or, worse, would tell her to leave. Instead she handed the silver frame to Lydia. "This is my daughter. Joan."

The words were simple, but the emotions they stirred were not. At the same time that she felt honored that Aunt Bertha had trusted her enough to mention Joan to her, Lydia wondered what had triggered today's tears. Joan's portrait was not normally on display. Lydia knew that from the times she'd entered this room to fetch something for Aunt Bertha. Why had the older woman retrieved it from wherever it had been hidden?

Lydia looked at the likeness. The old-fashioned clothing confirmed her suspicion that the picture had been taken more than two decades ago when Joan was still living in Cimarron Creek. If Travis's story was true, this was the last portrait Aunt Bertha had of her daughter.

"She's beautiful." Though she was more slender than Aunt Bertha, Joan had the same delicate features as her mother. And while many daguerreotypes showed solemn people in formal poses, Joan's smile and the tilt of her head left no doubt that she enjoyed life.

The older woman nodded, acknowledging the compliment as she wiped her eyes. "Everyone said she was the prettiest girl in town, but now she's gone." The sorrow in her voice left no doubt that while Aunt Bertha might not have spoken of her daughter once she left Cimarron Creek, she had never stopped grieving.

"Oh, Lydia." Another spate of weeping accompanied her words.

Though Lydia searched for something to do or say to comfort Aunt Bertha, she felt helpless in the face of her despair. Knowing it was far from enough, she stroked the older woman's back and murmured, "I'm so sorry."

Aunt Bertha reached for the picture that Lydia had laid on the bed and clutched it to her chest. "I would give everything I own to see Joan again, but that will never happen."

"Do you want to tell me about her?"

Aunt Bertha shook her head. "It hurts too much," she said as tears continued to roll down her cheeks.

Lydia closed her eyes and prayed for guidance. What could she say to a woman who'd lost her daughter and who'd grieved for twenty years? Words might accomplish nothing, but remembering how pleased Aunt Bertha had been with the first fudge Lydia had made, she reasoned that perhaps actions would. The question was, what should she do? It would take more than a plate of candy to cheer Aunt Bertha today.

While Aunt Bertha continued to sob, Lydia's gaze was drawn to the window, where she could see a soft breeze stirring the tree branches. Beyond it, the sky was a faultless blue without even a single cloud to mar its perfection. It was a day to be outside, celebrating life. Perhaps that was the answer.

She patted Aunt Bertha's back one last time, then rose. "You and I need a change of scenery," she said firmly. "We're going out, so put on your hat and gloves. I'll be back in a few minutes."

Lydia's first stop was the store. As she'd expected, Opal was doing well. She had served a couple customers, and though each of them had said she missed seeing Lydia, Opal was willing to continue selling candy for the rest of the day.

"No one even blinked an eye at me," she said with obvious pride. "I thought they might be snooty, figuring they were better than me, but all they cared about was getting a few sweets for their family."

Her heart lighter, Lydia made her way to the livery stable. As she had expected, Porter was the only person there at this hour. Though his father owned the livery, Porter did all the work.

"Uncle Charles isn't a silent partner like Aunt Bertha," Travis had told Lydia one day when he'd been bemoaning his father's outspokenness. "He's always telling Porter how to do things. The truth is, Porter has done more for the business than his father ever did. I wish Uncle Charles could see that and leave Porter alone."

"Good afternoon, Porter."

"Lydia!" Blue eyes so like Warner's revealed Porter's surprise. Though he was a couple inches shorter than his brother, Porter had the same light brown hair, blue eyes, and build as Warner. "I didn't expect

227

you. I thought you were at your store all afternoon."

"I usually am," she admitted, "but I decided I owed myself a break." Lydia looked around. While the livery had the same open rafters that she'd seen in similar establishments in Syracuse, it was cleaner and smelled fresher than those had. Travis had not been exaggerating when he'd claimed that Porter took exceptional care of his business. "I'd like to rent a horse and carriage for a couple hours."

"You came to the right place. I have the best horses in town." A wry smile crossed Porter's face. "The only horses too. But are you sure you want to go out alone? Cimarron Creek isn't as safe as it used to be when Sheriff Allen was around. He kept a tighter rein than Travis does."

"I won't be alone." And even if she were, Lydia doubted the person or persons responsible for the thefts and vandalism would bother her. Their work seemed to be done under cover of darkness.

"I see." Porter's confused expression belied his words. "Usually the gentleman hires the carriage."

She smiled as she realized that Porter's assumption that she would be riding with a man was the cause of his confusion. "There are no gentlemen involved. I'm taking Aunt Bertha for a ride."

The livery man grinned. "Well, in that case, I have just the rig for you, if you can handle it, that is." When Lydia assured him that she was comfortable driving horses, Porter led the way into the back of the building and pointed at a shiny cabriolet. Designed to be pulled by one horse, it was the perfect size for two passengers. "Aunt Bertha and Uncle Jonas used to rent this one." He began to pull the vehicle away from the wall. "You'll want the hood up today," he said with a gesture toward the folded leather hood. "The sun is mighty bright."

Lydia nodded her agreement.

"Look around if you like," Porter said. "I'll have this ready in no time."

Though she had no particular interest in the contents of a livery, Lydia wandered to the back of the building. A coat of white-wash covered the soot on the rear wall, leaving only the faint smell of smoke as evidence of the Founders' Day fire. Closer to the front of the building, stalls held half a dozen horses, while shelves crowded with merchandise lined one wall. Lydia recognized the jars of molasses and the bins of hay and oats. Wedged between two bins were several yellow bags that looked familiar, though she could not place them.

"Here you go," Porter called out.

Lydia turned and made her way to the front of the stable, admiring the beautiful chestnut mare now harnessed to the cabriolet.

"What do you think?" he asked.

"It's perfect." Just the sight of the meticulously cared for vehicle and the well-groomed horse made her smile. Surely they'd have the same effect on Aunt Bertha. "How much do I owe you?"

When Porter quoted a price that seemed too low, Lydia raised an eyebrow. "Are you sure that's all?"

He nodded. "Cimarron Creek isn't a big city like Syracuse or Dallas, so prices are lower here, and people are friendlier."

Lydia saw no reason to dispute Porter's statement. The truth was, most of Cimarron Creek's residents had been friendly, with the notable exception of Travis's father. No matter how cordial she had tried to be, he'd rebuffed every overture she made. But the day was too beautiful to worry about Abe Whitfield.

Lydia looked down as something brushed against her skirts. There, attempting to rub her legs, was a butterscotch-colored cat. She smiled. "That's the largest cat I've ever seen and the friendliest."

"See, I told you we're a friendly town. That's Homer, the best mouser you could want." Porter reached down and stroked the animal's back. "I haven't seen a mouse or rat since he came here."

"How long have you had him?" The gray she saw on Homer's head made Lydia suspect he was an elderly cat, although he moved with the ease of a young one.

"It's going on ten years now. He just showed up one day. The scrawniest kitten you ever did see. I gave him a saucer of milk and wound up with a friend." Porter gave Homer's head a rub before he stood. "Talking about Homer isn't getting you on your ride." He turned toward the cabriolet. "Here, let me help you."

When Lydia reached home, she was pleased to see Aunt Bertha waiting on the front porch, all signs of weeping gone. "You brought my favorite cabriolet," she said with a smile.

"I can't take any credit for that. Porter picked it out."

When Lydia started to get out so that she could help Aunt Bertha, the older woman shook her head. "I'm not that old," she said

231

and proceeded to demonstrate that she could indeed climb into the carriage without assistance. "The horse is different. Jonas and I used to rent a gray gelding, but this one's beautiful." She settled back in the seat. "Where are we going?"

Lydia shrugged. "I'm not sure. All I knew was that we needed to get out of town." And judging by the change in Aunt Bertha's demeanor, the decision had been a wise one.

"Let's go north. The road's especially pretty that way."

It was. The trees were denser here, not quite a forest but tall enough and thick enough that they gave the impression of riding under a green canopy. Though the shade was welcome after the summer's heat, what Lydia welcomed most was the feeling that they had left Cimarron Creek and its problems behind, entering a world that was free of strife.

"This is lovely," she said.

Aunt Bertha smiled. "The best is yet to come."

While the road had been almost flat when they left town, ten minutes later it began to climb a small hill. When they reached the top, Aunt Bertha touched Lydia's arm. "Stop and look back."

They were high enough now to see all of

Cimarron Creek spread below them, the trees standing proudly along each of the town's streets and in many of the yards. Beyond them fertile fields, some dotted with goats, others clad in differing shades of green from a variety of crops, bore testimony to the founders' wisdom in settling here.

"It looks so beautiful, so peaceful," Lydia said, her heart filling with joy as she gazed at the pastoral scene. This was what she had sought for Aunt Bertha, not simply a change of scenery, but a place that would soothe her spirit.

Aunt Bertha made a clucking noise. "Appearances can be deceptive. Looking at it, you'd never know there were secrets hidden along those streets, would you?"

But Lydia was not surprised, not when she held her own secrets, not when she knew one of Aunt Bertha's secrets was the reason Joan had left her home and her family. The question was, what other secrets did Cimarron Creek harbor?

15

"You're responsible for this, aren't you?" Pa scowled as he held out a familiar-looking white box. "She said she heard the fellas were playing dominoes here tonight, and she thought they might like something sweet. I told her no one would eat anything she made, but she just smiled and said she couldn't sell them to anyone. Something about a special size and flavor."

Pa brandished the box in front of Travis's face, and as he did, Travis saw two things: the chocolate creams were twice their normal size, and one was missing.

"What flavor was it?" he asked.

"Coffee."

Biting back a smile, Travis recalled once telling Lydia the only thing his father could be guaranteed to consume without finding fault with it was a cup of coffee. Not only had Lydia remembered but she'd turned that offhand comment into a new flavor of candy.

"So, how was it?" Travis asked.

Though Pa continued to scowl, he couldn't hide the twinkle in his eyes. "Not bad."

"Do you believe in miracles?"

Startled by the unexpected question, Lydia spun around, her heart beating at twice its normal rate. "Travis! I didn't know you were coming." Supper had been over for two hours, but Lydia was still in the kitchen, bruising mint leaves for the syrup that she would let steep overnight.

"What happened? Did you find Edgar?" That would indeed be a miracle.

"No. I'm sorry to have gotten your hopes up. There's no news about Edgar, but . . ." Travis paused. "Would you mind putting down that knife? I don't feel comfortable with a weapon pointed at me."

Lydia glanced at the red-handled knife and nodded. Laying it on the counter, she said, "It may look dangerous, but the blade is so dull that the only danger is to the mint leaves. Aunt Bertha told me to throw it out, but I didn't want to do that." Lydia hated waste of any kind. "Besides, it works better than a potato masher at releasing the oil."

As a result, the kitchen was filled with the pungent scent of mint. "What's the miracle?"

"It may not seem like one to you, but when I came home for supper, I discovered Pa with a box of candy."

Lydia nodded. "He tried to refuse it, but I wouldn't take it back. To be honest, I thought he'd throw it away, but I wanted him to know that I wasn't giving up on him. I guess the miracle is that he kept it long enough to show it to you."

"He did more than that. He'd already eaten a piece, and when I took one, he ate another. Trust me, Lydia, that was close to a miracle."

Lydia's heart began to sing with pleasure. Like Travis, she had feared that Abe Whitfield would not eat anything she had made, but she wanted to prove that she cared about him. That was why she'd made a special coffee cream filling and why she'd crafted candies sized for a man's hand.

"Tell me one thing, Travis. Did he call me the Cursed Enemy?"

Travis shook his head.

"Now that's a miracle."

It had been almost two weeks since what Lydia referred to as the Candy Episode.

Though she had hoped that it would mark a change in Travis's father's attitude toward her, she had seen no difference. When she greeted him after church, he remained silent, ignoring her as effectively as if she were invisible.

"He's always worse in the summer," Aunt Bertha told her. "I think the heat bothers his leg."

There was no doubt that late July in Texas was hot. Though there had been hot days in Syracuse, they paled compared to the unrelenting Texas sun. Lydia had seen the difference in her customers. While they still bought candy, tempers were shorter, with the result that two women had almost come to blows over the last pound of chocolate-covered mints. Fortunately, today was a few degrees cooler.

Lydia walked to the front of the store and smiled at the sight of her best customer's approach. "Opal," she called into the back room, "Hilda Gray's on her way. Be sure to use the Blue Willow teapot for her." Hilda had admired it, saying it was the prettiest of the pots in the store and that tea brewed in it tasted extra special. From that day on, Lydia had tried to ensure that the woman who ordered more custom-made candy than anyone else in Cimarron Creek was served tea from that particular pot.

"Of course." Lydia heard the sound of cupboard doors opening and closing. A few seconds later, Opal appeared in the showroom, a frown marring her smooth forehead. "The pot's not here. Maybe you took it home last night?"

Lydia shook her head. Though she'd stayed later than Opal yesterday, she had no reason to return the teapot to the mansion on Pecan Street. When she'd offered it to Lydia for the shop, Aunt Bertha had said the teapot brought back unhappy memories, memories Lydia suspected were of Joan.

"Could you have put it in a different cupboard?" Lydia asked. There had been fewer than normal customers sampling candy yesterday, and she had had no need to use the Blue Willow pot. But, though she and Opal looked on each of the shelves, the teapot was nowhere to be found.

"I'll wait on Hilda," Lydia said when she heard the doorbell tinkle. Somehow she'd convince the woman that tea tasted just as good from a different pot. "Would you check to see if anything else is gone?"

But nothing was, and that was odd. If someone had wanted the teapot, why hadn't they also taken the matching sugar and creamer? A steady stream of customers kept

Lydia from dwelling on the missing china, though the questions returned when she closed the store. And, judging from the expression on Travis's face when he met her, she wasn't the only one who'd had at least one unpleasant surprise today.

"Is something wrong?" she asked as they headed east on Oak Street. "You look a bit preoccupied."

He raised his eyebrows before nodding. "Sorry. I didn't realize it was so obvious. I had a strange day. Four shopkeepers reported thefts."

"That is unusual." Travis had told her that other than the occasional stolen chicken, theft was uncommon in Cimarron Creek. Homeowners felt secure enough that few locked their doors, and while shopkeepers did resort to lock and key, it was simply to discourage curious children from browsing through the merchandise when the stores were closed. It was probably coincidence that Lydia's teapot had gone missing the same day that others had items stolen.

"What was taken?" She doubted anyone else had lost items of minimal value.

"That's what's strange. It wasn't what you'd expect. Take Warner. He has expensive medicine in the apothecary, not to mention a very valuable scale, but the thief took his favorite pestle. It's not much good without the mortar. Cousin Jacob is missing three jars of orange marmalade from the mercantile." Travis chuckled. "He told me no one buys marmalade, even when he puts it on sale, so he can't figure out who'd bother to steal it. It just doesn't make sense."

Lydia agreed. The Blue Willow teapot was worth more than three jars of marmalade, but its value was far greater as part of the set. "Were there any signs of breaking and entering?" She and Opal had checked both doors and had found nothing.

"Not one." Travis paused when they reached the corner of Cedar. "That's part of what puzzles me. I spent the day questioning everyone who might have been nearby, but no one saw anything, and as far as I could tell, the thief simply walked into those buildings." Travis shook his head. "I could believe one of the store owners forgot to lock a door, but four on the same night? That seems unlikely. Four people wouldn't be careless at the same time."

"Five."

His eyes widened as he stared at Lydia. "What do you mean?"

"My Blue Willow teapot is missing, and I know the door was locked last night. You were there. You saw me lock it." Since

Opal's feet had been bothering her, Lydia had sent her home early and had done the after-closing cleanup herself. "Plus that, it was still locked this morning."

"Five in one night. That's just as improbable as the fact that the stolen items were of so little value." A frown marred Travis's normally handsome face. "It could have been someone who's good at picking locks, but the fact that he locked up after himself is strange. Why would someone do that?" Travis's frown deepened. "Maybe the townspeople made a mistake in hiring me, because I can't imagine who's behind this any more than I can figure out who killed Edgar."

Though Lydia hated the self-doubt she heard in Travis's voice, what wrenched her heart was the thought of Edgar being dead. While she'd told herself that was possible, perhaps even likely, Opal was so convinced that he was still alive that her optimism was wearing off on Lydia.

"You still think he was killed?"

Travis nodded. "It's the only thing that makes sense. A happily married man whose wife is expecting their first child isn't likely to leave town and abandon her."

"Why not? That's what he did to me." The words were out before Lydia could stop them, and yet, though she hadn't intended to tell anyone in Cimarron Creek about her past, she found she could not regret her impulsive statement. Somehow it seemed important that Travis know what had happened in Syracuse.

He looked steadily at her, his expression encouraging her to continue.

"Promise you won't tell anyone. What I'm about to tell you would only hurt Opal, and she doesn't deserve that." When Travis nodded, Lydia continued. "Edgar and I were supposed to be married."

"I suspected as much. I figured you were one of those mail-order brides and that you came out here to meet and marry Edgar."

"That's not the way it happened. I knew Edgar when we both lived in Syracuse." Lydia could see that revelation surprised Travis. What had Edgar told him of his past? Obviously not that he'd lived in Syracuse. "He wanted to start a new life in Texas, and since I had no family back East, I agreed. We'd planned to wait until school ended, then get married and come here."

Raised eyebrows met her words. "So, what changed your plan?"

"Edgar got into a fight. He was outside a tavern when he saw a man hitting a woman. By the time he reached her, the woman was lying on the ground, dead. Edgar's temper got the better of him and he attacked the other man. I don't know all the details, but I know the other man got the worst of the fight." Lydia shuddered at the memory of Edgar's bloodstained fists. "When it was over, the other man said Edgar was going to pay for what he'd done. He was the one who'd be blamed for the woman's death."

Travis remained silent, as if he knew Lydia hadn't finished. "I believed Edgar's story, but he knew the police wouldn't. You see, the other man was the son of one of the wealthiest families in town. They would never have let their son's reputation be tarnished."

Lydia wondered what would have happened if the fight had occurred in Cimarron Creek. Would everyone have rallied around a Whitfield or a Henderson if they were involved, regardless of who was responsible? She'd heard more than one person say the founding families were overly protective of their reputation.

When Travis said nothing, Lydia continued. "None of it makes sense. Edgar wasn't a drinker, but there he was on a street lined with taverns, and so was Richard Hale. When it was over, Edgar knew his only chance was to leave."

"And he left without you."

The way he phrased it made Lydia wonder if Travis had somehow guessed how she and Edgar had argued that night. She'd wanted to go with him, even though it would have meant leaving the school shorthanded, but he'd been adamant. "He said he'd be able to hide his trail if he went alone and that I'd only slow him down. He told me this was only a minor change in plans. I'd join him here as soon as I could, and we'd be married."

"But in the meantime he married Opal."

"Exactly. And now he's left her."

No wonder Lydia thought men could not be trusted. Travis shoved his fists into his pockets as he strode away from Aunt Bertha's house. Edgar had told Lydia he wasn't a drinker, but if he wasn't, why was he in that particular neighborhood? That had to have raised questions in Lydia's mind. Then he'd fled, leaving her to travel to Texas alone, which couldn't have been easy. And — worst of all — he'd broken his promise to marry her.

Somehow, though he'd claimed he wouldn't do it, Edgar had wound up working in a saloon. Although, to his credit, Travis had heard that Edgar hadn't so much as touched a drop of alcohol, despite working in a place where drinking was one of the major attractions. That said something for him, but it didn't outweigh the fact that he was now Opal's husband.

Why? For the life of him, Travis couldn't understand that. Though he had to admit that Edgar and Opal had seemed happy together, Opal didn't hold a candle to Lydia. He could almost understand the marriage when he'd believed Lydia was a mail order bride Edgar had never met, but how could a man who'd known Lydia as long as Edgar had marry someone else? It was time to send a telegram to Syracuse and learn the official version of the story.

Half an hour later, Travis hung his hat on the hook inside the front door, steeling himself for an evening with Pa. The man had been ornerier than normal the past few days, and with the way today had gone, Travis didn't expect anything different.

"What's going on in town?"

So much for a pleasant greeting. His father scowled as he looked up from the paper he'd been reading. "I heard some folks were robbed."

Travis should have expected that news to spread quickly. There were few secrets in Cimarron Creek, and something as juicy as multiple thefts was certain to fuel the grape-vine.

"Nothing big or expensive," he said, repeating what he'd told Lydia. "I can't figure out who'd bother stealing things like that."

Pa didn't bother to hide his scorn. "You could if you hadn't let yourself be blinded by a pretty face. It's as plain as can be that the girl's behind it."

"Lydia? That's ridiculous."

"No, it isn't. Just because she makes good candy doesn't mean she's honest."

At least Pa was acknowledging something positive about Lydia, and he hadn't referred to her as the Cursed Enemy. That was a step in the right direction. Travis ought to let the crazy idea that she was a thief go. Experience had taught him there was no reasoning with Pa when he was in a mood like this, and yet Travis couldn't simply dismiss the allegations. "Lydia isn't a thief. She was one of the people robbed."

"So she says." The smirk that accompanied his words left no doubt of Pa's opinion. "That's the best way to keep you from suspecting her — pretend she's a victim."

Travis didn't bother counting to ten. He could count to a hundred, a thousand, a million and it wouldn't lessen his anger.

"Whether or not you approve, I'm the sheriff here. It's my job to catch whoever is behind these thefts."

"Then do it and use your brain. Just because she's pretty doesn't mean she's not guilty. Face it, son, you're smitten."

Was he? The thought slammed into Travis with the strength of a speeding train. He wouldn't say he was smitten — the very word rankled — but he couldn't deny that Lydia was special. Never before had he met a woman like her, one who was strong at the same time she was vulnerable. Never before had a woman's smile warmed him the way Lydia's did. Never before had he cared so deeply whether that woman was happy.

Was that being smitten? Travis didn't know. What he knew was that he cared about Lydia and that he wanted her to learn that men could be trusted. Travis swallowed as he admitted one more thing: he wanted to be the man who made her happy, the one she trusted.

He wasn't thinking about marriage — of course he wasn't. Travis knew he would never marry. How could he risk making a woman's life as miserable as his mother's had been? But he could be a friend, a good friend.

There must be something he could do for his friend Lydia. As Travis stared at the kitchen table, a memory resurfaced.

"Did something happen to Aunt Bertha?" Catherine asked as she settled onto the bench in the rose garden. It was Sunday afternoon, one of the few times she and Lydia had to spend together. "She looks different. Happier."

Though Lydia suspected that part of the reason Aunt Bertha was more relaxed was that she had finally shed tears for her daughter, she wouldn't divulge her secret to anyone, not even Catherine.

"We've been taking rides out of town," she said. "Aunt Bertha seems to enjoy them. She claims they remind her of good times with her husband." Lydia glanced at the sky, registering the cumulus clouds with their dark underbellies. "We would have gone again this afternoon, but it looks too much like rain."

Catherine nodded. "I know. I need to go home soon. Thunderstorms make Mama nervous."

"How is she?" Lydia wouldn't ask about the trip to Europe, because with school starting in a few weeks, there was no time for that, even if Gussie were well enough.

The flash of anger that crossed Catherine's face surprised Lydia with its intensity. "She's no better. Every time I think she might be recovering, Dr. Harrington bleeds her again. He says it's the only way to get the bad humors out, but I can't help thinking he's making her worse."

Lydia tried not to shudder at the thought of what effect bleeding would have on a woman as weak as Gussie Whitfield. The procedure seemed barbaric, but unless Catherine's mother refused it, the doctor would probably continue to drain cups of blood from her.

"I wish there were something I could do. I know she enjoys the candy, but there must be more that I can do for her. For both of you," Lydia amended her statement. Catherine might be well physically, but her mother's illness had taken a toll on her emotionally. Lydia knew she could not heal Catherine's mother, but perhaps she could boost her spirits. "Would you and your mother like to join Aunt Bertha and me for a ride next Sunday?"

Catherine's face brightened. "That could be just what she needs." When she left a few minutes later, she gave Lydia a hug. "I'll tell Mama about the ride. If I'm right, she'll spend the next week practically counting the hours."

Lydia wasn't counting hours. Enjoying her sole day of rest, she was engrossed in *Northanger Abbey* when she heard a knock on the front door.

"Travis." Lydia smiled at the sight of the handsome sheriff standing on the porch, one hand behind his back. Though she'd seen him just a few hours earlier when they'd left the church, she couldn't stop her pulse from racing as he smiled back at her. "Aunt Bertha didn't say she was expecting you."

"I'm not here to see my aunt. I came to see you." His eyes darkened, and for an instant Lydia thought he was bringing bad news, but then the corners of his lips turned up. "After you told me what happened with Edgar, I sent some telegrams to Syracuse. It turns out he told you the truth. Apparently there were two witnesses. At first they were afraid to testify, but they both agreed that the killer was shorter than average and wore expensive clothes. When I asked if that description would fit Richard Hale, my sources said it would."

Travis shifted slightly, perhaps because he was uncomfortable with his hand behind his back. It was the first time Lydia had seen him stand that way, and though she wondered at the somewhat awkward position, it was of little importance compared to the story he was relating.

"The official verdict is that an unknown assailant killed the woman, and since she had no family or close friends, there was no one to question it. No one is looking for that assailant."

The relief that flowed through Lydia shocked her with its intensity. This was more than she had dreamed possible. Travis's report meant that Edgar no longer had to fear for his life. He was free. He and Opal could have a happy future, if only he'd return to Cimarron Creek.

"That's wonderful news, Travis. I don't know how to thank you."

His smile warmed her more than the summer sun. "Just doing my job, ma'am," he said, giving his lips a wry twist. "Here's the real reason I came." Travis brought his arm forward, revealing a bouquet of flowers clasped in his hand. "I thought you might like these. It may seem silly, since you have a rose garden here, but I always thought wildflowers were special. Don't ever tell Aunt Bertha, but my mother said she preferred them to roses."

Lydia inhaled deeply, trying to get her heartbeat back to normal. Travis was right.

Wildflowers were special, but the man who held them was even more special. She knew he was kind — the fact that he arranged his schedule to help her carry pans to and from the confectionary was proof of that, as was the fact that he'd sent multiple telegrams to Syracuse to ease her mind about Edgar's past — but the gift of flowers that he'd obviously picked was more than kind.

She stared at the man whose friendship had become such a vital part of her life, wondering why he'd brought flowers. They, along with books and candy, were traditional courting gifts, but Travis wasn't courting Lydia. Travis knew she was not ready for marriage and might never be. And, if that weren't enough, he'd admitted that he had no intention of marrying. The flowers were nothing more than a gesture of friendship. Lydia nodded, wondering why the thought filled her with disappointment.

Keeping a smile fixed on her face, she accepted the bouquet of multicolored blossoms. "I agree that they're special. I love knowing that wildflowers were planted by God, not man, but if these are like their northern cousins, they need to be put in water right away."

As Lydia walked toward the butler's pantry, Travis followed, watching but not commenting as she debated between two vases. Perhaps it was foolish to worry so much about choosing the perfect container, but this was the first time anyone had given her flowers, and they pleased her more than she'd thought possible. As if that weren't enough, the faint blush that stained Travis's cheeks was as endearing as the flowers.

When she'd decided that cut glass would complement the flowers better than painted china, Lydia continued to the kitchen and filled the vase with water, then carefully arranged the stems. Placing the finished bouquet on the table, she smiled. "Beautiful."

"Yes, indeed." The smile Travis gave her made Lydia's heart skip a beat. Some might say it was only a smile, but it was so warm that she felt as if she were melting like the chunks of chocolate she turned into fudge. And then she realized that he was staring at her, not the flowers. Color flooded her cheeks.

"I was talking about the flowers," she said, trying not to let her bemusement show.

Travis's smile widened. "I wasn't."

16

Travis was beginning to believe Pa was right. Not that he was smitten. He wasn't, despite the fact that he couldn't forget the warmth that had flooded through his veins when he'd witnessed Lydia's obvious pleasure over the bouquet he'd given her. When he'd remembered how happy his mother had been the first time he'd picked some bluebonnets and Indian paintbrush for her, Travis had hoped that a few flowers would bring a smile to Lydia's face.

They'd done that and more. She was always beautiful, but as she'd arranged the bouquet in the vase, her face had been luminous, her smile so radiant that it had taken every ounce of willpower Travis possessed not to draw her into his arms and kiss her. He'd wanted to. Oh, how he'd wanted to. But he hadn't. Friends did not kiss.

Frowning, Travis increased his pace. It was

early morning, the time of day when he walked the streets of Cimarron Creek, talking to residents while he kept an eye out for anything unusual. Almost everyone knew that he also patrolled at night, trying to discover who was responsible for the problems that continued to plague the town. But last night, just like every other night, he'd found nothing amiss.

Perhaps Pa was right when he claimed that Travis was the wrong man to be sheriff. He felt as if he'd accomplished nothing. Though he told himself that Edgar might have left of his own accord and was hiding, Travis didn't believe that. As painful as it was to contemplate, Travis believed foul play was the reason for Edgar's disappearance and that someone in Cimarron Creek was responsible for that foul play.

If he were a good sheriff, Travis should have been able to find at least a trace of Edgar. But even if he couldn't do that, he should have been able to figure out who was responsible for the thefts. So far he'd accomplished nothing other than realizing that the locks the shopkeepers used were easy to open.

When he'd discovered that, he'd insisted everyone replace theirs with sturdier ones. Cousin Jacob at the mercantile had been more than willing to order new locks for everyone, and Porter — whose skills extended beyond horses and carriages — had volunteered to help install them. But, though the stores now had better protection, Travis still had no idea who had broken into them and taken items with so little monetary value.

A good sheriff would have done better. The thought echoed through Travis's brain with each step he took. Though he forced a smile when Faith greeted him as he passed the saloon, Travis's mood was far from jovial. Even Faith's assertion that he was a good man to have found Opal a job outside the Silver Spur did nothing to boost his spirits. That had happened weeks ago. The only thing he'd accomplished since then was making Lydia smile. While that had been satisfying, it wasn't enough.

Knowing he would accomplish little if he remained in town, Travis crossed the street toward the livery. Perhaps a gallop on Hamlet would help clear his mind.

"Is Hamlet ready?" he asked as he entered the stable and looked for his cousin. Porter would probably be surprised to see him now, since it was usually late morning before Travis saddled up and rode outside the town itself.

"Hey, Travis! Good to see you." Porter grinned as his obviously well-fed cat rubbed his legs. "I was hoping you'd come in this morning. There's something I need to tell you."

As the grin faded and Porter's expression turned solemn, Travis knew whatever his cousin wanted to discuss, it was bad news. He looked around the livery, wondering if Porter had been the victim of robbery or vandalism.

"What is it?" Travis could see nothing out of the ordinary.

Porter picked up Homer and began to stroke his head. "You know I wouldn't say anything if it wasn't important, but you're like a brother to me, and brothers look out for each other. That's why I thought you needed to know that folks are starting to talk."

It was what Travis had feared. Someone had noticed him carrying flowers to Aunt Bertha's and had turned a simple act of friendship into something more serious. The next thing he knew, the women would be baking a wedding cake. He could only imagine how Lydia would react if the gossip made its way to her store.

"Just what are they saying?" It was good that Porter had warned him rather than letting him or Lydia be blindsided.

"That you shouldn't be sheriff."

Not Lydia. That was good, and yet though Travis steeled himself not to react, the accusation hurt. It was one thing to hear it from Pa, but knowing that the people he was trying to protect felt the same way was an unexpected blow.

"Are there any specific reasons people are saying that?" Travis wouldn't ask who'd voiced the concerns, but he needed to know why.

Porter nodded and began ticking off items on his fingers. "You haven't found Edgar Ellis, you don't know who set the fire here, and you haven't arrested anyone for stealing from the merchants."

It was Travis's turn to nod. "I'm doing the best I can."

"What if it isn't enough?"

"I always knew that boy had a good head on his shoulders, and this proves it." Aunt Bertha waved her hand in the direction of the front door. Though there was no one there, she smiled as if greeting a favorite visitor. "Some folks in town wondered if he'd ever get married. I can't say that I blame him for being gun-shy. You weren't here to see it, but his parents didn't set much of an example of a good marriage."

The smile turned to a frown, but she continued the one-sided conversation so quickly that Lydia had no chance to say anything. It wasn't the first time Aunt Bertha had indulged in what Lydia considered one of her speeches, and she'd learned nothing was gained by interrupting. The barrage of words would end whenever Aunt Bertha was finished and not a second earlier. Though she suspected Aunt Bertha was speaking of Travis, she wouldn't ask. She'd simply sit here in the parlor and listen.

"I'm not surprised his sister ran off with the first man who offered her a chance to get out of Cimarron Creek," Aunt Bertha announced. "I'd have done the same thing. Of course, that left him alone with his father. He has to be a saint to put up with him." She shook her head and clucked her tongue. "But I'm digressing. That seems to be one of the hazards of old age. I forget what I'm trying to say and go on a tangent. Stop me if I do it again."

Lydia nodded, though she knew the futility of trying to redirect Aunt Bertha's conversation.

"You wouldn't believe all the speculation I've heard about that dear boy. Honestly, Lydia, as much as I love this town, there are times when I could pull my hair out over all the gossip. When I heard what they were saying, I told those busybodies he was simply waiting for the right gal to catch his eye. Turns out I was right." She gave Lydia a quick smile. "I can't tell you how happy I am that Travis is courting you."

"Courting?" The word came out as little more than a squeak.

"What else would you call it? He didn't bring those flowers for me." Aunt Bertha nodded, her expression as satisfied as a cat with a saucer of cream. "It wouldn't make any sense for him to give you candy, but mark my words: he'll bring you more flowers."

"These are beautiful, Travis," Lydia said as he handed her a bouquet of wildflowers the next evening. He'd walked home from the store with her as usual, then had returned two hours later with the flowers. "I don't know what to say other than thank you."

She buried her nose in the blossoms, as much to hide her confusion as to sniff the delicate fragrance. When she looked up, she found Travis studying her. Had he realized how deeply the gift would affect her? There was a hint of amusement in those gray eyes, but she also saw something that, if she hadn't known better, she would have termed insecurity. That made no sense, for Travis was the most secure man she knew, a man who was comfortable in his own skin, one who willingly took on additional responsibility to help the rest of Cimarron Creek.

"No one's ever been so kind to me," she told Travis. It was true that Edgar always remembered her birthday, but he'd never brought her what Aunt Bertha would call courting gifts. "I feel like I'm being spoiled."

"Not spoiled. Treated well." The corners of Travis's lips lifted ever so slightly. "You deserve it, Lydia. I want you to realize that not all men are like Edgar. Some of us can be trusted to keep our promises."

She nodded, acknowledging the sincerity she heard in his words. Travis wasn't like Edgar. She knew that. If he made a promise, he would keep it. "You haven't promised me anything."

He seemed surprised by her words. "Oh, but I have. The day you arrived, I promised to make you feel welcome."

Lydia tried to recall everything Travis had said that day. "I don't remember that."

He shrugged. "Just because I didn't say the words aloud doesn't make them any less binding. When I saw you get off that stage-coach, I told myself it was my responsibility to welcome you. Besides, you looked like you needed a friend."

A friend. Despite what Aunt Bertha thought, that's what this was all about. Responsibility and friendship, not courtship. Lydia looked at the lovely flowers that she was gripping too tightly. When he'd brought her the first bouquet, she had thought it was a gesture of friendship, but then Travis had looked at her as if she were more than a friend. And he'd called her beautiful.

She'd cherished the memory of that moment, clutching it to her heart more tightly than she had the flower stems. She had dreamt about that moment, and when she'd wakened, it had been with a smile on her face as she thought of Travis and the warmth she had seen in his eyes. She should have known better. After all, Travis had told her he'd picked flowers for his mother when she needed cheering. That was what he'd sought to do — to cheer Lydia. And he'd succeeded.

Travis was her friend. Friendship was good. Of course it was.

Travis was her friend, just her friend, Lydia reminded herself the next day. As they walked to Cimarron Sweets in the early afternoon, they spoke of ordinary things. Travis told her about the dogs that had been chasing Nate's goats and how the farmer worried that his animals would be so stressed by the encounter that they'd shed too much fur.

"I shouldn't joke about it," Travis admitted, "because it's no laughing matter, but Nate is like an anxious parent. He'll be a good father someday."

It was an innocuous comment. In all likelihood, Travis meant nothing by it, but Lydia couldn't help wondering whether this was his subtle way of saying Nate would be a good suitor. She didn't doubt that. He would be a good suitor and a good husband — for some other woman. Nate was not the man for Lydia.

When Travis began to speak of Warner and how profitable the pharmacy was, Lydia quickly changed the subject. Though it might be nothing more than coincidence that he had chosen today to talk about the two men who'd asked permission to court her, Lydia did not believe it. This was Travis's way of saying that he was her friend, nothing more.

"Is something wrong, Lydia?" Opal asked a couple hours later. The young mother-to-be's forehead was creased with lines of worry.

Lydia shook her head, sorry that she had caused her assistant even momentary concern. Opal had enough worries without Lydia adding to them. Resolutely, Lydia fixed a smile on her face.

The smile was still there when Travis arrived to walk home with her. Though some evenings they took a longer way to Aunt Bertha's, tonight Lydia was in no mood to dally, and so she headed north on Main Street when they left the shop.

"Did you have many sales today?" Travis asked as they passed the building that served as both the mayor's office and the town's post office.

Lydia started to nod but stopped as something caught her eye. "What's that?" she asked, pointing to what appeared to be a flour sack propped against the side wall of Travis's office. Though the deep shade from the live oak that separated the two lots almost hid it, she had spotted the edge of the bag.

"I don't know, but I'm sure it wasn't there this morning." As part of his early morning patrol, Travis checked all sides of each of the town's commercial establishments.

Seconds later, they reached the bag. As

Lydia had thought, it was an ordinary flour sack, one of dozens the mercantile sold each month, but the lumpy sides told her this bag no longer contained flour.

Travis gave out a low whistle. "Recognize this?" he asked as he pulled out a Blue Willow teapot.

Though she had no doubt it was hers, Lydia inspected it carefully. "It's definitely mine." She lifted the lid and showed Travis the interior. "I noticed the tea stain the night before it was stolen and planned to bring some baking soda to scrub it."

Travis raised an eyebrow but said nothing more than, "Let's take this inside." He lifted the sack and led the way into his office. Once inside, he emptied it, placing each item on his desk, then pulling a file from the drawer. "Everything's here," he confirmed. "Each and every piece of merchandise that was stolen the night of July 27 is here."

Lydia looked at the list and the contents of the flour sack, confirming what Travis had said. "Why would anyone steal all those things and then return them? It makes no sense."

It made no sense, but then again, the initial thefts had made no sense. It was almost as if someone was playing, stealing things simply to prove that he could. But who would do that and why?

Travis had returned all the items to the flour sack and locked it in his office. Tomorrow he would return everything to the owners, but before he did that, he wanted time to think about what had happened. There had to be a clue somewhere.

Though he'd been tempted to bow out of tonight's dominoes game, he hadn't. That might actually hinder Travis's investigation. He'd discovered that concentrating on something else often sparked new ideas. Perhaps that would happen tonight.

"I thought you might enjoy something sweet with your coffee," Hilda Gray said as she placed a plate of candy on the table next to the coffeepot and four mugs that were as much a part of the games as the tiles. She gave her husband a fond look. "I know Porter will eat more than his share, so if the rest of you fellas want some, you'd better stake a claim right away. This is what's left over from my quilting bee today."

Travis gave Porter's wife a warm smile as he thanked her for the candy. Though he'd been surprised when Porter had announced he was planning to marry Hilda, Travis had to admit they seemed happy together. His surprise at the betrothal was simply because Porter had always had an eye for beautiful women and redheads. Hilda's hair was mousey brown, and her features were far more ordinary than those of the women he'd admired in the past. But she was a first-rate cook and a good mother, and she'd had a sizable dowry.

Watching the two of them together, Travis was grateful that Porter had looked beneath the surface. His cousin deserved and appeared to have found a good marriage. Though Travis didn't envy many men, he couldn't deny the pangs of longing that sometimes shot through him when he saw the way Hilda gazed at Porter. Would any woman ever look at him with such love?

Wrenching his thoughts back to less painful subjects, Travis reached for a piece of candy when Hilda left the small room that Porter had designated as his sanctuary.

"These chocolate creams are one of Lydia's specialties," Travis said as he popped one into his mouth.

"You would know. You spend enough time with her." Though Warner was normally even tempered, tonight his voice held more than a little rancor.

"Yes," Nate chimed in. "For a man who claimed he wasn't ready to get himself hitched, you sure do seem to be showing a lot of interest in Miss Crawford."

What had gotten into those two? They were acting as hostile as Widow Jenkins's bulldog. "It's called being friendly." Not smitten. Definitely not smitten, though Pa had repeated the accusation the day Travis had picked the second bouquet for Lydia.

Warner grabbed two pieces of candy and laid them in front of his place, then filled his mug with coffee, all the while scowling at Travis. "The way I see it, you're more than friends with Lydia. Half the town is talking about how you're courting her, the way you walk her to and from the store every day. What I don't understand is how you can do it. You knew I was interested in her."

"So was I," Nate admitted. Though he eyed the rapidly disappearing sweets, he settled for putting an extra spoonful of sugar in his coffee. "Problem was, she wouldn't have me. Said she wasn't ready to think about getting married."

Travis looked around the table. While both Nate and Warner were obviously annoyed, Porter leaned back in his chair, his grin as wide as the Cheshire cat's.

"It looks to me like my cousin outfoxed both of you," he said smoothly. When Nate and Warner bristled, Porter shrugged, then turned his gaze on Travis. "Ever since he pinned that star on his chest, Travis has been acting like he owns the town and everyone in it."

For some reason, Porter was spoiling for a fight tonight, but Travis had no intention of satisfying him. "That's ridiculous," he said, deliberately keeping his voice at a conversational level. "I'm simply doing my job." Though Travis expected Porter to voice his opinion of how poorly Travis was performing that job, he remained silent, perhaps because he'd already stirred the pot.

Warner reached for the tiles and began to mix them, the force with which he mixed them telling Travis how angry he was. "The last time I checked, your job doesn't include courting the prettiest girl in town. You ought to give Nate and me a chance."

Travis wasn't courting Lydia, and even if he were, they'd had their chance. Hadn't they both told him Lydia had refused their offers of courtship? And today, when he'd deliberately interjected their names into his conversation with Lydia, she had shown no interest in either man.

Travis turned to Nate. "I thought you had feelings for Catherine." Admittedly, Nate had never said anything to him, but Travis had seen the way he'd looked at Catherine, as if the sun rose and set on his cousin.

"I was, but then I saw Miss Crawford."

Fickle man. Just like Edgar Ellis. It was still difficult to believe that any man could prefer Opal, but there was no ignoring the fact that Edgar had broken his promises to Lydia and married the redhead.

Fixing his attention on Warner, Travis said, "It seems to me the only reason you were interested in Lydia was that your father was pressuring you to get married. Don't you think she deserves a man who cares about her, not just the fact that she's a pretty, single female?"

"And you're that man?" Warner chose to answer Travis's question with one of his own.

"I told you I'm her friend."

Porter's laugh echoed through the room. "You did. The question is whether any of us believe you."

17

"Ouch." Opal winced as she cupped a hand under her expanding belly. "He got in a good kick that time." The wince turned to a smile, the same sweet smile that Opal always wore when she spoke of her unborn child.

"Maybe *she* was running." Though Opal insisted her baby would be a boy, Lydia couldn't resist teasing her, occasionally reminding her that babies came in two varieties. Lydia stifled a yawn. Normally she would still be asleep, but Hilda Gray had placed an extra order for chocolate creams, so Lydia had come downstairs earlier than normal to help Opal box the candies.

"He's an active one, especially at night. I just wish Edgar wasn't missing all this." The smile that had brightened Opal's face faded. Though she continued to arrange the pieces of candy in the box, Lydia saw the way her lips tightened. "I know the sheriff thinks he's dead, but he ain't — isn't," she corrected herself.

Lydia nodded her approval. When Opal learned that Lydia had been a teacher, she'd asked her to help her speak correctly and had proven to be a good pupil.

"I don't care what anybody says. I'd know if Edgar was dead." Opal laid her hand over her heart. "I know in here that he's alive. I just don't know where he is."

For Opal's sake, Lydia hoped she was right. She picked two more candies from the cooling area on the table and placed them in the box she was filling. This one would go to Catherine and her mother. As Gussie's health continued to fail, Catherine claimed that sweet treats were one of the few pleasures she had.

"Can you think of any reason why Edgar might have left?" Lydia turned her attention back to Opal. "Did he fight with anyone?" It was likely Travis had posed these same questions, but Lydia couldn't stop herself from asking.

When she'd first learned of Edgar's disappearance, she had wanted to learn what had happened for her sake. Now she was more concerned about finding him for Opal and Travis. Opal needed to know where her husband was, and Travis needed to solve the town's biggest mystery to prove to himself and the increasingly skeptical towns-people that he was a good sheriff.

Cimarron Creek was buzzing with the story that the stolen merchandise had been found. Though publicly Travis speculated that someone close to the thief — perhaps even a family member — had found the cache and returned it anonymously to protect the thief, he'd told Lydia that his instincts said the thief himself had been responsible for the return. That had left them both puzzled about the type of person who would do such things.

"Fight?" Opal looked at Lydia, her eyes widening with surprise. "Edgar wasn't a fightin' man. That was one of the reasons Faith hired him. He wouldn't let no one — sorry, anyone — fight in the Spur. At the first sign, he'd throw the men out." Opal closed the now-filled box and wrapped a tie around it. "Before he came, Faith was always replacing broken glasses. All that changed when Edgar was around."

This was the first time Lydia had heard that story, and it warmed her heart. "Maybe one of those men decided to pay him back." It wouldn't be the first time an angry man became violent.

Opal shook her head. "I don't think so. Folks here don't hold grudges, at least not too many. Besides, I don't reckon those men remembered much the next day."

"But there had to be a reason Edgar left." Men didn't simply disappear for no good reason.

Her eyes shining with tears, Opal shook her head again. "I heard some folks say he didn't like being married. That's not true, Lydia. Edgar loved me, and he loved this baby, even if it isn't his."

As the words registered, Lydia felt the blood drain from her face. "What do you mean?" She steered Opal to a chair, then took the one next to her. The candy could wait. What mattered now was learning the truth about Edgar, Opal, and her baby.

Opal clasped her hands together, her expression leaving no doubt that she regretted her unplanned revelation. "No one knows what happened, not even Faith," she said slowly. "You've got to promise you won't tell anyone."

Lydia nodded. If there was one thing she was good at, it was keeping secrets.

"It happened a few days after Edgar came to town," Opal said. "It was a slow night at the Spur, so I went outside. Edgar wanted to come with me, but he couldn't leave. A couple of the regulars were short a man for poker, so he was playing." The tears that had been welling in Opal's eyes began to trickle down her cheeks. "I should have waited," she said as she brushed the tears aside. "I know that now, but I wanted some fresh air. I figured I'd walk up to the bridge and back — wouldn't take more than ten minutes." Opal's lips trembled, and Lydia wished she'd thought to pour her a cup of coffee. The simple act of sipping might help calm her.

"When I got to the park, a man came out of the shadows. It all happened so fast I don't remember much other than the pain."

Though Opal hadn't said the word, the meaning was clear. Lydia wrapped her arms around the girl and drew her close. "He violated you." It was a woman's worst nightmare.

"Yes."

"And you don't know who it was." In a town this size, Lydia would have thought Opal knew almost everyone, but the fact that she had not named him told Lydia she had not recognized her assailant.

"No. It was too dark to see much, and he didn't say anything. He knocked me to the ground and stuffed a bandana in my mouth so I couldn't scream. Then he . . ." She paused for a moment, perhaps gathering the courage to pronounce the ugly word. But instead, Opal said, "When I went back to the Spur, Edgar saw I was upset. I didn't want his pity, so I wouldn't tell him what happened. But when I realized I was gonna have a baby, he was the only one I could trust."

When Opal met Lydia's gaze, her eyes shone with pride. "He said we'd get married. That way he could protect me and the baby. It was more than pity, Lydia. He told me he loved me, but he didn't think he had anything to offer me. That's why he hadn't said anything before." Opal pursed her lips. "Edgar loved me and the baby. He wouldn't have left us. I know he wouldn't."

Her story rang true. Lydia knew Edgar had a chivalrous side. His desire to avenge the woman outside the tavern had been the reason for the fight that had driven him from Syracuse.

She had no trouble believing Edgar had wanted to protect Opal. As for loving her, that part also rang true. Opal was a very loveable woman. It wasn't difficult to imagine Edgar falling in love with her. But what had happened after that made Lydia cringe. Poor Opal! Lydia's heart ached at the thought of all she had endured: first rape, then the loss of her husband.

She looked directly at the young woman

and said, "You should tell Travis what happened. The man who did this to you is probably still in town. It's possible he'll attack someone else." For the first time, Lydia wondered if the reason Travis escorted her to and from the store was out of concern for her safety. He'd never hinted that he thought she was in any danger, but perhaps he knew more than Opal realized.

Opal shook her head. "I don't want to talk about it. Besides, there's nothing the sheriff can do now. I told you I don't know who it was."

"Still, he needs to know. You wouldn't want any other woman to suffer the way you did, would you?"

Opal closed her eyes for a moment. When she opened them, the tears were gone, replaced by determination. "All right. He can know, but you have to tell him."

As the door opened, Travis looked up from the wanted posters he'd been studying. While Cimarron Creek had its share of crime, at least there had been no stagecoach robberies and no more mysterious fires. Though Porter claimed otherwise, Travis was convinced that the Founders' Day fire at the livery had been the result of someone — probably Porter himself — dropping a still-smoldering cigar on a bale of hay. But thoughts of fires, mysterious or otherwise, vanished at the sight of his visitor.

"This is an unexpected pleasure," Travis said as he rose to greet Lydia.

"You might not say that when you hear why I've come. I'm here on business — sheriff's business." Though she took the chair he offered, her smile seemed strained, and he noticed that she had not removed her apron. As far as Travis knew, Lydia never left the store wearing it.

"Did you have another robbery?" As he'd feared would be the case, Travis had found no clues to who had taken the items from the Main Street businesses. The flour sack could have belonged to anyone, and the stolen merchandise had no telltale threads or smudges to help identify the thief.

"I wish it were that innocent." Lydia leaned forward, placing her clasped hands on the edge of his desk. "There's no easy way to say this, so I'm going to be blunt. Someone raped Opal early last February. Edgar's not the father of her baby."

Travis took a deep breath, trying to absorb the implication of Lydia's announcement. Though his first concern should have been for Opal, he found himself wondering how Lydia had reacted to the knowledge that

Edgar had married an already pregnant woman. Did she feel betrayed, or did she understand? He wouldn't ask such a personal question, though his own esteem for Edgar rose a notch. It took a strong man to step forward under those circumstances.

Nodding slowly, Travis asked, "Why didn't Opal come to me when it happened?"

"I'm not completely sure," Lydia admitted. "She says she can't identify her attacker, but I suspect that's only part of it. I imagine she was ashamed and afraid everyone would think she'd somehow encouraged the man."

Knowing the feelings many of the town's matrons had for the girls who worked at the Silver Spur, Travis suspected Opal's fears were well founded. Still, the attack had occurred, and even though it had happened six months earlier, Travis's job had just become more complicated.

"So now we have a rapist as well as a thief, a vandal, and a possible murderer in Cimarron Creek." He tried to keep his voice light, when all the while his mind was whirling with the realization that his hometown harbored yet another secret. "And to think I once believed this was a peaceful place."

Lydia's expression left no doubt that she shared his concerns. "Do you believe there's a connection between Opal's rape and Edgar's disappearance?"

He did indeed. "That's exactly what I was thinking. First Edgar's girl is attacked; then he vanishes. I don't think it's a coincidence."

Travis saw the question in Lydia's eyes and realized it had appeared when he'd referred to Opal as Edgar's girl. "I hate to say this, knowing what happened between you and Edgar, but everyone in town knew he was smitten with Opal the minute he set eyes on her, and she was just as infatuated. What if someone else had his eye on Opal and wanted to stake a claim?"

"By forcing himself on her? That sounds extreme. Why not simply court her?"

"You know the answer, Lydia. Opal worked in a saloon. Some men would claim that made her fair game. They'd say you don't marry a saloon girl. You just pay for her time."

"But this one didn't give her a choice. He took what he wanted and left her lying in the park like a bag of garbage."

The image made Travis clench his fists and wish it was the rapist's throat he was squeezing. "When I find him, you can be sure he'll pay for his crime. In the meantime, you and Catherine and all the other women need to be extra careful. If anyone tries to attack you, scream as loudly as you can and run. You may not get far, but the scream will alert others. That may be enough to discourage the attacker."

The alternative was one Travis did not want to consider.

"This chicken is delicious." Lydia smiled as she took another forkful of the succulent meat. Aunt Bertha had roasted it with a variety of herbs and served it with tender carrots, green beans, and fluffy mashed potatoes. "I don't know when I've had such a good meal." It was just what she needed after a drama-filled day.

Lydia's head was still reeling from Opal's revelation and the fact that Travis believed there was a connection between Opal's attack and Edgar's disappearance. Lydia couldn't have explained why she had asked the question, but once the words were spoken, she'd realized how right they felt, and when Travis had agreed that it was no coincidence, an unexpected warmth had flooded her veins. The circumstances were horrible, but it felt good — so very good — to be working with Travis. It made her feel that they were not simply friends but were also partners.

Their discussion was something she had

shared with no one, not Aunt Bertha and certainly not Opal. Though Lydia had told Opal that she'd reported the rape to Travis, she had not told the young woman of their concern. There was nothing Opal could do, and if she believed she was somehow responsible for Edgar going missing, she would only fret. That wouldn't be good for either her or her baby. And though Aunt Bertha would undoubtedly have had an opinion, it was best for everyone if Opal's story remained a secret.

Lydia nodded at Aunt Bertha as she swallowed a bite of chicken. "You're not only the town's matriarch, you're its best cook."

"Thank you, my dear. I —" Abruptly Aunt Bertha dropped her knife and grabbed her chest. Though a moment earlier she'd appeared healthy, her breathing turned rapid and shallow.

Lydia's heart began to pound with apprehension. "What's wrong?" She'd seen Aunt Bertha out of breath, but never had she seen her face so pale, and never had she seen her hands tremble like cottonwood leaves in a summer storm.

"My heart." The older woman struggled to speak. "Too fast." She pushed her plate to the side, then laid her head on the table. Though Aunt Bertha's pallor and trembling had alarmed Lydia, the sight of the oh-so-proper woman's etiquette breach filled her with fear. Something was terribly, terribly wrong.

She jumped to her feet. "I'll get the doctor."

"No. Not him." To Lydia's relief, Aunt Bertha's voice sounded stronger. "All he'll do is bleed me." She raised her head slowly, as if testing her neck's ability to support it. Though she was still pale, color was returning to her cheeks, and her hands were steady. "See. It's over now."

Lydia reached for Aunt Bertha's water glass and held it to her lips, urging her to take a sip. "Has this happened before?" she asked when the older woman managed to drink an ounce of the cool liquid.

"Not this bad."

That meant this wasn't the first time. For a second, Lydia felt herself grow light-headed, and in that moment she realized just how dear Aunt Bertha had become to her. She couldn't let her suffer and possibly die. Lydia's experience with illness had centered on measles, chicken pox, and whooping cough — maladies that had afflicted her students. She knew little about diseases of the heart, but what she knew was that they were serious and needed to be treated.

She put her arm around Aunt Bertha's shoulders. "We have to do something about this. Are you certain you don't want me to summon Dr. Harrington?"

"Positive."

Having seen how quickly Catherine's mother was declining under the doctor's care, Lydia understood Aunt Bertha's reluctance. Still, there had to be something she could do. Lydia thought quickly, nodding when she found a possible answer. "Why don't we see what Warner would suggest? You trust him, don't you?"

Though Lydia had expected resistance, Aunt Bertha's expression brightened as if she recognized the wisdom in Lydia's suggestion. "Of course."

Afraid that if she delayed even a few minutes, Aunt Bertha might change her mind, Lydia grabbed her hat and gloves and practically ran to the Grays' house. Fortunately, it was less than two blocks away from Aunt Bertha's home. Located next to one of the original three mansions, Charles and Mary Gray's home had the same classical style but only half the size of the house Jacob Whitfield currently owned.

"No imagination," Aunt Bertha had declared when she'd described the house Charles had built, "and Porter's just as bad. Their homes are imitations of Ellen and Thomas's. Ellen and Evelyn and I knew better," she said, referring to the wives of the founding fathers. "We insisted that each of our houses be unique."

But architecture didn't matter now. What mattered was finding a way to help Aunt Bertha. Taking a deep breath to slow her pulse, Lydia knocked on the front door of the house Warner shared with his parents. A few seconds later, Mary Gray opened the door.

"Is Warner home, Mrs. Gray? I need to talk to him."

Though Lydia's words came out more sharply than she had intended, the woman with the same light brown hair and blue eyes as both of her sons smiled. "Come in, Lydia. We were just finishing supper, but if you'd like to join us for a piece of pie, I believe there's one left. I put some of your peanut brittle in it." Like her daughter-in-law Hilda, Warner's mother was a regular customer of Cimarron Sweets, though she favored peanut and pecan brittle over chocolate concoctions.

"I'm sorry, but there's no time for that." Even though Aunt Bertha appeared to have

285

recovered from whatever ailed her, Lydia wasn't comfortable leaving her alone. The little she knew about heart problems included the fact that another attack could come without warning.

Mary's face sobered. "Has something happened to Bertha?"

"She's not feeling well. I thought Warner might be able to help."

Normally soft-spoken Mary Gray turned and yelled, "Warner, come quickly!"

Rapid footsteps answered the summons. "What's the rush, Ma?" When Warner spotted Lydia, his demeanor changed, and he put on what she thought of as his professional mantle. Gone was the smiling man who'd tried to court her. In his place was the town's trusted apothecary. "What's wrong?"

Lydia explained as best she could, concluding, "She refuses to let me summon the doctor. Is there anything you can do?"

Warner nodded. "We'll try digitalis. Doc Harrington doesn't believe in it, but I keep a small quantity on hand for emergencies like this. We've had others in town who needed it." His expression darkened. "Digitalis is very powerful but also very dangerous. It's critical to take the right amount. It can work wonders on the heart, but too much can be fatal."

When Lydia blanched, Warner assured her he'd show her the correct dosage and how to administer it to Aunt Bertha. He grabbed his hat and turned toward the door. "I'll get some from the store and will meet you at Aunt Bertha's house. I shouldn't be more than ten minutes."

Warner had not exaggerated the drug's power. Half an hour later, Aunt Bertha's color was fully restored, and she declared her heart was beating better than it had for the past five years.

"I feel almost young again," she told Warner, "and if that's not a miracle, I don't know what is."

"Just don't overdo," Warner cautioned. "I don't want to hear about you dancing in the streets."

He stayed another half hour, telling Lydia he wanted to ensure there were no side effects, and for that half hour, Aunt Bertha regaled them with her usual nonstop stories, focusing on the mischief Warner, Porter, and Travis had gotten into as boys.

"That's enough," Warner said, raising his hands in surrender. "If I stay any longer, Lydia will be convinced I was a ruffian."

Lydia gave him her warmest smile.

"Never. I know you for what you are: a good man."

Though Aunt Bertha nodded her agreement, Lydia could see she was tiring, and insisted on helping her up the stairs to her room. "Thank you, Lydia," she said when she was sitting in bed, propped up by two large pillows. "God knew what he was doing when he brought you to Cimarron Creek. I don't know what I'd do without you."

18

"I can't believe the difference in Aunt Bertha." Catherine took another sip of tea as she contemplated the assortment of candy samples Lydia had placed in front of her. Since it was rare for Catherine to come to Cimarron Sweets, Lydia had taken advantage of the lull between customers to join her for a cup of tea in the showroom.

"It's been weeks since Aunt Bertha came to the house," Catherine continued, "but she said she was feeling so well that she wanted to spend the whole afternoon with Mama. What happened?"

When Lydia finished explaining about Aunt Bertha's sudden weakness and the effect digitalis had on her, Catherine nodded. "Cousin Warner is a smart man. I wish he could help Mama, but the tonics he thought might strengthen her made no difference."

As tears welled in Catherine's eyes, Lydia searched for something to cheer her friend.

"What do you think about taking a longer than normal ride tomorrow? We could pack a picnic lunch and leave right after church."

"That's a great idea." Catherine's smile confirmed the wisdom of Lydia's change of subject. "I'll fry a chicken and bring some hard-boiled eggs." She glanced at the display case. "Do you think there'll be any fudge left?"

Lydia feigned indignation. "Do you think I would serve you leftover fudge? I'll make a new batch tonight. Would you prefer plain or a flavor?"

"Plain. That's Mama's favorite." Catherine sipped the tea, then smiled as she set the cup back on its saucer. "I know the perfect place to go. I had never been there, but Nate . . ."

As Catherine's smile faded, Lydia knew that no matter what her friend said, she still had strong feelings for the man she had hoped to marry. "Let's go somewhere else," she suggested.

Catherine shook her head. "It's a wonderful spot. We'll all enjoy being there."

And they did.

"He did it. I'm sure he did." Nate's blue eyes, typically filled with the amusement he seemed to find in even ordinary events, were

290

as cold as steel today. "The proof is here."

Travis had seen the barely banked fury when his friend had stormed into the sheriff's office, demanding Travis accompany him back to the ranch. It had been a silent ride, but once they arrived and Travis saw what had happened, Nate's silence had changed to bitter accusations.

As he pointed toward the three empty yellow bags casually discarded next to the feed trough, Nate's lips quivered ever so slightly. "That's the poison that killed my goats."

It was an ugly scene. A dozen of Nate's prized Angora goats lay on the ground, their legs stiff and bent in awkward positions, leaving no doubt that their deaths had been painful. Anger and regret rushed through Travis with equal force — anger that the animals had suffered, regret that there was nothing he could say to alleviate Nate's distress. The goats were more than a business for Nate. He took pride in having the finest Angoras in the Hill Country and cared for them almost as if they were pets. Their deaths were an emotional as well as a financial blow for the rancher.

"How do you know it's poison?" Travis asked as he inspected the bags. Though there were traces of a white powdery substance in them, the bags themselves had no markings.

"Because that's the same kind of bag the rat poison he sold me came in." Nate kicked a pebble, his frustration sending the small rock sailing across the pen. "I tell you, Travis, he did it. I know he's your cousin, and I thought he was my friend, but this tells a different story."

Nate gave the goats another look, then turned away, as if the sight were more than he could bear. Travis understood his friend's anger. Death, particularly senseless death, made his stomach turn. Though he could not condone it, he understood killing in the heat of anger, but to kill innocent animals made no sense.

"You can't let him get away with it," Nate insisted.

Travis turned toward the goats one last time before laying a hand on Nate's shoulder. "You can be sure I'll talk to him. What I don't understand is what you think Warner would gain by killing your goats."

Nate glared as if the answer should be obvious. "I think he wants to drive me out of town. That way he'd have less competition for Lydia's hand."

Though Travis couldn't imagine his cousin or anyone thinking Lydia would favor the suit of someone who inflicted a painful death on goats, he knew Nate didn't want to hear that. "I thought both of you had given up on Lydia."

It had been a little more than a week since the dominoes game when Nate and Warner had accused Travis of courting Lydia. As far as Travis knew, neither man had approached Lydia during that time.

"I can't speak for Warner," Nate said, his voice ragged with emotion, "but I haven't given up. I was planning to ask my sister to invite her to Sunday dinner so we could spend some time together."

Travis had to admire the man's persistence. "Be that as it may, you can't honestly believe Warner would kill your goats." His cousin was a peaceful man.

"They're dead, aren't they? And that's the poison he sells." Nate turned and pointed to the bags. "It looks pretty clear to me who's responsible. Do your job, Sheriff. Arrest him."

Travis entered the drugstore, tipping his hat to Mrs. Wilkins, who was buying another bottle of nerve tonic. When she had summoned Travis to her house to deal with the latest broken window, she had confided that the vandalism had upset her so much that she had had to resort to a patent medicine.

Though Warner wasn't convinced that the medicines were as effective as the manufacturers claimed, he stocked a variety of them and tried to steer Cimarron Creek's residents to the better ones.

This morning he was counseling Mrs. Wilkins on the recommended dosage and warning her about the dangers of ingesting too much. Travis could tell that the woman was paying little attention, and he hoped that the tonic was not as dangerous as Warner intimated. Dead goats were bad enough.

As soon as Mrs. Wilkins left, Travis locked the front door, flipped the sign to "closed," and turned toward his cousin.

"Why'd you do that?" Warner demanded, the cordial smile he'd worn for Mrs. Wilkins vanishing.

Travis approached the counter. As much as he hated the reason for this visit, it was his responsibility as sheriff to learn whether Nate's suspicions were well founded. "We need to talk. I thought you might prefer doing that here rather than in my office."

"What's going on?" Warner stared at Travis as if he were a stranger.

"A dozen of Nate's goats died last night."

Travis watched his cousin, wanting to see every nuance of his reaction. The shock looked genuine. "That's unfortunate," Warner said, his voice resonating with sincerity. "Nate must be upset. Do you know why they died?"

"They didn't just die. They were killed." Again, Warner appeared honestly surprised by Travis's announcement. "Someone gave them a hefty dose of the poison you sell in yellow bags. Nate found three empty bags next to the goats."

Furrows formed between Warner's eyes. "I don't know how that happened. I've only sold one bag this summer and that was to Nate. He'd been having trouble with rats in his house. I told him he ought to get a cat, but he has sneezing fits whenever he's around one, so I ordered what he wanted: the strongest poison I could find."

It all sounded plausible, except for the fact that although Nate had bought only one bag, there were three empty sacks near the goats' pen.

"You're sure you sold him only one bag?"

Warner nodded.

"When was that?"

Though Travis had expected Warner to check his records, he answered without hesitation. "The middle of May. I remember it, because it was the day I met Lydia." That must have been the day Nate had given her the toilet water.

"And you haven't sold any since then?"

"Nope." Warner shook his head. "I had to buy five bags, but the other four are still here. I'll show you." He led the way to his storeroom, gesturing toward the yellow bag on a bottom shelf. "There you go."

Travis crouched next to the shelf and pulled the bag out, intending to count the remaining sacks. "How do you explain this?" Though the shelf had appeared full, removing the bag revealed that the space behind it was stuffed with empty burlap sacks. Travis didn't have to guess where the other three bags had gone. He knew.

The blood drained from Warner's face. "I don't understand. Who would have done this?" Warner gestured toward the burlap filling the spot where the poison should have been.

"Someone who didn't want you to realize the poison was missing. Did you count the bags the day your pestle was stolen?"

Warner shook his head. "No. The shelf looked full."

"So they could have been taken that night." Or any other night, since the thief had proven he could enter the drugstore without leaving any sign. "You should probably install another set of locks."

Though Warner had replaced his locks at the same time as the other shopkeepers, Travis didn't want him to take any chances. Unlike the others, Warner stocked potentially dangerous merchandise.

"I'll order new locks today." Warner laid his hand on Travis's shoulder and waited until they were face-to-face. "You don't think I poisoned Nate's goats, do you?"

"No." Travis would stake his reputation on Warner's innocence. "But it's also clear that whoever did wants you to take the blame."

Lydia tried not to sigh at the realization that she'd checked the clock at least a dozen times in the last five minutes. It was silly the way she watched it each afternoon, practically counting the minutes until Travis arrived to walk home with her. Oh, she made a show of rearranging the display of candies in the glass-fronted case, and she did her best to carry on a conversation with Opal, but the simple fact was, she was waiting for Travis.

It was undoubtedly foolish to put such store in the time they spent together, but she couldn't deny how much she enjoyed those few minutes each day. As they walked, they'd talk about everything from town politics and Aunt Bertha's roses to whether Lydia should try making chocolate-covered peanuts. And while it was true that she discussed the same subjects with Catherine, that wasn't the same. Catherine and Travis were both friends, but being with Travis was special. Lydia had never had a friend like him, one who made her nerve endings sizzle like water on a hot griddle.

As the doorbell tinkled, Lydia smiled. He was here. She studied his face as she did each afternoon, then frowned. Opal might not have noticed, but Lydia knew Travis's expressions well enough to know that something was wrong. Though he returned her smile, his was strained, and there were furrows between his eyes.

"What happened?" It wasn't much of a greeting, but the words slipped out before Lydia could censor them.

Travis's lips curved in a wry grin. "You haven't heard? I thought the Cimarron Creek grapevine would have spread the news."

"I had the normal number of customers, but no one had anything unusual to report." Though Lydia had been taught to deplore gossip, it appeared to be a favorite pastime of many of the women who frequented her shop.

"I guess Nate didn't tell anyone. I wasn't sure what he'd do."

Sensing that Travis didn't want anyone, even Opal, to overhear Nate's story, Lydia bade her assistant farewell and led the way out the back of the store. When they were out of earshot, she turned to Travis. "What happened?"

His lips tightened. "Someone poisoned a dozen of Nate's goats and tried to make it look like Warner was responsible."

How awful! Lydia knew Nate prized his goats and that this must have been a blow to him. "I don't understand why anyone would kill Nate's goats. That's just plain mean." The fact that poison was involved meant the animals couldn't be used for food, and it wasn't the right season to be shearing them. The once valuable goats were now worthless. "It makes no sense, and it makes even less sense that Warner would be involved. I thought he and Nate were friends."

Travis gave her a wry smile. "Are you forgetting the fight at the Founders' Day celebration? They weren't friends then. They were rivals for your hand."

Lydia had hoped that everyone in town had forgotten that embarrassing moment, but at least one person hadn't. "That was over a month ago."

"They both still want to court you."

"And I told them both I wasn't interested in marriage." Admittedly, Lydia had started dreaming of a husband and children again, but neither Warner nor Nate starred in those dreams.

As if he'd read her thoughts, Travis said, "I know it will take a while for you to get over what happened with Edgar, but someday you'll be ready to marry."

"Maybe, but I can't imagine marrying either Nate or Warner."

Surely it wasn't Lydia's imagination that Travis looked pleased. "I see." When he cleared his throat, apparently uncomfortable with the direction of their conversation, Lydia decided to change the subject. Since the street was empty, she didn't need to worry about being overheard.

"Who do you think killed the goats?" Right now that was more important than the possibility that she might one day want to marry.

"I don't like admitting this," Travis said, "but I have no idea."

Lydia considered the goats' deaths. In terms of severity, it was between Opal's rape and the thefts and vandalism that had plagued the town for the last few months.

"I wonder if it's the same person who's behind what happened to Opal and Edgar, and the thefts from the stores."

Though Lydia was no expert on crime, teaching had brought her into contact with a variety of people. Most had been pleasant, but one mother's behavior had concerned Lydia enough that she'd spoken to the headmistress about her.

"Some people have a warped sense of right and wrong," the headmistress had said. "They're the dangerous ones, because you never know what they'll do."

Lydia wondered whether someone with a similarly twisted mind was at work here.

Travis looked as if he'd considered and dismissed that theory. "I agree there's likely a connection between Opal and Edgar, but I don't see how the other crimes are related. As far as I know, Nate has never set foot in the Silver Spur, so he may have never met either Edgar or Opal, except possibly at church."

"But Nate's the victim. He doesn't have to have any connection to Opal or Edgar. If I'm right, the person who's responsible is someone who knows him as well as Edgar and Opal."

They had reached Aunt Bertha's front door, but Travis made no move to open it.

Instead, though he appeared to consider Lydia's words, he frowned.

"That doesn't narrow the field very much. There are a fair number of people in Cimarron Creek who fit the bill, including me."

Lydia blinked, surprised that Travis felt the need to say that. "But you're not the person behind the crimes."

"Are you sure?"

It seemed as if he were testing her, although she had no idea why. "Of course I'm sure. You're an honest man who'd never do any of those things. I'm as sure of that as I am of my own name."

Though he made no reply, Travis seemed uncomfortable with her praise. Lydia softened her voice as she said, "I'm sure of one other thing, and that's that you need help. I balked when you advised me to hire an assistant, but you were right. Having Opal help has made my life a lot easier. I think you need to take your own advice, Travis. Hire a deputy."

She had thought he might dismiss the idea out of hand, but instead Travis looked thoughtful. "Who would you suggest?"

"Someone you trust."

As much as he hated to admit it, especially since Pa would see it as proof that Travis couldn't do his job, Lydia was right. He needed help. That was why he was on his way to Porter's house. It would be easier to approach both of his cousins at the same time, and he knew Warner would be there for his usual Wednesday supper.

"Are you looking for the other Musketeers?" Hilda asked when she opened the door. "They're out back."

Exactly what Travis had expected. The two men were standing at the far edge of the property smoking cigars.

Warner's eyes lit when he saw Travis. "I hope you've come with good news. Did you find out who killed Nate's goats and tried to place the blame on me?"

How he wished he could answer in the affirmative. "No, I didn't. That's why I'm here." Travis shook his head when Porter offered to get him a cigar. Unlike his cousins, he'd never developed a taste for tobacco.

"I need your help." He leaned against the fence, trying to appear casual. "I've been thinking about it for a while, and I realized Cimarron Creek needs a deputy sheriff."

Porter blew out smoke rings, smiling at their perfect shape. "Sheriff Allen didn't need help."

That was the response Travis would have expected from his father, not his cousin.

"True, but things are different now. We have a lot more crime than when Lionel was sheriff."

"And you think a deputy would change that? Maybe we need a new sheriff."

Warner stared at his brother, apparently as startled by his suggestion as Travis was. "You don't mean that, Porter."

"Of course not. I was only joking." He took another puff of his cigar. "I guess my joke fell flat. Sorry."

Travis wasn't sure why the joke — if it was a joke — hurt. It was no more than what Pa had been saying. But somehow it seemed worse coming from a man who was almost as close as a brother.

Warner cuffed his brother's ear as he'd done when they were boys. "No more jokes." Turning to Travis, he asked, "What do you want us to do other than agree that times have changed?"

Travis looked from Porter to Warner. They were more than his childhood friends; they were the other Musketeers. "I'd like you both to become my deputies. There's no one I trust more."

Porter studied the tip of his cigar, refusing to meet Travis's gaze. "You're not thinking straight, Travis. You know Pa wouldn't let me walk away from the livery."

"And I've got a drugstore to run." Warner echoed his brother's protest.

They were valid objections. Fortunately, Travis had anticipated their reaction. "I know. That's why I thought you both could do it part time. It wouldn't be forever, just until we catch whoever's behind all these crimes."

For a moment, the only sound was the soughing of the wind. Then, his eyes narrowing with what looked like suspicion, Porter asked, "You think it's one person?"

"I'm not sure." Travis wouldn't admit that Lydia's theory was beginning to make sense to him. "All I know is that I've got to find him or however many hims there are. I hoped you'd help."

Warner puffed on his cigar for a few seconds. When he spoke, Travis heard genuine regret in his voice. "I'd like to, but it would look mighty strange if I was investigating a crime that at least one person thinks I committed."

"And I'm his brother," Porter added. "No one would believe I could be impartial."

Unfortunately, they were right. Clapping Travis on the shoulder, Warner said, "Sorry, Travis, but you need to find yourself a different deputy."

The question was, who?

19

"She's gone!"

Lydia looked up from the bread she was slicing for breakfast toast, her heart sinking at the sight of Catherine's red-rimmed eyes. It was the first Sunday in September. If Lydia had been in Syracuse, there would have been signs of autumn's approach — oak trees shedding their leaves; cooler mornings, some with the hint of frost; flowers beginning to fade — but summer still dominated the Hill Country. The days were hot, most boasting the vibrant blue sky that never failed to make Lydia's spirits soar. When she'd awakened this morning, she had smiled at the realization that this was another day to celebrate the majesty of God's creation. But Catherine was not celebrating.

"Oh, Catherine." Lydia dropped the knife and rushed across the kitchen to wrap her arms around her friend. "Sit down," she said. When Catherine remained immobile, Lydia pulled out a chair and guided Catherine into it. Though shock was keeping her upright, her friend looked as if she might collapse. Not only was her face tear-stained, but her color was bright and her breathing shallow as if she'd run the three blocks from her house.

"What happened?" Lydia had no doubt about the cause of Catherine's tears, but she knew Catherine well enough to know she needed to talk, that telling the story would help release her sorrow.

Catherine buried her head in her hands, her shoulders shaking as she sobbed. A few seconds later, she looked up and brushed the tears from her cheeks. "I knew something was wrong when I woke. The house felt empty. It's never been like that before."

She fixed her gaze on Lydia, as if asking whether she understood. Lydia did not. Since she and her mother had lived in the boarding school, there was never a time when it felt empty. Even when the pupils went home for the holidays, there were always staff members bustling around. It was only because Mama had not started supper that Lydia had discovered that she'd collapsed on the floor of the pantry.

"There, there." Lydia pulled her chair

closer to Catherine and grasped her hands. The words were meaningless, but she hoped the physical contact would help her friend.

"When I went into Mama's room, she wasn't breathing." Tears began to well in Catherine's eyes. "He killed her, Lydia. I know he did."

It was a harsh accusation, but Lydia had no doubt Catherine believed it. This was not the first time she had expressed her distrust of the town's sole physician.

"Mama was feeling worse last night, so he bled her again. After that, she went to sleep, and she never woke up." Catherine gripped Lydia's hands so tightly they stung. "Promise me, no matter what happens to me, you won't let Doc Harrington treat me. Mama would still be alive if it weren't for him."

The anguish in Catherine's voice wrenched Lydia's heart. If only there were something she could say or do to comfort her. The doctors who'd treated her students had told Lydia that Heroic Medicine, as bleeding and purging were called, had been discontinued by most physicians when they'd learned that it did more harm than good, but nothing would be gained by telling Catherine that.

"You're healthy, Catherine. You don't need a doctor." Lydia wouldn't remind her that her mother had chosen to let the doctor treat her despite Catherine's advice.

Catherine stared at Lydia, her eyes so filled with pain that Lydia wanted to cry. "What am I going to do now?"

"I'll help you, and so will Aunt Bertha."

As if on cue, Aunt Bertha entered the room. "What happened?" Her smile faded at the sight of Catherine's stricken expression. "Gussie?" When Lydia nodded, Aunt Bertha extended her arms to Catherine. "Come here, child. Let me give you a hug." She wrapped her great-niece in her embrace. "It will be all right. Your mother is at peace now. Her pain is gone."

But Catherine's had only begun. Lydia remembered the days after her mother's death when she'd wandered aimlessly around her mother's room, picking up something Mama had loved, then putting it back, as if keeping everything the way Mama had left it would somehow bring her back. And through it all, there had been an emptiness deep inside her that she had feared would never be filled.

It was only days after the funeral that she had met Edgar. Thinking back, Lydia wondered whether the reason she'd been attracted to him was that Edgar helped fill some of those empty spots. Perhaps what she had believed was love was nothing more than the relief of not being alone, of having someone care about her.

While Aunt Bertha patted Catherine's back, comforting her as if she were a child, Lydia turned to practical matters. "I'll speak to Reverend Dunn," she told Catherine. "How soon would you like the funeral? Tomorrow afternoon?"

Catherine turned and shook her head. "No. It has to be in the morning. Mama loved sunrises."

And so on Tuesday morning as the sun began to make its way over the treetops, Lydia stood at Catherine's side while her mother was laid to rest. It seemed that most of the town had come to pay their respects. While Gussie had rarely left her home for the past year, she was still a Whitfield, and Whitfields were honored in this town.

When they'd filed out of the church into the cemetery, Aunt Bertha took her place on Catherine's right, with the entire Gray family next to her. Travis and his father had been among the first to arrive at the church, and to Lydia's surprise, Travis had taken her arm as they'd exited the church and now stood at her side, flanked by his father. Though she hadn't expected it, today Abe

Whitfield had even managed a civil greeting.

The graveyard service was mercifully short, and to Lydia's relief, no one seemed to expect Catherine to toss a shovelful of dirt onto her mother's casket. To Lydia's way of thinking, that was as primitive as the bleeding Catherine deplored. She'd found herself unable to lift the shovel at her mother's funeral, not wanting that to be her final memory of her mother.

Today the gravediggers lowered Gussie's coffin into the ground and the minister asked each of the mourners to place a wildflower in the grave as they left the cemetery. The actual burial would be done while everyone was at Aunt Bertha's house, partaking of the breakfast Lydia and Opal had prepared.

"I hate funerals," Travis said as he carried his plate back to the kitchen, where Lydia was working. Though the house was large, the dining room could not accommodate all the mourners, and so Lydia had decided that the seats there would be reserved for the older generation. The rest of the guests were invited to fill their plates and find other places to eat. Many of them, including Travis, chose to remain standing, although only he had come to the kitchen.

Lydia looked up from the cake slices she was arranging on a platter. "Aunt Bertha claims funerals are for the living, that they're a time to say farewell to loved ones."

As she pronounced the words, Lydia remembered Aunt Bertha's pained expression when she'd said that. Had she been thinking about her daughter? Though Aunt Bertha rarely spoke of Joan, she no longer hid her portrait but kept it on her bedside table. Was the constant reminder good or bad? Lydia did not know. She could only imagine how painful it must have been to have lost a child.

"I suppose she's right." Travis's words brought Lydia back to the present, and she realized he was responding to her comment. "At least Catherine knows what happened to her mother."

Lydia almost expected him to add a "but" to his statement. "Are you thinking about Joan and Edgar?"

"Yes. It's kind of hard not to on a day like this. I hate unresolved mysteries even more than I do funerals."

Hearing the pain and frustration in his voice, Lydia turned back to Travis. "I wish I could help you."

His eyes turned from silver to pewter as he managed a smile. "You do," he said softly, "in more ways than you know."

"Gussie would have been proud of the turnout," Aunt Bertha said two hours later when the house was once more empty. Lydia and Opal had washed the last of the dishes, while Aunt Bertha rested in the parlor. Now that Opal had returned to the Spur, Lydia joined the older woman. Though she had thought Aunt Bertha would be too tired by the morning's events to do anything but sit, she was busily tatting a dresser scarf, claiming her arthritis no longer pained her as much as it used to.

Aunt Bertha's smile was bittersweet. "I know I shouldn't have favorites, but Gussie was always my favorite niece, even if we were related only by marriage. She had a hard life, losing her husband and then having to raise Catherine alone, but I never heard her complain. She didn't even complain when Doc Harrington insisted on bleeding her. Instead, she always claimed she felt better a couple days later. Gussie may not have had a strong body, but she had a strong spirit. I only wish she'd lived long enough to see Catherine married." Aunt Bertha nodded as if she were about to make a grand announcement. "I saw Nate talking to Catherine, and it looked as if he was doing more than offering his condolences. That's enough to make this old lady dream about wedding bells."

Though Lydia hated to destroy Aunt Bertha's illusions, she knew little would be gained by letting her hope for something that was unlikely to happen. "I don't think Catherine is interested in Nate any longer. She doesn't trust him, and I can't say that I blame her. It's hard to trust a man who's fickle."

Aunt Bertha leaned forward, her eyes narrowing as she stared at Lydia. "You sound as if you're talking about someone other than Nate. Surely you don't believe Travis is fickle."

As a blush stained her cheeks, Lydia dipped her head and tried to regain her composure. It was silly the way even the mention of Travis made her so flustered. "Travis has never done anything to make me feel I can't trust him, but neither did my father."

Aunt Bertha laid down her tatting. "Do you want to talk about it?"

Perhaps it was the emotional impact of the funeral. Perhaps it was the discussion she'd had with Travis about farewells and the realization that she'd never put her father's memory to rest. Lydia wasn't certain. All she knew was that it felt right to tell Aunt Bertha about her parents.

Lydia gave a short nod. "There's not much to tell. When I was eight, he left my mother and me because he found another woman. For the longest time, I thought I had done something to make him leave, even though Mama insisted it wasn't my fault. When I became old enough to understand what had happened, my feelings of guilt turned to anger."

Aunt Bertha was silent for a moment, as if digesting what Lydia had revealed. "And that's why when things didn't work out with Edgar, you decided all men were louts."

Lydia stared at Aunt Bertha, startled by her seemingly casual statement. "How did you know about Edgar?"

Touching the side of her head, Aunt Bertha said, "My hair may be gray, but what's underneath is still functioning. I knew a smart woman like you wouldn't just pack up and leave her home without a good reason. Most times that reason is a man." She gave a little shrug. "It seemed like more than coincidence that you came to the same place as a single man from the North had a couple months earlier. Then, too, I saw the way you looked at Opal the first few days she worked here. It was more than curiosity over the woman you'd just hired. The way I saw it, you came out here expecting to marry Edgar. Am I right?"

"Yes, but now . . ." Lydia paused, trying to put her feelings into words. "I'm not sure Edgar would have been the right man for me."

Her smile one of satisfaction, Aunt Bertha nodded. "Because of Travis. I know you want to deny it, but I'm not blind any more than I'm dumb. I can see the sparks between you. What you feel for him is more than friendship."

"Is it?" Aunt Bertha sounded so confident, while Lydia was anything but. "I'm confused. I've never felt this way about anyone. He makes me feel special, and there are times when I believe God brought me here to meet him, but then I think I'm deluding myself."

For once Aunt Bertha had no reply, and so Lydia continued, voicing the fear that sent shivers down her spine. "It isn't only that I'm afraid of trusting men. The bigger problem is that I don't think I can trust myself. How can I when I thought I loved Edgar, but now I'm not sure I did?"

Aunt Bertha picked up her tatting and studied it for a moment. "I can't tell you that I've ever been in your situation, but I can tell you that you need to follow your heart. If I'd done that, I wouldn't have so many regrets." Her fingers flew as she plied the shuttle, turning ordinary white thread into beautiful lace.

"Regrets about your daughter?" Perhaps Lydia was being presumptuous in asking, but today was turning into a day for confidences.

"Yes." Aunt Bertha's fingers stilled as she looked around the room. "It hurts too much to talk about her here. Why don't you see if Porter can get my favorite carriage ready? We'll take a ride."

Less than an hour later, Lydia and Aunt Bertha reached the summit where they'd come the first time they'd ridden out of town. Aunt Bertha shielded her eyes with her hand as she looked down at Cimarron Creek. "Joan always loved this spot. She said she thought heaven would be like this."

"So why did she leave?" A woman who thought her hometown was heavenly was not someone Lydia would have expected to flee.

Aunt Bertha's lips flattened as she said, "She had no choice. Jonas wouldn't let the Henderson name be besmirched. He never believed Joan's story that it wasn't her fault. There were those who claimed Joan was the prettiest girl in town. I always thought that was true, but as her mother, I was hardly impartial. The boys seemed to think she was pretty. Joan always had a string of them following her around, but as far as I knew, there was no one special. That's why I was so shocked by what happened." Aunt Bertha shook her head. "I believed Joan was telling the truth, but Jonas was sure she'd led some fellow along, flirting with him and then giving him the one thing an unmarried girl should never give away."

Lydia had no trouble understanding Aunt Bertha's euphemism, and so she wasn't surprised when the older woman said, "When it was clear our daughter was going to have a baby, Jonas insisted she leave town." Tears fell from Aunt Bertha's eyes, and she covered her face with her hands for a moment as she sobbed.

Lydia's mind began to whirl as she considered the similarities — and the differences — between Joan's story and Opal's. Both had experienced the prospect of being an unwed mother and facing ostracism from the townspeople, but Edgar had come to Opal's rescue, protecting her and her unborn child from shame.

Joan had not had a champion. Not even her parents, and that surprised Lydia. The

Aunt Bertha she knew was a loving woman who'd gone out of her way to help Lydia, yet twenty years ago she had sent her daughter away rather than risk censure from the town's other residents.

Brushing the tears from her cheeks, Aunt Bertha looked at Lydia. "I'm not proud of my part. I should have taken a firmer stand, but I didn't. Perhaps if you'd met my husband, you would understand. I loved Jonas dearly, but I wasn't blind to his faults, either. When he made up his mind, there was no changing it. He was convinced Joan was a sinner. He claimed he wasn't punishing her by insisting that she leave. In his mind, he was protecting her from the consequences of her sin."

Aunt Bertha took a shallow breath. "When I realized that Jonas would not relent, I arranged for Joan to stay with my cousin in Ladreville until the baby was born. That way no one here would know what had happened. Sterling and his wife would arrange an adoption, and Joan would come home. Only she didn't. The day after the baby was born, Joan ran away, leaving the baby behind. I tried to find her — even hired a Pinkerton to search for her — but it was as if she'd never existed."

Two more fat tears made their way down

Aunt Bertha's cheeks. "Oh, Lydia, I'd give everything I own to see my daughter once more and tell her how sorry I am. I don't want to die without her knowing that I love her. I know God has forgiven me for what I've done, but I need her forgiveness too."

Impatiently, Aunt Bertha brushed the tears away. "Can you imagine what it's like for me knowing I have a granddaughter somewhere and that because of my weakness that girl has grown up without her mother's love?"

Like a single stone tossed into a pond, Aunt Bertha and Jonas's decision had created ever-widening ripples that affected far more than themselves and their daughter. Joan's daughter, the baby's adoptive parents, even Aunt Bertha's cousins had all been changed by that one decision.

Though it was obvious that Aunt Bertha regretted her part in Joan's banishment and that she'd paid for it through years of sorrow, Lydia's heart ached for Joan. What must it have been like to give up her child? That could not have been easy, and Lydia suspected her life afterwards had been a difficult one. Though she had no way of knowing whether Joan had been like Opal and cherished her baby regardless of the way it had been conceived, Lydia could not imagine Joan not having at least some regrets that she had not been able to watch her daughter grow from an infant to a toddler and finally to a woman.

But Joan had fled as soon as she'd given birth. Why? Aunt Bertha claimed the plan had been for Joan to come back to Cimarron Creek, yet she'd run away rather than return to her parents and her hometown. Where had Joan gone? Had she found a place where she was accepted, or had she succumbed to the dangers that threatened so many young women who were suddenly all alone?

Lydia shuddered, remembering some of the stories she'd heard. Aunt Bertha had probably heard the same tales of some girls' horrible fates. No wonder she had hired a Pinkerton.

Lydia took a deep breath and exhaled slowly, trying to calm her nerves. The Pinkerton's inability to find Joan greatly reduced the likelihood that she was still alive, and yet there had been no proof of Joan's death. That left uncertainty, and uncertainty, as Lydia knew from Edgar's disappearance, was painful. Aunt Bertha needed to know what had happened to her daughter.

"There must be something we can do to

find Joan," Lydia said, laying her hand on the older woman's arm in an attempt to comfort her.

"I don't know what. I've prayed every day that the Lord would send me an answer, but all I've heard is silence. Seeing Gussie die so young reminded me that my time on earth could end any day. Oh, Lydia, I want to see my daughter."

The utter despair in Aunt Bertha's voice threatened to break Lydia's heart. She took a deep breath as she searched for a way to help her. "If there are clues, they must be in that other town. What did you say the name was?"

"Ladreville."

"That's right, Ladreville. Have you been there since Joan left?"

Aunt Bertha shook her head.

"That's what we need to do." It might be a dead end, but at least they would have tried. "We'll go to Ladreville."

"We? You'd go with me?" A note of wonder colored Aunt Bertha's voice.

"Of course. You don't think I'd let you go alone, do you? I can't do that."

"You can't do that." Travis stared at the woman walking beside him, unsure which surprised him more: her plans or the casual way she'd announced them.

"Why not?" Lydia asked. "Aunt Bertha has done so much for me that it seems the least I can do is help her discover what happened to her daughter."

It was the day after Aunt Gussie's funeral. Though Lydia had closed Cimarron Sweets for the funeral, she and Opal had worked all day today and had had more customers than normal, with the result that they'd kept the store open an extra half hour. Now Travis was escorting her back to Aunt Bertha's and listening to her crazy plan.

"I don't disagree with your motivation," he told her. "I love Aunt Bertha as much as you do. The problem is that you two shouldn't travel that far alone. It's one thing for you to take a short ride out of town, but it's completely different to consider a journey of that length. Cimarron Creek and Ladreville aren't on the same stagecoach line. That means you'd have to go to Austin, then back to Ladreville. I can't imagine Aunt Bertha being able to do that comfortably. The alternative, which is to take a buggy, is too dangerous."

Though Travis had expected Lydia to begin protesting, she seemed to sense that he wasn't finished and simply raised an eyebrow.

"There are fewer bandits than in the past, but it's still too dangerous for two women alone. I'd worry about you every minute." He wouldn't tell her that he worried about her even when she was only a few blocks away from him. He worried about little things like a pan of hot syrup spilling and burning her, and he worried about the crazy man who was behind the spate of crimes deciding she would be his next target. But Lydia didn't need to know that.

She nodded slowly, as if she agreed with his assessment of the danger. "Then we'll hire someone to take us. There must be a man in Cimarron Creek who'd like to earn some extra money."

There were, but that didn't help ease Travis's worries. "The only ones I'd trust can't leave home for that long." And the rest . . . well, there was no reason to share his concerns with Lydia. He'd simply have to persuade her to wait.

"I know this is important to both you and Aunt Bertha. I want her to find the answers as much as you do. That's why I'm willing to take you to Ladreville, but you'll have to wait until I hire a deputy."

To Travis's relief, Lydia didn't ask when he thought that would happen. If she had, he would have had to admit that he had no idea. As he'd told Porter and Warner, they were the two men he trusted implicitly. The other men who might be candidates for deputy had serious flaws, or at least they did in Travis's mind. That was why he'd decided to advertise for a deputy. Someone with no previous ties to Cimarron Creek would have the impartiality he sought.

"All right," Lydia said. Though her reluctance was obvious, she made no protest. "What do I do in the meantime?"

"Pray."

20

Filled with a sense of urgency she couldn't explain, Lydia turned to Opal. "I want to check on Aunt Bertha. I shouldn't be gone more than half an hour." It was odd. Unlike the day when she'd found Aunt Bertha crying, Lydia had no sense that she was needed at the big house on the corner of Cedar and Pecan. Instead, the need that pulsed through her was to leave the store. The only reason she could imagine was to check on the woman who'd become as dear to her as if they were blood relatives.

In the days since Gussie's funeral, Aunt Bertha had recounted stories of Joan's childhood, but though she seemed unusually animated, Lydia had also noticed that Aunt Bertha's energy was flagging. When her daily dose of digitalis had not restored her to her prefuneral pace, Lydia had asked Warner about possibly increasing the amount of the powerful drug. His reaction had been instantaneous: adamant refusal.

Lydia understood Warner's reasoning. What she did not know was why she felt so anxious today. Fortunately, it was a slow time at the candy shop, and Opal would have no trouble waiting on customers while Lydia headed home.

As she closed the door behind her, Lydia started to turn left, then reversed herself. When she and Travis walked together, they avoided Cimarron Creek's business district by taking Oak east to Cedar, then following Cedar north to Aunt Bertha's house. Though there was no logical explanation for it, Lydia felt compelled to travel Main Street today. It was a few yards shorter than her normal route, but the odds of meeting customers and having to at least greet them meant that it could actually take longer. Still, she headed north on Main.

The light was on inside Travis's office, telling her he had returned from his early afternoon rounds. On an ordinary day, Lydia would have stopped in to see him, but not today. Though she waved as she passed the front window, she did not slow her pace.

The sense of urgency grew, and Lydia found herself looking in all directions, as if there were something important she must not miss. Everything looked normal. It was a typical Thursday in Cimarron Creek.

Lydia was halfway across Mesquite when she stopped, transfixed by the sight of a man heading toward her. She squinted, wondering if her eyes were deceiving her. Was it possible? Was this the reason she had felt compelled to leave the store? Lydia's pulse raced as she realized that other than the slight limp, he looked exactly the way she remembered him.

"Edgar?"

"Lydia?" he asked at the same time, his voice registering the surprise she heard in her own. There was no doubt about it. Edgar Ellis was back in Cimarron Creek. "What are you doing here?"

He sounded confused and angry at the same time. It was hardly the reaction Lydia had expected from the man who had once asked her to marry him. Apparently Edgar had forgotten how they'd planned that she would join him here.

Lydia looked around. For once Main Street was virtually deserted. While unusual at this time of day, that was also good. The fewer people who saw her reunion with Edgar, the better. She crossed the street, wanting to reassure herself that he was real, not an image she'd conjured.

"You know why I came. The question is, where have you been?"

Edgar's face was the one she remembered, the right eyebrow a little shaggier than the left, a small scar next to his nose. Only his eyes were different. Though still the same shade of blue she recalled, they now reflected pain and something more, perhaps disappointment. Whatever had happened to him, it had changed him.

"It's a long story."

"I imagine it is." Lydia hated the tart sound of her voice, yet she couldn't help it. The man she'd once believed loved her enough to share the rest of his life with her was standing only a foot away, and all she could think was that, though he looked like the Edgar of her dreams, she no longer felt anything other than curiosity about him.

Lydia fixed her gaze on Edgar, wanting to see his reaction to her next statement. "The sheriff and your wife will want to hear the story too."

He blanched. "You've changed, Lydia. You didn't used to be so . . . I'm not sure of the word."

"Angry, hurt, disillusioned? Any of those would describe the way I felt when I arrived in Cimarron Creek and discovered you'd married someone else." Though she had no trouble resurrecting the emotions that had colored those first few days, Lydia realized they'd lost the power to hurt her. Now she was filled with relief at the knowledge that Opal had been right when she'd said her husband was alive. Opal, dear, sweet Opal, would be overjoyed to see Edgar again, and her baby would have a father.

"I don't suppose saying I'm sorry would help, but I am sorry. The fact that you're here tells me you didn't get the letter I sent you."

"No, I didn't." And that, Lydia suspected, was a blessing in disguise. While it was true that she'd been hurt when she discovered that Edgar had married someone else, now that she was settled in Cimarron Creek, she couldn't imagine leaving.

"I couldn't mail it here and leave a trail," Edgar explained, "so I paid the stagecoach driver to post it at the end of the line. I guess he forgot."

He paused for a second, looking down the street as if searching for something. "Where's Opal? I went to the Silver Spur looking for her, but Faith said she was working in the confectionary. Since when does Cimarron Creek have a candy shop?"

"Since I opened one. Opal's my assistant."

When Edgar shook his head as if he hadn't

heard correctly, Lydia wondered whether his surprise was that she owned a store or that she had hired his wife. "You have a store here? You're staying even though . . ."

"Even though you didn't keep your promises?" Lydia finished the sentence for him. "Yes. I've discovered that I like being an entrepreneur. Maybe that's because I like the town. Cimarron Creek has become my home in ways that Syracuse never was." It was the first time Lydia had voiced the thought, but as she did, she realized how true it was.

She looked at the man she'd once hoped to marry, the man who was now another woman's husband, and realized she had no regrets. "Let's not waste any more time. You don't want Opal to hear about your return through the grapevine." Once he'd been reunited with his wife, she would tell him what Travis had learned from the authorities in Syracuse.

Edgar blanched as if the possibility of an active grapevine had not occurred to him and nodded as Lydia started to retrace her steps. When she reached the sheriff's office, she opened the door and gestured for Edgar to follow her.

"What are we doing here?" he demanded.

"This is where you need to be." There

would be more privacy here than at Cimarron Sweets.

"Edgar!" The shock on Travis's face as they entered his office mirrored Lydia's feelings when she'd seen the man they both believed dead. "Where on earth have you been?"

"Not yet." Lydia shook her head. "Let me get Opal. I'll close the store and bring her here so we can all hear his story at the same time."

Walking as quickly as she could without actually running and drawing unnecessary attention to herself, Lydia reached the candy shop in record time. Fortunately, there were no customers, and Opal was seated at the table in the back room.

"You're here sooner than I expected," she said, her expression relieved. "That must mean Mrs. Henderson is all right."

Lydia shook her head. "It's something else. You need to come to the sheriff's office with me."

Opal's eyes widened with fear and she laid a protective hand on her abdomen as if to shield her baby from the truth. "It's Edgar, isn't it? The sheriff found out what happened to him."

Lydia smiled, more pleased than she could express that she had brought good news.

"Opal, he's alive. Edgar's back in town."

The young woman's face turned radiant with happiness. "I knew it! I knew he wouldn't leave me."

Without waiting for Lydia, Opal ran down the street and into Travis's office. When Lydia arrived a minute later, she found Opal in Edgar's arms, her lips pressed to his.

Travis gave Lydia an amused look, then cleared his throat. "I know you two want some time alone, but I need to get Edgar's statement first. Let's let the ladies sit." Since there were only two guest chairs, Edgar stood behind Opal, his hands on her shoulders. Travis pulled out a sheet of paper and a pen. "Now, Edgar, tell us what happened. Why did you leave Cimarron Creek?"

"It wasn't my choice." Moving so that he could gaze into Opal's eyes, he said, "I would never have left you or the baby. You know that, don't you?" He clasped her hand in his. "I got a message that night from someone saying he might have a house for us. I knew how much you hated the idea of the baby being born in the saloon, so I'd been asking around, trying to find us a place of our own."

Once again Opal's eyes filled with tears, but she said nothing. So far Travis had written nothing on the pad.

"The note told me to meet him behind the saloon," Edgar continued. "When I went out, he grabbed me from behind and hit me on the head. The next thing I knew, I was lying in a ravine, not knowing who I was and feeling as if every bone in my body was broken."

As Opal gasped, Travis scribbled something. Though she did not speak, Lydia's heart ached for what Edgar had endured. He'd been battered in the fight in Syracuse, but this sounded much more serious. At least in Syracuse, he had had a chance to defend himself.

"It turned out that both arms and legs were broken, plus a couple ribs and my right wrist. My head had a huge knot on it." Lydia tried to imagine how a man with so many injuries had managed to move. It seemed that whoever was responsible had done his best to ensure that Edgar suffered.

"Oh, Edgar!" By now Opal's tears were flowing. "How did you survive?"

"I don't think I was meant to," he said, confirming what Lydia had feared. "I think he meant me to die slowly and painfully."

"But you didn't." Travis spoke for the first time since Edgar had begun his explanation.

"There were times when I wanted to, but

God had other plans for me. The rancher who owned the land said he felt an urge to visit that part of his spread. When he found me, I was in pretty bad shape. As best we could figure it, I'd been lying there for two days. Lucky for me, the rancher had learned something about doctoring during the war, so he set the bones and we waited for them to heal."

Though Lydia did not doubt the truth of Edgar's story, one point bothered her. "It doesn't take four months for bones to heal." Even a bad break mended in two. Why had Edgar stayed away so long?

"You're right," he agreed. "The problem was, even though I could walk again, I didn't know who I was or why someone would try to kill me. The rancher wanted to talk to the sheriff, but I wouldn't let him. At first I couldn't explain why, but I knew there was a reason lawmen couldn't get involved." He gave Travis an apologetic look before he turned back to Opal.

She gripped his hand and pulled it to her lips, pressing a kiss on it. "Oh, my dearest, how awful! I knew you were alive. I was sure of it. But I never dreamt of anything like this."

"So when did you recover your memory?" Travis asked. Though the question was casual, Lydia heard a measure of skepticism in his voice. Like her, Travis was bothered by the length of time Edgar had been gone. Unlike Opal, neither she nor Travis was completely convinced by Edgar's tale.

"It came in bits and pieces." Based on what Lydia had read about head injuries, that sounded plausible. "One day I remembered seeing several feet of snow on the ground and getting into a fight near a tavern."

"Syracuse." If he'd asked, Lydia could have given Edgar the exact date.

"Yes." He turned back to Opal, who seemed puzzled by the name. Had Edgar not mentioned the town where he'd lived? "I'll explain later," he told her before facing Travis. "Other memories came back, but I still had no idea what my name was or where I'd been living. Then one day I slipped on a muddy patch of ground and fell, hitting my head again." Edgar looked at Travis, as if challenging him to believe his story. "It was like that shook up everything inside and put it back in the right place." His face softened as he shifted his gaze to Opal. "That's when I remembered you and the baby."

Lydia had been watching Travis's face and realized his skepticism had not faded, though hers had. Edgar's story was close enough to what she'd read about recovery from head injuries that she believed it. "I've heard of things like that," she told Travis.

He raised an eyebrow when he turned to Edgar. "I suppose if I talk to this rancher, he'd corroborate your story."

"You don't believe me?" Edgar sounded surprised, perhaps because he'd once told Lydia that he valued honesty. He'd broken his promises to her, and it appeared he hadn't told Opal everything about his past, but this story rang true.

When Travis bristled, Lydia decided to intervene. "It's Travis's job to question everything and verify the truth."

Edgar nodded. "I see. He's Silas Lockhart of the Sleeping L ranch. That's half a day's ride from here. The place he found me was only about two hours from Cimarron Creek, but no one would have seen me unless they were looking."

Travis scribbled the information on his pad. "All right. I'll check with him. I'll be honest. What concerns me more than your whereabouts for the last four months is who was behind the attack."

Edgar's story left no doubt that it hadn't been a random attack. As Lydia and Travis had surmised previously, Edgar had been targeted. The question was, by whom and, though Travis did not say it, whether it was the same man who'd raped Opal.

"Do you remember anything that would help identify your assailant?" Travis asked.

Edgar shrugged. "It was a man. A strong one. That's all I remember."

Though she'd remained silent, gripping her husband's hand, Opal whimpered, making Lydia wonder whether she was remembering her own attack.

Travis continued his interrogation. "What about the note? Did you recognize the handwriting?"

This time Edgar shook his head. "Looked ordinary. Plain paper, careful printing."

"Printing?" Though Travis was conducting the investigation, Lydia couldn't help interjecting her question.

"Yes. Nice and neat, though. Not like a child."

Of course not. An adult had been responsible.

"Do you still have the note?" Travis asked.

Edgar shook his head again. "I put it in my pocket, but when I woke up in the field, it was gone."

Lydia wasn't surprised, and she suspected Travis wasn't either. The man who'd attacked Edgar wouldn't have wanted to leave any traces. He'd gone to a lot of trouble to take Edgar away from Cimarron Creek, but he couldn't have been certain that the blows to Edgar's head would result in amnesia or that he would die from his injuries.

Travis gave Edgar a long look, then nodded briskly. "I need to talk to Lockhart, but I'm inclined to believe you. If you remember anything else about the night you were attacked, let me know."

"I'd be glad to, Sheriff, but I won't be here. Opal and I are leaving before sunset. I need to find a place where she and the baby will be safe."

Surprise filled Opal's green eyes. "You think we're in danger?"

"Now that I'm back, yes. When whoever tried to kill me realizes he didn't succeed, he might try again. I can't take the risk that he'll hurt you too." Edgar drew Opal to her feet and stroked her cheek. "Pack whatever you want to take. We'll leave as soon as you're ready."

Travis shook his head. "I can't let you do that."

"I don't see how you can stop me, short of putting me over there." Edgar pointed to the town's solitary jail cell. "You don't have any reason to arrest me."

"You're right." A frown accompanied

Travis's admission. "But I wish you'd recon-sider."

"I've got to keep Opal safe." He turned back to Opal. "I'll go to the Spur with you, but first I need a moment alone with Lydia."

Lydia wasn't certain who was more surprised by Edgar's declaration: herself, Opal, or Travis. What did Edgar want to say that he needed privacy? Though Lydia had once had dozens of questions for him, they no longer seemed important. Travis appeared almost bemused, and Opal's reluctance to let her husband out of her sight even for a moment was palpable.

As the door closed, leaving her alone with Edgar, Lydia spoke. "I'm sorry for all you've gone through."

He appeared relieved that she had initi-ated the conversation. "I thought you might believe I deserved it after what I did."

"No one deserves what happened to you."

"Thank you for saying that, but I know I hurt you. I didn't plan to do that." Edgar's hands tightened into fists. "I loved you, Lydia. I hope you know that."

Loved. Past tense. It was what she had suspected. Lydia nodded, as much to en-courage Edgar to continue as to convey her understanding.

"When I met Opal, I realized that I loved

you like a sister or friend, not the way a man should love his wife. What I feel for Opal is different — deeper and stronger." Edgar's voice rang with sincerity. "Can you ever forgive me for not being honest enough to tell you the truth in enough time to save you the trip out here?"

"I already have." How could she blame Edgar when she'd discovered that what she felt for him was a mere shadow of her feelings for Travis? She wasn't sure where — if anywhere — those feelings were headed, but Lydia knew they were deeper than any she had ever had for Edgar.

She nodded slowly as she faced the man she had once thought would be her husband. "I'll admit I was hurt, but Cimarron Creek has become my home. I believe that coming here was part of God's plan for me."

As the lines of tension faded from Edgar's face, Lydia laid her hand on his cheek. It was a gesture of farewell and, at the same time, warning. "You were right to marry Opal, but you're wrong if you think leaving here will solve anything. Edgar, it's time for you to stop running away."

21

"What did you say to get him so riled?" Travis looked at Lydia, surprised that while Edgar was marching down the street, his anger apparent in the long strides that forced Opal to practically run to keep up with him, Lydia appeared perfectly calm. He'd worried that she might have been upset by the reunion with the man she'd expected to marry, but instead she appeared relieved.

Travis drew in a deep breath and exhaled slowly, letting his own relief settle over him. Until she'd emerged from the office, he hadn't realized how tense he'd been during the time Lydia had been alone with Edgar. It had felt like hours, although his watch claimed that only a few minutes had passed while they'd been behind the closed door. Travis had spent that time trying to distract Opal, who was clearly confused about why her husband wanted time alone with her employer. It seemed Edgar had neglected to mention his prior engagement to the woman he married.

A slight smile tilted the corners of Lydia's mouth. "I told him it was time to stop running, that he needed to stay and take a stand. If he'd done that in Syracuse, he wouldn't have spent all this time hiding."

Travis nodded, imagining how Edgar — or any man, for that matter — would react to such a message. The implication was that if he left Cimarron Creek, he was a coward. That would be difficult to accept coming from another man, but the fact that it was a woman — and not just any woman, but the one he'd once planned to marry — who'd voiced it made it particularly unpalatable.

"You're right," Travis told Lydia, "but I suspect Edgar disagreed."

She tipped her head to one side, the hint of a smile teasing her lips. "He didn't say anything, but I've always heard that actions speak louder than words." The hint turned into a full-fledged smile as Lydia looked at Edgar's rapidly retreating back.

"You know the man better than I do. What could we say to convince him to stay?" The idea of Edgar remaining in town made Travis's brain begin to spin with possibilities. "I need him here to help flush out his attacker. If he leaves, I may never discover who's responsible."

And Travis couldn't let that happen. Even if he were wrong and the same man wasn't responsible for Opal's rape and Nate's poisoned goats, the attacker was still a criminal. There was no way of knowing when he might strike again. Travis needed to find that man and put him behind bars to ensure that Cimarron Creek was safe. Or at least safer.

Lydia's smile faded. "I don't believe anything would convince Edgar when he's in this mood. He's only thinking about Opal and keeping her safe." She was silent for a moment before she asked, "Do you think whoever it is will try to hurt Edgar again?"

Travis shook his head. "Probably not. My guess is he wouldn't risk another attack on him. Once he realizes Edgar is still alive, he'll know Edgar will be on his guard. What I'm hoping for is that he might let something slip, especially if Edgar had a reason to be sniffing around."

While he and Opal had waited for Edgar and Lydia to emerge from his office, Opal had chattered about how everyone who frequented the Silver Spur respected Edgar and how he'd rarely had to use force, since he'd been able to spot potential fights before they began. At first Travis had only been half listening, but as she continued, his thoughts began to whirl. Edgar's return might be the answer to one of his prayers.

Travis raised an eyebrow as he fixed his gaze on Lydia. "How would you like to pay a visit to the Spur? There's something I need to discuss with Edgar and Opal."

Though she looked surprised by the suggestion, Lydia agreed, and five minutes later the four of them were seated in a corner booth, Edgar with his arm wrapped protectively around Opal, Travis and Lydia on the opposite side, a discreet distance between them.

Travis crossed his arms on the table and leaned forward. "I've got a proposition for you, Edgar. I know you want to keep Opal safe." The other man nodded, though the suspicion in his eyes did not fade. "As I see it, the only way to do that is to discover who attacked both her and you."

Suspicion turned to anger. "Who told you what happened to her?"

Opal patted the hand that clasped her shoulder. "It's all right, Edgar. I told Lydia, and she convinced me the sheriff needed to know."

As Lydia nodded, the faint scent of lavender teased Travis's senses. He would have expected the aroma of chocolate to cling to her, but somehow the toilet water was stronger.

"Travis and I believe the same person was responsible for both attacks," she told Edgar.

Though Travis hadn't expected it, Edgar appeared to accept Lydia's words. Perhaps it was because he'd known her longer or perhaps it was merely that Opal had rested her head against his shoulder, reminding him of his vow to protect her.

"We need to find the man." Travis stared at Edgar, waiting until the other man met his gaze. Though there was still a hint of defiance, it was now mixed with curiosity. "You can run, but you'll always be looking over your shoulder, wondering if he's on your trail. And until he's caught, there's always the chance that he'll hurt Opal again. No matter how hard you try, you won't be able to protect her every minute of every day."

As the words registered, Edgar nodded ever so slightly. Travis pressed his advantage. "Wouldn't it make more sense to stay here and track him down?"

"How would I do that? No one's going to answer my questions."

"They would if you were my deputy."

Edgar's eyes widened in shock. "You want me to be a deputy?"

"Yes. Lydia's been urging me to hire one. She says I can't handle everything alone, and she's right. She's almost always right," he added, smiling at Lydia. "From everything I've heard, you'd be a good deputy."

Edgar was silent for a moment, obviously trying to digest the idea. His expression gave no clue to his feelings until he turned to Opal. "What do you think?" The man rose in Travis's estimation. Few men he knew, including his cousin Porter, would have deferred to their wives.

The flush that stained Opal's cheeks told Travis she was both surprised and pleased by being consulted. "I think you'd make a fine deputy."

Before Edgar could respond, Travis spoke. "There's another part to this. A deputy shouldn't be living above the saloon. No offense to Faith, but it sends the wrong message." Though the solution he had in mind was only temporary, it might work. "Until you can find the right place for you and your family, I'd like you to move into my house. You've probably heard my father's not the easiest person to live with, but there's plenty of room."

This time Travis had no trouble reading

Edgar's expression. He was hooked, but once again he turned to his wife. "Is that all right with you?"

Opal nodded, her eyes sparkling with excitement. "It's more than all right. We'll be together and away from the saloon. That sounds perfect."

Edgar stretched his hand across the table to shake Travis's. "It seems you've got yourself a new deputy."

Some might call him impulsive for offering the job to Edgar, but the feeling of rightness that filled him told Travis he'd done well by hiring the man. "While you pack what you want to bring, I'll tell my father what's happening. Give me an hour." It wouldn't take that long to tell Pa, but the extra time would give his father a chance to cool down.

"You were quiet back there," Travis said as he walked Lydia back to the confectionary. "What do you think of my hiring Edgar?"

"It's a good idea." She tipped her head to one side in the gesture he found so endearing. "A year ago I would have scoffed at the thought of Edgar being a lawman, because he was often impulsive, but that was a year ago. He's changed. You only have to see him with Opal to know that. It's as plain as can be that he loves her in ways he never loved me."

Travis was surprised by her candor. Most women wouldn't have admitted such a thing, but Lydia wasn't most women. Perhaps he shouldn't say anything, but he couldn't stop himself from asking, "Does that bother you?"

"No. Even before he returned, I realized he's not the man for me."

Lydia looked up with a smile that made Travis's pulse race. Was it possible that she'd softened her stance on marriage? And if she did, what did that mean for him? As much as he wanted to explore both questions, now was not the time. Travis glanced at his watch as he opened the door to the shop for her. "I wish I could stay, but I need to prepare my father for Edgar and Opal's arrival."

"I hope it goes well."

It did not.

Even before Travis had finished his explanation, Pa's face had turned so red he worried that the man might have an apoplectic attack. "What's wrong with you, boy?" Pa demanded. "Do you have sawdust instead of a brain? Whatever made you decide to bring a whore and the Cursed Enemy under my roof?"

Travis took a deep breath. Counting to a

hundred wouldn't help, but maybe a few deep breaths would calm him enough that he could give his father a measured reply rather than an angry retort.

"First of all," he said slowly, "Opal's not a whore. Secondly, Edgar may have been born in the North, but he didn't fight at Gettysburg or anywhere else. And, thirdly and probably most importantly, this is not your roof. It's mine."

Pa glared at him for a moment. If he expected Travis to back down, he was wrong. Though Travis had spent the years since his mother died trying to placate his father, this was one time when he would not capitulate.

When the silence grew uncomfortable, Pa pounded his chair arm. " 'Pears to me you're trying to make living here uncomfortable for me. Next thing I know, you'll be telling me to move out."

Travis shook his head. "I'd never do that. You're my father, and you'll have a home with me as long as you want. All I ask is that you treat Opal and Edgar with civility."

Pa continued to glare at him. "You're asking a lot. It won't be easy."

Nothing with his father was.

"Edgar's back and he's now a deputy."

Catherine made no attempt to hide her surprise when Lydia told her what had happened. Though she should have been making a fresh batch of candy, Lydia hadn't wanted her friend to hear the news through the grapevine, and so she'd come to Catherine's house as soon as supper was over. Now they sat in the kitchen, glasses of buttermilk in front of them.

Shaking her head, Catherine said, "And I thought the most exciting thing that happened today was when Nate's nephews found a rattlesnake nest on the school grounds."

Lydia shuddered. She still hadn't become accustomed to the presence of poisonous snakes in Cimarron Creek. "I'm glad my news is happier. It was a relief to know Edgar's alive. Opal never gave up hope, but I had my doubts. So did Travis."

Catherine was silent for a moment, her expression thoughtful. When she spoke, her voice was soft. "I probably shouldn't say anything, but we're friends, aren't we?"

Lydia nodded, wondering where this was leading.

"It's just that I can't help noticing." Catherine paused again, as if she were choosing her words. "At first I thought I was mistaken, but it kept happening. Even now when we were discussing Edgar."

Feeling as if she were walking through a dense fog, unable to identify familiar landmarks, Lydia stared at her friend. "I have no idea what you're talking about."

"Travis," Catherine said, as if that would make everything clear. "I've seen the way you look when you're with him, but it happens even when he's not here. All you have to do is pronounce his name and your face changes. It softens, and your eyes get this faraway starry look."

Lydia felt the blood drain from her face. "I had no idea." Just as suddenly as the blood had drained, it rushed back, coloring her cheeks.

Reaching over to put her hand on Lydia's, Catherine smiled. "Don't be embarrassed. Your reaction is perfectly natural. Travis has stolen your heart."

He wasn't a coward, Travis told himself as he headed toward Aunt Bertha's house. He'd remained at home long enough to see Edgar and Opal settled in the bedroom farthest from Pa. He'd stayed through the unusually silent supper. Edgar and Opal hadn't seemed to mind. They'd spent most of the meal staring at each other, as if they still couldn't believe they'd been reunited.

Pa, perhaps mindful of Travis's admonition to be civil, had said nothing beyond "pass the biscuits," but Travis could see the anger stewing and had no desire to be there when it erupted. That wasn't cowardice; it was prudence. Besides, he wanted — no, he needed — to see Lydia again.

"Lydia's off visiting Catherine," Aunt Bertha said when she opened the door. "I tried to tell her she ought to move in with us rather than live alone, but Catherine refused. Said she couldn't impose on me. As if it would be an imposition." Aunt Bertha gestured toward the sweeping stairway. "I've got enough room to house half of Cimarron Creek. Besides, it would be good for both Catherine and Lydia. Young folks need to be together."

Without stopping to catch her breath, Aunt Bertha took Travis's arm and led him inside the house. "I know I'm no substitute for a pretty young girl, but I hope you'll keep me company for a few minutes. There's something I've been wanting to talk to you about."

Travis followed Aunt Bertha into the parlor, knowing there was no way to refuse her invitation. Even if he claimed sheriff's business, she would have insisted he could delay it for a few minutes. Experience had taught Travis it was easier to simply agree.

Declining her offer of a piece of candy, Travis settled into the chair Aunt Bertha indicated and waited for her to make whatever announcement she had planned. He didn't have to wait long.

"It's customary to ask a father's permission, but since that's not possible, I want you to know I approve. It's clear to me that you have feelings for her, and I don't believe I'm mistaken in thinking she returns them." Travis's confusion must have been evident, because Aunt Bertha cleared her throat and continued. "What I'm trying to say is that you have my permission to marry Lydia."

Marry Lydia. The idea had occupied Travis's thoughts for weeks, and though he'd tried to tell himself it was a bad idea, he had failed. Aunt Bertha was right. He did have feelings for Lydia. Oh, why mince words? He loved Lydia, and he wanted nothing more than to marry her.

"I can't."

Aunt Bertha's jaw dropped. "Why on earth not? You two are perfect for each other."

But they weren't. Lydia might be perfect for him, but he was far from perfect for her. She'd already been disappointed in love once. There was no way Travis would risk her future happiness by asking her to be his wife.

"You're right that I love her, but that's the reason I can't marry her. I can't bear the thought of Lydia ending up like my mother. I heard Ma crying, Aunt Bertha. I know how unhappy she was. She claimed it wasn't Pa's fault, but . . ."

"It wasn't his fault." Aunt Bertha did not let Travis finish his sentence. "Abe did his best to make her happy, but the one thing he couldn't do was be Chet."

"Chet? Who's Chet?" Travis had never heard the name.

"He's the man your mother loved." Aunt Bertha continued as if she hadn't dropped a bombshell. "Cynthia met him when she was in Houston visiting some cousins. The way she told the story, it was love at first sight. They planned to marry when the summer was over, but then Chet caught swamp fever and died. When she came back to Cimarron Creek, it was as if the life had been sucked out of her."

Aunt Bertha leaned forward slightly, her hands clasped in her lap. "Abe thought he could help her, and heaven knows Cynthia needed help. Both Jonas and I urged him to wait, but your father always was a stubborn man. He was determined to marry Cynthia, even knowing she might never love him. To give him his due, I think Abe made her as happy as she could be. It was clear Cynthia doted on both you and your sister, but I could see there was an emptiness deep inside her that nothing would fill."

Travis stared at the far wall, feeling as if the foundation of his life had been shifted. So much was clear now. It was no wonder Pa was as cantankerous as he was. Travis couldn't imagine what it must have been like, loving a woman yet knowing she would never return that love. It wasn't, however, difficult to understand how frustration and a sense of failure could change into anger.

And Ma? What must it have been like to have lost her true love? When she looked at Travis and his sister with their obvious resemblance to Pa, did she dream of what her children might have looked like if Chet had been their father? Travis's heart ached for both of his parents.

"You may look a lot like your pa," Aunt Bertha said, almost as if she'd read his thoughts, "but you're like your ma in one respect: there's only one true love for you. Don't let her slip away."

22

"I don't know how to thank you. I've never seen Aunt Bertha so excited." Lydia spoke softly, though she suspected there was no need and that Aunt Bertha was so caught up in her own thoughts in the backseat of the surrey that she would not hear anything either Lydia or Travis said. "I don't think she's slept more than a few hours each night since you told her we could go."

It had been over a week since Edgar's return to Cimarron Creek. While the town was still reeling from the news, the surprise had made it an exceptionally good week for Cimarron Sweets. The women had all wanted to talk to Opal, but rather than admit that they were indulging in gossip, they preferred to pretend that they'd developed a sudden yen for a pound of fudge or a dozen chocolate creams. No matter what excuse they used, when they left the store, they could be overheard discussing how well

Opal looked.

The focus on Opal pleased Lydia for several reasons. First, and most important, was that Opal was being accepted by the townspeople. Though they'd been polite in the past, Lydia had had the impression that they were watching Opal carefully, almost as if she were on probation. Edgar's return seemed to have changed that. Now Opal was being treated like a full-fledged resident of Cimarron Creek.

That was good. So too was the fact that with Opal being the center of attention, no one was taking particular notice of Lydia. Ever since the day Catherine had declared that she wore a special look when she spoke of Travis, Lydia had worried that others might guess her secret. It was true that she cared for him. It was true that his happiness was more important to her than her own. It was true that she sometimes dreamt of sharing her life with him. All those were true, but did they mean she was in love? Lydia wasn't sure.

What she was sure of was that Opal was a woman in love. There was no ignoring the change in her, the new lightness in her step, the way happiness practically bubbled out of her. Opal's face brightened, and she became almost beautiful each time Edgar entered the store. Though his duties as a deputy sheriff did not compel him to visit each of the business establishments on Main, Edgar had made it a habit to do so several times a day, thus giving him an excuse to check on his wife.

Opal was thriving, and so was Edgar. Each day his limp seemed less pronounced, perhaps because as his confidence grew, he forgot about his leg. All Lydia knew was that she had never seen either of them looking happier. Even Travis seemed less worried now that he had someone to help him keep the peace.

"It feels good to be out of Cimarron Creek," he said as they crested another hill. "I'm trying to put my worries aside."

Lydia glanced at the backseat, still amazed that the normally garrulous Aunt Bertha was content to sit so quietly, apparently enjoying the late September sunshine and the pastoral landscape. Though she had sighed heavily as they left Cimarron Creek, since then a small smile had creased her face.

Lydia turned to Travis. "Are you afraid Edgar's attacker will do something while we're gone?"

He shook his head. "I was thinking closer to home. I hope Pa won't cause Opal and

Edgar too much trouble."

Lydia had wondered what kind of reception Opal and Edgar — especially Edgar — would receive and had been surprised by Opal's description of their first days living with Travis and his father. "Opal says he's pleasant to her."

Raising an eyebrow, Travis asked, "Did she also tell you that he ignores Edgar?"

"No, but that's probably better than yelling at him." Opal would have hated having her husband referred to as the Cursed Enemy.

"No question about that," Travis agreed. "Edgar says he isn't bothered by the silence. He claims he's relieved to have Opal away from the Spur, but I can't help wondering if the truce — if you can call it that — will last."

Since they were both concerned about tiring Aunt Bertha, Lydia and Travis expected to be gone four or five days, perhaps longer if they found something that led them to Joan.

"Edgar can always walk away," she suggested.

"Or arrest Pa." Travis chuckled as he flicked the reins. "That would keep the town buzzing, wouldn't it?"

The hours passed more quickly than

Lydia had thought possible as she and Travis talked about everything and nothing at all. She heard about his sister and her daughter, while she shared amusing stories about her former pupils. It didn't seem to matter which subject they chose. What mattered was being with Travis and knowing they were helping Aunt Bertha.

When the sun reached its zenith, Travis chose a spot shaded by massive live oaks for their lunch stop, and the three of them devoured the fried chicken, hard-boiled eggs, peach pie, and cool tea that Aunt Bertha had prepared last night. As soon as Lydia had packed the remaining food, Travis assisted her and Aunt Bertha back into the surrey, then continued toward Ladreville. Though he'd explained it might have been possible to reach their destination in one day if they left early and made no stops, Travis had suggested they break the journey into two days for Aunt Bertha's benefit. And so they stopped at dusk, enjoying supper at a small hotel.

As she savored the beef stew and biscuits the innkeeper provided, Aunt Bertha smiled. "I haven't been this excited since the day before my wedding." She laid a hand over her heart, as if to slow its beat. "I can't wait to see Sterling and meet his wife. She and

I've exchanged dozens of letters over the years, so I feel like I know her, but we've never actually met. It seems like a dream come true that we'll be together tomorrow. I just know they're the key to finding Joan."

Though Lydia wanted to urge caution, she refused to do anything that would dampen Aunt Bertha's enthusiasm. They would reach Ladreville tomorrow, and then Aunt Bertha's questions would be answered. "I hope so."

Travis simply nodded, as if he shared Lydia's concerns, and continued to clean his plate. When he swallowed the last bite of the apple cobbler, he turned to Aunt Bertha. "Would you like to stretch your legs before retiring? I thought I'd take a short walk."

Aunt Bertha shook her head. "I'm going to try to sleep, but don't let that stop you and Lydia." She gave Lydia a quick smile. "Don't worry about waking me when you return. I'm a deep sleeper."

Though that was a lie and she would probably disturb the other woman when she entered the room they were sharing, Lydia simply nodded. "I'm worried about her," she said a few minutes later as she and Travis strolled down the road away from the hotel. A quarter moon shone from the ebony sky, its reflected light doing nothing to dispel the concerns that weighed so heavily on Lydia.

"What will she do if she can't find Joan?" Even though Aunt Bertha had once admitted that she knew it was unlikely she would discover anything that might lead her to her daughter, her excitement today told Lydia she had new hopes. Lydia hated the thought that those hopes might be dashed.

Travis laid his hand on top of the one Lydia had put on the crook of his elbow. "At least she'll have tried, and you'll be there to comfort her."

What comforted Lydia was the warmth of Travis's hand on hers. Though they often walked together, this was the first time he'd kept his hand on hers, and it felt good. Oh, so good.

"You've made a big difference in Aunt Bertha's life," Travis said. While it was difficult to see his face in the darkness, Lydia heard his voice deepen. "For that matter, you've made a big difference in mine."

She had? The thought caused Lydia's heart to skip a beat. There had been times when she had thought he might return the tender feelings she had developed for him, but never before had Travis said anything like this. "What do you mean?" Though she longed to know how she'd affected Travis,

Lydia focused on Aunt Bertha. "I feel like she's the one who gives, and I'm the taker."

Travis stopped and turned to face Lydia. "You're wrong about that. You've given Aunt Bertha a new reason to live. Before you came, she was lonely and discouraged. Now she's energized again. She reminds me of the Aunt Bertha I knew ten years ago."

Travis tightened his grip on Lydia's hand, the warmth of his palm sending pulses of delight through her veins. "I won't say you've taken her daughter's place, but you've become the granddaughter Aunt Bertha always wanted."

That was more than Lydia had dared hope for, and tears of joy filled her eyes as she said, "I couldn't love her more if she was my real grandmother. She made me feel welcome my first day in Cimarron Creek, and she hasn't stopped since."

"I notice you didn't say that about me."

Though Travis's voice held a mocking tone that told Lydia he was joking, she decided to answer seriously. "You were preoccupied the day I arrived."

He laughed. "That's one way to describe it. All I could think about when I went to meet the stagecoach was that trouble was coming."

"And then I stepped off it and proved you right."

"Hardly." His voice turned serious. "I was expecting my father. I knew he'd have nothing good to say, but instead of an angry old man, I saw a beautiful young woman. My life hasn't been the same since."

"Because now you can have all the fudge and toffee you want."

Travis laughed again. "That's true. I'm not discounting the appeal of your candies, but that's not the biggest change in my life. I don't know how you do it, Lydia, but somehow you make me laugh. That's the nicest gift anyone's ever given me."

As he looked down at her, Travis smiled. "It's too beautiful an evening to waste talking."

"What did you have in mind?"

His smile widened. "This."

Travis placed his finger under Lydia's chin and tipped it up. Then, slowly, as if he had all the time in the world, he lowered his lips to hers.

Lydia had heard about kisses. She'd dreamt about them. She'd even experienced one the day Edgar had asked her to marry him and another the day he'd left Syracuse. But never had she known a kiss like this one. The touch of Travis's lips on hers sent waves of pleasure up her arms and down her spine, turning her into a tingling mass of nerves. She tasted the sweetness of apple cobbler, smelled the fresh scent that was uniquely Travis's, and heard his faint intake of breath as he paused for a second before deepening the kiss.

It was wonderful, marvelous, stupendous. Though Lydia was a teacher who prided herself on her extensive vocabulary, the reality of Travis's kiss was greater than anything she had ever imagined. Words were inadequate to describe how she felt, how being so close to Travis made her senses sing. All that mattered were the unforgettable sensations his touch was creating.

When her legs threatened to buckle from sheer delight, Lydia leaned against Travis and felt the reassuring warmth of his arms around her. This was what a kiss was meant to be: sweet, sincere and oh, so special, because she was sharing it with Travis.

23

"You look as excited as me."

Lydia smiled at the woman seated next to her. Aunt Bertha was her talkative self, which was one of the reasons Lydia sat in the back of the surrey this morning. The other and equally important reason was that she feared the older woman would guess what had happened last night if she saw Lydia with Travis.

Ever since her conversation with Catherine, Lydia had been concerned that Aunt Bertha might guess the depth of her feelings for Travis. She suspected it would be even more difficult to hide those feelings if she were so close to Travis again. As it was, she had lain awake, reliving those wonderful moments when she'd been in his arms. Then, when she'd finally fallen asleep, she had dreamt of him, and this morning when he'd smiled at her across the breakfast table, she'd felt a blush rise to her cheeks.

It was silly. He hadn't promised her anything. He hadn't said he loved her, and as far as Lydia knew, he was still determined not to marry. But he had kissed her — kissed her as if she were a desirable woman, not simply a friend — and that had her acting like one of her pupils.

Lydia wasn't a young girl. She was a grown woman who ought to be able to control her emotions. She and Travis needed to talk, and when they did she would learn what, if anything, he meant by the kiss, but in the meantime, Aunt Bertha deserved all Lydia's attention.

"I am excited," she told the older woman. "It's another beautiful day for traveling, and I'm enjoying visiting a new part of the Hill Country." Lydia turned and gestured toward the verdant landscape. "It's not quite as hilly here as around Cimarron Creek, is it?"

Aunt Bertha nodded. "That's not the only difference you'll find when we get to Ladreville. Sterling and Ruth tell me it's a special town." Without waiting for Lydia's response, she continued. "I'm sure you know that this part of Texas has many German settlers. You can tell that from some of the towns' names. No one would ever think that Fredericksburg or New Braunfels were

Spanish settlements, would they? What makes Ladreville unique is that its founders came from Alsace-Lorraine. There are both French and Germans there."

Relieved that Aunt Bertha did not appear to have noticed her attraction to Travis, Lydia raised an eyebrow. "And they're not fighting? As I remember from my history books, the French and the Germans were at war more often than not."

"Sterling said there were some difficulties at first, and they still worship in different churches. Believe it or not, when Sterling arrived, his parishioners were unhappy that he was an American rather than a German. I never did hear how he overcame that, but he claims that's long since resolved, and even though a few of the old-timers still speak French or German at home, English has become their common language. Ruth says even though the War Between the States divided them as it did so many towns, they're all Americans. She claims it's a pretty and peaceful town." Aunt Bertha pursed her lips. "I wouldn't have sent Joan there if I hadn't been certain she would be safe. But she wasn't, was she?"

This was the first time Aunt Bertha had said anything like this, and the way her hands trembled told Lydia just how worried

she was. "You said she left of her own volition," she reminded the older woman.

"What if she didn't? What if someone
abducted her the way they did Edgar?"

It was a frightening thought and one that
would chill anyone's blood, especially a loving mother's. Lydia wondered if this fear
had plagued Aunt Bertha for twenty years
or if it was the result of what had happened
in Cimarron Creek recently. "Let's not bor-
row trouble," she said. "In just a few hours,
we'll be in Ladreville. You'll find the truth
there." And if God answered Lydia's
prayers, the truth would bring Aunt Bertha
peace.

It was late morning when they entered the
town where Joan Henderson had once lived.
Though she hadn't known what to expect,
Lydia found herself enchanted by the obvious European influence. The two-story half-
timbered buildings with their steeply
pitched roofs looked like something out of a
picture book, and while the residents were
dressed similarly to those who shopped at
Cimarron Sweets, the stores in Ladreville
bore little resemblance to the ones in
Cimarron Creek. Window boxes filled with
flowers and cascading vines combined with
the unusual architecture to make the shops
more appealing than any Lydia had seen.

She made a mental note to talk to the other shopkeepers in Cimarron Creek about adding window boxes next spring.

Ladreville might be charming, but the way Aunt Bertha wrung her hands told Lydia her anxiety was increasing the closer they came to Joan's last known residence.

"This must be it," Aunt Bertha said as they approached a block with two churches. "Sterling said the parsonage was next to his church on the corner of Rhinestrasse."

The settlers, apparently paying tribute to both their past and their present, had named the east-west streets after rivers: Rhinestrasse, rue de la Seine, and Potomac Street. When Lydia commented on the names, hoping to distract Aunt Bertha, the older woman told her the north-south streets were called Hochstrasse, rue du Marché, and Washington.

The town was picturesque, and as far as Lydia could tell, it was as peaceful as Ruth Russell had claimed. Lydia could only pray that it held the answers Aunt Bertha sought as well as storybook charm.

When they reached the middle of the block, Travis pulled on the reins, stopping the surrey in front of the simpler of the two churches. They had arrived. It was only after he'd helped both Lydia and Aunt Bertha out and offered his arm to Aunt Bertha that he turned to Lydia. "That looks like the sheriff's office across the street. Once I get you two settled, I'll pay him a call."

It was a good idea and told Lydia that while Travis had not joined the conversation, he'd heard what Aunt Bertha had said. If the current sheriff had been in Ladreville twenty years ago, he would know if there had been any suggestion of foul play when Joan Henderson left town. Even if he was new to the job, there might be records.

Before Lydia could comment on Travis's suggestion, a man and woman emerged from the parsonage. Aunt Bertha's little gasp left no doubt that she recognized her cousin. As they closed the distance, Lydia searched for a resemblance between them. While Aunt Bertha was short and plump, the man was tall and very thin. While Bertha's hair was silver, his was gunmetal gray. But as he came closer, Lydia saw that Sterling Russell's hazel eyes were the same shape as Aunt Bertha's. Though the man was fifteen years her junior, it was clear they shared a common heritage.

Pastor Russell pulled his cousin into a hug. "Bertha, I'm so glad you came. It's been far too long since I've seen you. Letters are a poor substitute for being together." He gave the blonde-haired woman who appeared to be in her early forties a fond glance. Though no one would call her beautiful, Ruth Russell's warm smile left no doubt that she seconded her husband's welcome. "I'd like you to meet my wife. Ruth is excited to finally meet the cousin who's written us so many letters."

Aunt Bertha returned the hug, then gestured toward Lydia and Travis. "It's thanks to these two wonderful young people that I was able to come."

When the introductions were complete, Ruth led everyone inside the parsonage. "I was hoping you'd arrive in time for the noon meal," she said as she gestured toward a dining room where five places were set at a table that could accommodate a dozen. "I have a pot roast just about ready. And no, I don't need any help," she said, forestalling the inevitable offer. "Even before I became Sterling's wife, I was used to feeding my family."

She gestured toward a small room that Lydia discovered had been outfitted with a basin, a ewer of warm water, and a newly laundered towel. "You can freshen up in there."

Minutes later they were all gathered around the table, bowing their heads as the minister offered thanks for their safe arrival and the food.

Throughout the meal, Lydia watched Aunt Bertha. Though the food was delicious and the conversation pleasant, she was more subdued than usual, and Lydia knew she was anxious to learn what she could about her daughter. But, seemingly mindful of being a guest rather than the hostess, Aunt Bertha said nothing until dessert was finished.

"I wondered . . ."

Before she could complete her sentence, Ruth looked from Aunt Bertha to Lydia and smiled. "I wasn't sure how many nights you'd be able to stay with us. We have two spare rooms. Sterling and I want you to be comfortable, so you'll each have your own." She turned to Travis. "Lawrence and Harriet Wood — he's the mayor and sheriff, she's my older sister — live right across the street. They've offered to have you stay with them to give the ladies privacy. Besides, Sterling and I thought you might want to talk to another sheriff."

Travis nodded. "I do indeed."

Travis liked Lawrence Wood on sight. The former Ranger who'd been Ladreville's mayor and sheriff for almost a quarter century was an easy man to like as long as you were on the right side of the law. Though his blond hair was now liberally laced with silver, the expression in Lawrence's deep blue eyes left no doubt that he had lost none of his determination with age.

"I wish I could help you," he said when Travis asked about Joan Henderson. "I remember the girl, because she used to go to church each Sunday and sit in the first pew with Ruth, despite the whispers that always seemed to accompany her. Folks in Ladreville weren't used to unwed mothers."

"Folks in Cimarron Creek still aren't." Travis suspected that was part of the reason Aunt Bertha had never admitted what had happened to Joan. "My aunt's worried that Joan may have met with foul play. Do you think that's possible?"

Lawrence was silent for a moment. "I suppose anything's possible, but I'd say it was highly unlikely. There were no strangers in town then. The couple who adopted the baby didn't arrive for another week."

"But it might not have been a stranger." Travis looked around Lawrence's office, not surprised at how similar it was to his. Though the exteriors of many of Ladreville's buildings were unusual, the interiors resembled those of Cimarron Creek.

"You got a reason for saying that?"

"Yes. We've had some problems in Cimarron Creek, and they all point to the perpetrator being someone local. The problem is, I can't figure out who's behind them."

"Sometimes an outsider's perspective helps. Want to talk?"

Travis did, but an hour later, though he and Lawrence had discussed a variety of possibilities, nothing felt right.

"Thanks, anyway." Even though he felt no closer to a solution, Travis appreciated the older man's ideas.

"Anything else you want to talk about? If not, I need to make my rounds."

When Lawrence left after showing Travis the room that would be his for as long as he was in Ladreville, Travis stretched out on the bed and closed his eyes. Though it felt strange to be trying to sleep while it was light outside, he couldn't deny the fatigue that had caught up with him. Even though Edgar had taken over some of his responsibilities, Travis rarely got a full night's sleep.

He had expected to sleep well last night, knowing Cimarron Creek was miles away and there was nothing he could do for its residents. Instead, Travis had lain awake for hours, his thoughts focused on one particular resident.

A grin lit his face as he remembered those wonderful moments when he'd held Lydia in his arms. Nothing in his life could compare to the sheer joy he'd felt when he'd wrapped his arms around her and pressed his lips to hers. If he lived to be a hundred, he knew he'd still recall the softness of her cheeks and the faint scent of lavender that clung to her hair. And then there were her lips. Even her finest chocolate could not compare to their sweetness.

Travis had thought about kissing Lydia. He'd even dreamt about it, but his thoughts and dreams paled against the reality of holding her so close that he could hear her heart beat and feel the warmth of her skin. It had been wonderful, unforgettable, life-changing, for the kisses they'd shared had confirmed his belief that Aunt Bertha was right: Lydia was the one and only woman for him.

It was too soon to talk of marriage. Even if Travis were certain Lydia was ready — and he was far from certain about that — she deserved a courtship. A real courtship, not the bungled attempts Warner and Nate had made. But before he could begin that, they needed to finish their business here.

"Normally I would give you our largest

guest room," Ruth told Aunt Bertha as she led the way up the stairs, "but I thought you might prefer the room where Joan stayed."

When Ruth opened the door to the room she had prepared for Aunt Bertha, Lydia saw the pleasure in the older woman's eyes. It was a simple room, furnished with an iron bedstead, a bureau with more than its share of dings, and a small bedside table. Compared to Aunt Bertha's bedchamber at home, this appeared to have been designed for a servant, and yet Aunt Bertha seemed to glow. She touched the bedspread almost reverently, then drew the curtain aside and looked out the window. "I know some things have changed, but I can't tell you what it means to know that this is what Joan saw each day."

Ruth patted her shoulder. "Take your time getting settled. When you're ready, come downstairs. I'll put some tea on to steep, and we'll talk."

Travis and Sterling had already excused themselves, leaving the women alone. Though part of her wished Travis were here, if only so she could convince herself that she had not imagined last night, Lydia suspected Ruth had been wise to plan a smaller gathering. Lydia had asked Aunt

Bertha whether she preferred to meet with only Ruth, but Aunt Bertha had insisted Lydia accompany her. And so here they were, three women seated in the parsonage parlor.

As she'd promised, Ruth provided a tea tray and an afternoon of reminiscences. Though it had been twenty years, the parson's wife made Joan's stay here come to life as she recounted tiny details that Aunt Bertha absorbed like a thirsty flower after a drought.

"We never talked about it," Ruth said when she'd told Aunt Bertha how Joan had insisted on helping prepare meals and clean the parsonage, "but I sensed that she wanted to keep the baby. Not at first, mind you, but as the months passed, she started calling it 'my baby.' "

Though Aunt Bertha's lips trembled with emotion, she said nothing, letting Ruth continue. "Joan held the baby for a few minutes after she was born. I've seen plenty of new mothers, but I've never seen so much sorrow mixed with joy. That's when I knew Joan didn't want to give her daughter to strangers."

Ruth paused for a second, her eyes searching Aunt Bertha's face for her reaction. Other than closing her eyes in what Lydia suspected was an attempt to compose herself, Aunt Bertha said nothing. For once in her life, the woman who often talked practically nonstop was speechless.

When Aunt Bertha opened her eyes again and nodded, Ruth continued her story. "I told Joan she didn't have to let them adopt the baby. I knew it might be impossible for her to return to Cimarron Creek, but I assured Joan that Sterling and I would help her. She just shook her head and said it was too late. The next morning she was gone."

"And you have no idea where she went." Lydia made it a statement rather than a question.

"None. She didn't come down for breakfast, and when I went upstairs, everything was gone. It was as if she'd never been here."

Tears trickled from the corners of Aunt Bertha's eyes as she spoke for the first time since Ruth had begun to recount Joan's final days in Ladreville. "Are you sure she left on her own?"

"Yes." Ruth's voice rang with conviction. "I probably should have realized what she intended, because she hadn't planned anything after the baby's birth. Before that, Joan would talk about what we were going to do for the next few weeks, but as the time for the baby drew near, she stopped planning."

When Aunt Bertha said nothing, Lydia asked one of the questions she would have wanted answered had it been her daughter who'd disappeared. "How did she leave? On a stagecoach?"

Ruth shook her head. "The coaches didn't come through here then. No horses were missing, so she must have walked." Her blue eyes radiated sorrow as she said, "Lawrence searched everywhere, but there were no traces. Joan simply vanished."

Though it wasn't what Aunt Bertha had hoped to learn, it was an answer.

24

Supper that night was quieter than lunch had been, with Aunt Bertha so lost in her thoughts that she barely responded to the conversation. Lydia saw signs of fatigue and was glad when at Ruth and Sterling's urging, Aunt Bertha agreed to stay another day. She might not admit it, but she needed time to rest as well as more time in Ladreville. Lydia knew without asking that Aunt Bertha would never return, that whatever memories she made while she was here would have to last for the rest of her life.

The next day Priscilla Webster, the tall, slender midwife whose strawberry blonde hair had only begun to be threaded with silver, recounted what she remembered of Joan's delivery.

"It was one of the easiest first births I've ever attended," she told Aunt Bertha. "Joan was such a sweet woman that it broke my heart to know she wasn't going to raise that child. She would have been a wonderful mother."

Today no tears rolled down Aunt Bertha's cheeks, leading Lydia to wonder if she'd spent the night crying and had run out of tears. Instead of moisture, her eyes were filled with sorrow. "It was my fault," she said, her voice harsh with regret. "I'll bear that guilt forever."

Though Lydia tried to comfort her, nothing she said had any effect. Aunt Bertha had found some answers, but they weren't the ones she'd prayed for.

"I should have expected it," she said the next day as they left Ladreville. Once again she and Lydia shared the backseat of the surrey. "I was twenty years too late."

When they stopped at the inn where they'd have supper and stay overnight, Aunt Bertha pleaded fatigue and asked for her food to be brought to her room. "I'm afraid I'm not good company today," she said when Lydia said she'd join her there. "I need to be alone."

"The pain will ease with time," Travis predicted as he and Lydia shared a meal of rabbit stewed with prunes.

Though Lydia knew there was truth to his words, she also knew the trip had reopened wounds that had barely healed, despite the passage of two decades. Children held a special place in a woman's heart, Lydia's mother had told her the day Lydia had asked why she hadn't tried to find her husband.

"I knew he'd made his decision about me, and I was afraid that if he saw me again, he'd insist on taking you," she said. "That would have been unbearable. I could live without him, but losing you would have broken my heart. Lydia, when you've carried a child beneath your heart for nine months, you'll know what I mean. That child is the best part of you." She had gripped Lydia's hand as she added, "I would have done anything to keep you safe and happy. Anything. And that feeling won't stop as long as I draw breath."

But Aunt Bertha hadn't been able to keep her daughter safe, and now she was bearing the pain of knowing that Joan hadn't wanted to give up her own daughter. Lydia's heart ached for the older woman.

"I'm afraid tonight's not a good night for a walk," Travis said when they'd finished their meal.

Lydia nodded. The steady rain that had started an hour before they arrived at the inn had intensified, turning the roads into muddy tracks. Perhaps that was for the best.

As much as she longed for another of those unforgettable kisses, Lydia felt almost guilty about the smiles she and Travis had exchanged today. It seemed wrong to be happy when Aunt Bertha was heartbroken.

By morning, the rain had ended and the sun had dried the road's surface. Aunt Bertha's mood appeared to have improved along with the weather, and she gave a running commentary on the countryside they were crossing, telling Lydia what she knew about each of the ranches they passed, pointing out the various birds that perched in trees, speculating on the probability of seeing a javelina. Until they reached Cimarron Creek and Travis helped her out of the surrey, the one subject she did not touch was the time they'd spent in Ladreville.

"Thank you, Travis," she said as he opened the front door for her. "I won't pretend the trip ended the way I had hoped, but I'm grateful we went. Talking to everyone and seeing where my granddaughter was born was helpful. Thank you."

Though Travis simply nodded, the pain Lydia saw reflected in his eyes told her he too wished the trip had been more fruitful.

"Would you make us some tea, Lydia?" Aunt Bertha asked when Travis had headed to the livery to return the surrey. She removed her hat and gloves, laying them carefully on the console table in the main hallway. "If there are any chocolate creams left, I'd like a couple of them too."

Ten minutes later, Lydia joined Aunt Bertha in the parlor. The woman's expression was so woebegone that instead of her normal chair on the opposite side of the table, Lydia took the seat next to Aunt Bertha on the horsehair settee and wrapped an arm around her shoulders. "I'm sorry we didn't find any clues to your daughter," she said.

Aunt Bertha nodded. "I knew it was a long shot. I wasn't lying to Travis when I said I was glad we'd gone. The trip made two things very clear to me. First, I won't see Joan again this side of heaven."

Lydia tightened her grip on Aunt Bertha's shoulders, wanting to dispute that belief. "It's always possible that she'll come back to you."

Shaking her head, Aunt Bertha said, "If Joan wanted to return, she would have done so by now. I said my farewells to her back in Ladreville. Now it's time to put the past behind me and focus on the future. I always wanted to plan a wedding."

The abrupt change of subject startled Lydia. "Whose wedding?"

"Why, yours, of course. I may be old, but I'm not blind. I saw what's happening between you and Travis. My nephew is a fine man, Lydia. More than that, he's the man God intends for you. That's the second thing that became clear to me while we were gone."

She gave Lydia a look that said she did not want to be interrupted. "I've always found Romans 8:28 to be a beautiful verse, and it's true, every word of it. God does have a plan for us, and he does bring something good out of even the worst times in our lives. I may not have found what I sought in Ladreville, but I heard God's message. He told me to put the past behind me and think about the future. If I do that, I know the future will be a happy one. I may not have Joan, but you and Travis will be my family."

"But . . ." Lydia wasn't certain what to say. Even though there had been no more kisses, Travis's hands had lingered on her waist when he'd helped her in and out of the surrey, and his eyes had sparkled when he'd caught her gaze. There'd been a hundred little things that drew them closer, and each of them had made Lydia feel special.

Aunt Bertha gave Lydia a smile tinged with regret. "There's no need to be embarrassed. Love is one of God's greatest gifts. Don't make the mistake I did with Joan and let it slip away. Whatever you do, don't waste your chance at happiness."

If his smile were any wider, his face would crack, Travis told himself as he drove the surrey back to the livery. He needed to stop smiling or someone would notice.

Someone did.

"You look like the trip agreed with you," Porter said when Travis hopped down from the buggy.

"It did." In ways he would never tell Porter. As long as he lived, Travis knew he'd never forget how good — how right — it felt to hold Lydia in his arms. Now they were back. Travis could begin his courtship.

"And Aunt Bertha got to visit her kinfolk."

"Yep." Visiting Sterling and Ruth had been the official reason for the trip, because, even though it had been twenty years, Aunt Bertha still didn't want anyone to know what had happened to Joan. "Her cousins are as nice as can be. They made us all feel welcome."

Porter looked up as he unfastened the horses' harnesses. "I don't understand why Lydia had to go."

Because she turned what might have been

a chore into the best five days Travis could remember. But that was something else Porter didn't need to know. He tried to deflect his cousin's attention with a question. "Did you ever try to figure out why Aunt Bertha does anything?"

"Can't say that I have." Porter chuckled as if recalling at least one incident. "Once she sets her mind on something, there's no gainsaying her."

"Exactly. By the way, that surrey drove as smoothly as you said. I couldn't have asked for a finer vehicle." While Porter preened from the praise, Travis's attention was snagged by the arrival of his cousin's cat. "Homer looks as sleek as ever."

"He's a good cat. With him around, I never worry about mice or rats spooking the horses. That old tomcat is worth his weight in gold." Porter shot Travis a speculative look. "You ought to see about getting yourself one. They're good companions."

"I may just do that." But before he did that, Travis had a different kind of companion in mind. After he paid Porter for the surrey rental, Travis headed home, whistling with each step he took. Aunt Bertha might not have found what she sought on the trip, but Travis had found more than he'd expected. The time with Lydia had shown him that she was the woman he wanted as his wife. But before he asked her to marry him, there was one thing he had to do.

"It's about time you got back," Pa groused as Travis entered the house. "Did Bertha find that daughter of hers?"

Travis blinked in surprise. He'd told no one the real reason for the trip. "No," he said shortly, "but how did you know that was why we went to Ladreville?"

Pa shrugged as if the answer should have been obvious. "Because I talk to Bertha. You don't think I stay in this house all day, do you? Some days I visit her, and we talk about . . ." Pa's words trailed off, making Travis wonder if he had been about to say "your mother." Instead, his lips curved and he snarled, "You've got a lot of nerve leaving me alone with those two."

While other things might have changed in five days, it was obvious Pa's attitude toward their guests had not. "I thought you liked Opal's cooking."

"It's better than yours. The gal wouldn't be so bad if it weren't for that husband of hers." Pa spat the words as if they were a curse. "That Yankee's got no right being in this house."

Travis tried not to sigh at the memory of how many times they'd had this particular discussion. "The war's been over for more than fifteen years. We're all Americans now."

"That's what she said." Pa thumped the floor with his cane. "It's easy for young whippersnappers like her to say that. She didn't watch her brothers in arms get killed."

Opal had endured something even worse, but that wasn't Travis's story to share. "Maybe not, but her husband was beaten and left for dead by someone who most likely spent his whole life right here in Cimarron Creek."

Pa frowned. "You don't know that for a fact."

"It's the only answer that makes sense. What doesn't make sense is your attitude. Why can't you admit that the war is over and treat Edgar and Lydia like everyone else?"

Gesturing toward his missing leg, Pa scowled. "That's why. I can't forget — not for a single minute — that the Cursed Enemy took away my leg. As long as I live, I will never welcome one of them beneath this roof."

"Then we've got a problem." This wasn't the way Travis had hoped to introduce the subject, but he couldn't let it go. "I've tolerated your treatment of Edgar because it's temporary. As soon as he can find a house, he and Opal will leave. It won't be the same with Lydia."

"Lydia?" Pa stared at Travis as if he'd suddenly sprouted horns. "You fixing to marry her?"

"If she'll have me, yes. Lydia's the best thing that ever happened to me. I love her, Pa, and I plan to ask her to marry me. If she accepts, I will expect you to treat her with respect. There will be no more silent treatment."

His face mottled with anger, Pa pointed an accusing finger at Travis. "The Bible says to honor thy father."

It was a familiar refrain. In the past, Travis had remained silent, but in the past his future happiness had not been at stake. Today he countered, "The Bible also says a man shall leave his mother and father and cleave unto his wife. The choice is yours, Pa."

"That's no choice. You told me I'd always have a home, and now you're forcing me out." He thumped the floor again. "So be it. I'll go back to Austin and live with Dorcas. At least she had the good sense to marry a Texan."

"Why don't you sleep on it? You might feel differently tomorrow."

"I won't. I'll be on the stagecoach tomorrow."

Perhaps it was wrong, but Travis felt nothing but relief.

25

"The house sure was quiet this morning," Opal said as she piped a yellow rose on top of a chocolate cream.

It was the Monday after Lydia and Aunt Bertha had returned from Ladreville, and life had begun to resume its rhythm. Lydia had spent Saturday at Cimarron Sweets, where a predictably larger than normal number of customers had come, ostensibly to buy candy for their families but actually to inquire about Lydia and Aunt Bertha's trip.

"I can't recall the last time she left town," Mary Gray said as she vacillated between a box of fudge and one of peanut brittle.

"Everyone needs a change of scenery" was Lydia's standard reply. Occasionally she would add something innocuous about the pleasure of visiting family, but she said little to satisfy Cimarron Creek's matrons' curiosity. She'd known they'd barrage Aunt Bertha with questions after church, and they had, but Aunt Bertha, being Aunt Bertha, had provided so many details about Ladreville itself that by the time she was finished, the women had forgotten their original question.

Aunt Bertha had been a bit more forthcoming with Catherine when she and Lydia had joined her for Sunday dinner, admitting that she had not accomplished everything she had hoped in Ladreville, but most of the time, Aunt Bertha had chosen not to speak of the trip. Instead, she had continued to sing Travis's praises whenever she managed to turn the conversation in that direction. Lydia would have appreciated some of the quiet Opal said she'd experienced.

"Edgar and Travis were out investigating Mrs. Pratt's missing hog, and Mr. Whitfield — well, he didn't say a word other than 'pass the jam.' "

"Does he usually talk?" Lydia's limited experience with Travis's father suggested that a quiet morning would be preferable to a tirade.

"Oh my, yes. That man could give Mrs. Henderson a run for her money with his talking. Most of the time he's complaining. He tells me I can't cook half as good as his wife, and he says Travis is wasting himself as sheriff, but it's all bluff. The truth is, he's a lonely man. Reminds me of Jake Haskell. Jake used to come into the Spur just so he'd have someone to talk to."

"I wonder if Travis realizes that." Lydia added a bit more blueberry syrup to the fondant, smiling when it turned the frosting into the exact shade of blue pansies. When Opal had asked for her help in filling an unusually large order of chocolate creams, Lydia had decided to make an extra dozen as a special gift for Aunt Bertha. Though candy wouldn't assuage the pain of not finding Joan, the chocolates topped with her favorite flower might cheer Aunt Bertha.

Travis and his father were a more difficult problem. Lydia knew there was friction between the two men and that Travis despaired of ever resolving it. That was one of the things he had talked about on the ride to Ladreville, how he feared that no matter what he did, he would never be able to please his father. But if Opal was right, the angry outbursts might be a symptom of a different problem, one that could be easier to fix.

Opal shrugged. "I don't know why he wouldn't realize it. It's plain as can be."

"To you, maybe, but that's because you're a woman. Men are different."

"You can say that again." As Opal waggled her eyebrows, both women laughed.

"You girls look like you're having a good morning."

Lydia started at the sound of Aunt Bertha's voice. Trying to act nonchalant, she slid the pansy-topped chocolates into a box. "We are. It feels good to be back to work. Opal did a great job while you and I were gone, but it's fortunate we came back when we did. Hilda Gray ordered twice the usual number of chocolates for her quilting bee."

Aunt Bertha chuckled. "My guess is she found an expensive new dress she wants to order, and half those candies are meant to butter up Porter."

Lydia couldn't help laughing. "So that's why some people call them butter creams."

"I don't understand it." Edgar scowled as he settled into the chair across from Travis. "Things were pretty quiet while you were gone, but you sure can't call today quiet."

Travis was equally surprised by the number of problems reported this morning. "At least you found the hog. Mrs. Pratt was counting on that to feed her family this winter." The missing animal had turned up in a neighbor's vegetable garden, happily rooting among the turnips. With the gate between the two houses closed, no one could explain how the hog had gotten out, but other than the loss of a few turnips, there had been a happy ending to that call.

Edgar nodded. "Mrs. Pratt was so glad to have him back that she promised to invite me and Opal for a ham dinner this year." Taking a slug of the coffee Travis brought to the office each day, Edgar nodded again. "It's been a mighty strange day. First the hog, then it turned out Mrs. Higgins's chicken wasn't missing at all. It was just roosting in the outhouse. Strange place, if you ask me."

"It didn't go there on its own." Travis knew that Mrs. Higgins, like almost everyone in Cimarron Creek, was careful to keep the door to her outhouse latched. The last thing anyone wanted was to discover a wild animal had decided to nest there.

"Someone put the chicken there, just like someone moved that hog out of its pen. I wish I knew why."

Travis didn't need another worry right now. He'd talked to Pa again this morning, trying to dissuade him, but his father was adamant about leaving on today's stagecoach. He'd groused about the fact that the stage only ran on weekdays, forcing him to spend the weekend with his ungrateful son, the whore, and the Cursed Enemy. This morning he'd been uncharacteristically silent, saying only that he'd made up his mind. Though Travis had sent Dorcas a telegram, alerting her to their father's decision, he still hoped that Pa would decide to remain in Cimarron Creek. It was, after all, his home.

Before Travis could say anything more, the door burst open. "I've got a problem," Warner said, his voice low but filled with anger. "Can you come with me now?"

Just what Travis didn't need: another problem. But as sheriff, he could not refuse. "Sure." He turned to Edgar. "I know you'll handle anything that comes up." He followed his cousin out of the office. "What's wrong, Warner?"

Warner shook his head. "Let's wait until we're inside. It's better if you see it." Less than a minute later, he ushered Travis into the back room of the pharmacy and pointed toward an empty spot on one of the cupboard shelves. "That was full yesterday. I know, because I checked the supply. Today's the day I normally dispense some to Aunt Bertha, and I wanted to be sure I had enough for her and the other widows who've been having heart palpitations. They don't take it every day, but I need to have some on hand in case someone has an attack."

As far as Travis knew, Aunt Bertha took only one medication. "Digitalis?"

"Yes. Now I only have enough for a couple days."

Staring at the empty spot, Travis shook his head. "I don't understand. It looks like everything's gone."

"Almost everything. I keep a small supply at home. Ever since the day Aunt Bertha had her attack, I wanted to be prepared. That way if she called me at night, I wouldn't have to come here."

Travis didn't claim to be an expert on medication, but he knew that his aunt's life depended on taking the digitalis each day. "Can you get a new supply before what you have at home runs out?"

"Yes, but that doesn't explain who took the rest." He pointed to the pharmacy's rear entrance. "There's no sign of a break-in."

Just like the last time, when the mortar had been missing along with Lydia's teapot and items from the other shops.

"I thought you changed the locks."

Warner nodded. "I did. Porter helped me like he did all the others. We added a second lock after the rat poison was taken. That one's a lot stronger than the others. Porter assured me it would be difficult for someone to pick."

To the best of Travis's knowledge, there had been no thefts since the rat poison. Though it was possible that other shopkeepers had yet to discover their losses, Travis doubted this robbery was like the first set. That time, the missing items had been small and not particularly valuable. Digitalis did not fit into that category.

"Who has keys?" he asked his cousin. A lock was no good if its keys were readily available.

"Just me. I carry one and keep the spare at home."

"In the old cigar box?"

Warner seemed surprised by the question. "How did you guess?"

"That's where you used to keep your treasures." When they'd been twelve, those treasures had included a couple marbles and an Indian arrowhead Warner had found when he, Porter, and Travis had been exploring the outskirts of town.

"I guess I'm predictable, but some things never change."

Some things did. Pa was gone, and Travis, the man who had once feared marriage, was planning a courtship. "I'll see what I can find. Sooner or later, whoever's behind this will make a mistake."

"I hope it's sooner."

"Me too."

When Travis returned to his office, Edgar handed him a folded piece of paper. "Mrs. Henderson would like to see you. I read it, just in case it was something I could handle, but she's specific about seeing you."

"No offense, Edgar."

"None taken. I figured to start my rounds once you came back."

Travis locked the office as he and Edgar left, knowing Edgar's first stop would be the candy store. He couldn't blame the man. If he hadn't been worried about Aunt Bertha and whether he'd discover something had been stolen from her house, Travis might have detoured there too.

"Come in, my boy." To Travis's relief, Aunt Bertha did not look distraught when she opened the door. She led the way to the parlor and gestured toward the settee. "Sit down, and before you wonder if I'm missing a hog or a chicken, let me assure you that I've asked you to come here as my attorney, not the sheriff."

Travis shook his head in amazement at the speed with which the grapevine moved. "I won't ask how you heard about the missing animals." He only hoped she never learned about the stolen digitalis. "Now, what can I do for you?"

She leaned forward, her green eyes serious. "I need you to promise you won't breathe a word of this to Lydia."

"Of course not. Attorney-client privilege says anything you tell me will remain confidential."

"Perfect." Aunt Bertha's relief was visible. "Here's what I want."

Travis listened, surprised and yet not surprised by her request. Everything she said made sense. "Are you certain?"

"Yes. Now, how soon can you make this happen?"

"How about tomorrow morning?"

"Perfect."

Lydia took a deep breath, trying to let the peace she normally found in church wash over her and quiet the thoughts that whirled through her. She and Aunt Bertha had been home for over a week now. Though the sorrow that had filled Aunt Bertha's eyes while they were in Ladreville had not disappeared, she seemed — if not happy — at least at peace.

Aunt Bertha had joked with Lydia that Travis was courting her. Lydia doubted that was the case, and yet she could not deny that her relationship with him had changed the night they'd kissed. Since then, they'd exchanged glances that made Lydia's heart beat faster, and then there'd been the casual touches. Though nothing more than a brush of fingertips or a palm that lingered an extra second on her waist, those touches had sent shivers of excitement up and down her spine.

Those had been wonderful, but so too were their conversations. Though he'd asked her not to tell anyone, Travis had shared the story of the missing digitalis.

"I don't understand it," he admitted. "It seems as if someone is targeting Warner, but I can't imagine why. When the mortar was taken, I thought it was simply part of the rash of thefts, but now the digitalis combined with the stolen poison makes me wonder."

"I'd almost forgotten about the poison."

Travis shook his head. "You can be sure Nate hasn't. There's a truce between him and Warner, but I know he hasn't forgotten that those yellow sacks came from Warner's store."

"Big yellow bags?"

"Fairly big." Travis gestured to give Lydia an idea of the size. "Why?"

"I remember seeing them somewhere, but I can't recall where it was." She looked up at Travis. "Don't you hate it when that happens, when the memory is just out of reach?"

Despite Lydia's inability to remember where she'd seen the bags of poison and her feeling that it was important to remember, it had been a wonderful week, starting with Aunt Bertha's reaction to the special candy Lydia had made for her. Though she'd expected Aunt Bertha to be pleased by the chocolates with their pansy decorations, Lydia hadn't expected the exuberant thanks she'd received. Aunt Bertha had hugged her, telling her the gift meant more than she could imagine. Today before they'd entered the church, she had regaled at least a dozen people with the story of her new box of candy.

"I'm a selfish old woman," she'd said with a wry smile. "Instead of sharing them with visitors, I've put the box on my bedside table. I eat a piece each night — a special treat from a very dear young lady. And," she added, lowering her voice as if to confide a secret, "I sometimes reach for one or two in the middle of the night. There's nothing quite like a piece of chocolate to help a body sleep."

The matrons had nodded their approval, the gleam in their eyes making Lydia suspect she'd have a number of orders for uniquely decorated chocolates when the store opened tomorrow.

Now Aunt Bertha sat at Lydia's right, her hands folded on top of her Bible, her eyes closed in silent prayer.

On the opposite side of the church, Opal and Edgar sat with Travis in the pew he normally occupied with his father. Though the grapevine had buzzed with the news of Abe Whitfield's departure, no one seemed to know why he'd gone to Austin. Opal speculated that he wanted to see his granddaughter again, but when Lydia had asked Travis, he'd said only that it was his father's decision.

Despite the resurgence of petty crimes, Travis seemed happier than Lydia could recall. Each day when they'd walked to and from the store, he'd given her looks that made her suspect he was remembering the kiss they'd shared on the way to Ladreville. If so, that made two of them. She couldn't forget how good that kiss had felt and how much she wished it could be repeated.

Pushing aside thoughts that had no place in church, Lydia prayed for peace, and for the next hour, she thought only of the hymns she sang and the sermon Reverend Dunn delivered. When the service ended and she and Aunt Bertha emerged from the church, Lydia found Travis apparently waiting for her.

"It's a beautiful day," he told her. "Much too nice to stay indoors. I wondered if you'd like to take a walk with me this afternoon."

Knowing Aunt Bertha would have her customary after-dinner nap, Lydia nodded. Though she often spent Sunday afternoons with Catherine, her friend had told Lydia she was spending the day with Nate and his family. "It's nothing romantic," Catherine assured her, "but I like his sister and the children."

"Thank you." Lydia smiled at Travis. "I'd enjoy that." She could think of nothing she'd rather do than spend this beautiful autumn day with him.

Two hours later, he crooked his arm for her as they descended the steps of Aunt Bertha's home and headed north on Cedar. When they reached the spot where the street dead-ended next to the creek that gave the town its name, Travis shook his head.

"I'm not sure this was a good idea. I thought we might walk along the creek, but I'd forgotten how different ladies' shoes are from mine. Do you think your shoes can handle that?" He gestured toward the uneven terrain that marked the creek's banks.

Lydia nodded. "They're sturdier than you might think, and if there's mud, I can always brush it off."

"If you're sure," Travis said, his voice holding a note of concern, "there's a place I wanted to show you." He led the way.

Cimarron Creek, Lydia had discovered, took a slow and meandering path alongside its eponymous town. The town itself was situated at the spot where the river made a right-angle turn, changing its flow before turning again. Upstream a few blocks, here at the end of Cedar Street, the creek bent once more. Lydia and Travis strolled along the creek's bank, stopping occasionally to watch a fish swim through the clear water, apparently undisturbed by the presence of humans so close. Lydia smiled when a jay flew by their heads, then perched on a branch and squawked, warning others of the arrival of intruders. The bird was clearly more bothered by their presence than the fish.

When they reached a small bend in the creek, Lydia stopped, entranced by the sight of a massive live oak tree shading the water, one branch extending so far that it practically touched the opposite bank.

"It's lovely," she told Travis. "This is the kind of place where I could spend hours."

Travis smiled. "It's always been special for me. My mother brought me here when I was maybe six or seven. She said it was her thinking spot, the place where she felt especially close to God." He moved next to the oak branch and laid an arm across it in an almost protective gesture. "After Ma died, I used to come here and talk to her. I suppose that sounds foolish. She's no more here than she's in the cemetery plot, but I feel closest to her here."

Lydia took a step toward Travis, wanting him to know how touched she was by his story. Though he hadn't said it, she sensed that this was the first time he'd brought anyone to this spot.

"I can see why both of you came here. It's beautiful and peaceful, the perfect place to reflect on the majesty of God's creation. Thank you for sharing it with me." Though Lydia knew she'd never come back alone, she also knew she'd cherish the memory of being here with Travis. It was another special moment in what had been a very special week.

Travis dropped his arm and closed the distance between them until he was standing only a few inches from Lydia. Though he'd been smiling, the smile faded, replaced by an expression so serious that she wondered if something was wrong.

"This isn't all I want to share with you," he said, his voice husky with emotion. "Dorcas said her husband had a flowery speech, but I've never been one for fancy words. I always thought I should say what I meant as plainly as possible so there'd be no misunderstanding."

Travis reached for Lydia's hands, clasping them between his. "When we left Ladreville, I told myself I'd go slowly, that you deserved to be courted, but I've discovered that I'm not a patient man. I don't want to wait for months to learn whether I have a chance with you."

He took a shallow breath, his gray eyes now the shade of thunderclouds. "I love you, Lydia, and I hope you'll do me the very great honor of becoming my wife."

Lydia's heart had skipped a beat when Travis had spoken of courtship, but now her breath caught as the full magnitude of his words registered. Aunt Bertha was right. Travis had been courting her. Lydia had been right too. The kiss they'd shared on the way to Ladreville and all the tender moments they'd had since then had meant as much to Travis as they did to her.

Travis wanted to marry her! Lydia wanted to shout the news from the rooftops, telling everyone in Cimarron Creek that she was the most fortunate of women. Instead, she found herself so overcome with emotion that she was unable to utter a single word.

When she'd dreamt of marriage proposals, Lydia had never imagined receiving one in such a beautiful spot. The day Edgar had asked her to marry him, they'd been in the school's parlor, but Travis wasn't Edgar. He was a man of spotless integrity, a man who would never disappoint her.

"I won't make promises I can't keep," Travis said as if he'd read her thoughts. "I can't promise we won't have arguments or times of sorrow, but I can promise that I'll never stop loving you, and I'll do everything I can to make you happy."

Travis's expression was solemn. "Before you give me your answer, there's something you need to know. I never thought I would marry, because I was afraid I wouldn't be able to make my wife happy. That's because I saw how often my mother cried. I worried that would happen to my wife, and I couldn't subject any woman to a life like that. I was convinced I'd die a bachelor. But then I met you, and suddenly I couldn't imagine my life without you."

Lydia smiled at the realization that Travis's feelings mirrored hers. When she pictured a future without him, it was bleak.

"Thank goodness Aunt Bertha set me straight," Travis continued. "She told me that Ma's unhappiness was not my father's fault."

As Travis explained about his mother's first love, Lydia's heart ached for Cynthia, who never recovered from Chet's death, for Abe, who tried but failed to make her happy, and for Travis, whose life had been colored by his parents' less-than-perfect marriage.

"That's such a sad story," she said.

"It is, but we don't have to repeat it." Travis tightened his grip on her hands, his eyes darkening to charcoal as he said, "Will you marry me?"

Though she wanted to answer yes, Lydia hesitated. "Are you sure about this, Travis? Even though most of the people seem to have accepted me, I'm still a Yankee. I don't think your father will ever forget or forgive that."

Travis nodded. "You're probably right. When I told Pa I wanted to marry you and that I expected him to welcome you into our home, he chose to leave."

This was worse than Lydia had feared. She had caused a rift — a seemingly irrevocable rift — between Travis and his father. And yet, though she heard regret in his voice, Travis's eyes shone with love.

"Pa made his choice. I wish he'd chosen differently, but I won't forfeit our future to placate my father. I love you, Lydia, and I know there'll never be another woman who touches my heart the way you do."

Just as there would never be a man who touched her heart the way Travis had.

His eyes still solemn, Travis raised her hands to his lips and pressed a kiss on them. "If you love me even a little, say you'll marry me."

Lydia smiled. "I love you a whole lot more than a little." Before she agreed to Travis's proposal, she needed to make certain he understood just how much she loved him. "You're the second man who's asked me to marry him, but I want you to know that I'm not your mother. You'll never be second place in my heart."

As Lydia spoke, Travis's expression lightened. She continued, "Loving you has made me realize that what I felt for Edgar were the feelings I would have for a brother, not the man I wanted to marry. Edgar is a good man, but he's not the right one for me. You are. I love you, Travis, in every way a woman can love a man. And, just as importantly, I trust you."

Though Travis looked as if he wanted to speak, Lydia shook her head. She needed to finish. "You know how hard it is for me to give my trust, but from the first day I met you, you've been honest and trustworthy. That's part of what I love about you. All of which is my long way of answering your question. Yes, I love you, and yes, I want to marry you."

As Travis wrapped his arms around her and lowered his lips to hers, Lydia knew this was where she was meant to be. Travis was the man God had chosen for her.

26

"This is the fastest I've ever seen news travel," Opal said the next morning as she cut another slab of fudge into perfectly even cubes. "I don't know who started it, but three different women stopped me on the way over here to ask if it was true that you're going to marry Travis."

Lydia smiled. It felt as if she'd done nothing but smile since she'd become engaged to Travis. She suspected she'd even smiled in her sleep last night. When she and Travis had returned from the creek, they'd shared their news with Aunt Bertha, who'd made no secret of her delight. Next they'd stopped at Travis's house to tell Opal and Edgar, and by the time they'd reached Catherine's home, she and Nate were just arriving back from visiting his sister. Any one of them could have been responsible for activating the grapevine, but Lydia suspected the honor belonged to Mary Gray. She'd found

Travis's aunt sitting in the parlor with Aunt Bertha when Travis brought her home.

It didn't matter who had spread the news. What mattered was the news itself and how it made her feel. Lydia could not remember ever being this happy. When she'd awakened this morning, she had felt as if everything in her life had led her to this moment. Cimarron Creek was where she was meant to be, and Travis was the man she was meant to marry. Lydia was almost giddy with happiness. That's why it made no sense for her stomach to feel so queasy.

"Did you package all the peppermint?" she asked Opal. A piece of that might settle her stomach.

Opal nodded. "There were just a couple broken pieces."

"That's probably all I need. My stomach's a bit upset this morning."

Opal grinned as she handed the slivers of mint to Lydia. "Nerves. I was the same way the day Edgar and I got married. My head and my heart knew it was the right thing to do, but my stomach had other ideas. Edgar didn't say anything, but I could tell he felt the same way."

Lydia was still sucking on a piece of peppermint when Edgar knocked on the door and entered the kitchen.

"I'm heading out of town and won't be back for lunch," he told Opal. "Travis said not to fix anything for him. Said he wasn't hungry."

Lydia smiled as Opal gave her an "I told you so" look. "You don't have to worry about your wife," she told Edgar. "She can eat with Aunt Bertha and me."

Though Lydia expected nothing more than a nod in response, a puzzled expression crossed Edgar's face and he took a step backward, almost as if he did not want to be near Lydia.

"What are you eating?" he asked.

"I'm not sure what Aunt Bertha has planned, but I wouldn't be surprised if it's chicken and dumplings."

Edgar shook his head. "Not for lunch. Now."

Though Opal appeared confused by her husband's brusque reply, she said nothing.

"Peppermint."

Edgar sniffed, then nodded as he turned to Opal. "Remember how I told you the strangest things trigger memories? That's what just happened. When I smelled the mint on Lydia's breath, it was like I was behind the Spur again. The man who attacked me smelled of mint."

Blood drained from Opal's face, and she

gripped the edge of the counter as if to keep from falling. "Me too. The man who hurt me had mint on his breath."

Lydia looked at her two friends. "We've got to tell Travis."

"His alibi is solid." Travis wasn't certain whether he was relieved or disappointed. As much as he hated the idea that one of his friends might have been responsible for the attacks on Opal and Edgar, he would have welcomed the end of his search for the perpetrator.

"Nate's the only man in Cimarron Creek who chews mint," Edgar had pointed out when he and Opal recounted their stories.

Though that was true, Travis's instincts told him the seemingly easy solution wasn't necessarily the correct one. After all, someone had done his best to implicate Warner when Nate's goats were poisoned.

"You didn't really think Nate was responsible, did you?" Lydia sat in one of the guest chairs on the opposite side of Travis's desk, the furrows in her forehead confirming that she shared his frustration.

Travis shook his head. "I didn't want to believe it. I'm almost as close to Nate as I am to Porter and Warner. They're my friends, and it's hard to believe someone you know that well could be behind such awful crimes."

When Lydia nodded, Travis continued. "After you told me the date, I looked at the notes I keep about the complaints I receive and remembered a couple things about the night Opal was raped. The grippe had been sweeping through town, and a couple of the shopkeepers who hadn't been able to open up that day asked me to keep an eye on their stores." There hadn't been any problems, but he'd been more tired than usual by evening and had wondered if he were catching the grippe.

"We were supposed to play dominoes at my house, but at the last minute Nate sent a message that his sister and her husband were ill and she needed him to take care of the boys. I was more than happy to cancel the game and call it an early night. I talked to Rachel today, and she confirmed that Nate spent the whole night with them."

"What about Edgar's attack?"

"That was another game night at my house. This time it was Nate who was sick. It must have been something he ate, but he was violently ill that night. Our game broke up early, and he was in such bad shape that I insisted he stay at my house. Even if he'd had a reason to attack Edgar, Nate was too weak to do it that night."

And that left Travis back where he'd been before with no clues.

Lydia leaned forward, a spark of excitement lighting her eyes. "It may only be coincidence, but I couldn't help noticing that both of the attacks took place on your game nights. I wonder if there's a connection."

It was an intriguing thought. "You think someone chose that night because they knew I'd be occupied."

Lydia shrugged. "How many people know you play dominoes every Tuesday?"

"Just about everyone in Cimarron Creek. Folks make it their business to know who goes where and when." Travis was silent for a moment, considering. "The only problem with that theory is that if Edgar and Opal's memories are accurate, the attacks took place after the games were over. One night we didn't play, the other we finished early."

"But the person who's responsible had no way of knowing that."

"True. I wonder —"

"Whether the thefts also took place on Tuesday."

Travis laughed as Lydia completed his sentence. "I've heard old married couples begin to think alike, but I never knew it would start even before the wedding. That's almost scary."

"Does that mean you've reconsidered the whole idea of marriage?"

Though the smile that accompanied Lydia's words told Travis she wasn't serious, he wouldn't let her think — not even for a moment — that he wasn't eager to marry her. "Never! You're stuck with me, Lydia. Forever and ever."

"And I couldn't be happier." Lydia's smile faded. "I just wish we could discover who's responsible. Now, about those other incidents . . ."

As he checked his records, Travis's frown deepened. "Almost all took place either Tuesday night or early Wednesday morning. There's no way of knowing when the chickens were stolen, and Mrs. Wilkins is such a sound sleeper that she didn't hear her windows being broken."

"So we have a pattern."

"But no suspects."

"I can't remember ever seeing Aunt Bertha so happy." Catherine smiled as she and Lydia did a final check of the kitchen. Opal, who'd insisted that a woman less than a month from giving birth should not be circulating with the guests, was supervising the half dozen women who had prepared everything from roast beef to mashed potatoes and squash to feed the expected crowd.

"I knew she'd be pleased by our engagement," Lydia admitted. "She's the one who told me Travis was the man God intended for me." And, according to Travis, Aunt Bertha was the one who'd freed him from his past to pursue his future. "I have to say, though, that when Aunt Bertha said we should celebrate, I never expected all this." As they entered the butler's pantry, Lydia gestured toward the stacks of plates and silverware prepared for the guests.

The whole town had been invited to the party in honor of Lydia and Travis's engagement. When Lydia had heard the scope of the plans, she'd objected, believing the effort would be too much for the older woman, but Aunt Bertha had countered by saying she would hire women to cook and others to prepare the house.

"Most of the guests will stay on the first floor," Aunt Bertha had said as she directed the women to clean every nook and cranny of the house, "but some will wander upstairs. It's been years since my house was open to the town, so there's bound to be some curiosity about it. I don't want anyone to find a speck of dust."

And they would not. Each room had been

scrubbed, then polished; an enormous quantity of food had been prepared; and countless bouquets of roses from the garden had been arranged and placed throughout the house. Everything was ready, waiting for the arrival of the other guest of honor.

Lydia smiled, thinking of the intricate planning Aunt Bertha had put into today's party. She had been like a general preparing for battle, barking out orders as if the fate of the world hinged on this one day. What might have been a simple celebration had turned into an elaborate affair, and yet Lydia could not complain, because as Catherine had pointed out, Aunt Bertha was happy. The sorrow that had lingered in her eyes after the trip to Ladreville was gone, at least temporarily, and for that Lydia gave thanks.

"I'm the luckiest man in Cimarron Creek," Travis announced when he arrived. His lips curved into a grin. "Make that all of Texas," he corrected himself. "Who else would have not one but three beautiful women at his side?"

Though Lydia knew that the puzzle of who was responsible for the attacks on Opal and Edgar weighed heavily on him and that he would undoubtedly be watching everyone who attended today's party, searching for clues to the man's identity, they'd agreed to say nothing about the latest twist in the investigation to Aunt Bertha. Today was a day for celebration, starting right now.

"Beautiful?" Catherine, who'd joined Aunt Bertha and Lydia to greet Travis, chuckled. "You need to have your eyes checked if you think I'm beautiful. Mourning clothes don't flatter anyone." Lydia had to concur. Though Catherine's dress was skillfully cut, the unrelieved black made her normally milky complexion appear sallow.

Aunt Bertha nodded. "That's why I don't want anyone wearing black for me. When it's my time to go, I want you to celebrate, knowing I'm in a better place. No black." She pretended to frown at Travis's finely cut black suit, though the clothing did not appear funereal but merely served to accentuate the breadth of his shoulders and the ever-changing color of his eyes. The frown quickly turned into a conspiratorial smile, as Aunt Bertha and Travis shared a secret. "I even put that in my will, didn't I, Travis?"

He nodded. "You did, indeed. But I still say you're a trio of beautiful women, even you, Catherine."

"You always were a smooth talker, Travis. I'm just glad you came to your senses and asked Lydia to marry you." Aunt Bertha touched Lydia's sleeve, her eyes shining with approval.

"And I'm grateful she accepted me," Travis said as he turned to Lydia, his smile widening as his gaze met hers.

For a moment as their eyes met, Lydia felt as if they were the only two people on Earth, as if God's wonderful creation had been made for them alone. It was a heady feeling, the result of the love she saw shining from Travis's eyes.

"You look especially beautiful today."

His words brought Lydia back to reality. "It's the dress," she said lightly, though she suspected Travis had not noticed that she was wearing new finery. "Aunt Bertha insisted I have a new one. This is the fanciest gown I've ever owned."

The town's dressmaker had outdone herself, creating a gown of pale blue silk with royal blue trim. From the small bustle to the intricately draped skirt, it was both elegant and flattering, as was the way she'd arranged her hair. Instead of pulling it back in a simple chignon, which was practical for days at Cimarron Sweets, Lydia had swept it off her neck, leaving a few curls to frame her face. Though Travis had not commented on that, she had seen the approval in his expression.

"Aunt Bertha deserves the credit," Lydia said.

"Nonsense. A dress can only do so much. Still, wait until you see what I have in mind for your wedding gown. You'll be the most beautiful bride Cimarron Creek has ever seen." Aunt Bertha nodded to punctuate her words.

As Catherine left to take her place in the parlor to serve as hostess while Travis, Lydia, and Aunt Bertha moved to the front porch to greet guests as they arrived, Travis said, "Lydia would be beautiful in feed sacks."

Lydia couldn't help blushing. Though her mother had told her she was pretty, no one had ever paid her such fulsome compliments. She wasn't beautiful — she knew that — and yet when she was with Travis, his love made her feel beautiful.

Aunt Bertha nodded briskly. "Your mother taught you well, Travis. I only wish she could be here to see this day. She'd approve of your bride-to-be as much as I do. Lydia will be a fine addition to the family." Aunt Bertha looked down the street, her smile fading slightly. "Where's your ornery old coot of a father? I know he went off to Austin to visit Dorcas, but he should be here today. Of course, if he were, I'd give him a piece of my mind."

"He probably knew that," Travis told her. "I wouldn't be surprised if that's why he stayed in Austin."

Lydia knew that was not the reason, but as much as she hated the idea of having caused a rift between the two men, there was nothing she could do. Fixing a smile on her face, she greeted the first guests, and before she knew it, the house was full of laughing and joking townspeople. It seemed as if all of Cimarron Creek had accepted Aunt Bertha's invitation.

The afternoon was as joyous as Aunt Bertha had predicted. Once the last guests arrived, Lydia and Travis circulated among the guests, accepting more congratulations and, in Travis's case, some good-natured ribbing about using his position as sheriff to ensure that Lydia accepted his proposal. They both laughed, as did the women who teased him.

"We're going to amend the wedding vows," Travis said with mock solemnity. "In addition to promising to love and honor me, Lydia will also promise to make at least one pound of candy for me every week that we're married."

Lydia joined the joking. "And Travis will

promise not to arrest me if a batch of lemon drops is too sour."

As everyone who heard their declarations chuckled, Lydia smiled again. Today was not simply a day of love and laughter. It was a day for family and friends, and for the first time, she realized how much her position in Cimarron Creek had changed. She was no longer an outsider. She was now part of the family. It was a wonderful feeling.

"I love you," she whispered to Travis as they moved toward another group of well-wishers.

"Not as much as I love you," he replied, giving her hand a little squeeze.

The day couldn't have been more perfect.

27

It was perhaps half an hour later that Lydia noticed how flushed Aunt Bertha had become. Leaving Travis to discuss cattle prices with several of the local ranchers, she crossed the room to the spindly chair where her benefactress was holding court.

"Are you all right?" she asked softly, not wanting to embarrass Aunt Bertha in front of her guests.

Though she kept a smile on her face, Aunt Bertha shook her head slightly. "I'm a bit warm. Would you mind getting me my fan? It's in the top right bureau drawer."

"Certainly." Moving as quickly as she could without causing any speculation, Lydia climbed the stairs and turned toward Aunt Bertha's room. From the corner of her eye, she spotted a woman at the other side of the hall. Though there'd been a steady stream of guests visiting the second story, the sight of this particular woman made Lydia pause. The rest of the quilting circle had come earlier, but she had not accompanied them.

"Were you looking for something, Hilda?" she asked.

Lydia's best customer came closer. Though she shook her head, she appeared flustered and did not meet Lydia's gaze. "I was just curious. I've never been up here. I wanted to see if the rooms were like Porter's parents'."

Aunt Bertha had predicted curiosity, though when she had mentioned people possibly venturing upstairs, Lydia had not expected family to be among them. She had assumed — obviously erroneously — that everyone in the extended Whitfield-Henderson clan was familiar with Aunt Bertha's home.

"And are they?" While Lydia had seen only the foyer of the elder Grays' home, she suspected that despite the similar exteriors, the interiors were quite different, if only because the Grays had built their home twenty years after the three original mansions were constructed.

Hilda shook her head. "Not as much as I expected. I think Papa Gray must have . . ." Her words trailed off, and her eyes widened in surprise.

"There you are, Hilda. I was looking for you."

Lydia turned, almost as surprised by Porter's disapproving tone as the fact that he was approaching from the opposite end of the hallway. The last time she had noticed him, he'd been at Hilda's side, sipping punch with his parents. Unless Porter had been upstairs for a while, he must have used the servants' staircase. And yet, why would he? The elegant curved stairway was the direct route from the parlor to the second story.

"Come, my dear." Porter's voice changed from harsh to ingratiating as he approached his wife. "I know you don't want to miss the rest of the party, but Susan's getting cranky, and you know how Aunt Bertha is about poorly behaved children. We'll never hear the last of it if we let Susan disrupt anything."

Though he had barely acknowledged her presence, Lydia nodded. Porter's statement explained why he'd used the other staircase. Knowing that the children would be bored by adult conversation but not wanting to exclude them from the celebration, Aunt Bertha had arranged for them to play in the summer kitchen, with three women from church taking turns supervising them. Since

Porter had obviously been with his daughter, it made sense that he'd taken the servants' stairway. That was the quickest way upstairs from the summer kitchen.

Porter raised an eyebrow as he turned toward Lydia. "You'll excuse us, won't you? Our daughter can be a handful." Hooking his arm with his wife's, Porter led the way to the back stairs, leaving Lydia to retrieve the fan from Aunt Bertha's room.

To her relief, the simple act of fanning seemed to return Aunt Bertha's color to normal, and though Lydia might have expected her to be fatigued by the long day, when the party ended two hours later, Aunt Bertha appeared almost as energetic as she had that morning.

Lydia could not say the same thing about herself. Though she had enjoyed the day, she now felt drained, and judging from the subtle signs of stress she saw in his expression, so did Travis. Being the center of attention was hard work.

Though Aunt Bertha invited him to stay, Travis threaded his fingers through Lydia's as he prepared to leave. "Thank you, Aunt Bertha," he said with a warm smile. "This was a wonderful party."

"It was my pleasure. I can't think of anything that would have made me happier." The older woman extended her arms to Lydia and enfolded her in a hug as she said, "We may not be related by blood, but you're the granddaughter of my heart."

As tears of joy filled her eyes, Lydia looked from Aunt Bertha to Travis. Thanks to these two wonderful people, for the first time in her life, she felt complete. The spaces deep inside her that she had once believed would remain empty forever were now filled by their love.

"I love you," she said softly. "Both of you."

Her eyes shining with happiness, Aunt Bertha nodded. "And we love you."

Something was wrong. Lydia could not dismiss the feeling. Just before she'd wakened, she had been dreaming of Travis. They were smiling at each other as they raced through a rainstorm, trying to reach the front door of a house Lydia had never seen yet one she somehow knew was their home. Travis had opened the door, but before they could step inside, Lydia had wakened and her heart began to pound with fear.

There was no rain. The morning was bright and sunny, but something was wrong. It wasn't a feeling. It was a fact. The house felt empty.

As she pressed her hand to her racing

heart, Lydia reminded herself that it was Sunday. That meant Opal would not be in the kitchen, occasionally clattering pans as she cut and weighed candies. Of course the house was empty. Lydia picked up her watch from the bedside table and nodded. On a normal day, Aunt Bertha would sleep at least another half hour. Today she'd probably remain in bed longer than that, since even though she hadn't wanted to admit it, yesterday's party must have been tiring.

It had been an unusual day for all of them. When Aunt Bertha had finally headed for bed, she'd worn a sheepish expression as she admitted that she'd eaten too much during the party and would forego her nightly chocolate cream. To the best of Lydia's knowledge, that was the first time that had happened since she'd begun making pansy-decorated candies. Perhaps Aunt Bertha was still sleeping off the effects of overeating.

Still . . .

Lydia swung her legs out of bed, slid her feet into her slippers, and reached for her wrapper. Compelled by an urgency she couldn't explain, she hurried down the hall until she reached Aunt Bertha's room. She put her ear to the door, listening for something — anything — that might have alarmed her, but there were no unusual sounds. No sounds at all. And that was wrong. Though Aunt Bertha snored, today there was no snoring, no sound of breathing.

Remembering how Catherine had described how empty her house felt the day her mother died, Lydia closed her eyes and prayed. *Please, Lord, don't let it be true.* But there was no sound other than the deafening pounding of Lydia's heart.

Forcing her eyes open, Lydia entered Aunt Bertha's bedroom and raced to the bed.

"No!" she cried as she stared at the empty shell of the woman she loved so dearly. The hair was Aunt Bertha's; the nightdress was the one Lydia had seen a dozen times when she'd carried laundry upstairs; but everything else about the dear woman looked different — horribly, horribly different. It couldn't be true, and yet it was.

Dressing as quickly as she could, Lydia tried but failed to erase the image of Aunt Bertha's still form. There had been no need to touch her, to search for a heartbeat or a breath. Aunt Bertha had breathed her last.

Lydia shuddered. She wouldn't cry. She wouldn't scream. But she had to tell someone. Not just someone. She had to tell Travis.

Moments later, she was pounding on his door.

"What's wrong?" She could see the surprise in his eyes when he noticed her hasty toilette. Unlike Lydia, Travis had dressed with care this morning and had donned his best suit in preparation for church services.

He ushered her into his home, and when Lydia said nothing, he asked again, "What's wrong?"

Lydia found the voice that had deserted her only a moment ago. "It's Aunt Bertha. She's dead." As she pronounced the words for the first time, her composure crumbled, and she began to sob. Even though she knew in her mind that Aunt Bertha was gone, somehow hearing herself say it made the fact real. Aunt Bertha was dead, and Lydia would not see her again this side of heaven. Oh, how was she going to bear that?

Instinctively, Travis opened his arms to embrace Lydia.

"We knew her heart was weak," he said softly as he stroked Lydia's back in an attempt to comfort her. "The party yesterday must have been more of a strain than we realized. Still, you saw how happy she was. It's the kind of passing she would have wanted. Think about it, Lydia. She went to sleep happy and never woke up. It was a peaceful end."

If only that were true! Lydia shook her head. "Something's wrong, Travis. I don't know what happened, but Aunt Bertha's body is so swollen I almost didn't recognize her."

Lydia shuddered at the memory. Aunt Bertha's face was contorted in a parody of a smile, and her body . . . Lydia didn't want to think of the swollen flesh.

Two sets of footsteps told Lydia that Opal and Edgar had heard her pounding on the door and had come to see what was happening. She stepped away from Travis, not wanting to leave the comfort of his arms but knowing there were things that had to be done. Death, particularly a death like this, involved others.

"It's Aunt Bertha," Travis told Opal and Edgar. "She died last night, and Lydia's worried about the cause of death. That means we need Doc Harrington. I can only do so much as sheriff. Doc's the one who investigates deaths." Travis turned toward Opal. "Will you go back to the house with Lydia? I'll bring the doctor. If anything else comes up, you're in charge, Edgar."

Lydia crossed her arms and held them close to her body, trying to still the tremors that coursed through her. This couldn't be happening, and yet it was.

Opal touched Lydia's hand. "We should go. It won't take Travis long to get the doctor. Mrs. Henderson would want you to be there."

But Mrs. Henderson was beyond caring what happened in her home. Lydia shuddered again as she followed Opal out the door. "I don't know what I'm going to do without her. She was my friend, my mother, and my grandmother all in one. And now she's gone."

Opal had no answer.

When the doctor arrived, Lydia understood why Catherine did not trust him. Lydia had met him only a few times, once when he was leaving church, another time when they'd passed on the street, and yesterday when he'd made a brief appearance at the engagement party. Though he'd been cordial on those occasions, today he strutted around the house as if he owned it before demanding to see "the body" as he referred to it.

Lydia bristled at his tone, anger helping to mute her grief. Did the man have no common decency? And then she noticed his hands. He was a doctor, and yet there was dirt beneath his fingernails. Aunt Bertha would have handed him a bar of soap and a brush and insisted he clean them. Though Lydia was tempted to do precisely that, she knew from Catherine's stories that the doctor would not comply. The sooner he was gone, the better.

Lydia led the way up the stairs and into Aunt Bertha's room, grateful that Travis was with them. He'd ensure that Doc treated Aunt Bertha with dignity.

"Harrumph!"

Lydia had no idea what the doctor meant by that. He stood in the doorway for a moment, his eyes scanning the room as if he were taking inventory. With a quick nod, he strode to the bed and yanked the blankets from Aunt Bertha's body. If he was surprised by the state of her body, he said nothing, merely stared at it for a few seconds.

"Was she taking digitalis?" he demanded.

Though Travis stood by her side, it was Lydia to whom the question was addressed and Lydia who answered. "Yes."

Doc Harrington nodded. "That's what killed her. She took too much. That's why there's all that swelling."

The doctor might think he knew what had happened, but he was wrong. "That's not possible," Lydia told him. "I gave her the normal amount last night." Warner had impressed on both of them the importance of the proper dosage, telling them that even a slight increase in the quantity could be fatal. That was why Lydia measured the powder so carefully before she dissolved it in water.

Doc Harrington glared at Lydia, obviously angered by her daring to challenge him. "Look, missy, the proof is there. She took more than she should have."

Lydia shook her head again. "I told you, that's not possible. We ran out of digitalis last night. With all the excitement of the party, I forgot to get a new supply. I was planning to ask Warner for more this morning."

The doctor was not convinced. "You can say what you want, missy, but I know what I see. Bertha Henderson died of an overdose of digitalis."

Without asking permission, he strode to her bureau and began opening drawers, rifling through the contents. Lydia took a deep breath, trying not to shout her horror at the thought that this man was pawing through Aunt Bertha's belongings with his dirty fingers.

"What are you doing?" Travis asked.

"Looking for where she had it stashed."

Travis took three steps and laid his hand on the doctor's shoulder, pulling him away from the bureau. "Lydia's already told you Aunt Bertha didn't have any more digitalis. Even if she had, she wouldn't have taken too much of it. She knew how dangerous it was."

Doc Harrington gave Travis a look that said as clearly as words that he was mistaken. "If the pain gets bad enough, people will do anything to stop it."

"Not Aunt Bertha." Lydia was as certain of that as she was of anything in her life. "She wouldn't have taken a chance of dying."

"So you say." The doctor shook off Travis's hand and moved to the bedside, where a box from Cimarron Sweets lay on top of Aunt Bertha's Bible. He opened the box, sniffed, then spun around, an expression that looked almost like glee lighting his face.

"You're right, missy. Mrs. Henderson didn't kill herself, but her death was no accident. This candy has digitalis in it." He held the open box under Travis's nose. "Smell it. The chocolate coating almost hides it, but if you take a deep breath, you can smell something sour. That's digitalis."

Doc Harrington closed the box and handed it to Travis. "There's only one person in this town who makes candy like this. It looks to me like your fiancée is a murderer."

28

"You're not going to arrest her, are you?"

Travis ushered the distraught woman into his home. It wasn't yet noon, and this was the second time a woman had pounded on his door.

"Surely you know Lydia would never harm Aunt Bertha," Catherine declared as she stepped inside. "Doc Harrington is an old fool. He knows nothing."

Travis wondered how Catherine had heard the news. He had planned to visit each of the family members, telling them of Aunt Bertha's passing, but it appeared that someone had already begun spreading the story.

Shaking his head, Travis offered Catherine a chair. With her color as high as it was, she looked as if she might keel over any moment. "Doc's right about the digitalis poisoning," he told Catherine. "I asked Warner, and he confirmed that swelling is a symptom, and when he sniffed the candy, he said that's what digitalis smells like in large doses."

Travis had confiscated the box of candy and had it locked in the small safe he kept in the sheriff's office. As much as he hated the fact that it pointed toward Lydia, he had to keep evidence secure.

"Lydia didn't do it," Catherine insisted.

"I know that, and you know that. That's why I don't want to put Lydia in jail, despite what the doctor says. But I have to do something. Until I discover who poisoned that candy and left it in Aunt Bertha's room, I have no choice but to close Lydia's store and insist that she never be alone. I can't risk anyone else in town being harmed."

Furrows formed between Catherine's eyes. "I can stay with Lydia if that will help, but I'm still puzzled by the murder. It makes no sense. Everyone liked Aunt Bertha. Why would anyone kill her?"

Travis was equally perplexed. "I don't know, but I intend to find out." The other crimes he'd been investigating were serious, but this one hit too close to home. Not only had someone poisoned his favorite aunt, but the same someone had gone to great lengths to frame Lydia. This was one crime

Travis had to solve . . . quickly.

Lydia took a deep breath and smoothed the skirt of her mourning gown, wishing she could settle her thoughts as easily as she had pressed the wrinkles from the navy blue gown she'd found in the attic. Though Catherine had offered her one of her black gowns, Lydia had refused. Since Aunt Bertha had been adamant about her loved ones not wearing black, Lydia would respect her wishes. The dark blue was somber enough to match her mood without being black.

Death was never easy, but sudden, senseless death was the worst. It had been two days since Lydia had discovered Aunt Bertha's lifeless body, two days in which she'd struggled to believe it was true. Though the uncontrollable sobs that had wracked her initially had subsided, Lydia now felt as if the foundation of her life had disappeared.

Everything had changed. Though she was still living in Aunt Bertha's house, nothing else was the same. Instead of the wonderfully kind woman who'd offered her a home, it was Catherine who now lived with her, since Travis insisted she not be alone. Instead of having a prosperous business on

Main Street, Lydia now had a shuttered store. Instead of being welcomed as part of the family, she was now a pariah, a woman accused of murdering her benefactress.

Lydia was more grateful than she could express for Catherine's company. Not only did Catherine continue to insist that no one who mattered could believe Lydia capable of poisoning Aunt Bertha, but she'd been a godsend, helping Lydia with the preparations for the funeral and the cold collation that would follow it. Though other members of the Whitfield and Henderson families had offered to take charge, muttering under their breaths that it was unseemly for Lydia to have any part in Aunt Bertha's funeral, Catherine had insisted that she and Lydia would handle everything.

"You know what Aunt Bertha would have wanted better than they do," she said quietly when Mary and Hilda Gray left, the frowns on their faces expressing their disapproval as clearly as their harrumphs. And so it had been Lydia who had chosen the flowers and candles that would help mask the smell of death, Lydia who'd selected the foods that would be offered to mourners after the funeral. And all the time it had felt wrong — so wrong — to have Aunt Bertha lying in a coffin in the same parlor that had been the site of such a happy event only a few days earlier.

As the hour for the funeral approached, the family began to gather. Catherine and Lydia had kept a vigil next to the coffin. Now they stood at the entrance to the parlor with Travis between them. Family had been invited to come an hour before the service began to pay their respects to the last member of the founding families.

"Why is she still here?" Charles Gray's face flushed as he pointed at Lydia, then turned his ire on Travis. "Don't you have any sense? Why would you let Aunt Bertha's murderer stay here?"

Keeping her hand on her husband's arm, Mary nodded. Though she said nothing, it was clear she shared Charles's views.

This was what Lydia had known would happen when Doc Harrington declared that some of her candies had been poisoned. She was once again the outsider.

"Lydia did not kill her." Travis's voice was steely as he laid a hand on the small of Lydia's back to support her. "She's here because Aunt Bertha considered her the granddaughter she never had."

When they'd returned from Ladreville, both Lydia and Travis had agreed there was no reason for anyone in Cimarron Creek to know why Joan had left town so many years ago and that Bertha Henderson did in fact have a granddaughter. Nothing good would come from those revelations.

Charles sniffed. "I thought you were a sensible man, Travis, but it's clear you've had your head turned by a pretty face. The town should never have made you sheriff."

"Watch what you say about my son."

Lydia felt Travis's surprise and knew her own was reflected on her face. While they'd both focused on Charles and his accusations, another man had entered the house.

"Pa!" Travis spun around and clapped his father on the shoulder. "Why didn't you tell me you were coming? I could have met your coach."

Lydia knew Travis had sent his father a telegram, telling him of his aunt's death. She also knew he hadn't expected a response. "I doubt anything would bring him back here," Travis had said when he returned from sending the message. Yet here he was.

Travis's father shrugged. "I figured you had other things to do. Obviously, I was right about that. Now, Charles, it appears you owe my son and his bride-to-be an apology."

"You won't catch me apologizing for

speaking the truth." Charles wrapped his arm around his wife and led her from the house.

"Good riddance." Travis's father shot an angry look at the departing couple. "Mark my words, they'll be back for the funeral, but only because people would talk if they weren't here." He turned to Travis and Lydia. "I may have played poker with him, but I never did like Charles. I always figured you shouldn't trust a man who played favorites with his sons the way he did. That's not right. He ought to have treated them the same, just the way I did you and Dorcas, but that's water under the bridge now."

Lydia looked into the parlor, where other members of the family had taken their seats. If they'd overheard the outburst — and she saw no way they could not have heard it — they gave no sign.

"Can I offer you something to eat?" She addressed Travis's father. "I remember how hungry and thirsty I was after riding on the stagecoach."

The older man nodded. "Just make sure there's no poisoned candy on my plate."

Lydia felt the blood drain from her face. She shouldn't have been surprised. Abe Whitfield had been nothing if not honest about his dislike of her, but surely that was no reason for such cruelty.

"Pa!" Travis glared at his father.

"Can't a man joke?"

"Not about that. There are too many people in town who believe Lydia was responsible."

"Then they're fools. Anyone with an ounce of brains would know that. Lydia had no reason to kill Aunt Bertha. The woman gave her food and shelter. Where's she going to live now?"

That was one worry Lydia did not have, since Catherine had already offered her home to Lydia until she and Travis married. It must be her imagination that Travis seemed uneasy with the question.

Would this day never end? It was more uncomfortable than any funeral Travis had ever attended. Sorrow mingled with suspicion, and in most cases it appeared that suspicion outweighed regret that the last of the first generation was gone. There'd been no mistaking the pointed looks that had been directed at Lydia, the whispers that had ceased when she moved close enough to overhear them. She must have known what was happening, and yet she'd given no sign, simply walked with quiet dignity to the front row seat that both Travis and

Catherine had insisted she take.

Her apparent composure hadn't surprised Travis. He'd known Lydia had an inner strength that was greater than she realized. What had surprised — shocked might be a more accurate word — him was Pa's defense of Lydia. The rest of the town, with the notable exception of Catherine, Edgar, and Opal, seemed ready to believe the worst of Lydia, but Pa had stood by her side during the wake, taken the seat next to her during the service, then escorted her to the cemetery. This was a side of Pa Travis hadn't seen since Ma died: a kinder, gentler man. The change could be temporary. In fact, it probably was, given Pa's hatred of all Northerners, but Travis hoped it would last.

At least the funeral was over. Now all that remained was another hour or so of people helping themselves to the cold collation while they shared memories of Bertha Henderson's life and speculation about the ending of it. Fortunately, Lydia didn't have to overhear the latter. As soon as they'd returned from the cemetery, she'd secreted herself in the kitchen, ostensibly because Opal needed help serving the food. Travis suspected the real reason was that Lydia had no desire to be the object of the town's scorn. The people who'd been so welcoming less than a week ago had withdrawn their support, reverting to cold suspicion.

"When are you gonna read Bertha's will?" Pa asked. He'd been circulating among the guests, his frown deepening with each encounter.

"I thought I'd wait until tomorrow." Though Pa had no way of knowing it, Bertha's will would undoubtedly become another point of contention, especially when the extent of her fortune became common knowledge.

"Why wait? You've got the whole family here. Waiting will only increase the speculation."

Pa had a point. And since Travis had kept the will in his coat pocket all day, there was no need to return to his office for it. "All right. Would you gather Jacob, Mary, Catherine, and the Gospels? Ask them to wait in the library."

"That's all? Charles won't be happy that he's not included."

Travis doubted Uncle Charles would be happy about anything unless he were the sole recipient of Aunt Bertha's fortune. "Aunt Bertha was very specific about who would hear her will. Only those who are mentioned are to be in the room. The reason I asked you to get the others is that you're part of the group."

Pa looked surprised but pleased. "We didn't see eye to eye on a lot of things, but I always admired Bertha. She dealt with misfortune better than most of us." He squared his shoulders. "I'll have everyone ready in five minutes."

That would give Travis the time he needed. He crossed the room, then drew Edgar aside. "There may be some unhappy people, both inside the library and out here."

His deputy nodded. "That's only natural. Mrs. Henderson was well liked."

"I wasn't talking about sorrow. I'm going to read her will. I imagine some will be disappointed by the contents. I can take care of them, but when folks realize what's happening, others will be angry that they're not mentioned at all. Do whatever you need to keep order here."

Edgar nodded again and touched his gun belt. "I'm ready."

And so was Travis. Almost. Pa and the others he'd listed were gone. As he'd predicted, Uncle Charles was furious, his face red, his fists clenched. Travis turned back to Edgar. "Under no circumstances is Charles Gray to join me."

"Understood."

There was only one more person to summon. Travis made his way to the kitchen and found her washing dishes with Opal. "Lydia, I need you to come with me." The words sounded harsher than he'd intended, more of a command than a request. But the truth was, it was a command.

She turned, obviously surprised. "Where? Why?"

"You'll see." As she dried her hands, he added, "It'll be all right. I promise." He would do whatever he had to do to ensure that was one promise he kept.

As they entered the library, Travis heard the small gasps when everyone saw the woman at his side, but only Aunt Mary reacted.

"If she's here, my husband deserves to be here too."

"I'm afraid not. Now please sit down, Aunt Mary." Travis waited until Lydia took the only empty chair, one that unfortunately placed her next to Aunt Mary. If he'd thought ahead, he might have asked Pa to save a seat, but he hadn't wanted anyone to realize Lydia was included until the last minute.

Pulling the document from his pocket, Travis looked at the attendees, waiting until he'd made eye contact with each of them before he said, "I've brought you all here for the reading of Aunt Bertha's will. I expect you will have questions, but I ask that you say nothing until I've finished."

There was another quiet murmur before everyone fell silent.

Travis opened the pages and began to read. "I, Bertha Amelia Henderson, née Bertha Amelia Russell, being of sound mind do hereby declare that this is my last will and testament." As Travis continued reading, he heard murmurs of astonishment at the extent of Bertha's wealth. She had divided a quarter of it among the surviving members of the second generation and the children of those who had predeceased her. Even split eight ways, it was still a substantial sum. Even Aunt Mary seemed pleased until Travis read the final line.

"I bequeath the remainder of my estate, including my home and its contents, to Lydia Victoria Crawford, who brought joy and peace to my final months on Earth."

There was a second of silence. Travis saw the shock on Lydia's face as she realized that she was now a wealthy woman. The others, with the exception of Pa and Catherine, looked dumbfounded. Whatever they had expected, it was not for an outsider to receive the majority of Aunt Bertha's sizeable estate.

The Gospels looked at each other, their discomfort apparent, though they said nothing. Aunt Mary was the first to regain her voice. She leapt from her seat and pointed an accusatory finger at Lydia. "You scheming hussy! You worked your way into her graces and then you killed her!"

29

Lydia stared at the woman who, until recently, had always been polite to her. She couldn't blame Mrs. Gray for the accusation. Aunt Bertha's generous — almost unbelievable — bequest gave Lydia a strong motive for killing her. She already had the opportunity. Everyone in town knew she was the only person who made candy, and the family was well aware that she was the one who administered Aunt Bertha's digitalis. No jury would believe she was innocent.

Lydia rose and turned to face the people who were serving as her jury today. Other than Travis, who had never taken a seat, and Mary Gray, who remained standing, they were all seated: five with expressions that clearly condemned her, only two friendly. It was almost ironic that Travis's father, who'd regarded Lydia as the enemy for as long as she'd been in Cimarron Creek, had become an ally.

"I didn't know about Aunt Bertha's will," she said firmly. It was likely no one would believe that any more than they would believe her innocence, but she had to set the record straight. "Aunt Bertha never said a word."

Mary Gray fisted her hands on her hips and glared at Lydia. "She wasn't your aunt. It's unseemly of you to speak of her that way."

Travis shook his head and moved to stand next to Lydia. "First of all, I was there when Aunt Bertha insisted that Lydia call her by that name, but how she referred to her is hardly the issue here. What Lydia said is true. She had no idea she was even mentioned in Aunt Bertha's will, much less that she was the major beneficiary. Aunt Bertha changed her will less than a month ago and insisted on total secrecy."

Though some of the others appeared to accept Travis's statement, Mary Gray was clearly unconvinced. "She must have known. You must have told her. Why, I'll bet that's why you decided to marry Lydia, so you would get Aunt Bertha's fortune. You two schemed together to kill her."

Lydia didn't wait for Travis to respond. "I

didn't kill Aunt Bertha, and neither did Travis." Though she kept her voice low and calm, Lydia would not accede to Mary Gray's insistence that she call Aunt Bertha Mrs. Henderson. "I loved her as if she were my own grandmother." It was clear that no one, with the exception of Travis, his father, and Catherine, believed her, but Lydia had to say it one more time.

Mary Gray shook her head. "Lies. All lies. It's clear as can be that this greedy Northerner is just like the carpetbaggers. She came here to rob us, and she did."

The woman who had once been one of Lydia's best customers glared at Travis's father, perhaps hoping he would support her. When he said nothing, she turned to his son. "You'd better arrest her, Sheriff." She spat the last word, turning Travis's title into an epithet. "Arrest her, if you're man enough to do it." Shifting slightly, Mary addressed the others. "My husband shouldn't have stopped Porter when he wanted to run for office. Our son would have been a much better sheriff than this one. If he'd been in charge, Aunt Bertha would still be alive."

Though the logic of that statement escaped Lydia, she heard a murmur of assent and hated the fact that people were questioning Travis's abilities. He was a good sheriff; Lydia knew that.

"You may be right, Aunt Mary." Though his words were conciliatory, his tone was pure steel. "The fact is, Porter is not the sheriff of Cimarron Creek. I am, and I know what I have to do." He looked around the room, fixing his gaze on each member of his family. "This meeting is adjourned. Catherine, would you please show everyone out? When they're gone, ask Edgar to come here. Lydia, you need to stay." There was no warmth in his voice, simply resolution, as Travis the sheriff took precedence over Travis her fiancé.

When the others had left, Lydia turned to Travis. "What are you going to do?"

He countered with a question of his own. "Do you trust me?"

"Of course I do. I would never have agreed to marry you if I didn't." Travis looked so serious that she wondered where he was leading. Did he want to break their engagement because of all the accusations? He'd told her once that the Whitfields and Hendersons felt strongly that the family names not be besmirched. A fiancée whom the town believed to be a murderer was nothing to brag about.

Though her heart ached at the thought, she had to make the offer. "Do you want me to release you from our engagement?"

Travis looked as if she'd struck him. "Never! But I need you to trust that what I'm about to do is for your benefit."

As if on cue, Edgar entered the library. Travis nodded at him. "Now that you're here, we can make this official. Lydia Crawford, you are under arrest."

"That was a good move, son. I'm proud of you."

Travis looked at the man seated across the breakfast table from him, surprised but pleased by his father's approval. This was the first time they'd had a chance to talk since Travis had locked the woman he loved in the town's sole jail cell. Though Opal had cooked the meal as she did each morning, she'd left the kitchen as soon it was ready, claiming she'd eaten earlier when she'd taken food to the jail for Edgar and Lydia. Now she was heading to Cimarron Sweets to check on something for Lydia.

"I hated to do it, but it was the only way I could keep her safe," Travis told his father. "Uncle Charles was angry before the will was read. There's no telling what he's like now that he knows how much Lydia inherited. I wouldn't put it past him to take justice in his own hands."

Pa nodded as if he agreed. "Did you tell Lydia that?"

"Sure did. She took it better than I expected. She even said this would give us a chance to figure out who really killed Aunt Bertha. We both think the murderer may become careless now that Lydia's in jail."

"Lydia's a smart woman. Brave too." Pa took another forkful of scrambled eggs as if he'd said nothing out of the ordinary. It was only Travis who stopped chewing, astonished by his father's words.

"Even though she's a Northerner?"

Pa shrugged. "I won't deny that I'd rather you marry a Texan, but as far as Yankees go, Lydia's not bad."

That was high praise — very high praise — coming from the man who only a few weeks ago had referred to Lydia as the Cursed Enemy. Travis had no idea what had caused the change in Pa's attitude, but he wasn't complaining.

He swallowed the last of his coffee, plunking the mug on the table and preparing to rise. "It's time I got back to her. We've got a murderer to catch."

To Travis's surprise, Pa shook his head. "Before you go, I have a question for you." Whatever it was, it was making Pa uncomfortable. That was almost as remarkable as the way he'd complimented Lydia.

"Sure." Travis leaned back in the chair, hoping his relaxed posture would allay whatever concerns were causing Pa's obvious discomfort. "What's up?"

Pa cleared his throat and stared at the far wall for a second before meeting Travis's gaze. "You once told me I'd have a home with you for the rest of my life. Is that offer still open?"

The day had just become stranger. "Yes, of course, but . . ." What had happened to the man who'd declared he would never share a home with any Northerner? He must know that Lydia's time in jail would be brief and that when she was once again free, Travis intended to marry her.

"I had a lot of time to think on that stagecoach." Pa took another slug of coffee, his expression solemn. "I kept remembering Aunt Bertha and what she said after you came back from Ladreville. She told me there was nothing worse than losing a child, that she should have been stronger and not let Joan leave."

Pa set the mug on the table and leaned toward Travis. "It's too late for Bertha, but it made me realize I don't want to face my Maker with regrets like hers. You're a fine man, Travis. I don't agree with everything you do, but I have to accept the fact that it's your life and you need to live it as you see best." Pa reached across the table and laid his hand on Travis's. "Will you let me stay?"

"Of course." As Travis squeezed his father's hand, his heart overflowing with gratitude, he gave a silent prayer of thanks. Aunt Bertha was right in believing Romans 8:28. Something good had come from the tragedy of her death. The proof was sitting across the table from Travis.

Life in a jail cell was worse than she'd imagined. Lydia frowned as she looked at her new home. The cot that served as both her bed and the cell's only seating was hard and uncomfortable. The window was so high that the only way she could see out of it was to stand on the cot. She'd tried that once, but when the cot began to wobble, Lydia had decided that a glimpse of freedom wasn't worth the risk of being injured, and she resigned herself to boredom.

Though Catherine and Opal had visited her, and Travis spent as much time here as he could, there were still hours with nothing to do but read. Oddly, though books had once been her refuge, Lydia found herself unable to concentrate on the written word.

It was not pleasant being in jail. Besides the small and uncomfortable surroundings, there was the absence of privacy. Admittedly, Travis and Edgar did their best. They hung a blanket over the bars at night so Lydia could sleep without being observed, and they'd gone outside when it was time for her morning ablutions. The worst part was the lack of freedom. Lydia hadn't realized how much she would miss being able to go wherever she wanted whenever she wanted. If it chafed on her when she'd been here less than a day, what would it be like if she had to spend weeks here? The only good thing Lydia could say was that being here gave her time with Travis. The problem was, they still had no idea who might have wanted Aunt Bertha dead.

"Thanks, Edgar," Travis said as he entered the sheriff's office. "I'll take over now."

As Edgar gave Travis a brief report of what had occurred overnight, Lydia watched the man she loved. Surely it wasn't her imagination that he was more relaxed this morning, and yet that made no sense. She was still locked in this cell, they were no closer to finding the killer, and Opal had reported a minor problem at the candy store.

"Did something happen?" Lydia asked when Edgar left. "You look different today."

Travis nodded, the happiness shining from his eyes leaving no doubt that what had transpired had been good. "It was as close to a miracle as I've ever seen. My father and I actually had a civil conversation. The bottom line is, he's staying here."

As relief washed over her, Lydia felt tears prick her eyes. "Oh, Travis, I'm so happy for you." She had prayed for an end to the men's estrangement, and her prayers had been answered.

Travis pulled his chair close to the cell and extended his hand through the bars, giving hers a quick squeeze. "I'll be happier when I can let you out of here. You know how much I hate seeing you in a cell. But let's not talk about that. Why don't you tell me why you looked preoccupied when I came in?"

Lydia hadn't thought anyone would notice. "It's nothing serious. When Opal stopped at Cimarron Sweets to make sure everything was okay, she saw a mouse. We were trying to decide what to do. She suggested getting a cat, but I'm afraid the cat hair would stick to the candy. Much as I hate the idea of any kind of poison in the store, I think that's what we need."

Travis nodded. "You'll sprinkle it on the floor, so it won't be near the candy."

"I know. It's just that the thought of any poison makes me cringe." The majority of Cimarron Creek believed she had deliberately poisoned Aunt Bertha.

"That's understandable, but you need to get rid of the mice. I'll stop by the apothecary this morning and see if Warner still has that last bag of rat poison. In the meantime, let's see if we can find something happier to discuss."

Lydia nodded. "I wish we could. All I can think about is Aunt Bertha."

Travis's expression left no doubt that he concurred. "I keep telling myself we must have missed a clue."

"And I keep wondering if we're asking the wrong question."

He blinked in surprise. "What do you mean? What question could there be other than who killed Aunt Bertha?"

Unable to sleep, Lydia had found herself pacing the cell last night, trying to make sense of everything that had happened.

"That's the main question, but I keep asking why someone would go to so much trouble to frame me."

This time Travis nodded as if he agreed. "It's probably the same reason that whoever attacked Opal and Edgar tried to throw suspicion on Nate."

"And whoever poisoned Nate's goats wanted Warner to take the blame. The person's a coward, but even more, he'll do anything to avoid getting caught."

"The pattern is so consistent that it appears that the same person is responsible for all the crimes."

Lydia agreed. "The problem is, I can't imagine the motive." She had thought of little else since she'd been on the wrong side of the bars. "I can understand lust being the reason for Opal's rape and that the man wanted to kill Edgar because he'd married her, but that doesn't explain Nate's goats or Aunt Bertha's murder, much less the robberies and broken windows."

Travis nodded. "On the surface they appear to be unrelated."

Perhaps they were, but Lydia's instincts said otherwise. "What if we look beneath the surface? What if we consider not the victims but the people who were blamed? I keep thinking there must be a connection between everyone who was framed, if only we could find it."

Travis didn't disagree with her. Instead, he settled back in his chair and said, "Let's start with Aunt Bertha. The first thing is to figure out who had the opportunity to poison her candy. Whoever did that had to know she kept chocolates on her bedside table."

"I'm afraid that's just about everyone in Cimarron Creek. She mentioned it after church on Sunday, and the story spread. After that, several women came into the store asking for a small box they could keep for themselves."

"And anyone could have bought chocolate creams with yellow roses."

Lydia started to nod, then stopped as her heart began to race. "Yellow roses? What are you talking about? Aunt Bertha's bedside chocolates had pansies on them."

Travis shook his head. "Not that day. The box on her night table had yellow roses."

"That makes no sense, Travis. Aunt Bertha's candies had blue pansies on them. When she finished the first box, I made a second batch for her, also with blue pansies."

Travis shook his head again as he rose and unlocked the safe, withdrawing the box of candy he'd taken from Aunt Bertha's room. "Look," he said as he lifted the lid and displayed the remaining four creams. Not one was decorated with pansies.

"Aunt Bertha must have gotten hungry

and eaten them during the middle of the night. Otherwise, she would have realized these weren't her candies." Lydia thought quickly, trying to put the pieces together. "I only sold creams with yellow roses to one person — Hilda Gray. They're the special design that she serves at her quilting bees."

"So anyone who was there could have taken them, filled them with digitalis, and put them in Aunt Bertha's room. I'm sure every one of the quilters was at the party."

"That's true. They did come to the party and they were all upstairs, but I can't see how they could have taken half a dozen or more without anyone at the quilting bee noticing. Usually the women eat two or three apiece. I know Hilda doesn't send extras home with them, because she told me Porter eats whatever's left. In fact, this month she ordered an additional dozen just for him."

The pieces were starting to fit together, and yet something felt wrong. A fragment of a memory teased the back of Lydia's brain.

"Maybe they weren't for Porter. Maybe Hilda planned to fill them with poison for Aunt Bertha. Poison is often a woman's weapon." Travis laid the box of candy back on his desk. "Do you remember if you saw

Hilda upstairs the day Aunt Bertha died?"

"She was there," Lydia said, "but so were a lot of other people. It seemed like half the town wanted to see the upstairs rooms. That's why Aunt Bertha insisted that all the rooms be left open, so they could peek inside. The one thing I remember is that Hilda seemed upset when I found her in the hallway."

Lydia could see Travis filing that away for future reference. "Do you think she was guilty or simply embarrassed because you caught her snooping?"

"I don't know." Lydia tried to imagine Hilda as a murderer. It was possible, and yet it didn't feel right to her. "She definitely wasn't responsible for Opal and Edgar's attacks. We know that was a man. And the bags of poison that killed Nate's goats were heavy. I saw that when Warner sold the first one to Nate. A woman could have lifted them, but it wouldn't have been easy."

Travis was silent for a moment, perhaps considering how thin Hilda was. "What if she was an accomplice? You said she ordered the extra candy. That sounds as if she was involved."

"Or perhaps she just wanted extra candy for her husband. Aunt Bertha said she might have been buttering him up because she wanted a new dress."

Travis nodded. "You're probably right. It's hard enough for one person to keep a secret in a town this size. If there were two people, I can't imagine someone else not hearing about it. Let's go back to our original premise that only one person is responsible for the crimes."

"And that's not Hilda."

"No." Travis frowned. "Aunt Bertha's murder has narrowed the possible suspects. A lot of people may have known that she keeps candy in her room, but only a few knew she took digitalis."

"Catherine and Warner. But neither of them would —" Before Lydia could complete her sentence, a gust of wind sent something skittering across her feet. Instinctively, she raised them and shrieked.

Travis chuckled as he reached into the cell and pulled out a dried leaf. "Nothing to worry about. We don't have mice here."

"That's what Porter said the first time I rented a buggy. He told me his cat made sure of that." Lydia paused as the elusive memory she'd tried so hard to recall came into focus. "Porter said that, but he had some yellow sacks on his shelves. I didn't think about it at the time, but they looked just like the one Warner sold to Nate. Why would Porter need rat poison when he has a cat?"

"Porter." Travis's brow furrowed as he considered the possibility. "You're right that he would have had no need for poison. He's proud of Homer's mouse- and rat-catching skills." The furrows deepened. "It's hard to imagine why he would have poisoned Nate's goats and even harder to picture Porter as a murderer. He and Warner have been like brothers to me."

"But brothers kill. I don't imagine Abel was expecting his brother to kill him." And while the yellow sacks she'd seen in the livery weren't proof of anything, they did shed suspicion on Porter.

Lydia thought back to the afternoon of the engagement party. "Porter was upstairs at the same time as Hilda. He was at the opposite side of the hallway, closer to Aunt Bertha's room. I didn't think about it at the time, but he could have been coming out of her room."

Though he appeared thoughtful, Lydia could see that Travis still wasn't convinced. "I know you don't like the idea of your cousin as the killer, but he had the opportunity to replace the good candy with poisoned pieces."

Travis nodded. "He probably knows as

much about digitalis as you and I do. Warner is always talking shop. I wouldn't be surprised if Warner told Porter Aunt Bertha was taking digitalis."

Though Travis's words were matter-of-fact, Lydia heard the pain in them as he came to grips with the idea that a man he trusted might be a killer. "Porter and Hilda were having dinner with his parents the night Aunt Bertha had her attack. It would make sense that Warner told them all what he'd prescribed.

"And Porter would have had little trouble stealing digitalis from the pharmacy. If I could guess where Warner kept his spare key, you can be sure his brother could too."

Lydia heard the sorrow in Travis's voice. "Don't forget the yellow sacks I saw at the livery," she said. "Chances are they were the ones that poisoned Nate's goats."

"True." Travis frowned, then pressed his fingertips between his eyes as if to straighten the furrows that had formed there. "It's beginning to look like Porter's our man. The fact that most of the incidents took place on Tuesday night makes sense. Hilda wouldn't have been concerned that Porter wasn't home, because she knew our dominoes games sometimes run late."

Travis's lips thinned with what Lydia

suspected was frustration. "The problem is, I don't understand why he'd do such things. I thought he was happy or at least content with his life. He has a wife and a child. He makes a good living and is a respected member of the community. Why would he rape Opal, attack Edgar, and poison Aunt Bertha?"

"I don't know. There's no way to know what's inside another's heart. We can speculate, but unless Porter tells us, we'll never be sure."

As Travis stared into the distance, Lydia reviewed all the crimes. There was still a problem, one fact that didn't fit the emerging picture. "How do we explain that the livery was the target of arson?"

Travis was silent for a moment, considering the question. "It could be totally unrelated, or it could be that Porter was clever and set it himself. He must have figured that no one would suspect someone who'd been a victim."

Rising, Travis strode from the jail cell to the opposite side of the office, his boot heels clicking on the floor. He stood at the window, staring outside for a few seconds, then spun around. "You're right," he said when he reached the cell again. "I hate the idea that Porter's responsible, but everything seems to point to him."

Lydia tried and failed to imagine Porter locked in this cell. His parents already questioned Travis's ability as sheriff. They'd claim Porter's arrest was further proof of Travis's incompetence.

"The problem is, we have no evidence other than the candy. The rest is supposition."

Travis shrugged. "So we need to find a way to catch him."

"You mean set a trap?"

"Exactly."

30

The news spread like wildfire. Within minutes of the shop's reopening, it was filled with curious customers.

"I never did believe you were guilty," Mrs. Higgins announced as she ordered a pound of taffy. "Bertha Henderson was nobody's fool. She would never have left you what she did if she didn't trust you."

Though tears still filled Lydia's eyes each time she thought of the horrible way Aunt Bertha had died, she managed a small smile. "She was a wonderful woman, and I loved her dearly."

"Of course you did." Mrs. Higgins patted Lydia's hand and increased her order to two pounds.

"I shouldn't ask, but I will anyway," Mrs. Wilkins said half an hour later while she vacillated between a pound of chocolate creams and one of fudge. "Was it horrible being in jail?"

This time Lydia's smile was genuine. "I've had more pleasant nights," she admitted. "The food was delicious, though, thanks to Opal."

Mrs. Wilkins nodded and bought both the creams and the fudge, leaving Lydia to speculate that being notorious was a good way to increase sales. The situation would have been more amusing if a murderer hadn't still been on the loose. Though Travis had seemed confident that their plan would work, Lydia knew she would not rest easily until Porter was behind bars.

"Are you going to keep the store open?" Rachel Henderson asked when she stopped in to buy some mints for Nate. "I can't convince him to stop chewing the leaves, but he never refuses when I offer him some of your mint drops." She glanced at the glass-fronted cabinet. "I see you have peppermint sticks too. I'll take half a dozen. If Nate doesn't want them, the boys will."

As she paid for the candy, Rachel repeated her question about keeping the store open.

"Why wouldn't I?" Though Lydia had expected the other questions, this one surprised her.

Rachel acted as if the answer should have been obvious. "You don't need the money."

"But the town needs good candy. Opal

and I plan to keep making candy as long as we have customers like you to buy it."

While she'd been in jail and had little to do but think, Lydia had decided to make Opal a partner. Not only did the young woman deserve recognition for the work she put into the shop, but it would give her a measure of independence. While Lydia trusted Edgar to provide for his wife and child, it never hurt a woman to have her own source of income. The tears of joy that had filled Opal's eyes and the look of pride on Edgar's face when Lydia had broached the subject confirmed the wisdom of her plan.

The only question had been who would care for Opal's baby while she was working. Though Lydia saw no problem in having the child at the house each morning while Opal cut and boxed candy, the store was a different situation. A crying baby would distract customers. But when Widow Jenkins had mentioned how much she missed having children in her home, Opal's eyes had widened. Within minutes, the two women had made arrangements for the kindly widow to serve as a surrogate grandmother.

"I heard the judge is coming tomorrow." Though she rarely entered the store, claiming her presence might discourage other women from patronizing Cimarron Sweets, today Faith Kohler left the Silver Spur long enough to buy two pounds of fudge.

"That's what Travis said." Lydia confirmed the official story. "Of course, there could be delays."

"You must be anxious to turn over the evidence." Faith wasn't pumping for information, merely stating a fact. The news that Travis had released Lydia when she produced evidence proving she was not the murderer had spread quickly. And though Travis had never said it, the rumor mill quickly embellished the story with the speculation that the evidence pointed to the true murderer.

"I am anxious," Lydia admitted. "I want life to get back to normal." Or as normal as it could be with Aunt Bertha gone.

As the parade of women continued throughout the day, Lydia noticed two things: first, though everyone was undoubtedly curious, no one asked what the evidence was, and second, neither Hilda nor Mary Gray set foot inside the store. The reason could be that they were aware of Porter's guilt, or it could simply be that they were angry at the bequest Lydia had received. She'd know which was true soon enough.

The day passed more quickly than Lydia had dared hope, and almost before she knew what was happening, Travis was walking her home. Since neither of them wanted Catherine involved, Lydia had suggested that Opal ask her to help put the finishing touches on the baby's layette tonight. Now that she didn't have to worry about Catherine stopping in for a chat, Lydia stood in the kitchen making candy as if it were a normal evening. But if she and Travis were right, this would be far from a normal evening.

Porter knew that Travis had released Lydia. Not wanting to rely on the rumor mill, Travis had paid him a casual visit and had mentioned both Lydia's release and the story about turning evidence over to the judge.

"He didn't give any sign of being concerned," Travis told Lydia as they walked home from the store. "If I didn't know better, I would have believed him innocent."

"Do you think he is?"

Travis shook his head. "No. Everything fits too neatly." He looked around the kitchen, clearly worried about what might happen. "I only wish there were another way to prove it."

"I know you do, but there isn't. I'll be

481

safe. You'll be here."

He nodded. "And don't forget the judge."

Lydia's mood lightened as she thought of the plans Travis had made. "The judge who'll just so happen to arrive a little early."

Travis grinned. "It helps that Herb was good friends with Uncle Jonas. He's the one who warned me to be careful what I put in a telegram and who taught me how to hide a message inside one. Herb will be here within an hour. He knows to come in the back way, so no one will realize he's arrived."

It had all gone as planned. While Lydia stirred a batch of fudge, the two men were seated inside the pantry where they could hear everything that was said in the kitchen.

The door swung open, without so much as a knock to announce the visitor's arrival.

Lydia turned as if the sight of Porter Gray in her kitchen were normal. Though the man's blue eyes shone with a disturbing light, she knew better than to admit she saw anything amiss. She needed to gain his confidence if the plan was going to work.

"Good evening, Porter." Lydia continued her stirring. "This fudge needs a few more minutes on the stove. Why don't you sit down while I finish it?" Years of teaching had taught her the value of disarming an angry or violent child through distraction.

But Porter was not so easily distracted. He took a step toward her, his posture menacing. "What evidence do you have? I know I didn't leave any."

Mistake number one. He'd just admitted his guilt. Pretending she hadn't noticed, Lydia gave the fudge a final stir. "There. Now all I have to do is spread it out to cool." She opened a drawer and pulled out the red-handled knife she used for spreading candy. "Once that's done, I can pour us both a cup of coffee. Do you want cream as well as sugar in yours?"

"You're trying to distract me, aren't you?"

Lydia shook her head. "I'm trying to be a good hostess. Now, why don't you take a seat at the table? You'll be more comfortable."

To her relief, Porter did as she'd suggested. Keeping one eye on him while she spread the fudge, Lydia continued, "Aunt Bertha always said visitors should be welcomed." As she'd expected, Porter's head jerked up at the mention of the murdered woman. Lydia gave no sign that she'd noticed his reaction. "She was a true lady. I don't understand why anyone would have wanted to kill her."

If Lydia had calculated accurately, Porter would take the bait and give her a clue to his motive for poisoning his great-aunt. Travis had speculated that while Porter had tried to shift the blame to others, he harbored a need to brag about his exploits.

"I should have been sheriff." Porter practically snarled the words. Though they formed a complete English sentence, Lydia saw no connection between them and Aunt Bertha's death. "I wanted to be sheriff."

Though Porter sounded like a spoiled child deprived of a toy, the light in his eyes left no doubt that there was more to Porter's mood than simple pique. It was up to Lydia to coax the full explanation from him.

She pulled two mugs from the cupboard and filled them with coffee, setting one in front of Porter, then placing hers on the opposite side of the table. When she'd taken a seat, Lydia picked up her mug as casually as if they were friends sharing an evening of coffee and conversation.

"If you were sheriff, who would run the livery?" she asked. "Everyone in Cimarron Creek knows you provide the best service in three counties."

Though Porter's eyes lit at the praise, a scowl quickly turned his expression sour again. "Pa doesn't. All he cares about is

Warner and that blasted pharmacy. He says Warner is respected."

"So are you." It was true that Porter Gray was both respected and well liked within the community. That would change when the townspeople learned what horrible things he had done, but for the moment, he was still an honored resident.

Porter shook his head. "Pa always said Warner was the smart one, but he was wrong. I'm just as smart as Warner. Smarter, even. He could never have done all that I have. Why, he doesn't even know how to pick a lock, but I broke into every store in town without anyone knowing I'd been there."

Porter had solved another part of the puzzle by admitting that he'd entered the stores, but even more importantly, he'd given Lydia a clue to the reason for his crimes. Jealousy was a powerful motive. Though Lydia had puzzled about why he had tried to implicate his brother for the goat poisoning, now she understood the depth of Porter's resentment and the reason. Aunt Bertha had claimed that Charles Gray favored his older son, and it appeared he did — with deadly results.

Porter took a slug of coffee, his eyes still filled with that distant and disturbed expression. "When Pa told me the sheriff had more power than Warner, I knew what I had to do. It didn't matter that he said my place was in the livery. I knew I had to become Cimarron Creek's next sheriff. Then he'd see that I was the better son."

Lydia wasn't certain where Porter's twisted logic was headed, but dealing with schoolchildren had taught her to do everything she could to defuse anger.

"Would you like a praline with your coffee?" Without waiting for a response, she rose and laid several on a plate. Placing it in front of Porter, she continued. "I always thought these looked a bit like sheriffs' stars."

He stared at the candy, the frown that seemed habitual tonight deepening. "You're wrong." He took a bite of the confection. "This tastes good, but it doesn't look like a sheriff's badge. Here's what a real star looks like." To Lydia's surprise, he pulled a piece of silvery metal from his pocket and extended it to her.

She examined it closely. "It certainly is shiny, but that one point looks a little bent. What happened?" And where had he gotten it? Though Travis had said he'd asked Porter and Warner to be deputies, both had refused. Besides, this was a sheriff's not a deputy's badge.

"I don't know how it got bent. It was like that when I got it."

"And where did you get it?" Lydia tried to make the question sound casual, but she couldn't forget that Travis and the judge were listening, possibly taking notes of everything Porter said.

"I got it from Lionel Allen. He wasn't using it anymore. I saw to that." Porter's laugh sent shivers down Lydia's spine. No sane man laughed like that.

Porter's laugh turned into a snicker. "Everyone thought he was such a great horseman, but when his horse spooked, he couldn't control it. I hated to hurt the horse, but the town needed a new sheriff."

Breaking off a piece of praline, Porter looked up at Lydia, anger once again coloring his eyes. "I never thought they'd be dumb enough to give the job to Travis. It should have been mine, but no, they thought just because he was a lawyer he should be a lawman. I had to show them they were wrong. Cimarron Creek has had a lot more crime since Travis pinned on that star."

Schooling her expression to hide her satisfaction that she and Travis had been right in believing the crime spree could be tied to one person, Lydia rose to refill

Porter's mug. "Were you responsible for that — the missing chickens, the broken windows, the poisoned goats, and the robbery of most of the stores?"

"Of course." There was pride in Porter's voice as he pronounced the two words. "I knew that when the townspeople saw Travis couldn't solve the crimes, they'd realize their mistake and turn to me."

"Very clever." And it was, although in a warped way. "Was that why Edgar had to disappear?" Lydia was careful not to say anything that sounded like an accusation of guilt. She needed Porter to confess what he'd done.

"No! Edgar had nothing to do with showing everyone Travis's incompetence. He was getting too close to Opal. Until he came to town, she only had eyes for me."

It was another of Porter's delusions. Lydia was certain Opal would have extended nothing more than common courtesy to him. While the other girls at the Spur might have flirted with him, Opal had told Lydia she kept her distance from the men, particularly married men.

Porter's grin sent a shiver of horror down Lydia's spine. "I could see from the way she looked at me that Opal knew I was a real man. She didn't have to say anything, because I knew what she wanted from me, so I gave it to her."

Struggling to keep her expression neutral, Lydia tried not to shudder at the way Porter attempted to justify his rape of Opal.

"But then she married Edgar," he said, his eyes flashing with fury. "I couldn't let him have my woman."

Lydia could only imagine how angry Porter must have been when instead of dying in that rancher's field, Edgar returned to Cimarron Creek. That anger would only have been fueled by the fact that Edgar and Opal were reunited and that he was now wearing a deputy's star. It was almost miraculous that he hadn't attacked Edgar again.

"Would you like another praline, Porter?" Lydia slid the dish a little closer to him, encouraging him to take a piece of candy, hoping that would keep him talking. "I still don't understand about Aunt Bertha."

"Push him as far as you can," Travis had counseled her, "but don't do anything to endanger yourself." Lydia felt as if she were watching a pot about to boil. Sensing that Porter was close to the breaking point, she rose as casually as she could. If his anger let loose, she wanted to be able to flee.

"I thought schoolmarms were supposed

to be smart," he said with a sneer. "You sure aren't. Anyone with half a brain could see that Bertha stood between me and becoming sheriff."

This was obviously another case of Porter's twisted logic, but this time Lydia was unable to untwist the threads. "You're right, Porter. I'm not as smart as you. I don't understand that."

He pounded one fist on the table. "She was the one who convinced everyone that Travis should be sheriff. If she was gone, they'd realize I'm the better man. Besides," he said with another of those chuckles that sent shivers down Lydia's spine, "after Travis watches you hang for her murder, he won't want to stay in Cimarron Creek. I'll take care of Edgar, and then I'll have Opal too."

"That's where you're wrong, Porter." The door behind Porter opened, and Travis stepped out. "Have you heard enough, Herb?"

"What?" Porter's reaction was faster than Lydia had thought possible, fueled by anger and his own madness. Before she knew what he intended, he jumped to his feet and wrapped his arm around her throat, pulling her close to him. His other hand reached behind her and grabbed the knife she'd left on the counter, placing the blade against her throat.

"It's all your fault, Travis," he announced as he glared at the man who wore the star. Though the judge had emerged from the pantry behind Travis, Porter did not appear to consider the older man a threat. "If you'd let me be sheriff, none of this would have happened. Pa would have seen that I was the better son, but no, you had to interfere."

Though her heart was beating at twice its normal rate, Lydia tried to keep her expression calm. She didn't want Travis to know how frightened she was by Porter's actions. Though the knife wasn't sharp, if he pressed it hard enough, he could keep her from breathing.

Travis took a step toward Porter, the tight line of his lips telling her he was battling to control his temper. "You're right, Porter. Your argument is with me. Lydia's no part of it. Let her go."

"So you can arrest me?" Porter laughed again. "I'm not stupid!"

"We can work this out." Travis kept his voice low and even, his technique reminding Lydia of how she'd dealt with angry children.

Porter shook his head. "The only way we can work this out is if you let me go and forget everything you heard." He turned toward the judge. "You too."

"You know I can't do that," Travis said, his voice still conciliatory, although Lydia noticed that he kept his hand close to his weapon. "But if you let Lydia go, I'll do what I can to get you a lighter sentence."

"So I'll spend the rest of my life in prison instead of hanging? That's not going to work, Travis. You've got to let me go free." He gave Travis a menacing look. "If you reach for that gun, I'll slit her throat."

As Travis looked at Lydia and nodded ever so slightly, she knew what he wanted her to do. They had one chance to disarm Porter. Taking a deep breath, she said a silent prayer that this would work, then let out a piercing scream. "Don't do it, Travis. I don't want to die."

Startled by her shriek, Porter loosened his grip. That was all Lydia needed. She broke free and ran to the opposite side of the kitchen at the same time that Travis pointed his weapon at Porter.

"Put your hands in the air, Porter. It's over."

He shook his head. "You're wrong again." And as Lydia watched in horror, Porter plunged the knife into his chest.

EPILOGUE

"I thought this day would never come." Travis kept his arm wrapped around Lydia's waist as they entered the house that was now their home.

It had been eight days since Porter had killed himself. Though the knife blade was dull, the tip had been sharp enough to puncture his skin, and he'd wielded it with such force that he'd punctured his heart. By the time Doc Harrington arrived, Porter was already gone.

The town had been shocked by Porter's death and the revelation that he had been behind all the problems, but more quickly than Lydia had expected, life had resumed its normal pace, and the horror of Porter Gray's crimes had been replaced by happier events: the birth of Opal's son and the plans for Lydia and Travis's wedding.

It had been a joy-filled day, with even the weather cooperating to make the ceremony and the reception that had followed one Cimarron Creek would long remember, but now the guests had left, and Lydia was ready to begin her new life, her life as Mrs. Travis Whitfield.

"I wish Aunt Bertha could have been here," she said as she and Travis walked down the hallway toward the magnificent curving staircase. "I know there were some who thought it unseemly that we married so soon."

Travis's voice was low and intimate, though his words were matter-of-fact. "You and I know that's what she would have wanted. That's what matters."

"I think she'd be happy that we're both living here now." Though she had spent months in this house, today for the first time Lydia felt as if this were truly her home.

Travis shook his head. "I don't *think* that. I know it. Aunt Bertha would say it was time a new generation enjoyed her home."

"And you're sure your father doesn't mind sharing his house with Opal and Edgar and little Abe?" When they'd decided to begin their married life here and Travis had turned his home into the deputy sheriff's residence, Lydia had told Travis she wouldn't mind if his father joined them, but Abe had refused, claiming that a newlywed couple needed time alone.

"Pa won't admit it, but he's tickled pink that they named the baby after him. When I saw him holding Abe yesterday, he looked as proud as if he were the boy's grandfather." As Travis turned Lydia so she was facing him, she saw both love and amusement reflected from his eyes. "Pa also told me he's expecting us to give him a real grandson within a year."

The thought of holding Travis's and her baby filled Lydia's heart with joy. "I hope you told him that babies come in two flavors, and he might get a granddaughter."

"And risk having him yell at me?" Travis's feigned horror made Lydia laugh. "Of course I didn't. There's time enough for that later." He placed his hands on her shoulders and looked into her eyes. "I don't want to talk about Pa any more. In fact, Mrs. Whitfield, I don't want to talk at all."

Though his expression left no doubt of his meaning, Lydia couldn't resist teasing her husband. "What did you have in mind?"

"This." When Travis drew her into his arms and pressed his lips to hers, there was no need for words. God had answered her prayers, leading her to the man she loved, the man who loved her, the man who'd shown her that promises were meant to be kept.

The women on the stagecoach had been wrong: coming to Cimarron Creek was not a mistake.

ABOUT THE AUTHOR

Dreams have always been an important part of **Amanda Cabot**'s life. For almost as long as she can remember, she dreamt of being an author. Fortunately for the world, her grade-school attempts as a playwright were not successful, and she turned her attention to novels. Her dream of selling a book before her thirtieth birthday came true, and she's been spinning tales ever since. She now has more than thirty novels to her credit under a variety of pen names.

Her books have been finalists for the ACFW Carol Award as well as the Booksellers' Best and have appeared on the CBA and ECPA bestseller lists.

A popular speaker, Amanda is a member of ACFW and a charter member of Romance Writers of America. She married her high school sweetheart, who shares her love of travel and who's driven thousands of miles to help her research her books. After years as Easterners, they fulfilled a longtime dream and now live in the American West.